# SPIN
## THE
# DAWN

# SPIN
## THE
# DAWN

## THE BLOOD OF STARS

### Book I

ELIZABETH LIM

Alfred A. Knopf
New York

THIS IS A BORZOI BOOK PUBLISHED BY ALFRED A. KNOPF

This is a work of fiction. Names, characters, places, and incidents either are the product of the author's imagination or are used fictitiously. Any resemblance to actual persons, living or dead, events, or locales is entirely coincidental.

Text copyright © 2019 by Elizabeth Lim
Jacket art copyright © 2019 by Tran Nguyen
Map copyright © 2019 by Virginia Allyn

All rights reserved. Published in the United States by Alfred A. Knopf, an imprint of Random House Children's Books, a division of Penguin Random House LLC, New York.

Knopf, Borzoi Books, and the colophon are registered trademarks of Penguin Random House LLC.

Visit us on the Web! GetUnderlined.com

Educators and librarians, for a variety of teaching tools, visit us at RHTeachersLibrarians.com

Library of Congress Cataloging-in-Publication Data is available upon request.
ISBN 978-0-525-64699-0 (trade) — ISBN 978-0-525-64700-3 (lib. bdg.) —
ISBN 978-0-525-64701-0 (ebook)

The text of this book is set in 11.35-point Sabon MT Pro.

Printed in the United States of America
July 2019
10 9 8 7 6 5 4 3 2 1

First Edition

*To Adrian, for changing my life*
*in the best of possible ways*

Rainmaker's Peak

MOUNTAINS OF THE MOON

Dhoya Forest

Temple of the Sun

Great Spice Road

SAMARAN

A'LAND

Samarand Passage

Niyan

Gangsu

Blakmarat Desert

Jingan River

Summer Palace

SINGING MOUNTAINS

# SPIN
## THE
# DAWN

Ask me to spin the finest yarn or thread, and I can do it faster than any man—even with my eyes closed. Yet ask me to tell a lie, and I will stumble and falter to think of one.

I have never had a talent for spinning tales.

My brother Keton knows this better than anyone. Even though his brows rise once or twice as I tell him everything—of the three impossible tasks I was given, of the demon and ghosts I encountered on my journey, and of the enchantment that surrounded our emperor—my brother believes me.

Baba, my father, does not. He sees through the shadows I hide behind. That beyond the smile I give Keton, my eyes are red and raw. They are swollen from crying for hours, days even. What he cannot see is that in spite of the tears drying on my cheeks, my heart is hard.

I dread reaching the end of my story, for it is full of knots that I haven't had the courage to cut free. Distant drums pound. They draw closer with every second, a stirring reminder of the little time I have left to make my choice.

If I go back, I leave behind who I am. I will never see my family again, never see my face in the mirror again, never hear my name called again.

But I would give up the sun and moon and stars if it meant saving *him*.

*Him*—the boy with no name and yet a thousand names. The boy whose hands are stained with the blood of stars.

The boy I love.

PART ONE

# THE TRIAL

# CHAPTER ONE

I had three brothers once.

Finlei was the oldest—the brave one. Nothing frightened him, not spiders or needles or a flogging from Baba's cane. He was the quickest of us four children, fast enough to catch a fly with only his thumb and a thimble. But along with his dauntlessness came a craving for adventure. He despised having to work in our shop, having to spend the sun's precious light sewing dresses and mending shirts. And he was careless with the needle, his fingers constantly bandaged from pricks and his work marred with uneven stitches. Stitches I would unpick and redo to save him from Baba's lectures.

Finlei didn't have the patience to become a tailor like Baba.

Sendo had patience, but not for sewing. My second brother was the poet in the family, and the only weaving he loved was of words, especially about the sea. He would tell stories about the beautiful garments Baba could sew, with such exquisite detail all the ladies in town clamored to buy them—only to find they didn't exist.

As punishment, Baba made him sit on the pier behind our shop, unraveling thread from silkworm cocoons. Often I stole out to sit with him, to listen to his tales of what lay beyond that never-ending horizon of water.

"What color is the ocean?" Sendo would ask me.

"Blue, silly. What else?"

"How will you be the best tailor in A'landi if you don't know your colors?" Sendo shook his head and pointed at the water. "Look again. Look into the depths of it."

"Sapphire," I said, studying the ocean's gentle crests and troughs. The water sparkled. "Sapphire, like the stones Lady Tainak wears around her neck. But there's a hint of green . . . jade green. And the foam curls up like pearls."

Sendo smiled. "That's better." He wrapped an arm around my shoulders and hugged me close. "One day, we'll sail the seas, you and I. And you'll see the blue in all the world."

Because of Sendo, blue was my favorite color. It painted the white of my walls when I opened my window each morning and saw the sea glittering in the sunlight. Sapphire or cerulean. Azure. Indigo. Sendo trained my eyes to see the variations in color, to appreciate the dullest brown to the brightest pink. How light could bend something into a thousand possibilities.

Sendo's heart was for the sea, not for becoming a tailor like Baba.

Keton was my third brother, and the closest to me in age. His songs and jokes made everyone laugh, no matter what mood we were in. He always got in trouble for dyeing our silks green instead of purple, for carelessly stepping on newly pressed dresses with dirty sandals, for forgetting to water the mulberry trees, and for never spinning yarn fine enough for Baba to knit into a sweater. Money slipped through his fingers like water. But Baba loved him best—even though Keton didn't have the discipline to become a tailor.

Then there was me—Maia. The obedient daughter. My earliest memories were of sitting contentedly with Mama as she worked the spinning wheel, listening to Finlei, Sendo, and

Keton playing outside while Baba taught me to roll Mama's thread so it wouldn't tangle.

My heart *was* for becoming a tailor: I learned to thread needles before I could walk, to make a line of perfect stitches before I could talk. I loved my needlework and was happy learning Baba's trade instead of going out with my brothers. Besides, when Finlei taught me to spar and shoot arrows, I always missed the target. Even though I soaked up Sendo's fairy tales and ghost stories, I could never tell one of my own. And I always fell for Keton's pranks, no matter how often my older brothers warned me of them.

Baba proudly told me I was born with a needle in one hand, a pair of scissors in the other. That if I hadn't been born a girl, I might have become the greatest tailor in A'landi, sought after by merchants from one coast of the continent to the other.

"A tailor's worth is not measured by his fame, but by the happiness he brings," Mama said, seeing how disappointed Baba's words made me. "You will hold the seams of our family together, Maia. No other tailor in the world can do that."

I remembered beaming at her. Back then, all I wanted was for my family to be happy and whole like this—always.

But then Mama died, and everything changed.

We had been living in Gangsun, a key city along the Great Spice Road, and our shop occupied an entire half block. Baba was a well-respected tailor, known throughout southern A'landi for his skill at dressmaking. But ill times fell upon us, my mother's death opening the first crack in Baba's strong will.

He began to drink heavily—a way to drown his sorrows, he said. That didn't last long—in his grief, Baba's health deteriorated until he was unable to stomach any sort of spirits. He returned to his work at the shop, but he was never quite the same.

Customers noticed the decline in quality of Baba's sewing and mentioned it to my brothers. Finlei and Sendo never told him; they didn't have the heart. But a few years before the Five Winters' War, when I was ten, Finlei convinced Baba to leave Gangsun and move into a shophouse in Port Kamalan, a small coastal town along the fringes of the Road. The fresh sea air would be good for Baba, he insisted.

Our new home occupied the corner of Yanamer and Tongsa Streets, across from a shop that made hand-pulled noodles so long you could get full on just one, and a bakery that sold the best steamed buns and milk bread in the world—at least it tasted that way to my brothers and me when we were hungry, which we often were. But what I loved most was the beautiful view of the ocean. Sometimes while I watched the waves roll along the piers, I secretly prayed that the sea would mend Baba's broken heart—the way it was slowly healing mine.

Business was best in the summers and winters, when all the caravans traveling east and west on the Great Spice Road stopped in Port Kamalan to enjoy our temperate weather. My father's little shop depended on a steady supply of indigo, saffron, ocher—colors for our dyes. It was a small town, so we not only tailored garments but also sold fabrics and threads. It had been a long time since Baba had crafted a gown worthy of a great lady, and when the war began, there was little business to be had anyway.

Misfortune followed us to our new home. Port Kamalan was far enough from the capital that I'd thought my brothers would never be drafted into the civil war that ravaged A'landi. But the hostilities between young Emperor Khanujin and the shansen, the country's most powerful warlord, showed no signs of abating, and the emperor needed more men to fight in his army.

Finlei and Sendo were of age, so they were conscripted first. I was young enough then that the idea of going to war was romantic to me. Having two brothers become soldiers felt honorable.

The day before they left, I was outside, painting on a swath of white cotton. The peach blossoms lining Yanamer Street made me sneeze, and I splattered the last of Baba's expensive indigo over my skirt.

Finlei laughed at me and wiped drops of paint from my nose.

"Don't fret," he said as I desperately tried to salvage as much of the paint as I could.

"It's eighty jens an ounce! And who knows when the dye merchants will be back?" I muttered, still scrubbing at my skirt. "It's getting too hot for them to cross the Road."

"Then I'll get you some during my travels," Finlei said. He tipped my chin toward him. "I'm going to see all of A'landi when I'm a soldier. Maybe I'll come back as a general."

"I hope you won't be away as long as that!" I exclaimed.

Finlei's face sobered. His eyes pooled black, and he pushed aside a wisp of my wind-tousled hair. "Take care of yourself, sister," he said, his voice carrying both humor and sadness. "Don't work so hard you—"

"Become the kite that never flies," I finished for him. "I know."

Finlei touched my cheek. "Watch over Keton. Make sure he doesn't get into trouble."

"Take care of Baba, too," Sendo added, coming up behind me. He'd plucked a flower from the trees in front of our shop, and placed it above my ear. "And work on your calligraphy. I'll be back soon to make sure your handwriting's improved." Sendo ruffled my hair. "You're the lady of the house now."

I bowed my head dutifully. "Yes, brothers."

"You make it sound like I'm useless," Keton cut in. Baba was shouting at him to finish his chores, and he winced.

A smile broke Finlei's serious face. "Can you prove otherwise?"

Keton put his hands on his hips, and we all laughed.

"We'll visit faraway places with the army," Sendo said, his hand on my shoulder. "What can I bring back for you? Dyes from West Gangseng, maybe? Or pearls from the Majestic Harbor?"

"No, no," I said. "Just come home safely. Both of you." But then I paused.

Sendo prodded me. "What is it, Maia?"

My cheeks were hot, and I lowered my eyes to stare at my hands. "If you get to see Emperor Khanujin," I began slowly, "draw his portrait, will you?"

Finlei's shoulders shook with mirth. "So you've heard how handsome he is from the village girls? Every one of them aspires to become one of the emperor's concubines."

I was so embarrassed I couldn't look at him. "I have no interest in becoming a concubine."

"You don't want to live in one of his four palaces?" Keton asked snidely. "I heard he has one for every season."

"Keton, that's enough," Sendo chided.

"I don't care about his palaces," I said, turning away from my youngest brother to Sendo. His eyes shone with gentleness—he'd always been my favorite brother, and I knew he would understand. "I want to know what he looks like so I can become his tailor one day. An imperial tailor."

Keton rolled his eyes at my confession. "That's as likely as you becoming his concubine!"

Finlei and Sendo glared at him.

"All right, then," Sendo promised, touching the freckles on my cheek. We were the only two of the family with freckles—a result of our hours daydreaming under the sun. "A portrait of the emperor for my talented sister, Maia."

I hugged him, knowing my request was very foolish but still hoping all the same.

If I'd known it was the last time we would all be together, I wouldn't have asked for anything.

. . .

Two years later, Baba received a notice that Finlei had been killed in battle. The imperial emblem stamped on the bottom of the letter was as red as freshly drawn blood, and hurriedly pressed so that the characters of Emperor Khanujin's name were smeared. Even months later, the memory would make me cry.

Then one night, with no warning, Keton ran away to join the army. All he left was a quickly scrawled note on top of my morning laundry—knowing it would be the first thing I saw when I woke.

*I've been useless too long. I'm going to find Sendo and bring him home. Take care of Baba.*

Tears filled my eyes, and I crumpled the note in my fist.

What did he know about fighting? Like me, he was lean as a reed, barely strong enough to hold up against the wind. He couldn't buy rice at the market without being swindled, and he always tried to talk his way out of a fight. How would he survive a war?

I was angry, too—because I couldn't go with him. If Keton thought *he* was useless, what was I? I couldn't fight in the army. And for all the thousands of hours I spent creating new stitches and drawing designs to sell, I could never become a master tailor. I could never take over Baba's shop. I was a girl. The best *I* could hope for was to marry well.

Baba never spoke of Keton's departure, would not speak of my youngest brother for months. But I saw how his fingers became stiff as stones; they could not even stretch wide enough to hold a pair of shears. He spent his days staring at the ocean as I took over our faltering shop. It was up to me to drum up business, to make sure my brothers had a home to return to.

No one had any need for silks and satins, not when our country was devouring itself from within. So I made hemp shirts for the local fishermen and linen dresses for their wives, and I spun flax into thread and mended soldiers' coats when they passed by. The fishermen gave us fish heads and sacks of rice in return for my work, and it didn't seem right to charge the soldiers.

Toward the end of every month, I helped the women who were preparing their gifts for the dead—usually paper clothing, which was tricky to sew—to burn before the prayer shrines in honor of their ancestors. I stitched paper into the shoes of passing merchants and strings of coins into their belts to ward off pickpockets. I even repaired amulets for travelers who asked it of me, though I didn't believe in magic. Not then.

On days when there was no business and our supplies of wheat and rice were running dangerously low, I took out my rattan basket and filled it with a few spools of thread, a bolt of muslin, and a needle. I roamed the streets, going from door to door, asking if anyone had mending to be done.

But few ships docked at the port. Dust and shadows wreathed the empty streets.

The lack of work didn't bother me as much as the awkward encounters I'd begun to endure on my way home. I used to love going into the bakery across from our shop, but that changed during the war. For now when I returned to Yanamer Street, Calu the baker's son would be there waiting for me.

I didn't like Calu. It wasn't because he didn't serve in the army—he hadn't passed the imperial health examination, so he couldn't. It was because as soon as I turned sixteen, he got it into his head that I was going to be his wife.

"I hate seeing you beg for work like this," Calu told me one day. He waved me inside his father's bakery. The fragrance from the breads and cakes wafted out the door, and my mouth watered at the smell of yeast, fermented rice flour, and roasted peanuts and sesame seeds.

"It's better than starving."

He wiped red-bean paste off his palm. Sweat from his temples dripped into the bowl of dough on his table. Normally it would have made me wrinkle my nose—if Calu's father saw how sloppy he was, he'd have a scolding—but I was too hungry to care.

"If you married me, you'd never starve."

His forwardness made me uncomfortable, and I thought with dread of Calu touching me, of bearing his children, of my embroidery frames collecting dust and my clothes growing sticky with sugar. I stifled a shudder.

"You would always have plenty to eat—your baba, too," Calu tried again, licking his lips. He smiled, his teeth yellow as butter. "I know how much you love my father's puff pastries, his steamed buns with lotus paste, his coconut buns."

My stomach grumbled, but I would not let my hunger overpower my heart. "Please stop asking. My answer isn't going to change."

That made Calu angry. "Too good for me, are you?"

"I have to run my father's shop," I said, trying to be gentle. "He needs me."

"A girl doesn't run a shop," he said, opening the steam basket to take out the latest batch of buns. Usually he would give Baba and me a few, but I knew he wouldn't today. "You might be a fine seamstress—the finest in the village—but with your brothers away fighting for the emperor, isn't it time to be sensible and settle down?" He reached for my hand. His fingers were powdery and damp. "Think of your father's health, Maia. You're being selfish. You could give him a better life."

I jerked away, stung. "My father would never give up his shop."

Calu huffed. "He'll have to, since you can't keep it running by yourself. You've gotten thin, Maia. Don't think I haven't noticed." He sneered, my rejection making him cruel. "Give me a kiss, and I'll throw you a bun."

I raised my chin. "I'm not a dog."

"Oh, *now* you're too proud to beg, eh? You'll let your father starve because you're so high-and-mighty—"

I was done listening. I fled the bakery and stormed across the street. My stomach growled again as I slammed Baba's shop door behind me. The hardest part was that I knew I was being selfish. I *should* marry Calu. But I wanted to save my family *myself*—like Mama said I would.

I crumpled against the door of our shophouse. What if I couldn't?

Baba found me there, sobbing quietly.

"What's the matter, Maia?"

I wiped my tears and stood. "Nothing, Baba."

"Did Calu ask you to marry him again?"

"There's no work," I said, evading the question. "We—"

"Calu is a good boy," he said, "but he is just that—a boy. And he is not worthy of you." He hovered over my embroidery frame, studying the dragon I'd been stitching. It was difficult working on cotton, rather than silk, but I'd striven to get every detail: its carplike scales, sharp talons, and demon eyes. I could tell Baba was impressed. "You are meant for more, Maia."

I turned away. "How can I be? I'm not a man."

"If you were, you would have been sent to war. The gods are protecting you."

I didn't believe him, but for his sake, I nodded and dried my tears.

A few weeks before my eighteenth birthday, good news came: the emperor announced a truce with the shansen. The Five Winters' War was over, at least for now.

But our joy at the news quickly turned to sorrow, for another notice arrived. One with a blood-red seal.

Sendo had died fighting in the mountains, only two days before the truce.

The news shattered Baba anew. He knelt before his altar for an entire night, cradling the shoes Mama had made for Finlei and Sendo when they were young. I didn't pray with him. I was too angry. If only the gods could have watched over Sendo for two more days!

Two more days.

"At least the war didn't take all my sons," Baba said heavily, patting my shoulder. "We must stay strong for Keton."

Yes, there was still Keton. My youngest brother returned

home a month after the truce. He arrived in a wagon, legs stretched out as the wheels creaked over the dirt road. His hair had been cropped, and he'd lost so much weight I barely recognized him. But what startled me most were the ghosts in his eyes, the same eyes that had once sparkled with jokes and mischief.

"Keton!" I shouted.

I ran to him with open arms, tears of happiness streaming down my cheeks. Until I realized why he lay there, propped up against sacks of rice and flour.

Grief swelled in my throat. My brother couldn't walk.

I climbed onto the wagon and threw my arms around him. He embraced me, but the emptiness in his eyes was clear to see.

The war had taken much from us. Too much. I'd thought I'd hardened my heart enough after Finlei's death, then after Sendo's—to be strong for Baba's sake. But a part of me cracked that day Keton returned.

I fled to my room and curled up against the wall. I sewed until my fingers bled, until the pain swallowed the sobs wracking me. But by the next morning, I had patched myself together. I needed to take care of Baba. And now Keton, too.

Five winters, and I had grown up without knowing it. I was as tall as Keton now, my hair straight and black like my mother's. Other families with girls my age hired matchmakers to find them husbands. Mine would have too, had Mama been alive and Baba still a successful tailor. But those days were long past.

When spring came, the emperor announced that he was to take the shansen's daughter, Lady Sarnai, as his wife. A'landi's bloodiest war would end with a wedding between Emperor Khanujin and his enemy's daughter. Baba and I didn't have the heart to celebrate.

Still, it was good news. Peace depended on harmony between the emperor and the shansen. I hoped a royal wedding would heal their rift—and bring more visitors traveling along the Great Spice Road.

That day, I placed the largest order of silk we could afford. It was a risky purchase, but I hoped—we *needed* business to get better before winter came.

My dream of becoming a tailor for the emperor had faded to a distant memory. Our only source of income now was my skill with the needle. I accepted that I was going to stay in Port Kamalan forever, resigned to my corner in Baba's shop.

I was wrong.

# CHAPTER TWO

A patchwork of thick, gray clouds drifted across the sky, the seams so tight I could barely see the light behind them. It was a gloomy day, odd for the beginning of summer, but no rain fell, so I continued my morning routine.

I carried a ladder under my arm, climbing it to check on each of the mulberry trees growing in our small yard. Spindly white silkworms fed on the leaves, but there were no cocoons to collect today. My little silkworms didn't produce much during the summer, so I wasn't too concerned that my basket remained empty.

During the war, silk had been too expensive to buy, and our shop didn't produce enough to sell, so most of our business had been in linen and hemp. Working with the rough fabrics had kept my fingers nimble and my art alive. But now that the war was over, we'd have to work more in silk again. I hoped my order would arrive soon.

"Baba," I called, "I'm going out to the market. Do you want anything?"

No answer. He was probably still asleep. He'd been staying up late, praying at the family altar, since Keton's return.

Our small market was busier than ever, and the peddlers wouldn't haggle down their prices. I took my time, hoping that would help me avoid a certain someone on the way home. But as I feared, Calu was there.

"Let me help you with that," he said, reaching for my basket.

"I don't need help."

Calu grabbed the handle and pulled. "Would you stop being so stubborn, Maia?"

"Careful! You'll spill everything."

As soon as Calu loosened his grip, I yanked the basket from him and rushed into our shop. I closed the door and started unloading the goods I'd purchased: bundles of linen and muslin, small books of paper for sketching, a handful of oranges, a bag of pink-yellow peaches given to me by our neighbors, salmon eyes (Baba's favorite), tuna eggs, and a short sack of rice.

I had been so busy fending off Calu I only now saw the carriage parked across the street—and the man waiting in our shop.

He was portly and cast a wide shadow. My eyes roamed over his attire, picking out the brass button missing among its brothers on his bright blue silk coat. I tended to take note of people's clothing more than their faces.

My shoulders straightened. "Good day, sir," I said, but the man was in no hurry to greet me. He was too busy eyeing the shop with disdain. Shame made my cheeks prickle with heat.

There was fabric strewn over the floors behind the counter, and a swath of cotton to be hand-painted hung askew in the dyeing rack. We had dismissed all outside help years ago, and there was no money to hire cleaning servants. I had stopped noticing the cobwebs in the corners and the peach blossoms that the wind had swept through the door scattered about the shop.

The man's gaze finally circled back to me. I pushed my hair

from my eyes and tossed my braid behind my shoulder in an effort to make myself more presentable. Then I bowed, as if my good manners might make up for the shop's shortcomings. I tried again. "Good day, sir. How can I help you?"

Finally, the man stepped toward my counter. A large jade pendant, in the shape of a fan, swayed from his sash. It had a giant red tassel made of knotted silken cords.

*An imperial official.* Yet he wasn't wearing the typical gray-and-navy tunic that most imperial servants wore. No, he was a eunuch.

What was one of His Majesty's eunuchs doing here?

I looked up, taking in his bulging eyes and the finely trimmed beard that did nothing to hide the scornful twist of his lips.

He raised his chin. "You are the daughter of Kalsang Tamarin."

I nodded. My temples were sweaty from being outside in the marketplace, and the scent of the oranges I'd bought tickled my stomach, which growled. Loudly.

The eunuch wrinkled his nose and said, "His Imperial Majesty, Emperor Khanujin, requests your father's presence in the Summer Palace."

Surprised, I dropped my basket on the floor. "My . . . my father is honored. What does His Imperial Majesty wish of him?"

The emperor's official cleared his throat. "Your family has served for many generations as court tailors. We have need of your father's services. Lord Tainak recommended him highly."

My heart pounded as my mind raced to recall the dress I'd made for Lady Tainak. Oh, yes, a jacket and skirt of the finest silk, with hand-painted cranes and magnolias. The order had been a boon during the winter, and I'd painstakingly rationed the payment so that it would feed us for weeks.

I didn't need to know any details to feel sure this job would save my family. My dream to sew for the emperor, lost for so long, bubbled in me again.

"Ah, Lady Tainak's gown," I said, biting my tongue before I divulged that *I'd* made it, not Baba. I couldn't contain my excitement—and curiosity. "What might His Majesty require of my father's services?"

The eunuch frowned at my boldness. "Where is he?"

"Sir, my father is indisposed, but I'd be happy to relay His Majesty's instructions—"

"Then I will speak with your brother."

I chose to ignore his insult. "My brother recently returned from fighting the Five Winters' War. He is resting."

The eunuch put his hands on his hips. "Tell your father to come, girl, before I lose my patience and report that he has insolently neglected a summons from the emperor."

I pursed my lips and bowed quickly. Then I rushed to find Baba.

As usual, he was kneeling at the small shrine by our kitchen stove, holding thin sticks of incense. He bowed three times, once to each of the three different wooden carvings of Amana, the mother goddess.

Mama had painted the Amana statues when I was a child. I'd helped her design the goddess's divine gowns: one of the sun, one of the moon, and one of the stars. Those statues were among the few things we had that had belonged to Mama, and Baba prayed to them every day and long into the night. He never spoke of Mama, but I knew he missed her terribly.

I didn't wish to interrupt his worship, but I had no choice. "Baba," I said, shaking his frail shoulders. "There's an imperial official here to see you."

I walked my father to the front of the shop. He was so weak

21

he leaned against my arm. He refused to use a cane, saying it wasn't his legs that were broken.

"Master Tamarin," the eunuch said stiffly. Baba's appearance did not impress him, and he showed it. "His Majesty is in need of a tailor. I have been ordered to bring you with me to the Summer Palace."

Trying not to chew on my lip, I stared at the floor. There was no way Baba could make the journey to the Summer Palace, not in his condition. I fidgeted, already knowing what Baba was going to say before he said it—

"Much as your presence honors me, I cannot go."

I watched the eunuch's nose turn up at Baba, his expression a mixture of disbelief and disdain. I bit my lip, knowing I shouldn't interfere, but my agitation grew. We *needed* this chance.

"*I* can," I blurted, just as the emperor's official was about to speak. "I know my father's trade. It was I who made Lady Tainak's gown."

Baba turned to me. "Maia!"

"I can sew," I insisted. "Better than anyone." I took a step toward the dyeing rack. Above it were richly embroidered scrolls that I had labored over for weeks and months. "Simply look at my work—"

Baba shook his head, warning me to stop.

"His Imperial Majesty's instructions were clear," the eunuch said with a sniff. "To bring the master tailor of the Tamarin family to the Summer Palace. A girl cannot become a master."

At my side, Baba curled his hands into fists. He said, in the strongest voice I'd heard from him in months, "And who are you to tell me who is a master of my craft?"

The eunuch puffed up his chest. "I am Minister Lorsa of His Imperial Majesty's Ministry of Culture."

"Since when do ministers play messenger?"

"You think too much of yourself, Master Tamarin," Lorsa replied coldly. "I've only come to you because Master Dingmar in Gangsun is ill. Your work might have been held in great esteem at one time, but your years lost to ale and wine have soured your family's good name. If not for Lord Tainak's recommendation, I would not be here at all."

I couldn't take it anymore. "You have no right to speak to him that way."

"Maia, Maia." Baba rested a hand on my shoulder. "There's mending in the back to be done."

It was his way of dismissing me. I gritted my teeth and turned, but I glared at the emperor's messenger and walked as slowly as I could.

"My carriage will be waiting outside on Yanamer Street," Lorsa was saying. "If you or your son is not there by tomorrow morning, I will be forced to give this generous offer to someone else. I have my doubts that your humble shop will survive the shame of failing our emperor."

Then he turned on his heel and left.

"Baba," I said, rushing to him as soon as the shop door closed. "You cannot go."

"The emperor's command cannot be ignored."

"It's an invitation," I said. "Not a command."

"That's how it is worded. But I know what will happen if we ignore it." Baba sighed. "Word will spread that we did not heed the emperor's calling. No one will come to the shop anymore, and we will lose everything."

He was right. It wasn't just about the money or the honor—it was a mandatory invitation. Like being drafted to fight in the Five Winters' War.

"Now that the war is over," Baba said, "the emperor needs to show the rest of the world that A'landi is great. He will do so by hiring the best of everyone: musicians, tailors, and painters. No expense will be spared. It is an honor to be invited. One I cannot refuse."

I said nothing. Baba was in no shape to travel to the palace, let alone become the emperor's new tailor. And Keton . . . Keton couldn't sew the most basic of stitches, let alone garments worthy of the imperial court.

But me? I *knew* I could do it. I *wanted* to be the imperial tailor.

I went to my room and scrubbed my sleeve over the smudges on my mirror so I could see myself clearly. Honestly.

Baba always said I took after Mama, not him. I'd never believed him. I looked at my straight nose, large round eyes, and full lips—yes, those were from Mama. But Mama had been the most beautiful woman I'd ever seen, while I . . . I'd grown up in a house full of men and didn't even know how to act like a girl.

Finlei used to tease that, from behind, I looked exactly like Keton—reedy as a boy. The freckles on my face and arms didn't help either. Girls were supposed to be delicate and pale. But maybe, *maybe* all this could work in my favor.

I couldn't sing or recite poetry. I couldn't dance. I didn't have grace, or charm or wiles. But I *could* sew. Heavens, I could sew.

It had to be me.

When Baba returned to his prayers, I rubbed my finger on the coal from the fireplace and smeared it across my eyebrows. By my worktable was a pair of shears. I grasped them but hesitated. My hands never trembled when they cut cloth—I could cut a straight line in my sleep—so why did they tremble now?

24

I touched the ends of my hair, which reached past my waist even when braided. I undid the ribbons and unwove the braids. The waves rolled down across my back, tickling my spine.

I lowered my hand, bringing the scissors down with it. What I wanted to do was crazy. I needed to be rational, needed to consider the consequences. But all I could hear was Minister Lorsa telling me I couldn't go. And Baba telling me I couldn't go.

My whole life, I'd been told what I *couldn't* do because I was a girl. Well, this was my chance to find out. The only thing I *could* do was take it.

I relaxed my grip on the scissors' bows and pressed the blades against the back of my neck. With one swift motion, I cut my hair at my shoulders. The strands whisked down my back, landing at my feet in a pool of black satin, which the breeze from an open window swept apart as easily as feathers.

My hands stopped trembling, and I tied my hair back the way Keton and all the boys his age did. A strange calm fell over me, as if I had cut away my fears along with my hair. I knew that wasn't true, but it was too late to panic. Now I needed proper clothes.

I brought a tray of plain winter melon soup and steamed fish to Keton's bed. He used to share his room with Finlei and Sendo. Our house had felt small then. Now it felt too big. Half my room was storage for fabrics and beads and dyes . . . and now Keton had this whole room to himself.

My brother was asleep. His lips were twisted into a grimace as he snored. He'd told us he felt no pain even though his legs were broken.

"How can I feel pain if I can't feel my legs?" he'd tried to joke.

I set down his dinner and pulled up his blanket so it covered his shoulders. Then I reached into his drawer and pulled out a pair of his trousers. I folded them over my arm and began tiptoeing out.

"Maia." Keton stirred.

I whirled around. "I thought you were asleep."

"You thought wrong." Keton's head settled back onto the pillow.

I sat beside him on the edge of his bed. "Are you hungry? I brought dinner."

"You're stealing my clothes," he observed, nodding at the pile on my arm. "What's this all about?"

I leaned into a shadow so he wouldn't see my hair, and pursed my lips. "There was an official in the shop earlier. He wants Baba to go to the Summer Palace to make clothes for Emperor Khanujin."

Keton closed his eyes. War had driven out the rebelliousness in my youngest brother, and he looked decades older than his nineteen years. "Baba hasn't sewn in years. He can't go."

"He won't," I confirmed. "I'm going."

Keton pushed himself up with his palms. "Demon's breath, Maia! Are you crazy? You can't—"

"I don't want to hear it."

"You can't go," my brother finished, raising his voice over mine. "You're a girl."

"Not anymore." I touched my hair; then I gritted my teeth. "I'm tired of being told I'm not worthy."

"It's not just a matter of being worthy," Keton said, coughing into his sleeve. "It's a matter of tradition. Besides, they wouldn't want a girl taking the emperor's measurements."

I blushed in spite of myself. "I'll go as you, Keton Tamarin."

"Baba would never agree to this."

"Baba doesn't have to know."

Keton shook his head. "And here I always thought you were the obedient one." He leaned back with a resigned sigh. "It's dangerous."

"Keton, please. I need to do this. For us. For—"

"*This* is exactly why you shouldn't go," my brother interrupted. "Stop trying to convince me. If you're going to act like a boy, you can't think like a girl. Don't stare at the floor so much. Look a man in the eyes when you speak, and never hesitate."

I quickly lifted my gaze. "I'm *not* trying to convince you! And I *don't* always hesitate." Then I looked down again.

Keton groaned.

"Sorry! I can't help it. It's habit."

"You're never going to pass as a boy," he said. "You bite your lips and stare at the floor. And when you're not staring at the floor, you're staring at the sky."

I looked up, indignant. "I am not!"

"More of that," Keton encouraged. "More shouting. Boys are angry and arrogant. They like to be the best at everything."

"I think that's just you, Keton."

"If only I had time to train you."

"I grew up with the three of you. I know what boys are like."

"Do you?" Keton frowned. "You're a village girl, Maia. You're inexperienced in the ways of the world. You've spent your life sewing in the corner of our shop."

"And now I'll be spending my days sewing in the back of the palace."

He made a face, as if that proved his point. "Just try not to talk too much. Don't draw attention to yourself." He leaned back, his arms behind his head. "People will see what they want to see."

The sad wisdom in his voice reminded me of Baba. "What do you mean?"

"Exactly that," he said. "You sew better than anyone in this world. Focus on that, not on whether you're a girl or boy." He propped himself up with his elbows, studying me. "Finlei was right. From the back you really do look like a boy. And with all your freckles, you're not pale like most girls. . . . Baba lets you spend too much time out in the sun—"

"Someone has to collect the silkworms," I said irritably.

"You don't have that many curves, either." He squinted at me. "And your voice isn't very melodious. You've never been good at music."

I almost threw his clothes at him for the insult. "I'm not trying to become a concubine."

Keton clucked his tongue. "Don't wrinkle your nose so much, and try not to smile."

"Like this?" I asked. I imitated the grimace he made when he was sleeping.

"Better." He leaned back, a small smile on his lips. But it disappeared as quickly as it had come. "Are you sure you want to do this? If the emperor finds out . . . if *anyone* finds out . . ."

"I'll be killed," I finished for him. "I know."

But this was the best way to take care of my family. My chance to become a real tailor, the best tailor in all of A'landi.

"It'll be good money," I said firmly. "I'll send all of it home. Besides . . ." I managed a smile. "I already cut my hair."

Keton sighed. "I can't believe *I'm* telling you this, but be careful."

"I will."

"I'll expect plenty of stories about the girls at court when you get back," my brother said lightly. "And about Emperor Khanujin." He tensed. "Maybe you'll even see the shansen."

"I promise," I said softly. "I'll come back full of stories."

I glanced at the cane I had bought Keton when he first came home a month ago. He'd never touched it. How could he use it, when he could barely move his legs?

"Take it," he said, watching me.

The wood was rough, and it bit into my palm. Good—some pain would remind me to stay on my guard.

"Promise me you'll try to walk?" I said to him. "A little every day."

"I'll take a step for every day that you're gone."

That was enough to solidify my decision. I kissed my brother on the forehead. "Then I'll hope to be gone a long time."

. . .

While Baba slept, Keton drilled me on how to act like a boy. How to laugh deeply from my stomach, how to grunt with satisfaction after a good meal, how to grimace after drinking a strong cup of wine. He taught me not to apologize for burping, not to hide when I was passing wind, and to spit whenever someone dared insult my honor.

Then finally, when he was too exhausted to continue the lesson, I went to my room and paced back and forth, going over all the things that could go wrong.

*If I'm caught, I'll be killed.*

*But Keton and Baba need me to do this.*

Secretly, I knew *I* needed it too. If I stayed here, I would become Calu's wife—a baker's wife—and my fingers would forget how to sew.

So with no more hesitation, I packed all that I might need. An extra change of Keton's clothes; my best threads, flosses, awls, and needles; my embroidery ribbons and pincushion; chalk, paintbrushes, paint pots, sketchbooks, and pens.

The sun was in a hurry to rise, or so it felt. Light washed out the blanket of stars above me. I watched the morning crawl over the sea, until it touched my street and my house.

I was ready, my belongings carefully packed into a bundle that I slung over my shoulder. As I headed for the door, I walked confidently—as Keton once did—with a limp to complete the impression, my body bowing over my cane for support.

"Wait," Baba rasped from behind. "Wait."

Guilt swelled in my chest. "I'm sorry, Baba."

Baba shook his head. "I expected it. You were always the strong one."

"No," I said quietly, "Finlei and Sendo were the strong ones."

"Finlei was brave. Sendo, too, in his own way. But you, Maia, you are strong. Like your mother. You hold us together."

My knees gave. "Baba . . ."

He clutched the side of the door, his other hand outstretched with what looked like a bundle of cloth. "Take this."

The bundle was made of silk so fine I thought it might melt at my touch. I undid the golden cord. Inside was—

A pair of scissors.

I looked at my father in confusion.

"They were your grandmother's," Baba said, wrapping the scissors again as if the sight of them pained him. "They never spoke to me. They were waiting for you."

"What do they—"

Baba silenced my questions. "You'll know when you need them."

I opened my mouth, about to tell him to take care of Keton, and to take care of himself. But Finlei and Sendo had left with such words on their lips, and they'd never returned. So I said nothing and simply nodded.

"Maia," Baba said, his hand on my shoulder. There was a light in his eyes I hadn't seen in years. "Be careful. The palace . . . it will be dangerous."

"I will be careful, Baba. I promise."

"Go, then. Show them what you can do."

I leaned on my cane, dragging my right leg behind me as I limped toward the carriage.

The sun was already bright, but I didn't have any hands free to shield my face. My features crumpled, and Lorsa grunted when he saw me.

"Keton Tamarin?" he said, looking me up and down. "You and your sister share a strong resemblance."

My whole body knotted up like a badly coiled rope. I forced a manly laugh, which turned more into a cough. "I hope that's all we share. After all, she can't sew and I can."

The eunuch harrumphed in agreement; then he tossed Baba a sack of jens.

"Get in," he said to me.

Keton was right. People only saw what they wanted to see.

One last glance at Baba, and at Keton's window. Then into the carriage I went, with no idea what awaited me. Only that I must succeed—at all costs.

# CHAPTER THREE

It was a five days' carriage ride from Port Kamalan to the Summer Palace. I was disappointed that there was no need to sail there, for, despite having grown up in a port town, I'd never been on a ship. I'd never ridden in a carriage, either—at least, not on such a long journey. My legs and back grew sore from sitting for so long, but I didn't dare complain. I was too excited. And anxious.

Would I be good enough to sew for the imperial court? And would I see Emperor Khanujin in the Summer Palace? I had to, if I was to become his tailor. I wasn't sure how I felt about that.

I did not know much about my sovereign. He was born in the dragon year, like Finlei, which meant he was twenty-three years of age. Stories said he'd been a fierce warrior during the Five Winters' War, that he could win a man's loyalty with just a nod, that he was so handsome even the sun paled in comparison. That everyone who saw him loved him.

But I wondered if these were all stories.

If the emperor were truly so wonderful, he wouldn't have led A'landi to war—even to save the country from breaking in two. Even to save his throne from the treacherous shansen.

A good emperor wouldn't have taken my brothers away from me.

I squeezed my fingers over my lap, the pressure making me wince. The pain kept me from falling apart, as I always wanted to when I remembered what the war had cost my family.

*Boys don't cry,* I scolded myself. I turned toward the window and wiped my nose with the back of my hand.

I tried to focus on other things. Having idle hands always made me anxious, so I busied myself with knitting a sweater. I was fast, and when I finished, I unraveled the yarn and knit another one, and then I practiced my embroidery on a scrap of cotton.

Minister Lorsa never answered the few questions I ventured to ask, and he made no conversation. He slept as much as a bear, and he smelled twice as bad. Everything he ate, he burped out, so I spent most of the trip with my head out the carriage window, savoring the changing smells of A'landi's terrain as I knit.

On the fifth day, I spotted the Summer Palace in the distance. It was the size of my thumbnail from where the carriage was, and lay cradled in a large valley along the Jingan River, between the Singing Mountains. I had heard tales of its grandeur—its sloping golden roofs, vermillion pillars, and ivory walls—and I trembled with excitement, staring as it gradually became larger and more real to me.

Above us, a hawk soared, black but for the tips of its wings, which looked brushed with snow. Something gold glinted on its talons—like a ring or a bracelet.

"What an odd bird," I mused. "Is it the emperor's? It must be . . . with that cuff. What is it doing so far from the woodlands?"

My voice stirred the sleeping Lorsa, and he scowled at me for waking him.

"Look," I said, pointing out the window. "A hawk."

"An annoyance," he muttered as the hawk let out a cry. "Cursed bird."

The hawk dipped, spreading its great wings as it swooped beside the carriage. It was so close I could see its eyes. They glowed yellow and were sharply intelligent—they caught my gaze and held it, as if the bird were studying my features and marking me.

I stared back. The hawk's expression was—almost human.

Mesmerized, I reached my fingers out to stroke its throat. With a sudden jerk, the hawk darted away. It soared back into the sky, disappearing behind a tree on the palace grounds.

The carriage dropped us off at the base of a hill. Wisteria vines swayed in the gentle breeze, scenting the air around the eighty-eight steps to the servants' entrance. The ascent, I later learned, was a way of keeping us in our place and reminding us we were far below Emperor Khanujin, the Son of Heaven.

I stretched my legs and let out a small groan, feeling the stiffness in my calves from sitting for so long.

"There's no one to carry you up the steps," Lorsa said with a smirk.

I didn't understand what he meant until I remembered I was holding Keton's cane. "Oh. Don't worry about me."

Lorsa certainly didn't. He swept up the steps, leaving me behind.

I hurried after him. Even though my shoulders ached from carrying my belongings, and my legs twisted and turned—confused by how to use Keton's cane—I didn't stop to rest.

This was where it would begin. Where I would restore honor to my family's name. Where I would prove that a girl *could* be the best tailor in A'landi.

. . .

The Summer Palace was a maze of golden-roofed pavilions, winding cobblestone paths, and brilliantly designed gardens. Blossoms in every shade of pink and purple bloomed, and butterflies flitted about.

Everywhere I looked were men in gray-and-navy tunics with long, thin black beards. Servants and minor officials, they walked slightly stooped, as if ready to bow at any moment. In contrast, the eunuchs in bright blue moved with their backs straight as needles, holding closed fans at their sides. A few welcomed me with kind smiles before Lorsa glared at them, but it was enough to make me breathe easier. Maybe not everyone in the palace was as unpleasant as Lorsa.

A maid passed, carrying a platter of almond cookies and steaming chestnut cakes, and my stomach grumbled as I followed Lorsa along the narrow path. The buildings became more tightly spaced, the trees and bushes slightly less manicured. We'd arrived at the servants' quarters.

Lorsa was impatient when I finally caught up with him in front of a wide, open archway. "This is the Hall of Supreme Diligence," he announced, "where you shall work."

I limped inside, greeted at the entrance by life-sized statues of the Three Great Sages, A'landi's legendary scholars. The hall's floor was cool as porcelain, the walls hung with painted scrolls: most of His Imperial Majesty's favorite aphorisms, and others of peonies and catfish and cranes. The open-air latticed windows let in sounds of the real birds outside. No hawks, but plenty of larks and thrushes, even as the evening fell.

It was the largest room I'd ever been in—at least ten times bigger than Calu's father's kitchen, and three times the size of Port Kamalan's temple. There were spinning wheels in the corner of the hall, and twelve tables, each equipped with a weaving loom, an embroidery frame, and a basket full of threads, needles, and pins. Workstations were separated by folding wooden screens with hooks for hanging and draping cloth.

Eleven tailors were seated already at their stations, and they stared at me, whispering.

I started to lower my gaze, then raised my chin and frowned.

"Are these also imperial tailors?" I asked Lorsa, hobbling as quickly as I could behind him.

"There will be only one." The eunuch continued to the other side of the hall, the side with less sunshine. He pointed at a table. "This will be your station until you are dismissed."

*Dismissed?* "I'm sorry, sir. I'm confused."

Lorsa peered at me. "You didn't think you were the only tailor called to His Majesty's attention, did you?"

"O-of course not," I stammered.

"Surely you did not presume His Majesty would employ a tailor without first testing him?"

I realized my mistake now. How naïve I was to think I'd been chosen—that it would be so effortless to save my family's honor.

No, no. That wasn't it at all.

I'd be competing for the position. These eleven other tailors—they were my rivals!

Finding my courage, I looked at them. Each was dressed in his finest. I saw splashes of jade and pearl, velvet coats, brocade scarves with silk tassels, and gold-studded belts . . . and I suddenly understood why they were staring at me. It wasn't because of my limp, or that I was the youngest by far.

I was the most poorly dressed! The dye on my shirt was

faded, the fabric worn, my pant cuffs rolled to my ankles—and my sleeves far too long.

What kind of tailor couldn't even hem his own pants and make a shirt that fit?

My cheeks heated, and I bowed my head in shame, fiercely wishing I'd thought to alter Keton's clothes in the carriage instead of knitting a silly sweater.

I set my basket and satchel on my table and began to unpack my supplies. The tailor across from me said to his neighbor, loudly enough for me to hear, "A hundred jens he'll be the first one to go."

A snicker. "Why would I bet *against* that?"

My face grew hotter, and I glared at them. Then, folding up my sleeves, I sat on my stool and faced Lorsa.

"Now that you twelve are finally assembled," the minister announced, "we may begin the trial. Only A'landi's very best tailor is invited to serve the imperial family. Master Huan held the position for thirty years, but his recent passing has left the position empty. His Imperial Majesty, in his infinite wisdom and glory, has invited tailors from across A'landi to compete for this high honor.

"Many of you have already served as court tailors, but the imperial tailor is among the most esteemed and privileged of His Majesty's loyal servants. It is a position that is held for life and brings much prosperity to the one who is deserving.

"Of the tailors here today, only one will fill the vacancy in His Imperial Majesty's staff and begin work for Lady Sarnai immediately."

*Lady Sarnai?* That didn't make any sense. "I thought the position was for His Majesty," I muttered.

"I heard you utter something, Keton Tamarin," Lorsa said, his beady eyes blinking at me.

I clamped my lips shut. For a dangerous moment, I'd forgotten to sound like my brother. Had Lorsa noticed?

"Speak up if you have something to say."

"Um." My mouth became suddenly dry. I cleared my throat and summoned my best deep, male voice. "I was under the impression, sir, that the position was for a tailor for Emperor Khanujin."

"Your job is to please the emperor," the eunuch corrected me. "And he wishes the new imperial tailor to furnish Lady Sarnai's wardrobe."

I dipped my head, but not before seeing the tailors in front of me exchange glances. "Understood, sir."

My question had stirred unrest among the other tailors. Not everyone was comfortable with the idea of serving the shansen's daughter, especially with the war having ended so recently.

Minister Lorsa went on: "Once the new imperial tailor has been selected, his first task will be to create Lady Sarnai's wedding gown, so it is of utmost importance that your designs during the trial please Lady Sarnai as well as His Majesty.

"We shall begin with a simple task. As Lady Sarnai comes from the much colder North, she has few garments appropriate for the Summer Palace's temperate weather. His Majesty wishes her to have a shawl appropriate for the evening's gentle breezes."

A *shawl*? How in the Nine Heavens was Lady Sarnai to determine a tailor's skill by a shawl?

"You have each been allotted a bolt of white silk. You may cut your silk as you see fit. His Imperial Majesty's seal has been printed on each corner of the swath; all four seals must be present in your design. Only the dyes, embroidery threads, and ribbons in the materials cabinets may be used for your design in this challenge. No tailor is permitted outside assistance. Have your pieces ready for inspection tomorrow morning."

*Tomorrow?* I looked around and saw every tailor's back stiffen. Clearly everyone was as shocked as I was, but no one dared say anything, so I kept quiet too.

"Lady Sarnai will arrive in the morning to determine the tailors invited to stay for the next round of the trial," Lorsa continued. "Do not forget that the shansen's is an inherited title, like the emperor's, part of an unbroken bloodline of A'landi's military leaders. Lady Sarnai will be addressed as Your Highness, is that understood?" The minister waited for us to murmur that it was. "Good. May the Sages inspire you to craft something worthy of her."

No gong or bell pealed, but the words rang of freedom to my ears. I got up, reaching for the bolt of cloth and my sketchbook. The other tailors were already furiously designing, but I had no idea what I was going to do for Lady Sarnai's shawl.

Being surrounded by eleven sweaty, zealously competitive men wasn't going to inspire me, so I gathered some supplies from the cabinet and left the Hall of Supreme Diligence to find my own way.

# CHAPTER FOUR

My new home was a narrow room shaped like an elbow, furnished with a cot and a three-legged table barely steady enough to hold a candle. There was also a small bronze vessel on the wooden windowsill with incense for prayer, a bamboo lantern hanging from the ceiling, and a porcelain washbasin in which a fly had drowned.

"At least it's clean," I said aloud. "And I don't have to share it with anyone."

It was the first time I'd been alone in nearly a week. I leaned my head against the painted wall, taking a moment to breathe before I addressed the real reason I needed time to myself.

Slowly, I undid my shirt buttons. My entire torso pounded with pain. My chest was fairly flat for a girl, but I'd taken the precaution of binding strips of linen around it, and after five days of travel, my discomfort was enormous. I didn't dare remove the strips, but I dipped my hands into the bowl of water and cleaned off my sweat.

I'd have to get used to the pain.

I buttoned my shirt again and emptied my satchel onto the bed. For once, the sight of my tools didn't inspire or comfort me. I heaved a sigh. There was no way I could embroider an entire shawl by tomorrow morning.

I could paint one, though.

I was about to rifle through my things for my brushes when the bundle with Baba's scissors caught my eye. Out of curiosity, I unwrapped it, holding out the scissors so they glinted in the dim light. The finger bows were thinner and more delicate than those of my own pair, but aside from the sun and moon engraved on the shanks, there was nothing special about them. Besides, I didn't need an extra pair of scissors, so I rewrapped them and shoved them under my cot.

"Now, where are the paint pots I took?" I muttered, rummaging through my supplies. "Did I leave them in the hall?"

I must have. With a groan, I limped back toward the Hall of Supreme Diligence. I'd hoped not to run into anyone on the way, but an old man waved at me as I passed him.

He was large and wide in girth, but his fingers appeared thin and nimble. A glance at his sash confirmed he was a fellow tailor: we wore pins and needles the way a general wore medals. I stopped to greet him. He was not someone who had bet against my abilities—that I knew of.

"You must be Master Tamarin's son," he said. "Your face is the easiest one to recognize. You barely look old enough to grow a beard!"

He said it so cheerfully I forgot my restraint and laughed.

"Wing Longhai," he introduced himself. "From the Bansai Province."

I recognized the name. Master Longhai was famous for making men's robes; he'd attired the most acclaimed scholars and the highest nobles. He'd even made a robe for Emperor Khanujin's father.

"Keton Tamarin," I replied. "From Port Kamalan, south of Gangsun."

Longhai smiled. His face was craggy, with deep grooves; his

skin was touched by the sun, more than was usual for a master tailor, which suggested that, like me, he came from humble beginnings. Even so, his clothes were very fine, and he gave off a faint smell of rice wine under a perfume of sandalwood and lotus.

"Ah," he said. "I thought you looked like you were from the South. I take it you've brought amulets for luck and fortitude? My wife wouldn't let me leave home without a stockpile of charms. Master Yindi already has a dozen hanging off his desk!"

I wrapped my hand over my cane. "I don't believe in such things."

"And you call yourself a Southerner?"

"Port Kamalan is very small," I replied tersely. "There's little place for magic there."

Longhai shook his head at me. "Magic might not have any place in Port Kamalan, but you're in the imperial court now. You'll change your mind. Especially after you meet the emperor's Lord Enchanter."

I raised an eyebrow. I knew little of enchanters, lord or not, other than that they were rare and drifted from land to land. They didn't sound like very loyal advisers to me, so I didn't understand why kings and emperors prized them so much.

Longhai must have noticed the skeptical look on my face, for he said, "The Lord Enchanter advises Emperor Khanujin on many matters. He served the emperor's father for years, yet he hasn't aged a day! Some of the tailors are trying to befriend him—they'll do anything for an edge."

"Wouldn't using magic be cheating?"

"An unfair advantage, I'd say. But cheating?" Longhai chuckled. "Do you think the emperor's trial will be a competition merely of skill?"

I shrugged. I'd always been skeptical of magic. But I tended to be skeptical of most things I couldn't stitch together with a needle and thread. "What else is there to test?"

"You have much to learn," he said, but not unkindly.

We walked together to the Hall of Supreme Diligence, skirting a garden full of winding paths and plum and pine trees.

"The Courtyard of Heavenly Peace. We aren't allowed past the waterfall there, not without permission." Longhai lowered his voice. "But that doesn't mean we can't take a peek."

He crouched with his head bent and nudged me to do the same; then he pointed. Far on the other side of the garden, a woman walked briskly as three servants trailed her.

She was beautiful, with ivory skin, cascading black hair, and a swanlike neck. And clearly highborn, given the servants and the regal way she walked. But her clothing was odd: she wore leather boots, a simple shift of pale blue broadcloth that barely covered her ankles, and a quilted fur coat over her shoulders, hardly appropriate for the mild weather.

The maids were pleading with her. "Your Highness, there isn't much time before your welcoming banquet. Will you not change?"

"What is wrong with what I'm wearing?" the lady replied. Her tone was sharp, and it left no room for argument.

Her maids chased after her. "Your Highness, please!"

The lady strode on, deaf to their pleas. Following her was the largest man I'd ever seen. He was big as a bear and dwarfed the entire pathway. His beard was sharply cropped, and his eyes were narrow, crested by thick, black eyebrows.

"Your Highness," he said in a deep, gravelly voice. "You should heed your maids' advice. Please. It is what your father would wish."

The lady stilled. She wouldn't look at her companion, but tension flared between them. She raised her chin. "You *would* take his side, wouldn't you, Lord Xina?"

I couldn't see whether Lord Xina nodded or bowed in response, but the lady turned to her head maid. "Very well," she said, her voice shakier than before. "I will see what garments His Majesty has to offer. However, I make no promise to wear any of them."

Longhai rose once the lady was out of earshot. "Well, well. I'd say that was worthwhile. We'll have an edge against the others tomorrow. That was Lady Sarnai, the shansen's daughter."

I tried not to show my surprise. *That* was the lady we'd have to sew for during the trial? I'd envisioned her as a warrior like her father—a girl who wore armor and breeches, had no trace of femininity, and had grown up wild and untamed. Lady Sarnai *did* look fierce, but she was also . . . beautiful.

A grin spread across Longhai's wrinkled face. "Not what you expected, I see."

"She's very graceful" was all I could manage. "What about the man behind her?"

"Lord Xina," Longhai replied in a pinched tone. "The shansen's favorite warrior and the son of his most trusted adviser. His presence is an insult to His Majesty."

"An insult?"

"There are rumors Lord Xina was betrothed to Lady Sarnai before the truce was called. That he is her lover. But it's all court gossip. No one knows for certain." The old tailor reached into his robes for a flask. He offered it to me, and after I declined, he took a long drink.

I pondered the way the shansen's daughter had spoken to Lord Xina—was the bitterness in her tone for her lover or for her father? Or both?

Longhai capped his flask. "Did you see her fur coat? Rabbit, fox, wolf, at least three different bears. Northerners only wear what they hunt—Lady Sarnai must be quite skilled." He heaved a sympathetic sigh. "She won't have an easy time adjusting to life here." He leaned closer to me, as if to share a secret. "But she does seem to enjoy aggravating His Majesty. She wore breeches to tea with the emperor and his ministers of war."

Lady Sarnai had nerve. I didn't know whether that made me respect her more—or less.

"I'm sure we'll hear about it tomorrow," Longhai said as we approached the hall.

I wished Longhai's station were next to mine, but he was on the opposite end of the room. So I returned to my table alone and took out my sketchbook to start designing a shawl, not bothering to greet the tailors around me. I had a feeling they resented my presence.

To my relief, they ignored me, too. Since I was the last tailor to arrive for the trial, I'd been assigned the worst table—farthest from the windows and toward the middle, where my work was practically on exhibit for everyone to see.

None of the tailors except for Longhai had introduced themselves to me, but through scraps of their conversations, I caught some names I recognized. Like Longhai, they were masters whose styles I'd grown up studying and emulating; these were men who'd been sewing since long before I was born.

Master Taraha and Master Yindi came from different schools of embroidery, but both were geniuses: Taraha specialized in flowers, and Yindi in double-sided embroidery. Master Boyen was brilliant at knotting; Master Delun wove brocades unlike any others. Master Norbu was a favorite of the nobility.

And me? When we'd lived in Gangsun, Baba had asked visiting friends to teach me their regional styles and crafts, and in Port Kamalan, I'd picked up techniques from every merchant and tailor who'd speak to me.

But I was no master, and I had no reputation.

"You!" a man barked, interrupting my worried thoughts. "Pretty boy!"

The hairs on my neck bristled, but I turned my head. Master Yindi was plump, though not as fat as Longhai, with a pudgy nose that seemed to be always wrinkled at something. He was bald, too, save for the gray sideburns slinking down his cheeks. Ironic, since his beard was so long it almost touched his knees.

"Look here," he said. "Can I have your silk? You'll be going home soon anyway, so you might as well give it over to someone who can use it."

Laughter erupted. It seemed they all agreed I'd be the first to be sent home. My mouth set in a thin line.

"Leave the boy alone," Longhai said above the noise. "If all of you are so great, you shouldn't need extra silk."

"Befriending the rabble, eh, Longhai?" Yindi said. "Wouldn't expect any less from you." He turned back to me. "Are you sure you won't prick yourself with a needle?" he taunted. "My chin hasn't been that smooth since I was a child."

"What happened to that leg of yours?" another tailor chimed in.

The ink on my page smeared. I flipped it and restarted my sketch. *People will see what they want to see,* I reminded myself. *Better a girlish boy than a boyish girl.*

"Are you deaf, pretty boy?"

"Or are you only crippled?"

Now I stopped sketching. "I fought in the war. And a broken leg doesn't mean I can't use my hands," I snapped defiantly. "I'd wager I can sew faster than any of you."

Master Yindi laughed. "We'll see about that. When I was your age, I was still washing shirts for my master. He wouldn't let me anywhere close to a loom." He snorted. "Let me see those hands of yours, pretty boy. I can tell a tailor from a washboy."

I spread my fingers wide to show my calluses. My brothers used to tease that I'd never find a husband because my fingers were rough as a man's.

"So?" I said. "A tailor or a washboy?"

Yindi harrumphed and, pinching his beard in one hand, returned to his stool.

Longhai came to my station, resting a hand on top of my screen. "Don't worry about Yindi," he said. "He's all bark."

"Master Longhai speaks wisely," Norbu interrupted, to my surprise. He had been quiet, and I hadn't seen him approach my table. "We won't get any work done if we waste our time picking on the boy." He gestured at the statues of the Three Sages. "The gods are listening to us, masters. Do you want to invoke their wrath?"

One by one, the tailors shook their heads. Even Yindi, whose desk dangled with charms to ward off demons and bad luck, frowned.

"Then get back to work."

Norbu had influence because he owned a shop in the capital, Jappor, with over a hundred tailors under his command. He was the wealthiest of us all, and the most powerful. His daughter had married an important official. He was practically nobility.

"I trust they'll leave you alone now," Norbu said once the chatter faded. He smiled at me, and I got the distinct sense I now owed him something.

"Thank you," I said.

He toyed with the threads I'd set on my table. Norbu reminded me of an overstuffed lizard—his body was long and thin, but his stomach was round, his eyes half open and half shut so they looked deceptively sleepy. He wasn't mean like Yindi, but I still wished he would leave my things alone.

"We heard that you're taking your father's place here in the trial," he said. "How noble of you. My own baba died before I was born, but Master Huan—the emperor's last tailor—was like a father to me."

I folded my hands, which were itching to work, to be polite. "I didn't realize he was your master."

"Long ago," Norbu replied, sniffling. "But it still pained me when they found his body in the Jingan River last month."

I swallowed. "I'm sorry to hear it."

"He worked in this very hall, you know, with dozens of his apprentices. Even I came sometimes to assist him." Norbu paused. "The maids swear his ghost haunts the palace some nights."

A shiver tingled across my arm. "I don't believe in ghosts."

"Neither do I." Norbu tilted his head, his marblelike eyes studying me. "Worry not about the others, young Tamarin. I'll keep my eye on you."

I was relieved when he finally left me alone, and I draped the silk shawl over my arm. Silk was naturally light on the skin. That was what made it so sought after, so expensive.

I was good at painting, like Master Longhai, but embroidery was my strength, like Master Yindi and Master Taraha.

I decided to paint a garden and embroider its flowers. Peonies, lilies, and chrysanthemums, with a lady holding a dragonfly on her finger. It was a scene I'd practiced dozens of times, and the paint would dry quickly. With only one day to complete the shawl, now was not the time to take an unnecessary risk.

The hours passed. Painting kept my hands and mind busy, but the endless prattle of the other tailors was a constant hum.

"This is servants' work," one grumbled. "I haven't had to knot tassels since I was a boy."

"Dyeing is worse."

"All to be tailor to the traitor's daughter. What glory is there in that?"

"The privilege of serving His Majesty is honor enough," Longhai cut in. "Any more honor, and we'd have to become priests at the High Temple."

On and on they talked, until it had to be past midnight. My eyelids drooped. I hadn't had a good night's sleep since leaving Port Kamalan.

*No, I need to stay alert. I'll never finish if I go to sleep now.*

I stretched my fingers and rubbed a sore muscle in my neck. My whole body was tense. Bending over my work for hours and hours was second nature to me, but not while surrounded by eleven other tailors. The temptation to peek at my neighbors' progress was great, and everyone's chatter made it difficult for me to focus.

I rolled my shoulders back and picked up my needle to embroider the edges of the shawl, taking care not to smudge the painted scene.

"I made a cloak for the Lady of Bandeiya embroidered with a thousand peonies," Master Taraha was saying, "and she loved it so much she paid me with the finest jade necklace. My daughter is lucky to have me as a father. I gave it to her as part of her dowry."

"I've personally met Lady Sarnai. I know what she prefers."

"I can't imagine the barbarian's daughter in such fine silk. What a waste."

I knotted my thread and yanked it free from its spool. If only they would stop chattering!

"And what about you, Keton Tamarin?" Yindi called out from the other side of the room. "You're a quiet one. Why do you want to win His Majesty's little contest?"

I froze. What could I say? I *was* here for the glory, but more to help my family.

*Don't be humble,* Keton had warned me. *A man is proud of his craft. To be less than so is to seem ashamed of it.*

I said, with as much arrogance as I could muster, "Because I'm the best tailor in A'landi."

I heard several of the men scoff. "You're barely a man."

"Youth itself is a talent," Norbu said, calming them. "I trust His Majesty's judgment."

Yindi was relentless. "And how are you the best tailor, young Tamarin?"

I swallowed but spoke boldly. "I can spin and weave and knot. I've studied all four schools of embroidery. I can do a hundred different stitches in my sleep, and I'm fast."

Someone sniffed. "A brilliant design isn't only about speed or intricate stitches."

"I know." I went on, "It's also about composition. And color—"

"You think you know more about color than I do?" Yindi

scoffed. "Well, pretty boy, we'll see what you come up with. My bet is that you won't last through the morning."

"I suppose he can taper and hem a pair of trousers with his eyes closed," Boyen muttered, just loudly enough for me to hear. "So why did he come dressed like a peasant?"

My ego faltered, but I caught Longhai's encouraging smile. "You'll see" was all I could muster.

*Don't draw any more attention,* I warned myself. *They already think there's something odd about you.*

My hands trembled. For the first time I could remember, I had trouble easing my thread into the needle's eye.

"Having difficulty, Tamarin?" Boyen mocked. "Maybe you should try licking the thread." He made a smacking sound. "It's what they teach the children to do."

I couldn't take it anymore. I grabbed my cane and started for the door.

"You can't be tired yet, young Tamarin?" Norbu said when I passed his station. "Why don't you get some tea?"

It was a good idea, and I nodded to thank him for it. The tea reserves were kept in an anteroom in the hall, and I filled a cup, taking a long sip.

When I returned to my table to pick up my shawl, I cried out. Someone had spilled tea over my fabric! The paints were smeared all over the silk. The lady I had painstakingly drawn to resemble Lady Sarnai was no more than a blob.

Who had done this? I looked at all the tailors, but they ignored me.

I bit my lip and bunched up the ruined silk. Tears welled in my eyes, but I wouldn't give them the satisfaction of knowing they had hurt me.

"Had enough, pretty boy?" Yindi shouted at me.

Norbu clapped his hands to get everyone's attention. "Young Tamarin, if you need extra silk, you are welcome to take my scraps. I'm going to sleep."

"Thank you," I whispered. "But I'll manage."

"Norbu," the others cried, "you're going to bed already?"

"I work best alone," he said, stifling a yawn. "And in the morning."

I shoved my damaged silk into my satchel and followed Norbu out, my face hot from trying to suffocate my tears.

The corridors were open to the balmy night air, poorly lit by moonlight and hanging lanterns. I counted the doors, all gray with bronze latches, until I reached my room.

I collapsed on my cot. This had been my one chance to become more than a seamstress who hemmed pants and sewed buttons in Port Kamalan. This had been my chance to become an imperial tailor, the best in all of A'landi, to have my designs worn by royalty and admired throughout the land.

And now?

I drew in a tight breath. Finlei wouldn't want me to give up like this. Neither would Sendo. And Keton . . . *I have to win this position to take care of Baba and Keton. So they won't starve and I won't have to marry Calu. So I won't be a failure.*

I dried my eyes on the edges of my sleeves, then got up and lit a candle to survey the damage to my shawl. The flowers I had spent the afternoon painting had smeared. Even if I blotted them out, my design was ruined. The only way to hide the damage was to start afresh, maybe embroider over the tea stain and smeared paint. A difficult task, given I only had the rest of the night to work.

Sitting cross-legged, I exhaled, took out a sheet of parchment from my satchel, and wearily started to sketch.

*Stay awake!*

I leaned my head against the wall, promising myself I would only take a short break. When next I blinked, my candle was out, a pool of wax at the bottom.

"Demon's breath!" I cursed. I must have fallen asleep.

I lit another candle and stared out at the moon to see how much time I had lost.

My temples throbbed and a low hum filled my head.

I reached for my bag, fumbling for needles and thread, but my finger caught the bow of Baba's scissors instead. *Strange.* I thought I had put them under my cot.

I slipped them into my satchel with the rest of my tools. But what good were scissors now that my shawl was ruined?

*Calm down,* I told myself. *What do you do whenever you're in a situation like this? You don't panic and make more mistakes. You calm down. You take a walk.*

Holding a lantern in one hand, I went back to the Hall of Supreme Diligence. It was empty now, and I walked by each of the other tailors' creations. Master Boyen's drapery was masterful, Master Garad's beading exquisite. Longhai had crafted a swan, embroidered trees around it—beautiful enough to hang as a work of art. And Yindi, impressively, had embroidered nearly the entire shawl.

The pages of my sketchbook rustled, far too tremulously to have been touched by the wind. Unnerved, I set it down and went to the closest window.

*No ghost,* I told myself. *Just a bird.*

With a sigh, I placed my lantern on my table and began to embroider.

The humming in my head was louder now. I looked down, feeling a strange trembling at my side. At first I thought it came from my scissors, but that was impossible, so I ignored it.

Then they started glowing.

I grasped them to snip a loose thread and found that I was unable to put them down. Suddenly, in my mind's eye, I could see the shawl, completed—just as I had sketched it. But there was no way I could accomplish it in the hours remaining.

*But you can,* a voice assured me. *My* voice, but more confident somehow.

The scissors glided over the shawl, possessed in a way that my hands could only follow. Invisible threads repaired the cloth's damage, giving it life anew, and colors from my paint pots soaked into the silk, while the smeared paints dissolved and scattered until my design was back in place.

Impossible as it appeared, the scissors not only cut but embroidered. The thin silver blades split and gathered my threads and flosses to dance through the silk, embroidering intricate flowers and birds, trees, and mountains with precision and elegance.

With magic.

Magic I couldn't stop. My hand wouldn't let go of the scissors, no matter how I tried to pry them away, no matter how much I wanted to put them down. I was under a spell, drunk with their power.

If not for the soreness that swelled between my fingers, I would have thought I was dreaming.

With a final snip, the scissors became dull again, their glow vanished.

Completely spent, I collapsed onto my table and slept.

# CHAPTER FIVE

Something sharp poked my side.

My eyelids flinched, but I didn't open them. Gods, if that was Keton jabbing me awake with a knitting needle . . .

A snicker. "You awake, pretty boy?"

Wait, that didn't sound like Keton. Of course not. I was in the palace, not back home with Baba and my brother.

Drowsily, I stirred. Drool had dried on the corner of my mouth, and as I wiped it clean with my sleeve, Master Boyen's round face loomed over me.

He smacked his lips. "Aw, did I wake you from your beauty sleep, *Master* Tamarin?"

My eyes flew open. Why did he emphasize *master* like that? Did he know I was a girl?

*No,* I thought as my mind sharpened. Word must have gotten around that I was no master. It didn't take much sleuthing to know that none of my father's sons had earned the title yet.

Boyen smirked at me. "You ought to pack up your things. You'll be going home, since your shawl's stained."

I jumped to my feet. My shawl! Where was it?

I vaguely remembered my scissors flashing and cutting . . . as if they'd been possessed by a spirit. No, no. That wasn't possible, I must have imagined it.

Heavens, I must have fallen asleep without finishing!

Frantically, I rummaged through my station for the shawl. Then I remembered: right before I'd put away my father's scissors, I'd tucked them into a basket with my threads from home.

I crouched, fishing the shawl out of its hiding place. It wasn't hard to find—its pale daffodil color peeked out from under my spools.

I unfolded it and gasped.

It wasn't a dream.

Stitches so perfect and embroidery so delicate it should have taken me a month. The couching was flawless, and my twelve colors were blended in graduated tones, making the scene of lilies and peonies look real. Even the lady had been repaired; she wore a vibrant violet robe amid the pink and red flowers, though when I looked closely, she resembled *me* more than Lady Sarnai.

But stupid, stupid me! My shawl was wrinkled. Why hadn't I folded it better?

Anxiously, I smoothed out the wrinkles. A servant brought me a pan with charcoal, and I pressed it over the shawl now, careful not to burn the fabric.

I was so busy ironing my shawl I didn't have time to eat the steaming bowl of porridge the servants had brought me. It wasn't like me to ignore a free meal—Baba always said my stomach ruled my heart—but much as the fragrant smell of breakfast tortured me, I knew I had to finish my shawl.

In the hall, the other tailors were buzzing.

"Did you hear about the banquet last night?" Master Garad asked. "Lady Sarnai refused to drink to the emperor's health."

"Well, he refused to drink to hers as well."

"A match made in heaven. The Tiger's daughter and the Dragon's son."

"She's the traitor's daughter. The emperor had better be careful or she'll claw his eyes out on their wedding night."

"You'd do well not to speak ill of the shansen's daughter," Yindi warned them.

"Afraid his demons are listening, Yindi?" Garad snickered. "We know you think the shansen's possessed, you superstitious old fool."

Yindi shrugged. "Just you wait and see."

They laughed, but I didn't join in, even though I was glad Yindi was the target, not me. He got up abruptly to iron his shawl, or so I thought until he stopped at my station.

Ignoring him, I lifted my shawl. The silk shimmered like pale gold. It was magnificent, but I didn't know whether to be proud or worried. Was this my work, or the work of magic?

"You made that in one night?" Norbu said. "Impressive. Very impressive. I'd say yours is the best of the lot. The best by far."

I couldn't help beaming. "Thank you, Master Norbu."

"Impressive indeed," Yindi allowed. Based on the dark look that flitted across his face, he knew he had underestimated me. My beam brightened, until he said—

"But Lady Sarnai hates yellow."

Then Master Yindi walked on.

The gibe stung, and my confidence wavered.

"He's just jealous," Norbu soothed. "It's stunning. Sure to win, I'd say."

I warmed to him a little. "I hope so." I tumbled onto my stool, thoroughly exhausted. I barely had a minute's rest before a gong sounded and Lorsa's voice rang out.

"Her Highness, Lady Sarnai!"

I scrambled to my feet, chanting with the other tailors, "Good morning, Lady Sarnai!"

The shansen's daughter entered the hall, followed by an entourage of attendants and guards. I hardly recognized her. The girl I'd spied last night was a warrior who despised the Summer Palace's decadence—its thousands of servants, gilded gates, and rules and etiquette.

Today, she was a princess. Rubies and emeralds sparkled from her wrists and ears, and strings of pearls tinkled from her headdress, a phoenix crown inlaid with gold dragons, jeweled flowers, and blue kingfisher feathers. It seemed the emperor—or Lady Sarnai's maids—had won the battle over her wardrobe.

"Good morning, tailors," she said, in a voice that was soft but not gentle. "You are gathered here to show me what A'landi's finest tailors have to offer. I warn you, I am not easily impressed. I did not grow up wearing silk. I've never appreciated a garment for its beauty or elegance. However, I expect the new imperial tailor to prove me wrong."

"Yes, Your Highness," we tailors said, our heads bowed. "Thank you for this chance, Your Highness."

Arriving behind Lady Sarnai, a tall young man slipped between Norbu's and Yindi's tables to circle our stations. The other tailors had brought their finest samples with them to display: brocade purses with golden tassels, collars embroidered with peonies and chrysanthemums, sashes embroidered with scenes from the Seven Classics—of women dancing and playing the zither. My station was embarrassingly bare. I'd been in such a rush to leave home, I hadn't even thought to bring some of my work to show the future empress.

Whoever the tall man was, he didn't stop at my table. Instead, he returned to Lady Sarnai's side as she proceeded to judge the first tailor.

"It was not my idea to have a shawl-making contest," I heard her say to him. "What a waste of a challenge."

"Emperor Khanujin noticed you had no summer clothing. He is only concerned with your welfare."

"So he says." She sniffed. "You Southerners and your traditions. All this fuss simply to pick a tailor."

The tall man smiled amicably. "His Majesty gave me the impression that this trial was your idea, Your Highness."

His tone was polite, but the audacity of his words now made me wonder who he was. Lady Sarnai hadn't bothered introducing him, so he couldn't be that important. Yet he wore all black, which indicated he was of high rank. The gold epaulets, fine boots, and black mantle slung over one shoulder suggested he was a soldier from beyond the West Far Dunes. But most soldiers didn't dress so fashionably—or richly.

Maybe he was a eunuch. If so, he had to be an important one. Or perhaps he was an ambassador. His features were slightly foreign; he had black hair like A'landans but it was curly, not straight, and despite his tanned, olive skin, his eyes were light—they snagged the glint of the sun.

That was how he caught me staring at him. Quickly, I looked back down at my feet, but not before I saw a smile form on his lips. He disappeared from my view, his movements lazy yet graceful, more like a cat than a nobleman.

I decided I didn't like him.

When I looked up next, Lady Sarnai had finished judging Master Delun's work. Lorsa followed behind her, obsequiously complimenting her on her taste. I kept my head bent and my back bowed—even though it was starting to ache. The other tailors did the same until Lady Sarnai visited their tables. One by one, our fates were determined.

"I wouldn't let my maid use that to clean my chamber pot," she said cruelly of another master's shawl. Her eyes, painted with lapis powder and darkened with charcoal, narrowed into a flinty stare. "Is this the best you could do?"

Then she told Nampo—the tailor who'd offered a bet against me: "There are only four colors in this design. Do you think me a peasant?"

"There are," Nampo said, stumbling over his words, "but that is the style, Your Highness. It is like calligraphy—"

"If I'd wanted calligraphy, I'd have asked for poets, not tailors." Lady Sarnai held a cup of tea in her palm, and she sipped it, keeping her lips thin with displeasure. "Master Nampo, you are dismissed."

By the time Lady Sarnai came to my table, my heart was palpitating.

I hadn't been so close when I saw her last night. We were about the same height and build; we might have passed for sisters were I not pretending to be a boy, and were she not the Jewel of the North, the shansen's only daughter.

"Keton Tamarin," I introduced myself, bowing even lower.

"Tamarin," she repeated. "I haven't heard of you."

We could not have been more than two years apart in age, yet it felt like twenty. I kept my head bowed. "I'm from Port Kamalan."

"I didn't ask."

I clamped my mouth shut, staying quiet as Lady Sarnai touched a corner of my shawl and raised it closer to study it.

She took a moment longer to consider it than she had with the other tailors. Or at least, that was how it felt.

I tried not to stare at her as I waited, but from a stolen glimpse, I could see there was too much powder on her face, particularly around her eyes, which were bloodshot and puffy.

Had she spent last night crying?

I wouldn't be happy either if my father had sold me off to be married. But to wed Emperor Khanujin . . . could that be so horrible?

*You're letting your imagination run wild, Maia,* I scolded myself. *What do you know of Lady Sarnai?*

"The design is extraordinary," Lady Sarnai said at last. "Your skill is to be commended, Master Tamarin. I have never seen work so fine. . . ."

I held my breath, waiting for her to announce my victory in front of all the tailors who'd spoken ill of me. I was just as good as they were. No, better.

Baba would be so proud.

Lady Sarnai twisted her lips. "But I simply despise yellow."

I blinked, certain I had misheard her.

"That is all," Lady Sarnai said before moving on. Minister Lorsa sniffed at me, a sign that I was sure to be dismissed.

My throat closed up, and my hands trembled. *No, no, no. I can't go home. I can't let Baba down. Our shop won't survive another winter unless I win, or unless I marry Calu.*

I was so distraught I hadn't noticed the tall man coming over to my station. A deep, quiet grunt escaped his mouth, and I looked up.

He was younger than I'd thought, and better-looking. He might even have been handsome, if not for something sly and mischievous about his expression. His nose looked like it had been broken once; the bridge was slightly crooked, which some-how highlighted the cunning of his eyes. They danced with the light, never steady enough for me to catch their color.

He gestured at my shawl with long, thin fingers. "You made this?"

His attention took me aback. "Y-yes, sir."

A dark eyebrow flitted up. "In a single day?"

I stiffened. Something about the tall man—and his questioning—made me forget my place. What did it matter, anyway, if I was about to be dismissed?

"The imperial seals are within the design," I said brashly. "If you'd like to check."

His cryptic smile returned. "No, no. I believe you."

With his hands behind his back, the tall man walked on.

I wrenched my attention away from him and looked to Lady Sarnai, standing in the front of the hall, her fan flipped open.

"I shall wear Master Yindi's shawl to dinner tonight with His Majesty," she announced.

I swallowed, trying to hide my disappointment.

Lorsa handed Yindi a red silk pouch. "As the winner, Master Yindi will receive a prize of five hundred jens to use toward the next challenge."

*Five hundred jens?* I couldn't even imagine such a sum!

Lorsa continued: "The others who will remain are Master Boyen, Master Garad, Master Longhai, Master Taraha, Master Norbu, and . . ." He paused, a bushy eyebrow rising.

I clenched my hands into fists, squeezing so hard my nails bit into my palms. *Holy Amana, please . . .*

"Keton Tamarin."

I let out a huge breath. *Thank you. Thank you.*

Lady Sarnai dangled another red silk pouch. "Master Tamarin is the second winner today. His shawl impressed me the most. A feat not easily accomplished."

Stunned, I almost dropped my cane in my hurry to stumble toward Lady Sarnai. The glares from the other tailors and the tall man's smug smile couldn't ruin this moment for me.

"Thank you, Your Highness," I said breathlessly. "Thank you."

She dropped the pouch into my hand and waved me away.

"I will not be so generous again," Lady Sarnai said. "There will only be one winner for each new challenge, until only one of you remains." She gestured at Yindi and me. "But now you all know which two tailors are the ones to defeat."

With that, she turned on her heel and left, the tall, thin man following her a few steps behind.

"Your next task will be given tomorrow morning," Minister Lorsa said. "It will not be as easy as this one, so I suggest that you do not inebriate yourselves too much tonight." His gaze turned to me. "Or fool yourselves into thinking you are safe from dismissal."

My smile faded then, along with the happiness from my victory.

I hadn't won because of my skill at tailoring. I'd won because I'd used *magic* scissors.

If not for the scissors, I would have been sent home—because someone had ruined my shawl, because I couldn't have finished in time, because I hadn't known Lady Sarnai hated yellow. Only by magic had I been able to repair my shawl and make it extraordinary enough to impress Lady Sarnai.

Magic was real. *Very* real. And the revelation that I'd somehow used it sent me reeling with a staggering sense of wonder—and fear.

# CHAPTER SIX

After the dismissed tailors were gone, I sat on my stool, hugging my arms to my chest.

Behind my wooden screen, my mask of confidence fell apart. Those magical scissors had turned my ruined shawl into one of the most extraordinary garments I had ever made.

I opened my satchel, folded my shawl, and stuffed it on top of Baba's scissors. They looked so ordinary, their blades so dull they didn't even glint in the light. I stared at them, bewildered by how tempted I was to use them again—to see what else they could do.

I closed my satchel and kicked it beneath my table.

Only two days ago, I hadn't believed in magic. I had never seen magic. Now here I was, itching to use those enchanted scissors again.

With them, I would certainly win the trial.

Shouldn't I be happy? I'd won five hundred jens and proven myself to the other tailors.

*No. I've proven nothing.* I swallowed. Now that I'd won, the tailors would be watching me closely. If someone found out I was using magical scissors, they'd tell Minister Lorsa. Then I'd be investigated . . . and exposed as a girl.

*I won't use them again,* I decided. *Not unless I absolutely must.*

"Congratulations," Longhai said, peeking over my screen. "What's the matter? You don't look too happy that you won."

"I am," I said, mustering a smile. I cleared my throat, and my fingers nervously drummed against my thigh until I clasped my hands together. "I am," I repeated, "but I was almost sent home. I had no idea Lady Sarnai hated yellow."

"Anyone else would simply be happy to have won," Longhai said, chuckling at my distress. "But I understand." He lowered his voice. "Yindi's been bribing the maids for information. That's how he knew."

It became painfully clear that knowing Lady Sarnai's preferences was vital to winning the trial. "I have no money for bribery."

Longhai laughed. "You have five hundred jens now! Besides, you don't need it, not when you can embroider like that."

His praise sent a sharp pang of guilt to my conscience.

"But be mindful of what you say," he went on. "The five sent home today were those speaking ill of Lady Sarnai last night. I doubt it's a coincidence."

"I appreciate the warning."

So, Lady Sarnai had eyes and ears in the hall.

My stomach rumbled, and after Longhai returned to his station, I reached for the porridge sitting on my desk. It was cold by now and had attracted a following of flies, but I ate it anyway.

One of the kitchen maids passed through the hall to pick up our bowls and teacups. She was slightly plump around the waist, with a youthful face and friendly eyes as round as the two loops her black braids made behind her head.

She stacked my teacup atop a tower of cups on her tray. "We placed bets on everyone. I bet on you."

"Me?" I looked up from my sketchbook. "Why?"

"Because you're young, and . . . and . . . you looked like you'd be talented." She blushed, and my brows furrowed with confusion. Before I could ask what she meant, she added, "I wasn't wrong. Your shawl was magnificent."

"Thank you," I said, more bitterly than I intended. "I doubt I'll be so lucky next time."

"Lady Sarnai's tastes change like the wind," the maid said, "or so her servants say." She leaned close to me, whispering, "But I still think you'll win."

I blinked, warmed by her earnestness. It had been a long time since I'd had a friend my own age. "That's very kind of you."

"My name's Ammi. I sew a little myself, but my embroidery has always been clumsy." She touched my shoulder bashfully. "I'd love to show you sometime—maybe you can help me improve."

"Um." Her closeness made me nervous. As tactfully as I could, I inched away from her. "I'd love to, but I'm going to be busy with the trial."

She smiled. "If you get hungry, come visit the kitchens. The Lord Enchanter himself comes sometimes. He's always poking about for herbs and spices. Usually the expensive ones."

I tilted my head, curious. "To make potions?"

"No," she said with a laugh. "To mask the smell of incense. His quarters are near the palace's main temple. He says it reeks of ash and smoke."

I raised a brow. "How interesting. Well, I have no desire to meet the Lord Enchanter."

"You've met him already," Ammi said. "He accompanies Lady Sarnai everywhere."

I froze. The tall, thin man was the Lord Enchanter? He'd

looked so young. It was hard to imagine he was a hundred years old—maybe even older, according to rumors.

"He'd tell the most unbelievable stories and flirt with all the maids. But since Lady Sarnai's arrived, he hasn't come into the kitchen as often."

I frowned. "Does he really work magic?"

"Yes," she said. "He can make a grain of rice turn into a pot of porridge, and a bone become a roasted chicken." Her dark eyes shone. "Or even make a sapling grow into a tree."

"You've seen this?"

"No, but I've heard. The Lord Enchanter was away for years during the war, and he doesn't make a show of his magic as much anymore."

"Why not?"

She lowered her voice. "The shansen's daughter thinks magic is of the demons."

I felt a stab of fear. Now I certainly couldn't use my scissors: I couldn't risk being discovered and offending Lady Sarnai.

"What do you think of magic?" Ammi said, leaning close to me again. She really was taking her time stacking my dishes.

Something clicked in my mind, and I recognized the strange way Ammi was acting. She was flirting with me!

My hand went to my collar, which felt suddenly tight. "I . . . I t-try not to think m-much of it."

"You're turning quite red, Master Tamarin," Ammi said with a giggle. Finally she lifted her tray and turned to go. "If you need anything, be sure to look for me in the kitchens."

After Ammi left, Longhai and Norbu appeared at my station. "Seems you've attracted an admirer. She's a forward one. Well, I suppose they have to be."

"What do you mean?"

Longhai shook his flask and made a face. It was empty. "Life in the kitchen isn't easy," he replied with a sigh. "Being the wife of a tailor would be a far better life than working in the kitchens."

"You're young," added Norbu. "You should enjoy yourself."

I looked at him bleakly. "I'm here to sew, not find a . . . a wife."

"Then make friends," Longhai encouraged. "You won't find many master tailors your age. You should meet more of the palace staff. The servants are younger, and I'm sure the guards would enjoy hearing your war stories."

I gritted my teeth. I didn't have any war stories. "Thank you for the advice, Master Longhai, but I prefer my own company right now."

"A pity," Longhai said. "We have the rest of the afternoon off, and Norbu's invited us all for lunch in Niyan."

"It's my treat," Norbu said enticingly. He was in a jolly mood. I supposed I should be too, since I'd won the challenge. And honestly, the thought of a hot, steaming bowl of noodles made my stomach rumble yet again.

I reached for my cane. "All right."

"Wonderful!" Norbu cried. "Afterward, we'll head to the bathhouse. Keton, I need to know the secret behind your marvelous embroidery."

I choked back a cry. "Actually . . . ," I began. My chest pounded, reminding me why I couldn't go with five men to the public bath. "Actually, I really shouldn't go into Niyan today. I . . . my leg isn't feeling so well. And . . . and all those . . . those stairs."

"Are you sure?" Norbu asked. "You should celebrate your

victory. The healing waters will be good for you. You can rest those tired fingers and toes."

"I'm sure," I said firmly. "Have a good time."

Norbu slapped me hard on the back. "All right then, young Tamarin. We'll miss you."

I forced a smile and waved. "Enjoy yourselves."

My hammering pulse slowed as I watched them leave. Now I had a full day to consider how to stay in the trial without using my scissors, and to learn more about Lady Sarnai.

I would take up Ammi's invitation to visit the kitchen, I decided. One of the maids *had* to know something about Lady Sarnai.

On my way to the kitchen I passed a courtyard, where magnolia and peach trees grew around a pond filled with carp and catfish and little frogs that leapt onto the lily pads.

How Baba and my brothers would have loved this pond. We'd had a small one in our garden in Gangsun—Sendo and I would feed the fish every morning, and Finlei and Keton would compete over who could catch more carp with his hands, tossing them back into the water before Baba saw.

The memory made me smile. I knelt by the pond and dipped my fingers into the water. A whiskered catfish swam to nip at my nails, and the tickle in my fingertips made me laugh. What was Baba doing now? And Keton?

How I missed my home by the sea.

I sighed and stood, wiping my wet fingers on my tunic. Across the pond, I spotted the tall, thin man—the *Lord Enchanter*—watching me. Our eyes met, and to my relief, he turned away.

Up ahead, I saw the glittering gold path that only Emperor

Khanujin could walk. It was littered with rosy plum blossoms, meaning he had recently passed this way.

I skirted it carefully, continuing toward the kitchens. But as I looked up—there, behind a magnolia tree, was the emperor!

I nearly dropped to my knees when I saw him, as I'd been taught as a child to do. But since he couldn't see me, I crouched behind a leafy bush to steal a glimpse of my sovereign.

He was tall and regal, easily the handsomest man I'd ever seen. His hair, tucked under a gold headdress fringed with rubies and pearls, shone like the finest black lacquer, and his eyes radiated with the warmth of midsummer. Yet while he bore the grace and dignity of a king, the strong slope of his shoulders bespoke a fearsome warrior.

All the stories were true, and I felt a bittersweet foolishness now for asking my brothers to draw me a portrait of him all those years ago. No drawing could have done the emperor justice. Even the sun seemed to fall differently upon him, so that he glowed like a god from the heavens.

Pulse quickening, I ventured a step closer. Something strange and beautiful drew me to the emperor—my body resonated with a heat and pleasure that did not feel entirely natural. So entranced was I that I forgot to pay attention to what he was wearing, nor did I see the dark shadow looming behind me—

"It's a capital crime to stare at the emperor."

I froze, recognizing the voice. My cheeks burned as I pulled my gaze away from Emperor Khanujin and turned to face the Lord Enchanter.

He'd followed me from the pond, his sleeves neatly folded up to showcase his long, elegant fingers. Unlike the emperor with his soft grace, he was all angles and shadow, the edges of his robe clinging to his thin frame. At least the light wasn't caught in his eyes this time, so I could see they burned blue, pale as the heart of a flame. Normally, blue was my favorite color—but not on him.

"Close the jaw, *xitara*," he said, smirking. "You look as if you're about to be slaughtered."

*Xitara?* Instantly, I snapped up and stepped back onto the path. I wasn't sure what etiquette the Lord Enchanter deserved, but I wasn't about to bow after being called a little lamb.

"You're the one with that girl on the shawl." He twisted to face me, his lean face widening to fit a grin. "You're very lucky you won."

I didn't like the way he was looking at me—as though he knew my secret.

*Then act like you have no secret,* I reminded myself.

"Luck had nothing to do with it," I said dismissively. "My shawl was extraordinary—Lady Sarnai said so herself."

"So she did," the Lord Enchanter agreed. His hands moved when he talked—a habit my mother had always told me was rude. "But it was *too* extraordinary . . . at least for the first challenge. Lady Sarnai doesn't want a trial with an obvious winner. She wants to prolong the process. A tip for you, for next time.

"And now everyone knows to be wary of you. Why else do you think she pointed you and Yindi out as the tailors to defeat? Lady Sarnai is cleverer than you think. She's creating enemies for you."

The muscles in my jaw stiffened. "Why are you telling me this?"

He shrugged. "Life in the palace is boring now that the war is over. I need something to do, and you intrigued me enough for me to lend a hand."

"I don't need your help," I said, anger simmering inside me

now. "A war is fun and games to you, isn't it? If not for you and the war, my brothers— *I* would be able to walk without this cane!"

I stormed off, stumbling in my haste to get away.

Forgetting my plan to visit the kitchen, I went back to my room and dumped my satchel out onto my bed, thinking I would mend my pants and shirts so I'd no longer look like a peasant. My magical scissors fell onto the pillow.

There was no humming, no glow this time.

They probably could have cut me an ensemble fit for a prince, but I shrugged off the temptation to use them.

I slid the scissors under my mattress and began to hem my pants the regular way.

As evening fell, I caught sight of a black hawk soaring across the clouds, a gold ring glinting above its talon. Its yellow eyes, bright as the moon, seemed to watch me.

I shut the curtains.

# CHAPTER SEVEN

I t was a good thing I'd refused to go out with Norbu and the others. After their bath, they'd gone to the local drinking house, where Master Taraha and Master Garad drank themselves into a stupor. Now they were spending the day retching. Even from my table, I could smell it.

"Too much mead and garlic shrimps," Norbu said, slapping Master Garad on the back. The tailor looked like he was going to vomit again.

Norbu grinned at me. "You missed a fun afternoon, young Tamarin. We had a contest to see who could eat and drink the most. Taraha and Garad, the gluttons, won. Or lost, judging by how sick they are now."

I forced a smile, but I couldn't help wondering if someone had planned the contest so Garad and Taraha would be too sick to work.

*Stop being so suspicious, Maia.*

Well, I had reason to be. I didn't want anyone getting too close. I couldn't afford to have someone find out I was Maia and not Keton.

The other tailors had nothing to lose from the trial.

I had everything.

. . .

"For the next challenge," Minister Lorsa announced, "His Majesty has requested a pair of embroidered slippers for Lady Sarnai. On each of your tables, you'll find a basket with leather, cloth, lint, and satin.

"To prove your skill, all colored embroidery threads have been removed from the work cabinet and replaced with white threads. If you desire any colors, you'll have to make them yourself. You have three days to complete the task."

I was already at a disadvantage. I'd never crafted a pair of slippers, so I swiftly calculated what I would need to do. Dyeing threads would take at least a day, and I had hardly brought enough colors to embroider slippers worthy of the future empress.

*You memorized the differences between seventy stitches when you were twelve years old,* I told myself. *You can figure out how to make a proper slipper.*

*And,* I added, *you can do it without having to use those scissors.*

If I were completely honest with myself, I was itching to try them again. It hadn't been easy sleeping with them under my bed, expecting them to start humming and glowing.

And I kept wondering—could I win without them?

At least I had one advantage: my foot was closer in size to Lady Sarnai's than any of the other tailors. I could use my own feet as models.

I traced my chalk over the leather sheet, outlining the sole of each of my feet, then arch-shaped pieces that would cover the toes and heel. Once I had my pattern pieces, I copied them to my bolt of satin twice: one for a lining, and the other for embroidering my designs.

Yindi's shrill voice had disappeared, and I hadn't heard Longhai's laughter in at least an hour. I stood, looking out the hall's latticed windows. The other tailors were already in the garden gathering supplies to begin dyeing threads. I'd have to do the same.

And I knew just where to go.

I grabbed my cane and hurried out. The clouds were gray, and the sky dark despite its being late morning. I hobbled out into the courtyard, following my nose to the kitchens.

Inside it was hot, with at least a dozen fires blazing at once and a hundred cooks and servants clamoring and rushing about. Sweat dribbled from my temples as different smells assaulted my nose—ducks and chickens hanging on strings from the ceiling, salted fish left on racks to dry.

"I'm looking for Ammi," I said to a cook who was frying dough and seasoning it with cumin. The smell made my mouth water, and oil crackled and popped, spitting onto my sleeves.

When he ignored me, I wandered past the cooks, deeper into the kitchen. Serving girls bustled about with their arms full of trays and plates, but no sign of Ammi.

After ten minutes of wandering, I noticed a storeroom full of tea. There Ammi was, steeping tea leaves in hot water with dried orange peel.

"Master Tamarin!" she exclaimed.

"I'm sorry to bother you," I began. "I was wondering whether you could help me with something."

She blew her hair out of her face. "I'll try. What do you need?"

"Spices. For my dyes."

"Spices?" Ammi wiped her hands on her apron. "Spices are expensive."

"Berries would also work. Roots, bark, mushrooms. Anything you could spare."

"Well, seeing as you're making slippers for Lady Sarnai—"

"How do you know that?"

She smiled. "Word gets around, especially in the kitchen."

"What can you tell me about Lady Sarnai?" I asked.

"Not much. The lady is impossible to please. Her maids complain that she enjoys tormenting them."

I'd feared as much. At least Lady Sarnai was consistent in tormenting *everyone*.

Ammi led me to where the spices were stored. "I'll distract the spice master," she said. "Be quick."

When she gave the signal, I slipped into the storeroom. There rested a fortune of spices. Cinnamon, black pepper, ginger, nutmeg, cassia, and an assortment of flavors I had never heard of. Safflower, saffron, cardamom. The colors were vibrant, but they weren't what I was looking for.

Outside, Ammi giggled, and there was a thump on the door. I needed to hurry.

I reached for a random jar on the shelf, praying it wouldn't be more pepper. No, it was chili. The next, turmeric. Then ginseng, licorice, fennel. I was running out of time!

I reached for another jar in the far corner. As soon as I opened it, I thanked the gods of luck.

Dried pea flowers. The cooks used them in sticky rice desserts to color the rice a rich shade of blue.

I poured a good handful of the dried flowers into my pocket and, ripping sheets from my sketchbook, wrapped up a few pinches of saffron, fennel seeds, and sorrel—all yellow dyes. Even if Lady Sarnai didn't like yellow, *I* did. I liked how it stained my fingertips with sunshine and brightened the other colors surrounding it.

Ammi had somehow orchestrated it so that a trio of servant girls giggled around me as I slid out the door.

"Ammi's so lucky she gets to serve the tailors."

"Will you come back and show us your winning shawl?"

"Ammi told us you're going to win the trial."

"I hope so." I laughed with them until I reached the exit.

Ammi winked at me, and I smiled my first real smile in days, mouthed a "Thank you," and made my way back to the Hall of Supreme Diligence.

. . .

"Where have you been?" Yindi demanded when I returned from the kitchen.

I was suddenly glad the spices were tucked in my pocket. "I went for a walk."

Yindi sniffed, his pudgy nose wrinkling. "I smell spices."

I shrugged. "One of the maids passed me a snack."

Yindi blocked me from returning to my worktable. He curled his beard around his fingers. "You surprised me, young Tamarin. Perhaps you do have some talent in you."

"Thank you," I muttered. I tried to move past him, but he continued to block me.

"However, a lad like you has to pay his dues before becoming His Majesty's imperial tailor," Yindi went on. "I don't know where you learned to sew like that, but you won't be taking the post away from me. I'm the best tailor in A'landi, and everyone knows it. I'm warning you not to get in my way. If you do, you'll regret it."

By now, I was convinced it was Yindi who had sabotaged my shawl. "I'm here to serve the emperor. Not to play your games."

"So be it," he said. "Don't say I didn't warn you."

As he stomped away, he blew out my candles, leaving my station in the dark.

"Make sure you don't set your work on fire," Yindi called after me with a laugh.

I relit the candles. I'd brought vermillion and emerald dyes with me, so I prepared those colored threads first. Then I steeped the flowers and spices from the kitchen in my paint pots; they would need several hours before they were ready to use.

I ironed out my satin, envisioning my design on its blank canvas. A mountain landscape to remind Lady Sarnai of home—it needed to astonish, so I would keep my stitches small to showcase my attention to detail and my mastery of elaborate needlework.

My fingers got to work. I began with the flowers: I always started with a simple cross, then filled in the petals and stem, drawing out the leaves. It took only a few minutes for each, but there were dozens to make. Next I would stitch the mountains, couching the thread down in long, jagged lines to outline their shape.

My needle swam in and out of the satin. Three stitches per pulse. In and out.

I worked through the night. The incense from Master Yindi's miniature shrine was strong, and my eyelids grew heavy. I tugged at my cheeks, pinching them to stay awake.

Close to dawn, I stretched my arms and my back, which was beginning to hurt from so many hours hunched over my work. As I stood, I saw the basic shape of a shoe on Norbu's table, but he hadn't begun to construct it. Perhaps he had experience making slippers, but I still thought it bold of him to waste this work session.

When at last the gong in the front of the hall sounded, my fingers were raw from sewing.

"Attention!" Lorsa shouted. "Stop your work at once."

Was it morning already? Light filtered in from the open windows, but I had barely noticed. I rubbed my eyes and turned to Minister Lorsa.

To my surprise, Lady Sarnai accompanied him, her expression cold and unreadable.

*Why is she here?* I wondered as the tailors and I murmured our greetings to the shansen's daughter.

"I've decided this challenge is too simple," Lady Sarnai announced. "I am flattered His Imperial Majesty has bidden you to embroider slippers for me, but I have plenty. So I have decided to ask for something more—unique.

"As empress, I will welcome visitors from all over the world. A'landan slippers are revered for their beauty and adherence to tradition. But in Samaran, the queens wear slippers made of iron, and in Agoria, the princesses wear shoes wrought of gold. *I* would like a pair that embodies such strength and power, yet is pleasing to the eye."

A servant entered and set down a stack of blue porcelain plates. Then another brought glass bowls, glass vases, and fluted wine vessels. Soon the front table was piled with objects from paper to straw to bronze, even flowers.

Master Taraha asked what everyone was wondering: "Your

Highness, a tailor does not usually work with porcelain or glass or—"

Lady Sarnai cut him off. "The imperial tailor is a master chosen by the gods. I expect him to be able to work with any material, whether it be glass or silk. Or even the air, should I ask it. If that is a problem, you are welcome to go home."

That ended the questions.

Lady Sarnai turned on her heel, and Minister Lorsa hurried after her.

As soon as they were gone, the tailors dashed for the table. I lurched forward, hobbling as fast as I could with my cane, but someone kicked it from my hand and I fell hard.

Longhai pulled me up with a strong hand. "Hurry, Tamarin, before everything's taken."

Master Garad had already snatched the straw, and the others went for the bronze and iron and paper. By the time I reached the table, only the glass and porcelain items were left. Norbu took the porcelain plates at the last minute, leaving me with glass.

Master Boyen peeked over my screen. He held a handful of orchids and was already weaving the leaves and stems into the shape of a slipper. "Ohhh, glass." He tsked with false sympathy. "That's going to be difficult."

"I'll manage," I said through my teeth.

"I'm looking forward to seeing what you do this time," Boyen said. "We were all so impressed by your shawl, even Yindi is jealous. Best not to rile the old man too much. Glass breaks so easily, and we don't know who spilled tea on your shawl, do we?"

I glared at him until he left.

Then, with a sigh, I set my materials on my table. What did

I have to work with? A pair of glass bowls and a tall, slender vase. Scoring and staining the glass would be easy enough. But making slippers with it?

I gripped the edge of my stool, envisioning slippers made out of glass. Each idea ended with them shattering.

Unless . . . they were already shattered.

My mind raced furiously to come up with a plan. I took a wide brush and painted the inside of the vase with my pea-flower-blue dye. As it dried, I ran to the kitchen and came back with a sticky rice mortar that I'd use for glue.

Carefully, I lined my work area with a long scrap of muslin. Then, holding up my cane, I slammed the vase over and over until a thousand broken shards glittered on my table like blue diamonds.

One by one, I glued the shards over the base of the slippers. The glass cut into my fingers, making them bleed, but I bandaged them with scraps and kept going. I wouldn't stop until every inch of the shoe sparkled.

I would create something stunning. And I didn't need my scissors to do it.

. . .

On the day of our judgment, Lady Sarnai returned in the morning, accompanied by Minister Lorsa and the Lord Enchanter. Seeing the Lord Enchanter did nothing to soothe my already anxious nerves, but I did my best to ignore him and attended to bandaging my fingers and sweeping the leftover glass from my table. I wanted to collapse on my stool out of exhaustion, but I stood in front of my station like the other tailors to await Minister Lorsa's announcement.

He declared, "Each tailor will wear his slippers to present to Lady Sarnai." Lorsa chuckled. "If he is unable to take eight steps in them, he will be sent home."

Relief washed over me as I slipped on my glass shoes. They fit easily and weren't too difficult to walk in, but I saw Longhai staring down in dismay at his large, swollen feet.

The old tailor had been kind to me. I didn't want to see him eliminated over this silly challenge.

Pretending to practice moving in my slippers, I walked across the hall toward my friend.

"Walk on your toes," I advised him quietly as I passed his station. "It's only a few steps."

Longhai sent me a grateful look. He wasn't the only one struggling. The sight of Yindi tottering about in his slippers, cursing his "demon's luck," almost made me pity him.

Lady Sarnai seemed amused by everyone's discomfort. But miraculously, nearly everyone walked in his slippers without breaking them, except Master Garad, whose feet were so wide that his straw slippers collapsed.

Lady Sarnai lifted her chin, and he was dismissed.

I noticed then that the Lord Enchanter had disappeared from her side. His stride was so quiet I barely noticed him approaching my station.

"You've quite a dainty pair of feet for a boy," he said, pointing at them with his shiny black boot. Light refracted off my blue glass slippers, like a thousand bright stars swirling across the wooden floor. "You made them all by yourself?"

"Yes, sir," I said, but I avoided looking up at him. I knew if I did, his pale, ever-changing eyes would snare me.

"They're exquisite," the Lord Enchanter allowed. "Few diamonds sparkle as much as your slippers, Master Tamarin." He folded his arms, his long fingers tapping against his elbow, and smiled. "Carry on, then."

I peeked over my screen to catch a glimpse of the other tailors' work. Taraha had used dozens of vibrant colors to embroider a hundred flowers onto each shoe. A masterpiece . . . but he stubbornly hadn't used any of the special materials Lady Sarnai had requested.

He was asked to go home.

Master Boyen had gotten the palace blacksmith to smelt his bronze pieces into soles, but they were so heavy they tore the delicately woven orchids as he shuffled his eight paces.

He was also sent home.

The walking test was over, so I took my slippers off and laid them on my table, covering them with the embroidered satin cloth.

Lady Sarnai *would* pick that exact moment to arrive at my table. "Where are your slippers?"

Startled, I jumped. "Your Highness—here . . . here they are."

I lifted the satin cover, expecting the shoes to glitter and sparkle, but a cloud passed over the sun, dulling their brilliance.

Lady Sarnai scoffed. "A bit simple for my taste. I'm disappointed, Master Tamarin. I had high hopes for you after seeing your shawl."

*No! Change her mind. Fast.* "I . . . I dyed them with pea flowers, Your Highness," I rambled, "which I understand grew near your father's castle—"

"Do not attempt to ingratiate yourself with me," Lady Sarnai said, but she'd stopped tapping her fan on her palm.

The sun had returned and sent beams of light dancing off my slippers across the table and screen. An arched eyebrow rose. "What are they made of?"

I picked up one of the slippers to show how it sparkled in the light. "Glass."

Lady Sarnai's eyes narrowed. "Glass will break."

Hastily, I slipped the slippers on again to show her they wouldn't. "They're—"

"Glass is a paradoxical material," the Lord Enchanter cut in. "Fragile, yet resilient. Like the slippers."

"You've taken a liking to the boy," Lady Sarnai mocked. "Shall I have him sent to you after hours?"

Unruffled, he said, "How thoughtful, Your Highness. I *have* been thinking about having new shoes made, but I think I'll stay with my current pair a little longer. I've no desire to walk on any more pins and needles than one does with you already."

I stifled a smile, but Lady Sarnai wasn't quite so amused. She snapped her fan open and returned to the front of the hall.

"Master Norbu, Master Longhai, and Master Yindi shall remain," she said.

I bit my lip, hating how my insides curled. Yindi sent me a smirk, but Lady Sarnai wasn't finished.

"And," she said, "I will keep Master Tamarin as well."

Gratitude and relief washed over me, but it was short-lived.

"Master Yindi has won for the second time," Lady Sarnai went on. "He shall join me at the banquet tonight in my honor. To the rest of you who remain—do not disappoint me again."

My inner voice nagged. *You were almost sent home.*
*You could have won—if you had used the scissors.*

# CHAPTER EIGHT

'd been in the palace a week, and gone from home for nearly two. I missed Baba and Keton terribly; sometimes after leaving the hall, I composed letters to them in my head. It sounded silly, but it lessened my pangs of loneliness.

Now that there were only four tailors left, I had time to write an actual letter. I sat by a pond of carp surrounded by plum trees, which was quickly becoming my favorite spot in the palace, with a sheet of parchment on my lap, and my brush . . . but I didn't know what to say.

> *Dear Baba—and Maia,*
> *The emperor has asked twelve men to compete for*
> *the position of imperial tailor, and I had to make a pair*
> *of slippers last night—out of glass! Can you believe it?*
> *I didn't use those scissors you gave me.*

I hesitated and folded an arm over the pond's stone edge. "Oh, Baba, did you know what they can do? I need to win, but what if I can't without them?" I wrung my hands. "No, I can't write that."

> *I didn't use those scissors you gave me, and my slippers*
> *passed the challenge. I hope the money I sent home will*
> *be enough to last through the summer.*

My brush trembled as I bit my lip, reading aloud as I wrote my last line:

*And, Maia, twelve steps. One for each day I've been gone.*

A deep voice startled me. "Do you often make conversation with yourself?"

Stuffing my letter into my pocket, I lurched up and almost fell into the pond. I knew without turning around that it was the Lord Enchanter. His voice was growing familiar to me.

"I see you've survived another round," he said when I faced him. He wore black yet again—a good color for skulking in the shadows and catching people unaware.

"It would have been a shame if you'd been sent home," he continued. "Lucky for you, I decided to interfere."

I bit back a retort. It was true, he *had* helped me. Remembering his rank, I bent my back into a stiff bow and said, as politely as I could muster, "Thank you, sir."

"Bowing?" He eyed me. "Someone must have told you who I am. Pity. Now you're as formal and boring as the rest, and calling me *sir*."

"I do not know how else to address you."

His mouth set into a wry smile. "My full name would be too complicated for you to pronounce. You may call me Edan."

"Edan," I repeated. The name sounded foreign on my tongue.

He made a slight bow. "I serve as His Imperial Majesty's resident Lord Enchanter. To the West, I am known as His Most Illustrious; to the East, I am His Most Illuminating; and in every other corner of the world, I am His Most Formidable."

I drew in a sharp breath. What had Sendo told me about sorcerers? All I could remember was that they served kings all over the world, and they drank the blood of young girls.

Finlei had always scoffed at such tales, but the thought made me shiver.

*Have courage, Maia,* I reminded myself. If Edan wanted a young girl, he'd have plenty to choose from in the palace.

Besides, the man I saw looked far too young to have traveled the world. I was sure his boasts were hot air and nothing else.

"I've never heard of you," I muttered.

Edan laughed. "You're skeptical. That's wise. But odd coming from one so young."

"My brother told me fairy tales of magic when he . . ." I couldn't bring myself to say *was alive.* My tone darkened. "But that's what they are . . . just fairy tales."

"The A'landans are superstitious people. Constantly praying to their dead ancestors. If you believe in spirits and ghosts, I don't see why you wouldn't believe in magic."

I *did* believe in magic. I just wouldn't admit it to him, of all people. "What I believe in is hard work and providing for my family."

"You'll do well in that," Edan said. "I've seen your work. Very impressive. I found the shawl especially . . . interesting."

That sly look again, as if he knew my secret. My cheeks betrayed me by reddening. No, he couldn't possibly know. I struggled to sound nonchalant. "What do you know of sewing?"

"What do I know, indeed?" Edan said mischievously. "I seem to bring out the worst in you. With everyone else, you appear to be quite—"

"The *xitara*?" I said flatly.

Edan laughed. "I was going to say agreeable."

How I wished he would go away. "Looks are deceiving."

"I couldn't have put it better myself." He grabbed my cane and rapped my leg—the one that was supposed to be irreparably broken—and I cried out.

"Hey!" I was so upset I forgot to keep my voice deep and manly. "Give that back!"

"Why? You don't need it."

Scowling, I made a show of limping, holding on to a hedge for support.

Edan tossed me back my cane. He was watching me intently. "You think I haven't noticed that you favor your right foot half the time, and your left foot the other half? Only a fool would miss it, but to your good fortune, this palace is full of fools."

My anger evaporated, replaced by fear. "Please don't—"

"But that's not the real secret, is it?"

The color drained from my face. I stopped staring down and looked directly into Edan's eyes. They were amber now, thick and bright as the sap of a tree. They bored into me. "I don't know what you mean, sir."

"You're not Keton Tamarin, and you're certainly not old Kalsang Tamarin. His two oldest sons died in battle, but I heard he had a daughter who managed the shop quite well during the war. . . ."

My stomach flipped.

Edan leaned closer, his eyes blue and cool yet piercing. I could have sworn they had been yellow only seconds ago. "Would I be correct in presuming you are Maia Tamarin?"

My lips parted, but Edan put a finger to them before I said a word.

"Think carefully before lying to an enchanter," he warned

me. "Sometimes it helps to look in a mirror." He whisked one out and raised it to my face.

My hand jumped to my mouth. The reflection was me—but with my hair long again, and my brother, the *real* Keton, behind me.

"What magic is this?" I demanded.

"Simply a reflection of the truth," he replied. "We enchanters see more than most. I knew you weren't Keton Tamarin. You're that girl you painted on your shawl."

I pushed aside the mirror. "I was trying to paint Lady Sarnai."

"Hmm," he said, studying me. "The resemblance isn't striking, but it's there. Curious."

"There is no resemblance," I snapped. "I'm not a girl."

"I'm not going to tell anyone."

"You think I trust you?"

"You should." Edan loosened his collar. It was high and looked uncomfortable, given the heat, but there was no perspiration on his forehead. I was wearing my lightest linen and already sweating. "Come, what keeps you from trusting me?"

I could think of a thousand reasons, so I had no idea what possessed me to blurt, "My . . . my brother said that sorcerers drink the blood of young girls."

Edan simply burst out laughing. When he collected himself, he said, rather sternly, "The trial is down to four tailors. If you're going to win, it's time to show off a little."

My brows furrowed, and I lowered my defenses. "You told me my shawl was too good."

"For the first challenge," Edan corrected. "I didn't mean for you to become so underwhelming for the second one."

"I wasn't—" I groaned. There was no point in trying to

explain to him how difficult it was to create a miracle in three days—without using magical scissors, anyway. "Why do you want me to win?" I asked instead.

He smiled mysteriously. "An enchanter never reveals his intentions. Let's just say"—he pulled out my scissors from his sleeve—"*these* wouldn't belong to any ordinary seamstress."

"How did you get those?" I stood on my toes, reaching to get the scissors back. "Those are mine!"

"So there *is* some fire in you." His smile widened. "Why should I give them back? Are they special to you?"

My pulse quickened. Those scissors worked miracles. I couldn't allow the emperor's Lord Enchanter to learn my other secret and get me kicked out of the trial.

"My father gave them to me," I said, still reaching.

"Anything else special about them?"

"No," I insisted.

He lowered the scissors an inch. "Say *please*."

"Please," I said grudgingly.

Edan held them out. I snatched the scissors back and thrust them into my pocket.

"You're not a good liar, Maia Tamarin." Edan tilted his head. "Those scissors are charmed. Any enchanter could smell their magic on you."

"I don't know what you're talking about."

I turned to go, but Edan blocked my path. "The slippers you made were very good, but with the scissors, you could have put Yindi, Norbu, and Longhai to shame." Still not letting me pass, he crouched so our eyes were level. "If you think I'm going to send you home for it, you're quite mistaken. You've piqued my curiosity, *Master* Tamarin. Enchanted objects do not work for just anyone."

"What would you know about it?" I asked, trying to keep my voice sharp even though I was secretly curious.

"Plenty." Edan chuckled. "If you want to win the trial, *xitara*, you're going to need my help."

I bristled at his arrogance. "Will you stop calling me that?"

"You don't like it?"

"Why would I like being called a little lamb?"

"Ah. You know your Old A'landan." Looking suddenly amused, Edan tapped his chin. It was pointed, despite the squareness of his jaw. Not an unpleasing combination—but odd all the same. "I'll consider it—if you win."

"I *will* win," I replied. "And without *your* help."

"You're a strange one, you know." He watched me with crossed arms and a smirk. "When the other tailors arrived, they tried their best to bribe me with jewels, silks, furs, even one of their daughters—all for some help. But you refuse when I give it freely."

"You're not helping me," I said through my teeth. "You're tormenting me."

That dry chuckle again. "As you say, Master Tamarin. But a suggestion—try putting a pebble in your shoe so you at least remember which leg is supposed to be broken."

With that, he bowed to me as if I were as highborn a lady as the emperor's bride-to-be. Then he walked away, whistling a tune.

Accept help from someone so insufferable? I scoffed.

That he would even suggest it baffled me.

I turned on my heel, refusing to glance back at him. But I did watch my footing for the rest of the day—and hoped, anxiously, that I could trust him to keep my secrets.

# CHAPTER NINE

The next morning was blisteringly hot, which was no excuse for Yindi and Norbu to lounge about the hall with their shirts off, but they did it anyway. I averted my eyes, especially from Norbu, whose hairy belly really wasn't something I wanted to see.

For once I was grateful when Minister Lorsa arrived to announce our next challenge.

"His Majesty will soon have the pleasure of welcoming important dignitaries from the Far West. As such, Her Highness, Lady Sarnai, requires new clothes to greet them. She is aware that you are all capable of sewing garments in our local A'landan style, but she wishes to explore your range. The tailor who makes her a jacket that best embodies the Spice Road from one end to the other will win this challenge."

My mind was already reeling. A'landi was the eastern end of the Great Spice Road, and Frevera the western end. What little I knew of fashion on that side of the world meant plunging necklines, a prince's ransom of lace and brocade, and tight bodices—the opposite of A'landi's modest, flowing styles.

Lorsa continued: "The four of you may go to the market this afternoon to purchase supplies. You will be given a stipend of three hundred jens, and half a week to complete the jacket."

He paused, the way he always did before he said something unpleasant. "Oh, and one more thing: it must be made of paper."

. . .

"Paper!" Longhai muttered as we walked into town. "Of all things . . ." He stroked his beard, then reached into his pocket for his wine flask. "She's not going to wear paper to greet foreign dignitaries. You know, I'm beginning to suspect she's using the trial as a way to postpone her marriage to Emperor Khanujin."

I clicked my tongue. Edan had said as much.

I'd taken Edan's advice about the pebble in the shoe, but now the pain of walking was real, making me too slow even for Longhai, who broke from my side to walk with Yindi.

With a sigh, I continued alone. The trek from the palace into Niyan wasn't easy—eighty-eight steps down from the palace, then two hundred more steps down Chrysanthemum Hill. Another mile below sprawled Tangsah Marketplace.

Despite the breeze from the nearby Jingan River, the humidity gathered on my temples, pearls of sweat dripping down my cheeks onto my shoulders. The pins I used to fasten the bindings around my chest pricked my side, and I couldn't help rubbing my irritated skin. My bandages smelled and chafed, but I forgot about my discomfort as soon as I saw Tangsah.

I hadn't been in a real marketplace since we'd lived in Gangsun. Vendors stretched from street to street, some in bright sloping tents in every shade of orange, some in carts trundling down the paved roads. Ahead were jade carvers, drapery masters, and glassblowers, interspersed with donkeys and wild

chickens and children milling about, and farther out were ac-
robats and fire-eaters. There was no order to the market, but I
already loved it.

"Quite the spectacle, isn't it?" Longhai said, reappearing at
my side. "It's second only to the capital." He pointed at the far
side of Tangsah Marketplace and added, "The merchants in
the silk quarter will try to cheat you when they find out you're
working in the palace. Don't pay more than half what they're
asking. And don't act like it's your first time here."

I shifted the weight from my foot to my cane. "Is it that
obvious?"

"Yes," Longhai said. He paused. "You have real talent,
Keton, but you're young. If we weren't in this silly competition,
I would take you to be my apprentice." He shrugged his wide
shoulders. "This contest wearies me. We are craftsmen. We
should learn from one another, not cut each other's throats."

Before I could reply, Norbu slipped between us. "Are you
coming to the alehouse with us, young Tamarin? I'll buy you a
drink, if it means learning your embroidery secrets. That shawl
was marvelous."

I fumbled with my cane. "I need to spend the day buying
supplies."

"Such a killjoy." Yindi sniffed. "We have the day off and
three hundred jens each. We should enjoy it."

"Easy for you to say," Longhai said. "You won the last two
challenges. I'm rather inclined to follow young Tamarin myself."

But he didn't. Longhai had a weakness for drink. I had a
feeling Yindi and Norbu were using it against him.

"Aren't you hot wearing all that?" Yindi said, waving at my
tunic. I'd been wearing at least three layers to help obscure my
chest.

"This is cool weather to me," I lied, hoping he wouldn't notice the sweat pooling on the back of my neck.

Yindi crossed his arms, his flat, pudgy nose wrinkling as usual. "You're an odd one, Tamarin." He shook his head and disappeared into the drinking house with Norbu.

I stole a peek inside: it was full of men, some gambling at tiles and others drunkenly reciting poetry. In the center was Norbu, hobnobbing with the magistrates and nobles while his servant did his shopping.

"Doesn't he ever work?" I asked Longhai before he too went inside.

"Don't underestimate Norbu," Longhai said. "How do you think he is the richest tailor in A'landi? Certainly not by spending all day at the loom."

I retreated to the shade of a tangerine farmer's tent and stared at my map. Then I tightened my money pouch around my neck; Tangsah was infamous for its pickpockets.

Passing several bakers' shops and tents, I spied sesame cakes and honeycomb cookies. The palace fed me well, but there was nothing like honeycomb cookies fresh off the griddle.

I shook off the craving. *Silk, not cookies,* I reminded myself. *Thread, not cakes.*

With renewed determination, I set out to buy my supplies. After a few hours, my basket was heavy. I'd used up almost all the money Lorsa had given us on dyes, new needles, gold foil to make metallic thread, and a smaller frame for more intricate embroidery.

I had two jens and thirty fen left. Just enough to buy myself some lunch. I stopped by the baker whose steamed vegetable buns looked and smelled freshest, and got an apple from the farmer next door with my remaining fen.

There was a tap on my basket, and I jerked back, immediately assuming it was a pickpocket. It was Edan.

"What are you doing here?" I demanded.

"Why do you need any of this when you have those scissors of yours?" he said, frowning at the contents of my basket.

I hurried away from the farmer's stall. "I'm not going to use them."

He followed me. "Now that's a foolish idea if I've ever heard one."

"Lady Sarnai hates magic. I'm not being sent home over a pair of scissors. And I refuse to cheat." I glared at the Lord Enchanter. He was grinning and munching on a shiny yellow apple. *My* apple! "Do you ever take anything seriously?"

"I take everything seriously. Especially magic. If I had enchanted scissors like yours, the trial would be over by now."

"You couldn't sew to save your life," I retorted, reaching for my apple.

"Ah, but I wouldn't need to." He closed the snack in his fist, then opened his fingers. My apple had disappeared.

I tried not to dwell on how he had done that; it would give him too much satisfaction. "Shouldn't you be in the palace? Advising and protecting the emperor, or whatever it is you do?"

"His Majesty doesn't need my protection—or advice. He's a grown man." Edan grinned. "As I'm sure you've noticed."

The sun made everything feel very hot. Flustered, I said, "Emperor Khanujin is a great man. There is much about him to admire."

"Such as? His grace and wit? His charm and beauty? I daresay someone's infatuated." Edan peered at me inquisitively. "Have you spoken to him?"

My cheeks bloomed bright red. "N-no."

"Would you like to?" Edan touched his chin. "I could arrange it."

I remembered then what Lady Sarnai had said about Edan—that he'd taken a liking to me. *No,* I thought. He simply enjoyed tormenting me because he knew my secret. That I was a girl.

Was that why I was so petulant around him? Or had it been so long since I'd had my brothers to look after me that I didn't trust him? That I *couldn't* trust him?

"Are you so bored that you have nothing to do but follow me around?"

"My duty is to protect A'landi and ensure that the royal wedding takes place. I *follow you around* to look after A'landi's best interests."

"I thought you were following Lady Sarnai."

"Ah," Edan said, looking pleased. "I see someone's been listening to court intrigue. Very good, Maia."

"Will you not call me that in public?" I whispered harshly.

His lips stretched into a smile. "Very well. But I may in private?"

"Hmph." I crossed my arms. "I don't see the lady anywhere nearby."

"She is bathing in the holy waters of the Sacred Moon Temple. It wouldn't do for me to have followed her there, so I took the opportunity to replenish my supplies."

Edan held out his hands, which were empty. Before I could retort "What supplies?" a falcon dove into the marketplace, landing on his shoulder. His gaze still on me, Edan untied the scroll knotted on the falcon's left claw and stroked the bird's white throat.

I held my breath as Edan read the note. His expression gave nothing away, but he let out a small, inaudible breath.

"I hope you find someone to help you carry your goods home, Mistress—I mean, *Master* Tamarin. I would offer, but I'm afraid I've been summoned back to the palace. And as you know, one must obey the emperor."

"Even you?" I said. "The almighty Lord Enchanter?"

"Even me." Edan swooped a bow. The falcon on his shoulder craned its neck, peering at me with its round yellow eyes. "Another time, Master Tamarin."

"I hope not," I muttered.

Edan chuckled, having heard me. "Careful of pickpockets!" he called from behind.

Worried, I dug my hand into my pocket, only to find a new apple—and fifty jens.

I whirled around, but Edan was gone.

I let out an exasperated sigh. Never had I met anyone so insufferably pleased with himself.

I took a bite of my new apple. And yet, maybe he wasn't all bad.

Maybe.

# CHAPTER TEN

The following morning, just as we began drawing up designs and celebrating that we'd have the next few days free of the shansen's daughter, who should stride into the Hall of Supreme Diligence but Lady Sarnai, unannounced and unexpected. Scissors clattered to the ground, and Longhai threw his flask behind his table as we all leapt to our feet in alarm.

Lady Sarnai swept past us, wearing a white cloak made entirely of dove feathers, a quiver of scarlet arrows hanging on her shoulder and a bow in her hand. Minister Lorsa was noticeably absent from her side today. Only a maid accompanied her, one who looked as if she would rather be doing anything than carrying the four dead birds gathered in her arms.

As Lady Sarnai's dark eyes descended on us, the maid slung a dead falcon on Norbu's table, Yindi's, Longhai's, then mine. My bird landed with a thump, its sharp yellow eyes open and hollow, its gray-spotted wings spread wide enough to cover the breadth of my table. I swallowed, thinking of the black hawk I'd seen my very first day in the palace.

Lady Sarnai sniffed. "I desire these feathers to be incorporated into a silk sash for His Majesty. To wear over his ceremonial robes to the temple."

I hid a grimace. Surely, Lady Sarnai knew this would be a

great insult to the emperor? It was forbidden to wear any signs of death into a temple.

"Master Longhai," she said. "You look ill at ease. Does my request distress you?"

"No, Lady Sarnai," he said quickly.

"Curious," she murmured. "The sight of my morning's spoils made your Lord Enchanter so uncomfortable he excused himself from my company for the day."

I flinched at this news, remembering the falcon in the market. Had these birds been Edan's pets?

Lady Sarnai picked on me next. "The Lord Enchanter is such an enigmatic creature. What secrets simmer beneath that vile countenance, I wonder. Master Tamarin, I understand the two of you have become acquainted."

I opened my mouth to protest.

But Lady Sarnai went on: "It would be wise to stay away from him. Magic is the art of demons, no matter how the Lord Enchanter denies it. And as you know, any outside assistance is forbidden in the trial."

"Yes, Your Highness."

"Good." A sigh escaped her, and for a moment she looked quite miserable. But that cold mask returned, and she said, "I'll leave you all to work."

I did not enjoy depluming the dead falcon, but the other tailors seemed to have no problems with the task. Longhai worked swiftly and was already arranging the feathers around his worktable. I heard snipping sounds from Norbu's side of the room and couldn't help but cringe every time his blades cut.

Not long after Lady Sarnai left, Minister Lorsa appeared. "Kneel!" he barked at us, and we immediately dashed to the center of the room and touched our foreheads to the floor.

"What's going on?" I whispered to Longhai.

I had my answer before the old man could reply.

Emperor Khanujin had arrived.

The warmth of that first time I'd seen him washed over me once again. Only for a fleeting moment did I sense that it was strange, as if I were caught in some sort of spell that muddled my thoughts. I basked in his presence and hoped he would never leave.

"Your Imperial Majesty," we shouted, "may you live ten thousand years!"

"Ruler of a Thousand Lands," Lorsa's voice rang. "Khagan of Kings, Son of Heaven, Favored of Amana, Glorious Sovereign of A'landi."

The titles went on and on. I didn't dare look up, not even when the emperor finally spoke.

"Rise."

I was the last to obey. I unbent my knees and stood, only to see Edan behind the emperor. He tilted his head at my left leg, reminding me it was supposed to be crippled.

As I adjusted my position, I noticed Edan observing the feathers on our tables. The smirk he usually wore turned to a frown, and his arms stiffened at his sides.

"I understand that Her Highness, Lady Sarnai, visited the Hall of Supreme Diligence this morning," Emperor Khanujin said.

"Yes, Your Majesty," replied Lorsa. "She had an additional task for the tailors."

"What was it?"

"She wished to surprise you with a feather sash to wear to your morning prayers."

Emperor Khanujin regarded Lorsa. "And did you not think

to inform Lady Sarnai that it is forbidden to hunt any bird on imperial grounds?"

Lorsa's face darkened, and he lowered his eyes. "My humblest apologies, Your Majesty," he babbled, falling on his knees and kissing His Majesty's feet until he was told to rise.

Cautiously, I looked at the emperor and observed the dozens of jade and gold pendants adorning his neck and sash. One didn't shine as brilliantly as the rest.

It was bronze, and I made out the outline of a bird engraved on it. No wonder he was unhappy that Lady Sarnai hunted them in his gardens.

"I am grateful for Lady Sarnai's generosity," Emperor Khanujin said, addressing us tailors now, "but I have no need for a new ceremonial sash. I wear my father's, out of respect for the sacrifices he made to unite this country." He paused. "Reuniting A'landi is now *my* responsibility. You may find it contrary to tradition that Lady Sarnai is overseeing the selection of the next imperial tailor, but her happiness is of the utmost importance to maintaining the peace of our realm. I trust you will do your best to please her."

"Yes, Your Majesty," I intoned with the rest of the tailors.

"You come from all parts of A'landi, and some of you have journeyed far. I look forward to welcoming one of you into the palace."

My heart was fluttering so fast I almost didn't see Edan's wink as he followed the emperor out.

I shook myself from my trance. There was something strange about Emperor Khanujin. *Strange and wonderful,* I thought.

Or strange and terrible.

· · ·

It was late when I finally left the hall. My fingers were stiff from hours of knitting lace and folding silk ribbon flowers for Lady Sarnai's jacket, and my mind was swimming from lack of sleep. As I opened the door to my room, all I could think about was collapsing onto my bed and—

I reared back in surprise. My cot was aglow, and the walls seemed to be humming softly.

My magic scissors.

I yanked them out of the bundle under my mattress. Seeing them again, I felt my fingers almost instinctively slipping into the bows. It was so tempting. Lady Sarnai loathed magic, but Longhai had said it wasn't cheating, and Edan had encouraged me to use them.

I shook my head vigorously. *You're listening to Edan now, Maia? What's gotten into you?*

I needed to get rid of the scissors.

Before I could change my mind, I rewrapped them, took the bundle, and crept out into the gardens. I couldn't throw them into a well, no matter how much I wished to be rid of them. The scissors had belonged to my grandmother, and Baba had given them to me. Maybe I would bury them—if only for a little while.

I had just passed the magnolia courtyard when I heard a lady weeping. The sound was soft, almost lost amid crickets chirping.

The sniffling stopped, replaced by a voice I knew all too well. "Who's there?"

*Lady Sarnai.* Her commanding tone made me freeze. I swallowed, aware I was somewhere I shouldn't be, and yet something in her voice betrayed a trace of—fear?

But Lady Sarnai was her father's daughter. She didn't let up. "Show yourself."

I stepped out from behind the bush. "M-my apologies, Y-Your Highness. I . . . I got lost on my way back to the hall and—"

Lady Sarnai was the same height as me, but her voice—raw and thick with anger—made me feel small. "Did the emperor send you to spy on me?"

My eyes widened. "N-no, Your Highness. I thought you were one of the maids."

Lady Sarnai scoffed, but she clenched her handkerchief and said nothing, looking so miserable my heart softened toward her.

"You're homesick?" I said gently. "I am too."

"You couldn't possibly understand how I'm feeling." Lady Sarnai dabbed her eyes, then said harshly, "Don't tell me you fought in the war, that you were away from your home for years. I don't care."

I wondered now if her coldness—that flat, emotionless face she wore whenever she came to the Hall of Supreme Diligence—was a mask.

Lady Sarnai missed home. I could see it in the dark pools of her wet eyes.

She was angry and sad that her father had sacrificed her to make peace with Emperor Khanujin. And if Longhai was right about her relationship with Lord Xina, she had even more reason to be miserable.

"Lady Sarnai," I began hesitantly, "I know it's difficult for you here. But His Majesty is doing his best to make you happy. He's a kind man, and—"

"A kind man?" She laughed bitterly. "That enchanter has you all fooled."

I frowned. "He would make you happy," I repeated. "If you only let him."

"What do you know about happiness?" she snapped. "You're

a man. Now that the war is over, you can do what you want. You've proven yourself to A'landi. The world is open to you."

"I'm . . . I'm a simple tailor."

"A tailor who's been invited to sew for the emperor. A girl couldn't do that. A girl isn't fit to be anything more than a prize. My father promised he'd never force me to marry. He taught me to hunt and to fight like a man. I was just as good as all my brothers. And now?" Lady Sarnai wrung her hands. "He broke his promise to me. At first I thought it was because the war and magic had blackened his heart, but that is just the way of men. For what is a promise if it's made to a woman?"

Her words rang so true to me, I almost staggered back.

"I made a promise to my—my sister," I said, catching myself at the last moment. "That I would win this competition so she could have a better life. It isn't one I intend to break."

"We'll see about that." Lady Sarnai straightened, gathering her poise. "Leave me."

I bowed and obeyed.

I couldn't say my encounter with Lady Sarnai made me like her any more than before. Yes, I had glimpsed a vulnerable side of her, but she was still the cold and heartless daughter of the shansen. Yet something *had* changed.

Now I pitied her.

# CHAPTER ELEVEN

After my meeting with Lady Sarnai, I took care not to stray too far from the Hall of Supreme Diligence. I had a feeling she wouldn't be so forgiving if I ran into her again.

It was alone in the hall that Edan found me working on her jacket. The paper Minister Lorsa had given us was stiff, which was good for painting but cumbersome for the wide, flowing sleeves of my design.

"What are you doing here?" I asked, looking up when Edan's shadow blocked the early-morning light.

"The emperor's at his prayers. I thought I'd go for a walk."

"You're here to check up on me, aren't you?" I said, dipping my brush into the pot of gold paint.

"Not just you," Edan said. "On the others, too."

"They're still sleeping." I tilted my head at the empty wine gourds on Longhai's table. "They were up late drinking, as usual."

I swirled my brush and held it to the side of the pot so the excess would drain off. Setting it to the jacket, I swiftly painted a set of leaves patterned on imperial brocade, an embossed fabric with golden weaving.

Edan leaned over me. "You're quite the artist," he said approvingly. "Did your brother teach you to paint like this?"

I frowned at him. "You never told me how you knew my brothers died in the war."

"It's my business to know things," he said. For a moment, he looked weary—the way Keton did whenever someone mentioned the war. It made me wonder if Edan had fought beside the emperor.

I drew a ragged breath and turned back to my work, not wanting to expose my grief to Edan. "Shouldn't you be following Lady Sarnai?"

"Someone's prickly today," he said, folding his arms. His demeanor was serene and cool again. "You'll be pleased to know His Majesty has decided to supervise the contests from now on."

"Why would I be pleased?" I said, but my heart skipped a beat as I continued painting. I had often wished it were Emperor Khanujin I saw daily, instead of his Lord Enchanter.

My sketchbook suddenly appeared in Edan's hand, and he flipped through page after page of my drawings of Emperor Khanujin. *Designs* for his wardrobe, to be precise, but I'd taken care to draw his face on each.

I jumped to my feet, horrified. "That's mine! Where did you— Give that back!"

"Drawing portraits of His Majesty in your spare time?" Edan said airily. "It doesn't surprise me. Every girl in A'landi is besotted with our boy king."

My face burning, I snatched my sketchbook from him. "Boy king?" I huffed. "He's older than you."

"He *looks* older than me," Edan corrected. "And as you've said, looks are often deceiving."

I shoved my sketchbook into my pocket. "I'm not besotted with him."

Edan chuckled at me. "Impersonating a man doesn't make you one. I know very well you aren't immune to the emperor's charms."

"You make Emperor Khanujin sound like he's cast an enchantment," I countered. "If he has, shouldn't he work on charming Lady Sarnai?"

I expected a snide retort from the Lord Enchanter, but Edan admitted, "Her resistance to him is strange. Everyone usually loves the emperor, at least when I'm around."

What an odd thing to say.

He shrugged a shoulder. "Perhaps Lady Sarnai has charms of her own."

I hesitated. "I heard you were unhappy about the falcons she shot."

Edan cocked an eyebrow. "So you've been talking about me?" he asked, then laughed at my discomfort. "You'll have to work on your habit of blushing, *Master* Tamarin."

"I wasn't talking about you," I said defensively. "Lady Sarnai brought it up."

"What else have you learned about me?"

"Nothing. Except that you enjoy tormenting me."

"I'm *helping* you."

"I didn't ask for your help."

"Not even with your little infatuation for Emperor Khanujin?" Edan's eyes flickered, this time green as the leaves behind him. "Given how little love Lady Sarnai has for him, maybe he'll take on some concubines." He gave me a sly, sidelong glance. "I could put you at the top of the list if you'd like."

I flashed him my fiercest scowl. "I'm going to be the imperial tailor."

"Master Huan served His Majesty's father for thirty years. Do you think you can stay here for as long without revealing what you really are?"

I swallowed. Truthfully, I hadn't thought about it, but I couldn't tell Edan that. "Yes."

"Then you are very naïve."

"Who are you to tell me what I can and can't do?" I huffed. "I've managed perfectly so far."

"You haven't been here long," Edan reminded me. "And," he added smugly, "you've had help. If not for me, you'd be in a carriage on the way home by now. Or locked up in the dungeons."

I harrumphed, but the words made me press my brush to the jacket harder than I meant to.

"I suppose if you stayed on, I could help with your disguise," Edan mused. "I'm already helping you as it is."

"What exactly do you get out of this?"

Edan found a coin in his pocket and tossed it with one hand. "Minister Lorsa and I made a bet." He tilted his head back. "The winner gets a pig."

My brush sagged, drawing a line I hadn't meant to. "You're betting my future over a pig?"

"Pigs are smarter than people give them credit for! Where I grew up, we almost worshipped them." He sounded so serious I couldn't tell if he was joking. "Besides, I don't like Lorsa much. It would be fun to see him lose a pig." He smiled. "With that in mind, I suggest you move your jacket away from the window. There's a storm coming."

I looked up. "I see no rain clouds."

"If nothing else, you can trust an enchanter to tell the weather accurately."

"I'll take my chances."

Edan made a face. "At the very least, move the jacket away

from all that incense by Yindi's station. You don't want your work to smell like a prayer ritual."

"You're a sacrilegious one," I muttered. "What does it matter? Lady Sarnai never wears anything we make her."

"She's trying to amuse herself."

"The way you amuse yourself betting pigs on my future?"

"Not quite. Though I'd win faster if you called upon those special scissors of yours."

I wrung my brush free of water. "I've buried them."

"Buried them?" He grinned, tossing the coin one last time. "How many times have I told you not to lie to an enchanter, Maia Tamarin?"

"*Master* Tamarin. And I don't need them."

"You're used to being underestimated, so you want to prove yourself. Don't let that be your crutch. Accept help when you need it."

"I will. Now would you please go?"

He bowed, his black hair netting the sunlight as he bent. "As you wish, Master Tamarin." He winked at me. "As you wish."

· · ·

Much as I resented him, Edan was right about the weather. Soon after dusk, the clouds darkened. Thunder boomed, followed by streaks of lightning ripping across the sky. Rain pattered against the roof, and I quickly moved my jacket away from the windows and shut them.

I prayed the paint would dry despite the humidity. I'd spent a small fortune on the color, a deep violet that was one of A'landi's most prized exports on the Great Spice Road.

"Where's Norbu?" I asked Longhai. "His jacket's not here."

"I haven't seen him. Neither has Yindi." Longhai took a swig from his gourd, a larger one than his previous—a "gift" from Norbu, I suspected. "Hope he's not caught in the rain."

I didn't have time to worry about Norbu. I set my jacket on my table and inspected it with a critical eye. Stiff enough to stand on its own, the jacket had rippling sleeves and an embroidered collar like in the Freverish courts, and tonight I would twine strips of silk into its lace belt. Every detail was a marriage between one end of the Spice Road and the other.

*Not bad.* Best of all, I'd made it by myself with no help from any special scissors.

*But think of what you could've done with the scissors,* my inner voice nagged me.

I ignored it. If Lady Sarnai discovered that I was using magic, I would be dismissed.

Then again, if I lost the trial, I'd be sent home. There were four of us left now. Surely there'd be at least one more challenge before an imperial tailor was chosen?

I worked late, long after Longhai and Yindi had gone to bed, and the warm rain tinkling down the roofs became a patter, then a mist. Since no one was here, I decided to try on my jacket to make sure the belt would hold the paper folds together. As I tied the belt about my waist, a black hawk with white-tipped wings cried out and circled in the night sky.

"There it is again!" I peered out the window, but it'd already flown out of sight. I slipped outside to look for the bird.

Shadows crawled over the palace grounds, and the round red lanterns that lit the corridor beamed like glowing stars. In the distance I heard crickets chirping, and the soft rustle of the wind against the trees. The hawk was nowhere to be seen.

Disappointed, I suddenly became aware that I'd forgotten

111

my cane and had worn my jacket out of the hall. I slipped it off, and as I turned back, a terrible sight made me gasp.

Smoke. Not from the kitchens, but billowing out of the Hall of Supreme Diligence. The hall was on fire!

I dropped my jacket and dashed for the nearest fire bell. "Fire! Fire!"

Still shouting, I pulled open the door. Flames danced near Yindi's worktable. I saw his jacket hanging on one of the wooden screens, and Longhai's stretched out on his table. They'd be ruined if I didn't do something!

Barreling inside was not the smartest thing to do, but I did it anyway, ignoring the pain from the pebble in my shoe and racing to rescue their jackets.

I grabbed them and hurried toward the door. The ground smoldered under my feet, and the smoke was thick, searing my lungs and obscuring my sight.

Disoriented, I spun. I'd made sure to leave the door open when I entered, but now it was closed!

I threw my body against it, but it wouldn't budge.

I pushed again, grunting. "Let me out!" I shouted, coughing into my sleeve. "Someone, anyone—help!"

Flames licked the wooden stand on which one of the Three Sages stood. The wood beneath it creaked and snapped. Like bones breaking. The giant statue rumbled and toppled onto the ground. It rolled, faster and faster—toward me.

Nowhere to run. I climbed onto a table and leapt for the lantern hanging above me. It swung, barely strong enough to hold my weight. I kicked up my dangling feet just as the Sage bowled beneath me into the fire.

The lantern snapped, and I tumbled onto the table.

Smoke filled my lungs. Coughing, I swerved toward the closest window—one that, thank Amana, had no screens. I pushed the jackets out first, then squeezed my body through, but the pattern of the latticework caught at my hips.

*No, no, no.* I wriggled. I panicked. *So close.*

"Norbu?" I shouted, seeing a figure outside. "Norbu, is that you?"

No answer.

I sucked in my stomach and drove my hips through the window. With one last push, I rolled away from the hall, panting and struggling to catch my breath. Then I saw Norbu coming out of the shadows.

"Norbu!" I shouted. "Thank Amana you're—"

Norbu stepped on my wrist, pinning my hand to the ground.

Squirming, I kicked and cried, "Norbu, what are you—"

I stopped. He was carrying one of the heavy metal pans we used for smoothing our fabrics. I tried to yank my wrist away, but he was too strong. Too quick.

He raised the pan high, then brought it crashing down onto my hand.

Pain shot up from the tips of my fingers and flooded my brain. I screamed, but Norbu's other foot covered my mouth, muffling the sound before it pierced the commotion behind us.

The last thing I saw was Norbu slipping out behind the hall. Then everything went black.

# CHAPTER TWELVE

I couldn't move my hand. It felt like a pincushion, punctured by scorching needles from every side. Tears pricked the corners of my eyes, and my heart beat so fast I could hardly breathe. I tried to scream, but my mouth was gagged.

Something touched my broken hand, subduing the pain just enough for me to breathe.

I blinked, my vision bleary. I was lying on a bench, with a pillow slightly elevating my head.

Where was I? Not in my room. The smells here were crisper, an undertone of cinnamon and musk. The colors were a blur—splashes of periwinkle, an ocher wall, a tower of books with faded crimson spines. I shut my eyes, then opened them again.

*How did I get here?*

A voice. Male. Calm. "Ah, you're awake."

Edan's thin face focused into view.

"Drink this." He dribbled tea over the cloth in my mouth. It filtered down my throat, warm, but not hot enough to burn. It was surprisingly sweet, the taste of the medicine masked by tangerine nectar and ginger.

"I infused the tea with willow bark shavings," Edan said. "That should help with the pain." He untied the cord restraining my arm and lifted my hand. "Are you going to scream?"

114

I blinked. *No.*

"Now, I warn you," he said, releasing the gag, "I hate it when girls scream."

"I'm. Not. A. Girl," I said between breaths.

"I hate it even more when boys scream."

I tried to wiggle my fingers, but they wouldn't move. A tide of panic set my heart racing again. "I can't—"

"Don't worry," Edan said. "Now, *xitara,* don't get the wrong idea." He brought my fingertips to his lips and blew on them.

"What are you—"

He set my hand down. "It should take a few minutes. It might feel a little odd. Best for you not to think about it."

"Think about what?"

"The burns aren't as bad as I feared," he went on, ignoring me. "But the joints and muscles are in poor shape."

"Think about what?" I repeated.

Then I felt it. A sharp twinge in the muscles of my hand. The twinge became a tingling—more painful than pleasurable, but the sensation was odd, as if my bones were reconstructing themselves. Feeling returned to me finger by finger, and blood rushed to my palm as the swelling went down and my veins blued. I held my breath until it was over; then I gasped. "How did you—"

Edan poured water liberally over my hand, washing away the blood and soothing the bruises. "Healing was never my gift, but I learned enough to be useful."

I sat up. "I meant, how did you find me?"

"Oh," he said. "I heard you scream. Good thing you did. My hearing is very sensitive, you know."

I was barely listening. I wished he hadn't taken away my gag. The pain in my hand spiked, and I wanted to scream again, but

115

I wouldn't—not in front of Edan. So I clenched my teeth together and clamped my lips closed.

Slowly, the bruises faded before my eyes, the ones over my knuckles taking longest to disappear. I watched, so mesmerized that I almost forgot the pain.

"There," Edan announced. "Good as new. Almost, anyway."

I stared at my hand.

"No 'thank you'?" said Edan mildly.

"Thank you," I breathed, flipping my hand back and forth. Even my calluses were gone. It would be a nuisance developing new ones, but better than having a broken hand. "Thank you."

"Hmph," Edan said. Brusquely, he took my hand and studied it. "Not bad. Healing works best directly after the injury is sustained, you see. Once the blood and bones settle in the wrong place, it's difficult to convince them to return."

"What does that mean?"

"It means enchantments are usually only temporary. Which is why I'll have to watch over your hand very carefully."

I cleared my throat, suddenly made uncomfortable by Edan's attention, and put on my most businesslike voice. "I want to repay you for healing me. I don't have much money, but—"

He let out a short laugh. "Save your jens. Enchanters have little need for money, or anything else. I don't need any payment."

"What about help mending?" I persisted. I gestured at his clothes. "Or a new garment that's a bit more colorful than the black you always wear."

"A new cloak could be tempting," he mused. "Though, come to think of it, a favor from you might prove useful one day, especially given you've those scissors. I'll think on it, Maia Tamarin. Thank you."

His long fingers brushed the back of my injured hand, wrapping bandages over me. My stomach swooped from the intimacy of it, and when he was done, I drew my hand back.

"Thank *you*," I said quietly.

Edan merely smiled. For the first time, I wished he would keep talking. This silence felt heavy, awkward. "Finish your tea."

I hesitated.

"Toads and turds, girl, it's not poison. Drink the whole thing."

I gulped down the rest of the tea and wiped my mouth on my sleeve. "When will I be able to sew again?"

Edan sat on the stool beside me. "You should be fine in a few days. Take it easy for now."

"Can't." I flexed my fingers. My bones and muscles were in place, but that didn't mean it didn't hurt. "I need to win."

"And why do you need to win so badly?" Edan asked.

"For my family," I said. "Times have been hard."

"Ah, so it's not for yourself?"

"A little for myself, too," I admitted.

"If you're worried about the pain, you do have magic scissors."

I frowned. "I want to win without magic."

"I don't see why that's so important to you," said Edan.

"It isn't fair to the others," I replied. "Or to me. I didn't spend years learning to be a tailor so I could have my work done for me by magic."

"Don't be foolish. If it makes you feel better, Norbu is working magic too."

"What?" The muscles in my throat tightened. "How?"

"You'll find everyone in high places uses a smidgeon of magic every now and then. Even Emperor Khanujin's head chef. Most delectable duck you'll ever taste." Edan smacked his lips. "Don't close your fist. It'll leave scars."

I opened up my hand again. I wished he would take a step back. He was too close. I set aside my cup. "That didn't answer my question."

"Didn't it?" His playful eyes flickered blue—blue as the ocean in Port Kamalan. Deep and clear.

Edan watched me, expectantly awaiting my reply. I flushed and pretended to clutch my head. "What did you give me?"

"It's mostly something to numb the pain."

"Mostly?" I repeated.

With a grin, he leaned back, watching my face ease as the pain subsided, minute by minute. Then he picked up my cup, studying the leaves inside. "Is Maia your birth name?"

"It is."

"I'm not sure it suits you."

I twisted my lips tightly. "It means *obedient*."

He set down the cup. "Which is why I said I'm not sure it suits you," he said. "You have a remarkable journey ahead of you, Maia. I can see it in your tea leaves."

As usual, it was difficult for me to tell whether Edan was playing with me. "I need to get back," I said thickly. "There's only one more day for this challenge, and given the fire . . ."

The truth was, I didn't want to stay in Edan's chambers any longer. I was growing all too aware of the mysterious heat rising to my neck.

"Anxious about your jacket?" Edan said. "Your scissors would finish the job in an hour."

I peeled myself off the bench, stretching my legs over an expensive-looking carpet. "Will you stop badgering me about the scissors? I don't want to use them."

Edan laughed and clapped at me. "I have to say, being a boy suits you."

I opened my mouth, then closed it. He was right, I realized. As a girl, I would never have talked back to the Lord Enchanter. Would I? Or was it Edan who brought out this boldness in me? I suspected he provoked me on purpose. That he enjoyed it.

"Your skill is greater than the magic in the scissors," Edan said. Something about his expression softened, as if he respected my decision. "But if you want to win for your family, you'll need the scissors. If you want to win against Norbu, you'll need the scissors."

"How does he use magic?"

Edan stifled a yawn. "Don't worry about that for now."

"How can I not?" I said, wincing as I tried to curl my newly healed fingers. Now that the fogginess in my head was clearing, I couldn't stop thinking about how calmly Norbu had broken my hand. As if he'd done such a thing before.

I glanced about me, only now noticing my surroundings. Books everywhere, neatly ordered on their shelves, and scrolls that were labeled and tied with different-colored cords. Pockets of dried herbs and jasmine to mask the faint smell of incense that wafted in from outside. There was also a dagger with a silvery sheath, a thin wooden flute, and a painted horse figurine that looked like a child's toy.

I reached out with my good hand for one of the books. "Is this your room?"

"Yes, while I'm here." Edan yawned. "Stop being nosy, now. You should sleep."

"I'm not tired."

"Well, I am. Sleep. It'll help your hand recover."

I started to protest, but he touched my forehead, and the world folded into darkness.

· · ·

Norbu was not pleased to see me back in the Hall of Supreme Diligence, but he hid it well enough. He was there with the others, cleaning up the mess from the fire. His table had been burned, but he didn't look half as troubled as Longhai and Yindi—both had dark shadows under their eyes.

"Back so soon from the infirmary?" Norbu said coolly. "We worried you'd died." He glanced at my hand and noted the missing cane. "A broken hand to go with your broken leg?"

"You're the one who broke it," I retorted, appalled by the man's audacity.

"Me?" Norbu scoffed. "I was asleep in my bed the entire time. Ask the others."

"I saw you," I hissed. "You broke my hand."

"You've a vivid imagination, young Tamarin." He laughed, but I'd heard the edge in his tone as he discredited me. "Come, let me walk you to your stat—"

I pushed his hand away and started for my table. Behind Norbu, Longhai passed me a sympathetic look, but he didn't speak up.

I couldn't blame him. Norbu was a famous tailor and a powerful man; I was no one. Except for Edan, who would believe that he'd broken my hand? Still, now I knew Norbu was using magic. It didn't give me power over him, but it made me determined to beat him.

Norbu called after me, "I take it you are ambidextrous."

I ignored him, sifting through the remains of my station. A

fallen Sage had smashed my wooden screen, but my loom was intact. My embroidery frame was ruined.

I bent to retrieve my cane. The fire had singed its wood, but it was still usable. Leaning on its familiar support, I picked up one of my spools, still warm to the touch. Edan had said it would take time for my hand to heal, but even holding a spool of thread was painful. Using my good hand, I bundled together the few things that had survived.

"Longhai and Yindi found their jackets outside," Norbu said. He'd followed me, of course. "And yours. Some good soul must have tried to save them."

"It's a good thing you put *your* jacket aside, Norbu," I said through my teeth. "Otherwise, all your hard work might have been ruined in the fire."

"The gods watch over me," Norbu said, pressing his hands together. "I am very grateful."

I snorted loudly enough for him to hear. "You sabotaged us."

Norbu straightened, looking shocked. "Excuse me?"

"You started the fire," I said. "I heard you outside—"

"I think it more likely *you* started the fire, Master Tamarin," Norbu interrupted. "You were the only one working late, after all. And your jacket is practically unscathed."

"Me?" I nearly shouted. "You—"

Longhai touched my shoulder and shook his head.

"First you accuse me of breaking your hand, now of starting the fire." Norbu sighed. "I know you must be angry, young Tamarin, but that does not give you the right to slander my name. I will forgive you this time, since the night has taken its toll on everyone." He paused. "Now, if you'll excuse me, I have to work."

With that, he left me alone with Yindi and Longhai.

"I'm sorry," I said, drawing a sharp breath when I saw how

badly burnt their jackets were. My efforts to save them had been in vain. "I tried to—" I stopped, startled by the sound of Yindi angrily tearing his jacket in half.

Longhai barely flinched. Defeat stung his eyes.

"Don't," I said, putting my hands over Longhai's jacket before he, too, gave up. "You still have half the night."

"I know when to bow out gracefully," he replied. "It's something you learn with age."

"Norbu started the fire," I whispered. "I know it. You can't let him win."

Longhai's wide shoulders fell. "I already knew it was him."

My brows furrowed. "How?"

"His clothes reeked of smoke even though he said he'd been nowhere near," Longhai said. He swept a pile of ash with his foot. "How did *you* know?"

I thought about the hawk's piercing cry—how it had sounded like a warning. But who would believe me if I told them that?

I coughed from the smoke, covering my mouth with my sleeve. "I'd gone out to get fresh air, then I saw the smoke. I rushed in to get your jackets . . . and I saw Norbu just outside the hall."

"I'm going to admit defeat. Yindi will too." Longhai eyed my bandaged hand. "And you should as well."

"You can't give up without trying," I implored him. "Maybe Emperor Khanujin will postpone the trial. You can't let Norbu win."

"Norbu is a man with two faces," Longhai said. "I thought he had changed, but he is as ruthless as before. Do you know how Master Huan died, Keton?"

I shook my head.

"The servants found him drowned in the river just outside Niyan. Everyone assumed he fell into the river because he was drunk." He hesitated, and the grooves on his face deepened. "But I knew Master Huan. He never drank, not while he was the imperial tailor. He was poisoned."

I caught my breath. "How?"

"I don't know," Longhai said. "But Norbu was the last man seen with him."

He sighed, and I realized I had misjudged his friendship with Norbu.

"I've been trying to get it out of him the past few weeks, but the sly dog won't talk." He turned to me. "You'll learn that certain things aren't worth the trouble. I have my business and my family, and I will not risk my reputation for the sake of any contest. And you—you are young. Come with me and become my apprentice. You could make a good name for yourself. But you'll have no future if Norbu does *that* to your hand again."

His offer was tempting, but I hung back.

"I'm staying," I said firmly. "I can't let him win."

"Then Amana be with you." He gripped my shoulder. "May the Sages give you the strength to win."

Yindi had been quiet throughout our exchange, but now he walked up to us. His eyes were wide and wild. "The fire is a sign from the gods to leave. Nothing good will come of this wedding."

"Norbu made that fire, you fool," said Longhai. "And Norbu has played us all."

"No," Yindi said. "The shansen is playing us all. There are demon forces behind him. And once he brings them to A'landi, it will be too late."

"You've been listening to too many soldiers talk."

123

"Why do you say the shansen has demons?" I asked. "Doesn't he hate magic, like his daughter?"

"Lies." Yindi sniffed. "How can he hate what gives him power? Once the shansen places his daughter on the throne, he will have the emperor killed, just as he had his father and brother murdered by demons. Then he will steal his Lord Enchanter for himself. Just you wait and see."

A chill swept over me, but Longhai dismissed Yindi's warning.

"Enough of this," he said. "You are upset. We all are. But the palace has eyes and ears, and you are ranting like a mad fool. Leave now with dignity."

Yindi glared at him, and at me. "Just you wait and see," he repeated, directing the warning at me. Then he left without another word.

Longhai lingered, his round, jolly face the gravest I'd ever seen it. "Good luck to you, Master Tamarin. May you have all the prosperity and happiness that you deserve. Look for me if you're ever in Bansai."

I bowed my head. Then Longhai, too, was gone.

Turning to the empty hall, I gathered my jacket and what was left of my materials. I had only a few precious hours before Lady Sarnai would appear with Emperor Khanujin to judge our creations.

It had always been Norbu. I saw that now. Norbu who had ruined my shawl, Norbu who'd taken the other tailors out drinking so they couldn't work as hard, Norbu who had started the fire and locked me in the hall. Norbu who had broken my hand.

If not for Edan's help, Norbu would have won the trial.

Gods help me, as long as I could sew, that was not going to happen.

# CHAPTER THIRTEEN

As soon as I saw Norbu's jacket, I knew I had no chance.

It was magnificent. Sleeveless and daring. The collar was made of snow-white swan feathers, and the skirt rippled with pearls and ermine trimming fit for an empress.

Even Lady Sarnai was impressed. She showed little sign of emotion at the news that the Hall of Supreme Diligence had burned, forcing two tailors to resign. But when she saw Norbu's jacket, she actually smiled.

My heart sank. My only ally, Edan, wasn't here. Only now did I realize how much I had relied on his presence at these challenges.

I'd worked all night after Longhai and Yindi left, but because of my hand I'd had to forgo many of the details to finish in time. I'd planned to add lace to the neckline and sleeves and sew golden buttons to match the gilded leaves I'd painstakingly drawn over the violet paint to make the paper look like brocade. Now, seeing Norbu's feathers and pearls and fur, I realized my design was far too plain.

Lady Sarnai fluttered her fan, pretending to think. I simmered with agitation as I waited. I already knew whom she would choose, even though I couldn't bear to hear the words.

"Master Norbu's jacket is the superior one in this challenge," she finally said, confirming my fears. Lorsa started for

125

me, but Lady Sarnai raised her fan. "*However*, given the fire, another challenge may be necessary for me to make a proper decision."

I stole a glance at Emperor Khanujin, certain he'd be furious with the shansen's daughter for trying again to postpone the wedding. To my surprise, he nodded. "Very well. There will be one final challenge. But *I* will deliver it."

Lady Sarnai's eyes narrowed. "Your Majesty, you left the selection of the tailor to me, did you not?"

"I did," replied Emperor Khanujin, "but paper jackets and glass shoes are not indicative of either tailor's true talent." He waited, as if daring Lady Sarnai to object. When she didn't, he addressed Norbu and me: "No rules this time. Simply craft something for Lady Sarnai to the best of your ability. Something meaningful to you, that captures her beauty. Have it ready in a week's time."

I bowed. "Yes, Your Majesty."

Norbu echoed my words, smiling.

For the first time in my life, I wanted to spit at someone. If only the emperor hadn't been around, I really might have.

"What shall we do with the jackets?" Minister Lorsa asked once Emperor Khanujin had left.

"Ask Master Norbu," Lady Sarnai said.

Norbu bared his teeth, his smile widening. "It would greatly honor me if mine was burned at the temple."

"Very well," Lady Sarnai said. "Since the emperor is so dedicated to visiting the temple and praying to his heavenly ancestors, I'm sure they will welcome the gift."

Bile rose in my throat. Edan had to be right about Norbu using magic; no tailor in his right mind would offer to destroy such a jacket unless he had something to hide. Much as it pained me, I bowed. "Please burn mine, too, Your Highness."

My voice nearly came out as a whisper. All my hard work, burned! And to think I'd risked my life to save this jacket from the fire. I couldn't bear the irony of it.

I watched the servants take away my jacket, and after Lady Sarnai exited the room, Lorsa approached me. His tone was dismissive, as if I'd already lost. "Her Highness wishes you to take her measurements. Meet her in the Orchid Pavilion."

Now? Dread unfolded in the pit of my stomach, but I nodded.

. . .

The Orchid Pavilion was in the heart of the Summer Palace, surrounded by shady willow trees, a medley of birds in gilded cages, a spectacular garden, and a courtyard of royal apartments where the shansen's daughter resided.

I was sweating by the time I reached it. Lady Sarnai's head maid cast me a disapproving look. "You're late," she said. "Her Highness hates it when her visitors are late."

*Late?* I had come as soon as Lorsa told me.

"I'm sorry," I mumbled.

The head maid thrust a handkerchief in front of my face, and I dabbed my sweat with it. Then the doors, tended by a guard on each side, slid open.

Lady Sarnai's chambers were the grandest I'd seen yet. A rosewood table accompanied every silk-cushioned chair, and a square table in the front overflowed with ivory gambling tiles and hand-painted cards. In the corner were trunks that I imagined must be filled with gifts from His Majesty: the finest silks, jade combs, pearl hairpins, bronze cosmetic boxes, and sashes in every color.

Lady Sarnai was waiting for me by the largest window, seated before an embroidery frame. I couldn't see her work from where I stood, but she seemed skilled with the needle—more skilled than I'd expected from a lady of her rank.

"Come closer," she said. "You cannot take my measurements standing at the door."

I also couldn't take her measurements when she was fully clothed, but I said nothing about this. Lady Sarnai stood so a maid could remove her outer robe, and I unrolled my marked string. As Edan had noticed, Lady Sarnai's proportions were not so different from my own.

Knowing the maids watched me closely, I took her measurements, noting her girth and height but averting my eyes from her bare neck and arms. One misconstrued glance was all it would take to send me into the dungeons. How terrible it would be if I, a girl, were jailed for staring lewdly at Lady Sarnai!

But not looking made my task difficult, and when my fingers brushed against the lady's arm as I measured for sleeve length, she spoke: "You've a gentle touch for a man, Master Tamarin."

I immediately panicked and bowed, as if the comment were a death sentence. "I'm . . . I'm sorry. I didn't mean to—"

"Relax. For one so timid, you're curiously on edge."

I bit my lip. "This trial means much to my family, Your Highness."

"Ah," she said. "You have considerable skill for your age, Master Tamarin. I would say the gods must smile on you, but I noticed no shrine or amulets for luck on your table. Are you not superstitious?"

"I believe in hard work, Your Highness. Hard work and honesty."

She laughed at that. "I see they've forgotten demon lore in the South, but one does not grow up in the North without being wary. All the beasts in the northern forests and jungles are said to be part demon." She smiled tightly. "I would know. My own father sought to unleash their powers on Emperor Khanujin, but . . . one does not bargain with demons without paying a steep price."

I bowed my head, hoping it would hide my stricken face. Why was she telling me this?

I stared at my feet and prayed for dismissal, but Lady Sarnai let the silence linger before noticing the stiffness in my fingers. "What is wrong with your hand?"

"I . . . I was hurt in the fire."

"Pity. I hope it won't interfere with your sewing."

"It won't." I stepped to the side and stole a glance at Lady Sarnai's embroidery. It was only half finished, but I recognized the shape of a tiger—the shansen's emblem. I flipped my gaze back to the lady before she noticed.

She fluttered her fan at her neck. "I don't know much about you, Master Tamarin. I was given reports on all the tailors, but the one on you—and your father—was lacking." She closed the fan. "You are obviously talented. Why have you not tried to make more of a name for yourself?"

"A'landi was at war, Your Highness," I said tightly. "I was called to battle."

"In the Five Winters' War?"

I finished my measurements, rolled up my string. "Yes."

"Your two older brothers were killed in battle. Minister Lorsa mentioned this to me."

I said nothing. I had no idea why she wanted to keep me here, asking me questions she already knew the answers to.

"You must hate my father for taking them away," Lady Sarnai said. "And Emperor Khanujin for sending you to war at such a young age."

"It was my duty to serve in the war. I hold no anger toward the shansen—or Emperor Khanujin."

"Then you are a good man. Far better than most." Lady Sarnai closed her fan and waved for her maids to leave. "I've found that most men say one thing but mean another." She peered at me. "But *you* don't lie, Master Tamarin. You hide instead. You have a secret, I sense."

I was beginning to feel more and more ill at ease. "Your Highness, if there's nothing else—"

"Keep it," Lady Sarnai interjected. "I'm not interested in your secrets. The Lord Enchanter's, however . . . they interest me very much. And it interests me that he's noticed you."

"Only out of boredom," I said curtly. It was the truth—Edan had told me as much. "I doubt he takes a real interest in anyone."

"He is a disagreeable man," Lady Sarnai conceded. "I wonder if you'll do something for me. . . ." She waited for me to nod. "I noticed you staring at my needlework when you entered."

"Your work is very fine," I said honestly. "The Northern style is the one I'm least familiar with. I could not help but be curious."

"You should take a closer look," said Lady Sarnai, gesturing at her work. "Tell me what your keen eyes see."

I walked over to her frame, dreading that I'd find some secret message embroidered into the scene and be blackmailed for knowing she was betraying Emperor Khanujin. But her work was simply a scene of three animals. The elegance and boldness of her patterns surprised me. The Northern style had never been considered one of A'landi's great schools of embroidery, which were all inclined toward more intricate and layered designs, yet the elegance . . .

"Describe it for me."

"A tiger," I said aloud. "That is your father. And a dragon— Emperor Khanujin."

There were also the beginnings of a bird; it flew over them, its talons clutching a pearl that both the tiger and the dragon were reaching for.

"You look confused," said Lady Sarnai. "The pearl represents A'landi, and the bird is causing a rift between the tiger and dragon, you see. Just as magic creates a rift between the North and South." She leaned forward. "You Southerners and I may have our differences, but we are pious people. The presence of magic in A'landi is unnatural. It brings strife between the emperor and my father."

I remembered Yindi's warning about the shansen. "But not all magic is the work of demons, is it, Your Highness? Not all of it is bad?"

A dark look passed over Lady Sarnai's face, and I wondered what she had seen with her father. "Magic is the root of all that is wicked in this world. And enchanters are at the center of it. After all, what are demons but enchanters who have fallen from grace?" She scoffed. "I wouldn't expect a country boy such as you to understand."

I lowered my head. "Yes, Your Highness."

"My father never trusted Emperor Khanujin," she said, "but he never told me why. Never told me why he started the war in the first place." She pursed her lips, and I thought I read sadness in her dark eyes. It was hard to think of her—a highborn lady—as a prisoner.

"I remember meeting Khanujin once, when we were children. He was a sickly boy, especially when compared to his older brother—the heir. His skin was yellow as sand, and he could barely mount a horse. But look at him now. So . . ."

She didn't choose a word, and I didn't dare offer the one I was thinking: *magnificent*.

Lady Sarnai paused, as if waiting for my reaction. But for the life of me, I could not fathom what point she was trying to make.

What must it have been like for her, to go from a princess of A'landi to the daughter of a traitor? For centuries, a shansen was chosen from her family to serve as A'landi's military leader and protect the country from its hostile Northern neighbors. But when Khanujin's father and brother died, the current shansen refused to pledge allegiance to Khanujin. And so the Five Winters' War began.

It hurt to remember a time when my country was whole, and my family was whole. Even now, with the truce, no one knew why the shansen would not serve Khanujin. But Lady Sarnai suggested it had something to do with magic.

"I'd like you to get to know Edan better," Lady Sarnai finally went on. "Find out his weaknesses, his strengths. Find out what binds him to Emperor Khanujin. What is the source of his loyalty?"

I took a step back. "I . . . I doubt he would tell me."

"He is a fickle creature," Lady Sarnai agreed, "but I have a feeling he would open up to you. You're not a bad-looking boy, and the Lord Enchanter must be lonely."

I must have looked horrified, for Lady Sarnai laughed. She

pressed her fingers together. "You have done well in the trial, Master Tamarin, but Master Norbu has done better. Prove to me that you can be useful, and I may be persuaded to look more favorably upon you."

"Your Highness," I said, "I was under the impression that the trial was a matter of skill."

"It *is* a matter of skill," Lady Sarnai said, opening her fan.

It was the most beautiful one I had seen yet. The flowers were painted with such tiny details that it must have taken the artist months to complete.

"But craftsmanship is a luxury of peace," Lady Sarnai said, tipping the fan toward a candle's flame. "Artisans such as you are soldiers in times of war. Do not forget that."

"How could I?" I whispered, my heart aching as I watched the hungry flames lick at Lady Sarnai's fan. "I grew up learning the hardships of war."

"Quite so." She tossed the burning fan into a bronze incense pot.

I had to grip my legs to keep from reaching out to save the fan. I watched its long wooden handle crackle in the flames, and the silk painting blister and burn, melting until it was no more than an ember.

"War comes at a great cost," Lady Sarnai said, "and from that sacrifice comes peace. Sometimes we must let go of what we value for the future of our country. Be it a beautiful fan, or our honor, or our lives. In the end, we all belong to the gods anyway."

Her tone darkened, and I pondered what had crossed her mind—if she was regretting her promise to marry Emperor Khanujin.

"I need a tailor who can be a soldier for me when I need one, as well as a craftsman," she said. "Can you do this for me? Can you prove that you will be useful in times of war and peace?"

"Yes, Your Highness," I said rigidly. "I can."

"Good. I look forward to seeing what you create for me, Master Tamarin."

I bowed and, without turning my back on Lady Sarnai, shuffled out of the room. Once I was outside, I wondered whether my meeting with her had been a test of sorts. And whether I had passed—

Or failed miserably.

# CHAPTER FOURTEEN

While the Hall of Supreme Diligence was being rebuilt, Norbu and I were assigned new workrooms not far from Lady Sarnai's apartments. But I couldn't go there now. I needed to disappear from her watchful eye.

So I planted myself in the courtyard near my quarters, taking comfort in a letter from Baba. It was short, and he didn't mention Keton, but his words at the end were enough to make my heart burst.

> *The emperor's trial will be hard on you, but know that no matter whether you are chosen to stay or must come home, you are already the best tailor in A'landi to me. You've seized the wind, as I always knew you would.*

I held the letter to my heart. "Seize the wind," I whispered. "Don't become the kite that never flies." Those were Finlei's words. How often he used to say them to me.

I regretted not being as close to him as Sendo. Finlei had always been the most protective of my brothers, yet also the one who'd urge me to leave Baba's shop. "You can't be the best tailor in the world if all you do is sew," he'd say. "Come, let's go on an adventure to free that imagination of yours."

I could count on one hand how many times I'd taken him up

on the offer. What a stubborn girl I'd been back then. I wouldn't hesitate now.

"I'm not in Baba's shop anymore, brother," I whispered. I hoped, wherever Finlei was, he'd be proud of me for that.

Carefully, I folded up Baba's letter. Reading it had fired my determination anew, and I reached for my sketchbook to begin a new design for the final challenge.

I couldn't be sent home, not when Emperor Khanujin had given me another chance. I was so close. This final garment needed to be amazing—worthy of the gods.

But it was impossible to concentrate when my conscience pricked me every other minute about Lady Sarnai's order. I didn't want to spy on Edan!

*But you should, if you really want to win.*

Disgusted with myself, I scratched out my design and crumpled the page. Then crumpled another, and another. And another.

I let out a grunt of frustration.

"I heard Khanujin's given you a second chance."

I whirled around to face the intruder. For once, I wasn't surprised to see him. In fact, I was almost relieved. "Where have you been?"

"Asleep," Edan said. "Healing twenty-odd crushed bones is hard work, even for me."

He took my hand, and I instantly stiffened.

"Relax," he said, bringing my hand closer to his face for inspection. "It's healing nicely, but it's only been a few days. You need to rest more."

I pulled my hand back. "How can I rest when I have another challenge? I almost lost."

Edan cleared his throat. "The emperor did a fine job of extending the trial. Very noble of him, though I wouldn't have expected anything less." I caught the slightest tinge of sarcasm in Edan's voice. "He said you remind him a little of himself."

I turned back to my work, but curiosity bade me ask, "How so?"

"A young man trying hard to succeed. No one ever expected Khanujin to become king, you know. He had to learn much in a short time. Just like you . . . He didn't want to dismiss you just yet." When I didn't respond, Edan shielded his face from the sun and said, "Do you always work outside?"

"Only to sketch. I find it inspiring."

He looked over my shoulder at my drawing. "A water-themed dress?"

"It's inspired by home." I sighed. "It doesn't matter anyway. Norbu is going to win."

"Oh?" Edan feigned ignorance. "Because his designs are best?"

A needle of envy pricked me. "Yes. He's a master tailor. The greatest in A'landi."

"He *is* a master tailor," Edan allowed, "but so are you. Given a month on each of these challenges, I'm sure you both could work miracles. But not in a week. Not without help, anyway." He exhaled. "Don't you remember what I told you?"

"You said Norbu is using magic. But how?"

"Norbu has paint that creates illusions," Edan revealed. "Very elementary stuff. It only lasts a few hours. A day or two at most. Until now, he's been careful to survive each challenge, not to win."

It made sense now. That was why Norbu never had anything to show until the day of the challenge. Why he was always so secretive about his work. Why he'd wanted his jacket burned.

"Magic is a wild, untamed energy that exists all around us," Edan explained, "and certain people are more sensitive to it than others. We enchanters wear talismans that allow us to channel it, and on rare occasions, we enchant everyday objects, such as your scissors, to help us with our work, or to enable others temporary access to magic."

My brows knitted in confusion. Edan wore no rings or amulets, as Emperor Khanujin did. "I don't see a talisman on you."

"The answer to that would give you too much power over me," Edan said with a smile. "Now, don't scrunch up your face like that. You'll get wrinkles."

He waited until I let go of my frown. "*I* would need no magic paint to create an illusion, whereas an ordinary person such as Norbu would. He'd have to give something up, say a thimble or two of blood, every time he wants to use it. Must have cost him a fortune to obtain."

"How come no one else can tell that his designs are illusions?"

"Oh, he's a fine tailor on his own, so he uses magic sparingly. But I can see it well enough, and borrowed magic can always be undone." Edan tapped his chin with his knuckles, looking pensive. "I suspect you could expose him with a bucket of water—since he's using paint, after all."

"I've used magic too," I reminded him quietly. It made me uncomfortable to remember.

"So you have." He leaned close. "But your scissors aren't *borrowed* magic."

"What do you mean?"

"You didn't pay in blood." A dimple formed on the left corner of his mouth. "That means a little bit of magic sings in you."

I didn't know where my grandmother's scissors came from, or whether Baba had known they were magic. "It was so easy," I whispered. "Using the scissors . . . The shawl I made looked like my own work. But it wasn't. Not really. I don't know if I should feel proud or ashamed or—"

The dimple disappeared. "Feel lucky," said Edan. "Your scissors chose to speak to you. It is a gift, one you may need." His voice turned soft. "One that can go away if you are no longer worthy of its power."

The sadness in Edan's words struck a chord in me and made me wonder if he thought of his own magic as a gift. Why had I ever distrusted him? He'd always been my ally here in the palace. He'd always believed in me.

And Lady Sarnai had asked me to betray him.

"You're quiet," Edan noted. "Does what I say bother you?"

"No, it's not that." I shifted my stance. The pebble in my shoe hurt more than ever.

"Then something else?" His roguish smile returned, a shade more somber than usual, but I could tell he was trying to lighten the mood. "Shall I coax the truth out of you? Perhaps a serum would help—"

I couldn't take it anymore. "Lady Sarnai asked me to spy on you," I blurted.

A beat. Then, curse him, he burst out laughing.

"What's so funny?" I put my hands on my hips. "You don't believe me?"

"When did she ask this of you?" Edan said between laughs.

Already I was regretting my decision to tell him. "This morning."

"Then she's even more of a fool than I suspected."

"Why is that? She has good reason to distrust you."

"She does," he agreed. "But you? You'd be the worst spy in

the world, Maia Tamarin, given your complete inability to tell a lie." Still bemused, he said, "Why'd you decide to tell me? Dare I believe you've finally softened toward me?"

I flashed him my most irritated scowl. Edan had a way of making my temper flare. "My loyalty is to the emperor. You are his loyal servant. That's why I told you."

"And here I thought it was because of our growing friendship, and my affection for you."

I muttered, "I liked you better when I thought you were a eunuch."

Edan looked half offended, half amused. "You thought I was a eunuch?"

"A tall one," I said, turning up my nose. "And one who dressed far above his station."

"I'm far too good-looking to be a eunuch," Edan protested.

"I would disagree. Some are quite handsome, and you . . ." I searched for the right insult. "Emperor Khanujin's better-looking than you."

The quirk that tugged at his lips was completely unreadable to me. I couldn't tell whether I'd stung him—or amused him.

"Is it true that the shansen called upon demons to murder the emperor's father?"

The quirk in Edan's lips vanished. "Who told you that?"

"Lady Sarnai. She said her father had to pay a steep price for dealing with demons."

"It's true the shansen has dealt with demons," said Edan carefully. "Whether he called upon them to kill Khanujin's family is a different story. But it's strange that you should hear it from Lady Sarnai."

"I think she despises her father for using magic. And you, for being an enchanter."

"She despises everyone," Edan said, more cheerfully.

I frowned at how casually he took my news. "She told me demons are fallen enchanters."

"Are you worried about me now, Maia?" Edan laughed. "There's nothing to fear. I'm in no danger of becoming a demon, I can assure you. And I'm far more powerful than any demon the shansen could recruit."

For once, I took heart in his arrogance. I wanted to believe him, so I did.

"Be careful, Maia," he said quietly. The sudden change in his tone startled me. "Lady Sarnai will know you've betrayed her trust. I'd care if something happened to you."

I didn't like how tongue-tied I suddenly became. I raised a brow and echoed, "You'd care?"

Edan drew back. "Yes," he said, airily now. "Girl or not, you're a very talented tailor. And you have some aptitude for magic. Enough that I feel somewhat responsible for you."

I rolled my eyes. "You know, she reminds me of you."

Edan frowned, as if I'd mortally insulted him. "What do you mean by that?"

"Both of you enjoy mocking others. She uses this trial as a way of insulting Emperor Khanujin, and you—you enjoy—"

"I do not mock the emperor," said Edan. "Ever."

*You mock me,* I thought.

"If Lady Sarnai and I have anything in common, it's that we have little say in our futures. She uses her frustration to undermine the betrothal, and I use my boredom to study."

"Study what?"

His sharp eyes focused on me. "People who interest me."

"You don't seem like someone who would be interested in a sewing contest."

"I wasn't," he said, "until I saw those scissors of yours."

I already knew what he was going to say. "I won't use them, Edan—"

"It isn't cheating."

"Lady Sarnai hates magic."

"Given the choice between two tailors using magic, she should choose the one who uses it better. Your scissors reflect your skill; Norbu's paint doesn't. And you're not here for the same reason as the others. Longhai, Norbu, Yindi—they've sought the position for glory. You—you want to restore honor to your family's name. And I suppose you want to prove to yourself that you can be as good as any man."

I did. Though I lacked the courage to say it aloud.

"But thank you for warning me about Lady Sarnai," Edan said. "I appreciate it."

His sincerity took me slightly aback. "Don't presume that I did it because we're friends."

"Enchanters don't have friends," Edan said, clearing his throat. I got the sense he'd revealed something he hadn't wanted to. "Good night, Mistress Tamarin."

*"Master,"* I called after him. He was going to be the doom of me one day. I just knew it.

. . .

The door to my room should not have been ajar. I was always careful to close it, especially since I was not privileged enough to have a lock. I pushed my way inside, heart pounding. Something was wrong.

The few possessions I'd brought with me were flung carelessly over my bed—my sketches, the letter I'd received from home, and Baba's scissors among them. I almost wished the intruder were a thief, but the reality was much worse.

Norbu.

"Get out," I told him coldly.

He gave me a false, cheerful smile. "And why would I want to do that?" he taunted. "A pity you didn't burn in the hall. How is that hand of yours, by the way? Did the Lord Enchanter heal it for you?" He brushed his fingers across my pillow. "How did you pay him for his services?"

It was all I could do not to punch him. "Get out," I said again.

Norbu didn't move. "Do you know the price for lying to the emperor?" he said slowly, as if reveling in each word. "Your bones would be picked apart one by one, your eyes clawed out by ravens while you're alive."

"I don't know what you're talking about."

His smile widened. "You run well for someone with a lame leg, young Tamarin, given your injuries from the war."

My breath caught in my throat. "I don't—"

"Something about you has always seemed off, but I couldn't figure out what," Norbu interrupted. "I never heard of Old Master Tamarin having a son with such skill as yours. So I made some inquiries. Your father lost two sons to the Five Winters' War. Only a crippled son survived. No one could tell me about his skill with the needle, so I left it at that . . . until our encounter the other night. I spied you running across the hall, and it gave me pause. The pieces didn't come together immediately, but then I learned from Minister Lorsa that Old Tamarin had another child—" He held up one of my linen chest strips. "A daughter who just happened to work as his seamstress."

My knees weakened. I wanted to accuse him of lying, but my tongue had turned to lead.

Norbu laughed. "You sew better than most girls. That is the best compliment I'll give you. Concede the trial, and I won't say a word to His Majesty about who you really are."

"Why?" I spat. "Are you afraid you might lose to a woman?"

"No." Norbu's face contorted with cruelty. "But after losing two sons, I wonder how your father would cope with the death of his daughter."

The words twisted an invisible dagger into my gut. "Go on and tell the emperor," I said, but my voice shook. "And I'll . . . I'll tell how you poisoned Master Huan."

Norbu let out a cackle. "Longhai's been telling you stories, eh? You can't prove it. Neither of you can."

I curled my fists, hiding a wince when my muscles reminded me they were still healing. "You're not denying it."

"It was his time to go. His designs were old, and His Majesty needed a new tailor anyway."

"That new tailor won't be you!"

I almost accused him of using magic, but I stopped myself. If I could prove it at the trial, maybe I could send him home.

Laughing, Norbu touched my cheek and pressed his thigh against my leg. "I always thought you were a pretty boy. Perhaps a little kiss?"

I slammed my heel into his toes and slapped him as hard as I could. "I'm warning you," I said, grabbing my scissors off my bed. I pointed them into his ribs. "Leave. Now."

Norbu laughed. "Don't worry. I won't let your secret out . . . yet." He stood at the door, then turned back. "I have some respect for you, even. A pity how far you'll fall."

He slipped out and was gone.

The panic that had kept me frozen in place thawed into a tight, hard knot. Trembling, I splashed cold water on my face. Even that didn't startle the shadows from my heart.

I couldn't let Norbu win. Even if he knew my secret, I couldn't be afraid of him.

I would win this final challenge. No matter what it took.

# CHAPTER FIFTEEN

It was impossible to sleep with Norbu's threat looming over me. Every sound rattled me. The mice skittering outside my door, the leaves rustling on the roof. Still, no one came for me, which meant Norbu hadn't told the emperor my secret. Yet.

*The more you worry about it, the less you'll be able to concentrate on actually beating him,* I scolded myself. Catching sight of my scissors, I bolted up. *And you will.*

I stayed awake, sketching until morning light streaked the walls of my chamber. Charcoal stained my palm, and my fingers were sore from drawing, but finally, the perfect dress formed on the page. Tucking my sketchbook under my arm, I hastened to my new workroom and began laying out fabrics over the cutting table.

I constructed the bodice first, layering sheaths of shimmering pale blue silk over satin, then sewing them all together. It gave the effect of a glittering ocean—the view I'd grown up with.

I worked more slowly because of my weak hand, but my seams were still perfect, so tight not even a needle could pierce them. I beaded the collar with a hundred tiny pearls, their luster like the sheen of the stars, and silver-embroidered lace.

Around midday, a light knock broke my concentration.

I assumed it was Edan. I'd gotten used to his unannounced visits, and truthfully I looked forward to them, especially now. Perhaps he could give me advice on what to do about Norbu.

Not Edan. Ammi, with lunch.

The kitchen maid wore a bright smile. Setting her tray on the round wooden table, she let out a gasp and picked up the bodice on my lap. She breathed, holding it to her, "Is this for Lady Sarnai's dress? It's the most beautiful thing I've ever seen."

"You think so?" I said, inhaling. "I'm not done yet."

Ammi passed it back to me. "What more will you do?"

I was glad of a break, so I showed Ammi my sketch. "Do you think she'd like it?"

"Even the goddess Amana would love it," Ammi said firmly.

I sighed. "Somehow I think even Amana is less picky than Lady Sarnai."

We giggled together, and for a moment I forgot I was a boy. I cut my laugh short, but Ammi didn't seem to notice my lapse in character.

"Will you be able to finish it in a week?" she said.

That was my main worry. I bit my lip. "I'll do my best."

"Norbu hasn't even started," she told me. "I went to bring him lunch, and he wasn't there."

I swallowed, knowing why Norbu had yet to work on his dress. "Do you know where he's gone?"

"No, but no one is to leave the palace today. Lord Xina has returned. The emperor is not happy about the visit—the gates are closed until he departs."

"I see. Thank you, Ammi. You've been more helpful than you know."

Ammi's shoulders heaved, the way mine always did when there was something on my mind that should be kept there. "I saw the Lord Enchanter watching you during the challenge," she blurted. "Why didn't you tell me—" She bit her lip. "I would have understood, but I assumed . . ."

"You think I'm with Edan?" I didn't know whether to be horrified or amused. "The Lord Enchanter?"

"I won't tell," she said quickly. "It explains so much, anyway." She cleared her throat, looking very red. "He'd always flirt with the maids, but I always wondered why he never chased any of them. Heaven knows they've thrown themselves at him."

I started to tell her that she was out of her mind to think I was involved in some forbidden romance with Edan, but then I stopped. If Ammi thought me a boy who wasn't interested in girls, we could be friends. I desperately wanted a friend in the palace.

"He is very handsome," I admitted, a little startled to realize it wasn't a lie. I pursed my lips. What else could I say about Edan? He was tall and lean, not as warriorlike as the emperor, but he looked just as strong. No, I couldn't say that! I couldn't comment on his eyes, either, on their ever-changing colors.

"He looks out for you," Ammi said with a giggle. "You're blushing."

"Am not!" I said. Eager to change the subject, I raised my sketch of Lady Sarnai's dress again. "Now tell me, as a girl who's grown up watching the court, would a lady of Lady Sarnai's station prefer wider sleeves or sleeves that come off the shoulder like what's in fashion in the West now . . . ?"

Ammi stayed until she was missed, giving me advice on what the ladies in court wore and on what might please Lady Sarnai. After she left, I sewed until the blisters on my fingers burst and

I had to bandage them. I would need the scissors to complete the task in time.

I fluttered a sheet of sapphire silk onto my table and then reached for the scissors—the light reflected from the blades and shimmered against the walls behind me. As I raised them, they began to glow.

. . .

Only after I steamed and pressed my dress and carried it to Lady Sarnai's apartments did I realize I had barely eaten or slept in days.

I wasn't hungry or tired, though. Only anxious.

Norbu was already there, his dress mounted on a wooden mannequin. He'd chosen a heavier silk; from afar it almost looked like velvet, a deep burgundy the color of blood. As always, every piece of the dress was beautiful—the blouse trimmed with black fur along the collar, the sash beaded with drops of carved scarlet lacquer and jade, and the skirt embroidered with gold phoenixes sweeping up its skillfully draped folds. But *my* dress was stunning.

I was covering my work with a sheet to protect it from the sun when, from the corner of my eye, I saw Norbu stop to greet me.

He kicked at the skirts. "Not bad for a *boy* with a broken hand," he said, touching my forearm.

I jerked. "Get away from me."

His lips puckered, but he let me go. Lady Sarnai, Edan, and Minister Lorsa had arrived. Where was the emperor?

I glanced at Edan, but his gaze was on my dress. Was that a smile on his lips?

I looked away, my eye catching sight of a teapot on one of

Lady Sarnai's side tables. I hoped I wouldn't need to pour it over Norbu's dress to unmask his illusion. It seemed clear that mine was better.

"Master Norbu," Lady Sarnai said, "your dress is one that my mother would have worn."

She moved to my corner of the room. How could she be so graceful while also so cruel? I couldn't help admiring her as much as I disliked her.

I lifted the sheet covering my dress and heard a few sharp intakes of breath from Lady Sarnai's maids. "It's marvelous," they whispered to one another.

"Have you ever seen anything so spectacular?"

"All the ladies in court will want one just like it."

I leaned on my cane, drinking in their praise. For the hundredth time, I tried to look at my dress objectively and find a reason for Lady Sarnai to reject it. I couldn't think of any.

My dress was a soft pearlescent blue, one of the many shades of the sea Sendo had taught me to see as a girl. The outer layer, a short robe wrapped under a sash fastened by a silver cord, was a richer sapphire, the long sleeves embroidered with tiny rose blossoms and soaring cranes with magnificent white wings. On the skirts were opal-petaled water lilies and golden fish swimming in a silvery pool above the hem embellished with seed pearls and layers of lace, like ripples of water.

For an empress, I was sure all would agree mine was more appropriate than Norbu's. Certainly, more beautiful by far.

I exhaled, sure I had finally beaten him.

"Very fine work," Lady Sarnai murmured. "Master Tamarin, truly you've outdone yourself."

Her face was soft, almost kind. Was she in a better mood now that Lord Xina was here?

"Alas," she said, "this trial must come to an end. Both Master Tamarin and Master Norbu are skilled beyond measure, but I feel one would serve me better than the other." The softness dissolved, and she sent a sharp glance at Minister Lorsa.

The eunuch clasped his hands and announced, "Master Norbu has won the position."

My knees buckled, and blood rushed to my ears, making my heart pound in my head. *What?* After everything that had happened, it couldn't be. I couldn't fail Baba and Keton, not like this.

"H-he can't win," I stammered. "Master Norbu's dress is an illusion."

Before anyone could stop me, I reached for Lady Sarnai's pot of tea and splashed its contents at Norbu's dress.

The dress wilted, the rich burgundy fading as the texture of the silk thinned and roughened. Slowly, the fur and beading disappeared, and the gold phoenixes shriveled until they were threadbare, leaving behind little more than a sheath of white silk sewn into the form of a dress.

"Well, there we have it," Edan said, a beat after Minister Lorsa sniffed with disbelief. "Magic, and a rather poor display of one at that. Master Tamarin is the more skilled tailor. That is clear to all."

Lady Sarnai crossed her arms, her lips curling into a tight grimace. "Regardless, I prefer Master Norbu's service."

"But, Your Highness," Edan said thinly, "we all know how strongly you feel about the use of enchantment."

"This is *my* decision," she insisted. "The emperor and I agreed upon this in the truce."

"His Majesty and your father agreed you could select a tailor," said Edan sharply, "not a spy. Master Norbu, I take it, was more compliant than Master Tamarin in accepting your terms."

Lady Sarnai's jaw locked, and she glared at me.

Meanwhile, Norbu made no move to leave. "Master Tamarin?" he asked calmly. "Don't you mean *Mistress* Tamarin?" He was fast for such a large man, and I moved too late. He ripped at the buttons on my tunic, exposing the straps over my chest.

Lady Sarnai gasped, and the maids covered their mouths with their hands.

A cold tide of alarm seized me. For a moment, I couldn't breathe. I stood immobile—in shock, as the world spun.

"She's a girl, Your Highness," Norbu said. "She lied to you all."

"No—" I started.

Lady Sarnai raised a hand, silencing everyone. "Lord Enchanter," she said, beckoning Edan to her. "Is this true?"

I wasn't sure whether it was an accusation that he'd known, or whether Lady Sarnai simply wanted him to inspect me. Edan looked at me unflinchingly.

"Yes," he said. "It's true."

My chest squeezed tight. I met Lady Sarnai's eyes, waiting for the chilly dismissal I'd come to expect from the shansen's daughter. But for once, her brows unfurrowed, and her lips eased out of their usual frown. Time stretched. There was something in her stare I'd never seen before: compassion.

I dared hope that she might take pity on me. After all, I was a girl—like her. One who'd risked everything to break free of the roles this world expected of her. She would understand better than anyone.

Then Lady Sarnai fluttered a hand, and my heart sank. "Take her away."

"Please, Your Highness!" I shouted. "Please—don't."

Her bodyguards grabbed me, and I turned to Edan. But he spoke not a word in my defense. Nothing, as Norbu smirked and the servants watched with widened eyes.

"What will her punishment be?" Edan simply asked Lady Sarnai.

The shansen's daughter paused, considering. "Forty lashes to her back—wake her if she faints and restart the count. I'll ask His Majesty to have her hanged in the morning."

I let out a strangled cry.

Edan bowed to Lady Sarnai. It was curt, but obedient. "As you wish."

# CHAPTER SIXTEEN

There were forty-nine steps down into the palace dungeon. I don't know why I counted. Perhaps to calm myself. A hopeless goal.

My heart hammered so fast that I was out of breath and panting by the time the guards dragged me down the last step. The smell of rot made my insides curdle, and I could hear cockroaches and rats skittering on the cold stones.

A thread of fear bristled up my neck. *I won't be afraid,* I told myself. *I won't be afraid.*

My eyes strained to adjust to the darkness, and I barely saw the guards rounding on me. They struck me in the ribs and kicked me to my knees so that I landed in a rotten pile of hay, coughing and whimpering.

One guard grabbed me by my hair and chained my ankle to the wall. "We used these shackles last for a maid who stole from His Majesty. He ordered her hands chopped off. Wonder what he'll do to you."

I coughed until I could breathe again. I couldn't imagine Emperor Khanujin ordering such a brutal punishment. But what did I really know of him?

What did I know of anyone?

Edan hadn't spoken out to help me.

That hurt more than any whipping. But he had warned me

not to think of him as a friend, hadn't he? I should have listened.

*No matter what happens, I won't scream. I won't let them break me.*

Easier thought than done.

The guards tore away my tunic and ripped off my chest strips—so fast I'd barely crossed my arms to cover myself when the whip burned into my skin, a stinging line of fire. Blood splattered onto the cold stone floor. I tried not to look at it, tried to focus on keeping my arms over my chest, and on the unthinkable count to forty. It helped that cold tears spilled down my face, blurring my sight.

The guards picked up their rhythm. Faster. Harder. Each lash bit into me, gashing my back, and I chewed on my lip so hard my mouth grew hot with blood. On the seventh lash, I screamed. The world went black, then exploded into color, over and over with each lash, and at some point, I stopped remembering to breathe between each scream.

"That's enough!" a voice thundered.

I barely recognized who it was. My back was on fire. I collapsed.

My shackles clattered away and Edan draped his cloak over me. He was carrying me somewhere. Torches burned from the walls, the light hurting my eyes. But the air was still dank and still cold.

Then a metal door shuddered open, and five steps in, Edan stopped. Gently, he sat down, cradling me on his lap.

"Go away," I said, but my words came out garbled. Even I couldn't understand them.

"Open up." He held my chin up as he dribbled something in my mouth. "Come, Maia. Swallow. You need to drink this."

155

The taste was so bitter I nearly spat it out. Edan hadn't bothered sweetening whatever concoction it was that he'd brought this time.

But the pain did dull. Slowly.

With a great exhale, I shifted away from him, but his hold on me was firm. He touched my bare back with his fingers.

"I should have gotten here earlier," he said, his jaw clenched.

I clutched his cloak, pulling the folds over my chest. "Am I to be hanged?"

"This is where they keep the highborn prisoners," Edan said, avoiding the question. "It's a little nicer than where you were earlier."

The smell was still rank, but there was a small window that let in light.

I turned away from him. "What happened to Norbu?"

"He's been taken away. His Majesty was displeased to hear his loyalty could be so easily bought."

"So he'll be executed."

"That is the penalty for conspiring against the emperor."

I lifted my gaze, but my words faltered. "Will I be executed?"

Edan's voice was tight. "I've asked Khanujin to hear your testimony first."

"What for?" I said. "Everyone knows I'm a girl."

He didn't reply.

Strange, how little fear I felt. I supposed the lashes helped. Or whatever enchantment Edan was casting over me as he touched my cheek.

"Will you stay?" I asked quietly.

Edan wiped the corners of my mouth with his handkerchief. "Until you fall asleep, yes."

Tiredly, I laid my head against his chest. He didn't move.

Didn't wrap his arms around me, or push me away. But his heartbeat quickened a notch.

"I'm sorry, Maia," he whispered.

It might have meant more to me had I known that this was the first time Edan the Lord Enchanter had ever apologized to anyone.

. . .

When I awoke, it was morning. The guards outside were shouting at one another, and Edan was gone.

Gingerly, I touched my back. The skin was numb, the gashes already healing. Even the strips of linen around my chest had woven themselves together again.

Magic.

I swallowed hard, remembering Edan's visit. Remembering what awaited me in a few short hours.

It was difficult to stand. My back ached, and fiery pain shot down my legs as I limped to the door and pressed my ear to the keyhole.

I heard sweeping and splashing.

"Hurry, you laggards!" someone yelled. "His Majesty is here."

More sweeping. More splashing. Then silence.

Nervously, I raked my hands through my hair and backed into the corner. It was hard for me to imagine the emperor stepping into a dungeon.

But here he was, in front of my cell.

Gray light flickered over Emperor Khanujin's face as the guards opened the door. The gold trim of his robes glittered against the bleak cell walls.

"Your Majesty," I croaked, forcing my battered body into a

bow. My mouth was dry, and I must have smelled awful. I dared not look up at him.

His voice was hard. "Master Tamarin, you find yourself in the unfortunate position of having lied to me. A capital offense."

I hung my head. I'd known from the beginning what would happen if I was caught and found out. I had to be strong.

"You fooled Lady Sarnai into thinking you were your father's son. You are not Keton Tamarin."

"No, Your Majesty." I stared at my hands. "My name is Maia. I am the youngest child of Kalsang Tamarin."

"His daughter," the emperor murmured. "Yes, it makes sense now. I always thought there was something different about you. Perhaps it was your eyes." He stepped forward, into a stripe of light. "They don't belong to a boy who fought in my war."

Daylight shimmered over the pearl and ruby beads tinkling down the emperor's headdress as he cocked his head to one side, his gaze settling on my bloodied rags. "Given your lashing, I hope you'll still be able to sew."

He held out my scissors. They were dull even in the light—a pair of ordinary shears, or so it seemed. I held my breath.

"My Lord Enchanter said you are able to wield limited magic," he said. "Is this true?"

"Yes, Your Majesty."

He touched my chin and lifted it. A little thrill coursed through me, making me draw in a sharp breath. I looked up into his eyes in surprise.

There I was, ensnared again by the emperor's mysterious magnificence. Even in the dungeon, he was radiant—his touch was enough to make me forget my pain, my shame. My fear.

"A pity you did not tell me earlier," Emperor Khanujin murmured. "Such a talent is rare, especially in a girl." He brushed his hand to the side of my lips, and I thought I might faint from the tenderness of it. Then he withdrew his hand, but our eyes were still locked.

"You should be hanged. But—" He paused. "But you have a gift I need. So I will commute the sentence, for now."

I tilted my chin up. "Sire?"

"You will reassume your brother's identity. The imperial tailor's position is closed to women, and must remain so. Edan will make everyone forget your deception. But I will remember."

I swallowed, nodding in spite of my confusion.

"The future of A'landi depends on my marriage to the shansen's daughter. Whatever she requests of you, you will do. You live now only because of your talent with these scissors." The emperor forced them into my hand. "Fail me, and you *will* be hanged. As will your father and brother. Do you understand?"

"Yes, Your Majesty," I whispered.

I was in a daze—I couldn't sort out my thoughts. What would I have to do for Lady Sarnai that was so important the emperor was going to spare me?

But my tongue could not form the proper words in Emperor Khanujin's presence. Only when he was out of sight was his spell broken.

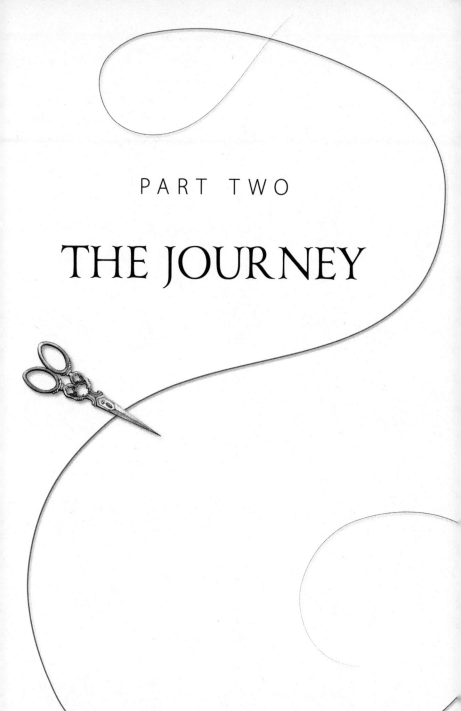

PART TWO

# THE JOURNEY

# CHAPTER SEVENTEEN

Being named the imperial tailor should have been one of the happiest moments of my life, but my bargain with the emperor cast a cloud over my victory. I had to please Lady Sarnai. Or else Baba and Keton would die.

I wasn't looking forward to working with the shansen's daughter. Then again, she'd already made me craft shoes out of glass, jackets out of paper—and I'd survived.

How bad could another dress be?

My heart beat wildly as I approached the Great Hall of Wonders. The largest audience chamber in the Summer Palace, it spanned a wide courtyard and was several stories tall, the stairs carved with statues of golden birds, elephants, and tigers. Inside were mosaic walls (a gift from A'landi's friends in Samaran), brilliant vermillion carpets that stretched as far as my eyes could see, windows that glowed with diffused sunlight, and three prominently displayed jade sculptures of the goddess Amana.

Edan cleared his throat, appearing behind me. "I'm happy to see you're out of that vile place."

I whirled to face the enchanter. For once, no grin tilted his mouth, no mischief twinkled in his eye. Instead he stood, his arms folded, and fixed me with a solemn look.

I hesitated. "Did you really make everyone forget that I'm a girl?"

He bent his head to the side. "Whatever His Majesty wishes will be done."

"Just like that?" I frowned. "With a wave of your hand. Or a snap of your fingers."

Edan shrugged. He looked tired, the area around his eyes weary and dark. I wondered whether the magic he'd cast to make everyone forget I was a girl explained the shadows clinging to his face.

"It's a bit more complicated than that" was all he would say. Before I could respond, he gestured at the passageway leading to the main chamber. "Come with me."

I followed nervously, treading across the carpet as if I were moving through a thicket of thorns. I recognized a few faces: Minister Lorsa, Lady Sarnai, and Emperor Khanujin. Lord Xina, who, as Ammi had mentioned, was visiting. The other members of the court were strangers to me: eunuchs, important officials, and one or two foreign dignitaries.

I kept waiting for someone to shout, "She's a girl! She's an impostor!" But it was as Edan had promised: no one blinked twice at my name, or at my face.

Still, each step was heavier than the last. When I finally reached the emperor's throne, I was breathing hard, as if I had walked a hundred miles, not a hundred steps.

"The trial has come to an end," Emperor Khanujin announced as I knelt before him. "I have decided to award the position of imperial tailor to Keton Tamarin, who will receive a remittance of twenty thousand jens a year."

*Twenty thousand jens a year!* For a moment, I let myself revel in knowing that Baba and Keton would never starve again. That now I was a master, one whose skill no one could doubt.

"Rise, Master Tamarin," continued the emperor. "Now that you serve the Son of Heaven as a tailor of the imperial realm, you are a master of your craft to all."

I forced a smile as I stood. "Thank you, Your Majesty."

"Thank *you*, Master Tamarin," Emperor Khanujin said. His ministers and officials echoed the words. "Lady Sarnai, you asked that I find the most talented tailor in A'landi to sew a wedding garment for you. Master Tamarin is yours to command."

Lady Sarnai said nothing. Like Edan, she stood beside the emperor's throne, but she was staring at something—or someone—so hard I thought her gaze might pierce the walls. I could not see who had captured her attention, but I did recognize the man's voice. It was deep, each word like a growl.

"The shansen wishes to know when the marriage will proceed," said Lord Xina, "and whether Lady Sarnai's conditions have been met."

I tensed, wondering if I'd imagined a note of anguish in his words. How must it feel for him, knowing that Lady Sarnai's tactics to delay her marriage to the emperor had failed, and that the woman he loved would soon be wed to another man?

"You may report to the shansen that his daughter requests a wedding dress," the emperor replied tersely, "to be completed by—"

Lady Sarnai suddenly spoke. "There will be *three* dresses."

Her gaze left Lord Xina and settled on me. There was a gleam in her eyes that I did not like.

A murmur of terror bubbled in my chest. Slowly, the shansen's daughter glided down the three steps from the emperor's throne until she was level with me, so close I could smell the jasmine oil used to perfume her hair. So close I could see the glimmer of confusion flicker across her brow when she held me in her gaze.

I held my breath, knowing exactly what she was trying to remember. Edan's enchantment had worked on everyone else, but if Lady Sarnai—

Her expression cleared, and she shook off whatever bothered her about me. It wasn't as important as what she wanted to say.

"Perhaps you know the legend of the god of thieves?" she asked. "He was so skilled he boasted that he could steal Amana's children: the sun, the moon, and the stars. The gods laughed at him, but he was undeterred. He captured the first two of Amana's children easily, but the stars—they danced in the sky and were difficult to catch. So he shot arrows into them, and caught their essence as they bled into the sky. Amana was so enraged that she buried the world in darkness. Even when the god of thieves gave back what he had stolen, she was not appeased.

"So he called upon Heaven's tailor to make Amana a gift. He had kept slivers of the sun, the moon, and the stars, and he asked the tailor to make three dresses so beautiful they blinded the mortal eye. The tailor succeeded. The dresses were so dazzling Amana forgave the thief and returned light to the world, but only for half the day—for the fragments the thief had given to make the dresses meant the day could never be whole again. A lesson never to anger the mother goddess."

Lady Sarnai paused now, and her red lips formed a dangerous smile. "You are the best tailor in A'landi, Master Tamarin. Make me the dresses of Amana."

I heard Lady Sarnai's mocking tone and struggled to stay calm. *Every* tailor knew the story of Amana's dresses. And every tailor knew that no human hands had ever made them.

166

"One woven with the laughter of the sun," I whispered. "Another embroidered with the tears of the moon, and lastly, one painted with the blood of the stars."

"As I understand it," said Lady Sarnai calmly, "you will need to journey far to acquire the necessary materials for each gown."

"But Your Highness," I blurted, "these dresses are myths. One cannot spin sunlight into thread, nor moonlight—"

"Have you ever tried?"

I swallowed hard. "No, Your Highness."

"I am aware that many have tried and failed to make these three gowns. Pray your fate will be different."

They hadn't just failed. They had disappeared or died—all pursuing something that couldn't be done. And for what? So many legends surrounded the dresses. Some said Amana would grant a wish—no matter how impossible—to the tailor who made them. Others said the dresses would awaken unspeakable power, enough to bring about the end of the world.

I suppressed a shudder. "Yes, Your Highness."

"My father will arrive the night of the red sun. That will give you a good month for each dress. I'm sure the emperor has informed you how important this task is, and what happens if you fail." Her tone hardened. "Do not disappoint me."

"All the palace's resources will be available to you, Master Tamarin," said the emperor, sounding unfazed by Lady Sarnai's demands.

I was hardly listening. All the jens in the world would not buy me the sun and the moon and the stars. What she was asking was impossible!

Lady Sarnai cocked her head to one side. "You look concerned, Master Tamarin. Perhaps the Lord Enchanter can be persuaded to aid you."

A shiver twisted down my spine. Lady Sarnai had wanted me to spy on Edan before, and now she wanted me to ask for his help. It couldn't be a good change of heart—not for either of us.

I folded my arms and bowed, hoping my bent head would hide my rising panic.

"Lord Enchanter," she said, "my young tailor is about to embark on a journey to procure materials for my three dresses. Can he count on your assistance?"

"I'm afraid, Your Highness," Edan said, somewhat testily, "that it is impossible for me to leave the emperor's side for a prolonged period."

"Ah, you don't trust your precious Khanujin with me. It bothers you, doesn't it, that I haven't fallen for his charms. Perhaps if you're not here, things might be different."

A dark look flickered across the emperor's face, and I heard a chorus of stifled gasps behind me. But Edan remained composed. "With all due respect, Your Highness, I must refuse."

Lady Sarnai clucked her tongue. "A pity. You may be the only one who could help poor Master Tamarin. He finds my request quite daunting."

"Perhaps you should change it, then." Edan's mouth set in a thin line as he finally regarded me. "The imperial tailor's skill with the thread and needle is beyond compare. I'm certain he could design something else that would please you."

"Unfortunately, my mind is made up," Lady Sarnai said. "I desire Amana's dresses. I have the utmost confidence that Master Tamarin has the talent necessary to sew them. Think how disappointed His Majesty would be if the truce fell apart because our young tailor perished before he could make my wedding dresses."

"Disappointed indeed." Emperor Khanujin spoke for him. "But the Lord Enchanter best serves the realm while at my side."

Edan's fists curled, but his expression didn't change. He bowed his head, listening as the emperor continued: "I will confer with Edan this afternoon as to how best to satisfy your request. Now, if there is nothing else, Lady Sarnai, my ministers and I have other matters to attend to."

"Master Tamarin, do you have any questions?" she asked.

"No," I whispered, slightly dazed.

"Then there is nothing else." Lady Sarnai smiled sweetly and fluttered her hands to dismiss me. To my surprise, Edan followed.

"I can't go with you," he hissed once we were outside.

"I didn't ask you to," I shot back. "I know it's an impossible task, even for you."

His face folded into a mask of rage. I'd never seen him angry before. It frightened me how black his eyes became, like onyx, too dark to penetrate. "It's not impossible; it's a trap meant to get me away from Khanujin, to send me on a fool's errand."

"Then I'll go alone," I retorted.

He gritted his teeth. "No, you don't understand. The emperor has threatened to execute you if you fail. But he wouldn't need to. Most likely, you'll be killed on your quest."

Killed. Like Finlei and Sendo. They died in the service of A'landi, just as I would.

I bit the inside of my lip, but I wouldn't let Edan's warning dissuade me. "Making Amana's dresses . . . it's never been done. I assumed it would be impossible. But you just said it wasn't."

"That doesn't mean it should be done."

"Then help me," I said. "At least tell me: Where can I find

sunlight so pure it can be spun? And moonlight so dense it can be woven? And the blood of stars . . . I don't even know where to begin with that one."

We found ourselves crossing a pond, and Edan stopped to lean on the rail of the wooden bridge, his lips pursed. "Let's start with the sun," he said finally. "To the lucky few who've seen one, a Niwa spider is known as a golden wheel spider. The silk from its webs is worth thousands of jens per ounce, because it is fire-resistant, among other things. A useful characteristic when one is seeking to gather the laughter of the sun."

Hope bubbled in my chest. "So where can I find a Niwa spider?"

"In the Halakmarat Desert. They're rare, but finding one is only the first step." Edan pulled away from the bridge to face me. "You should leave," he said quietly. "Run away."

His tone surprised me. He sounded almost . . . concerned. "My father and brother are counting on me." I swallowed. "His Majesty said I need to fulfill Lady Sarnai's demands or else he'll . . ." My voice drifted off. *He'll kill them.*

Edan sighed. "Then I'll come with you."

I looked up at him, startled. "I thought you said you couldn't leave the emperor."

"I *shouldn't*," he corrected. "Despite my title, I'm hardly more than a servant myself," he added bitterly. "One who needs permission from Khanujin to leave his side."

Before I could ask what he meant, he went on. "Helping you is the best way to ensure that war does not break out again. Besides, His Majesty would not refuse you an escort."

I blushed. "Even if that escort is you?"

"I'm hoping if I word my request carefully enough, he won't forbid *me* specifically to come with you."

"Why won't he give you permission to leave?"

Edan grimaced. "It's complicated. I protect A'landi by serving the emperor. If I leave, Khanujin will be vulnerable. He doesn't like being vulnerable."

"But—"

"That's all you need to know. Don't pry into my affairs, Maia. You'll find yourself in a dangerous position."

He seemed unusually on edge. "I'm planning to leave tomorrow," I said.

"We'll leave in three days," he corrected, tapping the lantern on one edge of the bridge. The wobbling light made the water in the pond flicker.

Three days? I frowned. I was eager to leave the palace, which was starting to feel more like a cage each day.

"I'll need time to prepare for the journey," he went on. "I'll give you a list of the things you'll need."

"I know what I need. The laughter of the sun, the tears of the moon, and the blood of the stars."

"Precisely," Edan said, not detecting my sarcasm. "It takes a while to devise a plan to acquire all those things. You use the time wisely. Spin or stitch or whatever it is you need to do."

"I don't have anything to sew with yet . . . which is why I need to set out as soon as possible."

Edan considered this. "Day after tomorrow, then," he compromised. "I'll seek you out with the list when I'm ready."

. . .

True to his word, he came to find me the next day just after sunrise. I was awake and already sketching. From the slight rise in his brow, I guessed he was impressed.

"You're up early," he said.

"I'm always up early."

"Here," he said, passing me a thin piece of parchment.

" 'Walnuts from the kitchen,' " I read with surprise. "Walnuts?"

"Ask for the largest ones possible. I'll need three—no, make that four. Read on."

" 'Gloves, to be knit from spider silk—' "

"You'll have to make those," he interrupted, "first thing—the desert will be our initial stop."

" 'Sturdy shoes, preferably made of leather, with sturdy laces. A carpet with some fringes, one color or two, will be sufficient.' " I frowned. "Why do we need a carpet?"

"The shoes and carpet, you'll have to make too," Edan said instead of explaining. "Guess you'll be busy."

"Lastly, my scissors." I set the list down. "Can I ask you something? Why is Lady Sarnai so fixated on these enchanted dresses if she hates magic?"

"Because she doesn't believe you can make them," Edan said tightly. "Because she's hoping we'll die on the trip." A bit more cheerfully, he added, "We'll just have to prove her wrong, won't we?"

"I'm not sure *I* believe they can be made."

"Tell me," Edan said, "for a girl with so much imagination, why are you so skeptical of magic?"

"I'm not skeptical. Not anymore. I just don't *trust* it."

"Disappointing," Edan murmured. "After all the times it's saved you."

I heaved a sigh, feeling I owed him an explanation. "I don't even trust the gods. Not to listen, anyway. My father prays to Amana every morning, every night. When my brothers went to war, I prayed too—to every god, then to every fairy, every spirit I could think of—to bring them back from the war safe. But

Finlei and Sendo died, and Keton—" A lump rose in my throat, strangling my words. "He came home, but he may never walk again. What is there left to believe?"

"It is wishful thinking to hope the gods might listen to you." Edan's tone was gentle. "Just as others are naïve to think magic works miracles. It is not always so. But . . ." He paused, a grin forming on his lips. "But sometimes, especially at the hands of a powerful enchanter such as myself, miracles do happen. Perhaps on our journey, we will find a way to help your family."

I thought of how Edan had healed my hand. Maybe there *was* some hope for Keton. And Baba.

"The journey shouldn't take longer than two months. Which should leave you a good three weeks to make the gowns after we return."

The idea of two months alone with Edan made me nervous. I fidgeted as if I were sitting on a pincushion. "Maybe we could join a caravan."

"With strangers?" Edan said. "Best not to attract attention. There shouldn't be too many bandits along the Spice Road this time of year, but we can't take any chances. We'll be faster on our own. So while I know you must be itching to discard your"—he looked me up and down—"your *manly* disguise, it might be wise to retain it a little longer." He tilted his head, considering. "Though trading in the Samarand Passage would be easier if you were a girl."

I folded my arms over my chest. "Why?"

"I could barter you for at least five camels," Edan mused. "Steal you back after a few hours before the merchant makes you one of his wives."

I balked. "There is no way—"

"Fine, stay a boy." He hid a smile at my distress.

"I can manage," I said stiffly. "Where are we going?"

"To three corners of the continent," Edan said. "For sunlight, we'll go west through the Samarand Passage into the Halakmarat Desert, then north to the border of Agoria for moonlight, then, for the stars, south to the Forgotten Isles of Lapzur in Lake Paduan." He turned for the door. "We'll purchase what you'll need to make everything on the list. And Maia . . ." He lingered on my name. "Bring the scissors."

"I said I would."

"Just making sure you don't forget." He winked. "You'll need them."

# CHAPTER EIGHTEEN

For once, Edan didn't sneak up on me. He arrived at the palace gates punctually at dawn the next day, leading two sturdy, well-fed horses, packed and saddled.

He'd traded his usual all-black attire for an ill-fitting, dull green tunic and trousers that had seen better days. His hair was hidden under a tawny muslin cloak, stray curls escaping from the hood. Several leather pouches dangled off his belt, a satchel was slung on his left shoulder, and under his arm he carried a thick stack of books belted tightly together.

"I hardly recognize you without your court finery," I greeted him. "I didn't think you owned anything except black silk."

"I thought it wise not to look too prosperous," Edan replied, stifling a yawn. "I welcome any opportunity to sleep a few extra minutes rather than dress finely. Mornings don't become me."

"I can see that."

The sun was beginning to pierce the mantle of fog above us. Edan loaded the books onto his horse's back, then threw a glance over his shoulder.

"We should go," he said. "The guards are half asleep now, and I'd rather not have to waste more magic or face their questioning when they're alert."

So he hadn't told His Majesty he was coming with me.

He helped me onto my saddle and handed me a pair of leather straps. "Pull back to stop, left or right to turn. Don't let go."

I gripped the reins. "How do you know I've never ridden a horse before?"

He pointed at how stiffly I sat on my saddle, and at how my feet were digging into my poor horse's body. "Relax, and give a good kick with your heels when you need to go. Don't fall asleep or you'll fall off."

I nodded and timidly patted my horse's mane. His coat was deep amber, like the sands of the desert we would be passing through. "What's his name?"

"Pumpkin."

"And yours?"

Edan flashed a grin at his horse, which was significantly larger than mine and had a beautiful black coat with a silvery mane. "Valiant Grace."

"Naturally," I muttered as he leapt onto his saddle with one elegant motion and was off.

I gave Pumpkin a kick, but he neighed and tried to unseat me before setting off with a lurch. I clung to him, bouncing awkwardly as he trotted on. At least he knew to follow Edan.

. . .

It felt like forever before Edan called for a break. "We won't take as many after today," he warned me.

"I'm not . . . tired," I said between breaths. "We can . . . keep . . . going."

Edan cast me a knowing look. "Five minutes. Sit up straight and catch your breath."

I rolled my neck back and stretched my legs, already sore

from only an hour of riding. To my dismay, we were barely out of Niyan! I could still see the faint outline of the Summer Palace in the distance, tiny as a butterfly, its sloping golden roofs and scarlet gates bright specks before the expansive city. I gulped. "How many days until the Samarand Passage?"

"Three," Edan replied. "But at the pace we're going now, maybe seven."

I winced.

"We'll trade the horses for camels once we get there. The Halakmarat Desert begins on the cusp of A'landi's borders; we'll have to go some way into the desert if we hope to find a golden wheel spider." He fished in a pocket for his map. "Deeper still to reach the Temple of the Sun."

I stared at the map in disbelief. "Two months won't be enough time to make this journey."

"Trust me," Edan said, rolling up the map. "It will be a little tight, but I've allowed for one or two . . . shortcuts." He noted my skepticism. "Magical ones. You'll see."

I inhaled, basking in the cool breeze from the Jingan River. "I hope so."

The Great Spice Road began wide. The farther we traveled, the narrower it became, but Edan was constantly ten paces ahead of me, so riding side by side was never an issue. We'd left early enough that traffic consisted of only a few local merchants pushing wheelbarrows, and it would only get lighter, since we were taking the southern fork of the Road through the Halakmarat Desert, which was less traveled and less patrolled.

Once I stopped worrying if I'd fall off Pumpkin every other minute, I ambitiously took out my needlework to work on a pattern for Lady Sarnai's first dress. A futile endeavor. It was impossible to keep a steady hand while on horseback.

Frustrated, I gave up on sewing and watched the land around me change.

As we traveled deeper inland, the sun burned my back, gnats bit my fingers so many times they itched like mad, and the cool breeze from the river disappeared. I should have been miserable, but the landscape left me breathless. Rocks as red as the setting sun, lizards that dashed through the soft peaked dunes, their eyes bulging whenever they stopped to stare at me, and trees that grew shorter and shorter, until their roots lay supine over the coarse earth.

We stopped to make camp before sunset, and I was so exhausted I fell asleep soon after pitching my tent.

When I woke, night was fading, the first glimmers of the sun peeking over the horizon and shining through the folds of my tent. I rolled to my side and reached into my satchel for my brush and a piece of parchment.

*Dear Baba and Maia,*

*I think more and more of Finlei and Sendo these days now that I am traveling the Road. Last night, I slept under the stars for the first time since ~~they went~~ after the war. I woke once or twice in the middle of the night, sure Finlei had wrapped a blanket over my shoulders and Sendo was there at my side to comfort me with a story—the way he used to when I had a bad dream. But there was just sand, and the ghostly silence of this empty land.*

I lifted my brush, not wanting to continue the letter on such a melancholy note. On the bottom of the page, I drew a picture of my horse and the sand dunes and lizards. Best not to mention Edan, who'd vanished into his tent just after dinner and still hadn't awoken.

*We won't have water for days in the desert. Imagine!*
*Me in the desert, after growing up by Port Kamalan's*
*sea. I miss you so much, Baba. And Maia—thirty-eight*
*steps.*

I folded my letter in half. Blowing sand settled into the crease as I tucked the letter into my satchel. I'd been in the desert long enough to know it was useless trying to sweep it clean.

I crawled out of my tent then and laid my head back against the sand, watching the stars fade. Remembering that Finlei and Sendo were dead made me homesick for Port Kamalan, and here, wandering in the vast world, I somehow felt closer to Baba and Keton than I ever had in the palace. Strangely, even though I was bound to return to finish Lady Sarnai's dresses, I'd never felt so free.

Two months of this lay ahead. I started counting the days, unsure of what was to come.

. . .

The Samarand Passage rested on the fringe of the Halakmarat Desert, marked by two jutting rocks. It appeared to be nothing but a large expanse of sand, naked trees, and dying grass—but within was a small trading town. There we exchanged our horses for camels. I wasn't sad to see Pumpkin go—four days in his company had left my thighs and knees blue with bruises. Now it *really* hurt to walk.

Seeing the Halakmarat Desert on the horizon—how *large*

the sun was here—made my stomach flutter with excitement. This was the farthest west in A'landi I had ever been! Already I'd seen more of the world than I'd ever dreamed I would.

"Come," Edan said, "we have a few stops to make."

Edan pulled up his hood, and I did the same. The winds here were strong, carrying sand from the desert, and the arid air chafed my skin.

The marketplace was on one long block with an inn at the end. I peered into a stall that sold sticky rice wrapped in palm leaves, and jugs of date milk for travelers preparing to go into the desert. The price of water made my eyebrows jump. Edan didn't stop to buy any, and I wondered what we would do for water. Then again, I'd never seen the Lord Enchanter stop to fill his canteen, and yet somehow it was always full.

"Where are we going?"

"To get supplies."

I frowned and looked back. "But the marketplace is that way."

Edan ignored me, making for the drinking house.

"Don't worry," he reassured me. "This is one of the more respectable establishments. No fighting's allowed, and everyone's required to keep his shirt on."

I smiled nervously as a group of drunken men jostled past. "That makes me feel so much better."

I'd never seen such a motley crowd of men. Merchants, gamblers, soldiers, and even a monk or two. About a third were A'landan, a good number were Agorian, and a few, I noticed with a gulp, looked like Balardans—barbarians who'd been fighting A'landi for years. They had helped the shansen in his campaign against Emperor Khanujin.

180

Edan pointed at a man drinking alone in the corner. "Best leather merchant in town. Go talk to him. You need to make a pair of shoes." He touched my shoulder and leaned closer. "A bargaining tip—don't smile so much. You do it when you're nervous, but these merchants will just think you're a dolt."

I frowned at him. "Where are you going?"

"Silk merchants," Edan said, heading toward a group of men playing cards.

I grunted—I'd far rather haggle with the silk sellers.

"Chess?" the leather merchant asked when I stopped at his table. He was already preparing the pieces for his next game.

I scratched at a mosquito bite on my arm and ignored the offer to play. Chess had always been Finlei's game, not mine—but I wasn't terrible. In fact, in all of Port Kamalan, Finlei was the only one who could beat me.

I put on my fiercest haggling expression. "I was told you have leather to sell."

"This is a drinking house, boy," replied the merchant. He had a face like his goods—tough, with many creases. "If you're not here to play, I'm not in the mood for business."

I took the stool across from him. It was like old times. Usually merchants who ended up in Port Kamalan were too tired to be difficult, but I'd dealt with the worst of them. "How about a game, then? If I win, you'll give me a swath of your best leather. Free of charge."

"There must be sand in your eyes." The merchant laughed and took another swig of his wine. He reminded me of Longhai, but I could see that behind his friendly drawl he was out to cheat me. "I never mix business with pleasure."

"Even for this?" I took out my pouch of jens from the palace and loosened the opening just enough for the merchant to see what was inside.

His eyes widened. "That's enough to buy twenty swaths of leather, boy."

"Oh, would you prefer to sell now?"

He stared at my pouch greedily. "Not a chance."

*Good. I'll get a free swath of leather. And prove to Edan I'm a better haggler than he is.* "You start."

While he made his move, I studied my side of the board. Chess was a battle of two armies; capturing the opponent's general meant victory. Finlei had been a master, and the only way to beat him was to make him think he was winning until the very end—when he couldn't breach the defenses I'd constructed around my general.

The strategy worked. It was a close game, but I beat the merchant tidily. Trying not to swagger with pride, I rolled my newly acquired swath of leather under my arm and went to find Edan.

The drinking house had grown even more crowded. Everywhere, men shouted "More food! More drink!" at the serving boys, who juggled gourds of wine and bowls of steaming noodles, and men who were already drunk shouted too, reciting bad poetry louder than it ought to have been heard. But as I threaded through the chaos, a familiar laugh cut through the din of several men gambling behind a bamboo screen.

My heart jumped wildly in my chest. *Norbu?*

A straw hat obscured his hair, and he wore a robe far coarser than the ones he'd donned in the palace, but I would recognize that silhouette—and that laugh—anywhere.

His heavy-lidded gaze fixed upon me, and I glanced away quickly, but not fast enough. Norbu caught me staring. His eyes lifted slightly, and his mouth curled into a sneer, one that raised goose bumps on my arms.

He whispered something to the Balardans next to him before slipping out of the gambling room. My heart hammering, I tried to follow. But by the time I'd squeezed through the crowd, Norbu had vanished.

And I had found Edan—or rather, heard him. He was in the back, his long legs splayed across the carpet, laughing and drinking and playing cards with the silk merchants. I stalked toward him, but Edan pretended not to see me.

"Have you heard?" one of the merchants was saying to him. "Emperor Khanujin's taken ill. No one's seen him for days. He won't leave his room."

As usual, my companion wore an inscrutable smile—either it meant nothing, or he knew something no one else did. "Well," he said, ignoring me, "we must hope His Majesty's health improves before he leaves for the Autumn Palace."

"Yes," the merchant said solemnly. "He was always sickly as a child, I remember. Word had it his father was glad Prince Khanujin was the second in line. Never thought the boy would make it to his adult years. I pray he marries Lady Sarnai quickly and produces an heir."

Edan replied, "Yes, a prayer for His Majesty's health."

The silk merchant gave Edan a hug. "Always a pleasure doing business with you, Gallan. Try not to overpay next time."

"Overpay?" I echoed as soon as Edan joined me. He pushed through the rear door, heading to a stall to pick up his purchase.

"The man doesn't know what he's talking about," he replied. "I got all this for two hundred jens. Compliments of my friends at the card table."

I surveyed his prize: ten yards of wild silk. "Did you cheat?"

"An enchanter never reveals his secrets," Edan replied mysteriously.

"I'd say someone pulled the wool over your eyes." I crossed my arms. "I could've gotten all this for fifty in Port Kamalan. I wish you'd let *me* handle the silk merchants."

His smirk fell apart. Rather sulkily, he asked, "How much did *you* pay?"

My turn to smirk. I held out my merchandise. "All the leather we need. Finest quality. Free."

"Free?"

"I won at chess. Fair and square."

"Remind me not to underestimate you." Edan grinned, looking a little proud.

Heat rose to my cheeks, but I didn't grin back. I glanced around, making sure we were alone, then asked, "Who is Gallan?"

"One of my many names," Edan said dismissively. "Don't call me Edan when we're away from the palace."

"Why not? What should I call you?"

"Anything else." Edan hesitated, looking suddenly pensive. "The emperor won't be pleased I'm gone. He may dispatch people to come find me. Or worse, if word gets out that I'm missing, the shansen might try to capture me."

I swallowed uneasily. "I should tell you, I saw Norbu just now. In the drinking house."

"Norbu?" Edan raised an eyebrow.

I nodded. "I thought he was to be executed."

"It's possible he bribed his way out of prison," considered Edan. "With his wealth and reputation, it wouldn't be unheard of. You needn't worry about him, though. He won't remember you're a woman."

That wasn't why I was worried. "He was with a group of *Balardans*."

A shrug. "He probably hired them to take him out of A'landi. Depending on how he escaped, the emperor's soldiers might be after him. We're the least of his concerns. And more importantly, he's the least of yours."

I hoped so.

With a long sigh, I glanced at the sky. The sun was setting now, its rim a deep burnt crimson. In three months' time, when the sun burned bright red, the shansen would arrive at the Autumn Palace, and Emperor Khanujin and Lady Sarnai would be wed.

A reminder my time was short.

After Edan picked up our camels, we led them out of town and made camp by a small pond just outside the Samarand Passage. It was shallow and overrun with flies, but I filled my canteens to the brim. Edan had warned me his enchantment on our canteens wouldn't last through the desert, and the pond would be the last reliable source of water for days.

"That worried look will be permanently etched on your face if you don't stop frowning," he remarked as I sat cross-legged, cutting a pattern for the bodice of one of the dresses.

"Easy for you to say," I retorted. "You're not the one with the impossible task of pleasing Lady Sarnai. Bet she's counting the days until she can order my death sentence."

"Well, Emperor Khanujin certainly won't welcome me with open arms if you fail. I *did* disobey him by coming with you."

True, and I hadn't been grateful.

I set the collar down on my lap. "I heard the merchant say His Majesty was ill."

Edan cracked his knuckles, something I had never seen him do. "Emperor Khanujin is prone to illness from time to time. Your gods will watch over him."

"Shouldn't you go back to heal him?"

"I would guess he's more angry than unwell."

I didn't understand what he meant, but the edge in his voice was a warning not to pry. "Well, thank you for coming with me."

"Thank me after you make the dresses."

I shook my head. "I still don't believe it's possible. The gods live in a separate world from us," I explained. "Our worlds do not touch."

"Except through magic," he corrected me. "I wasn't lying when I told you Amana's dresses *can* be made."

"You also said they shouldn't be."

"True," Edan said. "Those dresses have great power—power that is not meant to exist in the mortal world. But it's good you're reluctant. That just might keep you alive."

I'd never seen him so serious. "Are you trying to frighten me?"

"No." Edan's grim expression didn't change. "I want you to know that some journeys have ends, but not this one. This one will change you. Irrevocably."

"Don't all journeys change you?"

"It isn't the same." He leaned forward. "I, too, once journeyed beyond the stars."

"What did you find?"

His voice turned lethally soft. "That it's just the beginning."

He stood and walked away. "If ever you change your mind and want to go back, say the word. I will not question it."

"What do you mean, it's just the beginning?" I called after him.

But of course, Edan did not reply.

# CHAPTER NINETEEN

Edan was back to his usual cheerful self the next day, and to my relief, he said nothing about our conversation the night before. I was eager to resume our travels. The sooner we completed our journey, the sooner I could get back to the palace to make the dresses, and relieve myself of the heavy burden of securing peace for A'landi.

The camels were faster than our horses, and a good deal more pleasant to ride. I didn't even mind the smell. The hump took some getting used to, but my camel—whom I named Milk—wasn't half as finicky as Pumpkin.

"Milk?" commented Edan on my camel's new name. His silhouette was dark and lean against the sun. "I'm naming mine Snowfoot." He gestured at the white fur over his camel's hooves.

"What about Pestilence?" I suggested sweetly.

Edan's lips bent into a grin. "Teasing me now, are you? That's a good development."

I reached to pet Milk's small, petal-shaped ears. Her long, honey-colored lashes batted when I touched them, and an irritated snort escaped the thin slits of her nostrils. I sat back, chastened. Milk walked with a steady enough gait that I could take out my sketchbook and start drafting the dress of the sun. I remembered helping Mama design a dress for our statue of

Amana at home when I was younger, but sewing the dress from scratch would be different from fitting one onto a statue. The tales said little about how Amana's dress looked, except that the skirt flared like rays of the sun. That was enough of a clue to start fleshing out some ideas.

As we progressed into the Halakmarat Desert, sweat trickled down the crook of my neck. I wasn't made for the desert, as the camels were—or as Edan was, apparently. While I suffered and reddened under the sun, his smooth, bronze skin didn't even sweat.

It made me wonder about him. Like me, Edan kept his satchel always close at his side. Only, his was full of vials of various powders and liquids I couldn't begin to name. Like my spools and needles, I supposed. We each had our craft.

I'd begun to understand how his eyes changed color with his mood. Black when he was angry, irises like thunderclouds. Yellow when he used magic—with pupils as round as full moons. Blue when he was calm, like the pale sky above us.

I'd thought I'd learn more about his past now that we were traveling companions, but he'd only grown more mysterious. He always disappeared at dusk, and he was always awake before I was, despite his claim that he detested rising early. And these days, he always looked so tired.

"You've been quiet," I remarked.

"Talking depletes my energy," Edan replied, flipping a page of his book. "I dislike the desert more than most terrains."

"Why?"

"It's dry. And windy. Then there's the sun. The desert is where his power shines brightest, where he reminds you how small and insignificant you are. Over time, he'll burn away everything you have, from your hope to your dignity, to your very life." He stopped, his lips twisting to an apologetic grimace. "I suppose I've spent too much time in deserts."

I mustered a smile. The heat *was* intense. "I thought you didn't believe in A'landi's gods."

"I'm not A'landan," Edan said. "But the sun is worshipped in many lands. He's a brilliant, brutal deity. And now we are in the heart of his kingdom."

"Was it always a desert here? I heard that A'landi was once surrounded by forest."

Edan put down his book, and the sinking sun left us in shadow. Dusk was coming. "Why do you ask?"

"Because . . ." My voice trailed off. "I thought you'd know. You seem to have been here before. . . ."

"I've been many places before."

"So you've said," I replied, remembering how I'd thought he'd looked too young to have accomplished so much—that his boasts were merely hot air. Now I wasn't so sure. "When were you here?"

His eyes caught a glint of sunlight, and he turned, grinning at me. "The more I tell you, the less charming you'll find me."

I rolled my eyes, but a bloom of heat prickled my neck. "I don't find you charming."

"Ah, then there's even less to be said."

I wasn't giving up that easily. "I heard you've served Emperor Khanujin's family for three generations."

"It's impolite to ask a man his age," Edan said, a note of amusement touching his voice. "Why are you so curious about me all of a sudden?"

I nudged Milk a few steps forward, until we were beside Edan. A memory flashed of the little flute and the wooden horse figurine I'd seen in Edan's chamber—were they remnants of his past, of the boy he must have been once?

"I thought we should get to know each other," I said. "It's not like we have any alternatives for company."

"Ah, you should have brought more books to read, then. Would you like one of mine?"

I was sorely tempted to take it and throw it at his head. "Look, if you're going to protect me over the next two months, it might be helpful for me to know what you can do."

He tilted his head, considering. "I don't feel hot or cold, except in extreme conditions . . . My eyesight is exceptional for a human. My hearing is particularly sensitive, and my sense of smell is above average—highly astute when it comes to magic—but I have no use for taste. *There*, now you know more about enchanters than almost everyone in the world."

I blinked. "That doesn't tell me anything, really. Where are you from—"

"Nowhere and everywhere," Edan interrupted, reaching into his saddlebag. He tossed his canteen to me. "Your voice is getting hoarse."

It was the same gingery tea he had forced me to drink before. Only slightly stronger. I licked my lips clean and made a face. "You have no taste. No wonder you're so fond of drinking foul-tasting tea."

"Who said it was tea?" Edan rubbed his hands, reveling in my horrified expression. "Ginger's often used in potions. Truth serums, love potions . . ."

I made a gasping sound. "What am I drinking?"

He reached for the canteen and took a sip. "Ginger tea."

I gritted my teeth. "You're impossible."

"So gullible." He laughed and put the canteen away. "I would never need to use a truth serum on you, Maia. You couldn't tell a lie to save your life."

"I can't say the same for you."

"Yes, well, that's true to some extent."

The way he said it sounded almost sad. I snuck a glance at him. Dark circles bloomed under his glassy blue eyes.

"You look tired," I said.

"Most high enchanters have trouble sleeping. It's nothing to worry yourself over."

"What keeps you up at night?" I asked. "You're never in your tent."

A cloud passed over his face. "Demons and ghosts." With a faint smile, he added, "And not having enough books to read."

The winds grew stronger, stirring up desert sand until every inch of me itched with it. Even when I breathed, I inhaled more sand than air.

"This looks like a good place to make camp," Edan said suddenly. He hopped off his camel. "There's a sandstorm up ahead. If we stop now, we'll avoid the worst of it."

We raised our two tents and I crawled inside mine, certain I shed a pound of sand just taking off my cloak.

"Hungry?" Edan asked, following me inside. He unrolled what looked like a small tablecloth, barely larger than a chessboard. "We can't use this too often—magic must be conserved. But I thought we should reward ourselves for a good day's travel." He sat cross-legged on the sand. "Imagine what you'd like to eat and clap your hands once."

I stared at him with disbelief.

"Try it. I would do it myself, but I'm not a good cook, having little taste and all."

Had it been Keton, I would have braced myself for a practical joke. My brother used to tease me relentlessly about my appetite, especially when we were poor and had little to eat. "If only you could spin all that thread into noodles, we'd never be hungry again."

But Keton wasn't here; he was back home with Baba. How I hoped he was doing better. How I hoped he would tease me again, if I ever made it home.

Edan was waiting, so I closed my eyes and imagined my mother's chicken porridge, steaming with chives and ginger, Keton's favorite dumplings with chili oil, and enough sweets to last me a week: steamed coconut buns, fried flatbread, sticky rice with nuts and sliced apricots. Oh, and water. Jugs and jugs of water.

I clapped. And waited.

My nose caught a whiff of ginger. Then I opened my eyes. My jaw dropped—everything I'd imagined appeared before me.

"You went a little overboard," Edan said, with a hint of approval.

The food flowed off the cloth. "Is it . . . real?"

He passed me a bowl. "See for yourself."

My hands curved over the bowl, and a sharp pang of hunger stirred inside me. I picked up a dumpling, bit at its skin, chewed, swallowed. My shoulders melted with contentment, and I ate ravenously, not bothering to ask any more questions.

Edan laughed at me.

"What's so funny?"

"The way you look." He reached for a handful of dates and currants. "I haven't seen anyone so gluttonous since the end of the Great Famine. Maybe you should have become a palace taster instead of a tailor."

"I can't help it if you can't taste anything." I gulped a spoonful of porridge, then greedily turned for one of the coconut buns.

Edan wasn't touching the chicken, I realized. He chewed the fruit slowly, as if he was ruminating on something.

I set down my coconut bun. "Did you grow up during the Great Famine?"

"A different sort of famine," Edan said. "My stepmother was a terrible cook, my father a terrible farmer. I grew up half wild, on a diet of grass and sand. Yams, when I could find them."

It was the most he'd ever told me about his past. "Is that why you're not eating much?"

"No, I'm just not as hungry as you are," he teased. "Eat up. No more talk of famines."

As he reached for a piece of flatbread, a gold bracelet peeked out from under his sleeve. No, not a bracelet. A cuff—plain, with no ornamentation or jewels. I'd never seen it before. His sleeves had always covered his wrists. Could it be the talisman he'd said he couldn't show me?

"You mentioned that enchanters channel their magic through talismans," I began. "I noticed that Emperor Khanujin always wears an amulet with a bird on it. He isn't an enchanter. What is it?"

Edan dug his fingers into the pale sand. "Something to protect him," he said dismissively.

"Why does he need an amulet? I thought it was your duty to protect him."

"It is my duty to *serve* him," Edan corrected. "There is a difference."

I looked at Edan's wrist again; I wondered about that gold

cuff. I picked up my bowl once more, swallowing a mouthful before I dared to ask, "Would you do anything he asked?"

Edan straightened. His bread was on his lap, untouched. He seemed to have forgotten about it—or lost his appetite. "I came here with you, didn't I? Despite his telling me not to."

I frowned. "That just shows you're good at evading direct commands."

"Yes," Edan muttered, more to himself than to me. "Unfortunately, Khanujin has learned to be quite accurate in his speech."

"So you have to obey him?"

"Yes."

"Or what?"

"That's enough questions for today, *xitara*," Edan said. "It's nearly dark, and contrary to what you think, I *am* going to retire to my tent." He rose, pulling up his hood. "Be careful of snakes and scorpions." A pause. "But tell me if you see any spiders."

He disappeared into his tent.

I didn't see any spiders.

. . .

By our seventh day in the desert, I understood why Edan despised it here. Every breath stung my lungs, and my skin burned so hot it was agony to even move. Edan had become brutal about rationing our food and water, which confused me. I'd seen the powers of his tablecloth. I could have imagined buckets and buckets of crisp cool water. Anything to quench my thirst.

"Must we conserve water like this?" I pleaded.

"Magic is scarce the deeper we go into the desert."

"Will it get better?"

"Mostly."

*Mostly.* I rubbed my neck, which was tender to the touch. My head hurt, and my throat yearned for water, but I refused to show weakness. I wouldn't slow us down.

So it surprised me when, a few hours before dusk, Edan declared that we would stop and make camp. He was usually adamant about traveling until nightfall.

There was nothing special about where we were. As far as I could see, there was only sand and more sand, but something had made Edan perk up.

He fished in his satchel for an empty jar.

"What's the jar for?" I asked. My voice was unrecognizable. Dry and crackly.

"Spider hunting," Edan replied, as if it were the most natural thing in the world. "Golden wheel spiders are extremely rare, but I have a feeling luck is on our side."

"How will we find one?"

"By being observant." He lay on his stomach, scooping up a handful of sand and letting it cascade through the seams of his fingers. "We're getting close."

"You might as well look for a needle in a pile of straw."

"Leave it to me, then."

I shielded my eyes with my hand. The sand was hot. "You're going to get burned if you stay there for long."

"I don't burn," he said. "But you do." He reached into his satchel for a tiny lidded pot and tossed it my way. "It's salve. There isn't much, but the heat will get worse before it gets better and you're not used to the desert life. Put some on and wrap your face from the sun. Trust me, it'll help."

The salve smelled like coconut, with honey and a hint of rose. Gingerly, I rubbed some on my nose and cheeks. My discomfort melted away. It *did* soothe my burns. I pursed my lips, touched. "Thank you."

"Don't thank me," he said with a wry grin. "It's more for me than you. I'd rather spare myself the sight of your face blistering and filling with pus."

"Oh, you—" I thought of a thousand names to call Edan, but as I saw the corners of his lips lift mischievously and his eyes sparkle that deep blue I secretly relished, none made it past my lips. So I huffed and stalked off to set up my tent.

"Make sure you apply it every morning and night," he called after me. "I don't want to travel with a mummy."

. . .

A little after sunrise, Edan prodded me awake. Something squirmed in the jar in his hand.

I waved him away with a shriek. "What are you—"

"It's a nocturnal spider," he interrupted. "While you were sleeping, I was working."

I rubbed my eyes, now seeing the spider in the jar. Spindly legs, milky white fangs, and a bulbous body nearly as large as my palm.

Edan set the jar on the ground. The spider blended perfectly with the pale yellow sand.

"A golden wheel spider," he said. "Aptly named for the way it spreads its legs and cartwheels across the sand. It's fast."

He casually slid the jar under his arm. "You'll need to spin its silk," he said. "I'll show you where its burrow is. If you see any of its brothers and sisters, don't touch them. The bite is lethal."

I followed him, bringing my scissors. The burrow wasn't far

from our camp, surrounded by red-brown rocks that jutted like teeth out of the sand. A shiny silver web arched from one rock to another. Carefully, I knelt and wound the scissor blades, coiling the precious web without breaking a single strand.

Once there was no more silk to twirl onto the scissors, I stepped back for Edan to release the spider in the jar. But he was studying it.

"Are you going to let it go?"

"Just a minute," he said, passing me a small glass vial. "Open it, please."

Using a slender wooden spoon, he deftly swabbed the spider's fangs, collecting a viscous sample from its mouth.

I crouched beside him as he deposited the sample in my vial. "Is collecting poisons part of your work for the emperor?"

"It's not poison," Edan said quite seriously, "and I'm collecting it for myself." He crouched with the spider still in its jar. "Stand back."

Gently, he lifted the jar's lid, then tilted it onto the sand. The golden spider cartwheeled out of sight, kicking up sand with its eight legs.

In Edan's hand were three neatly tied spools of the Niwa silk I'd just spun. I was so entranced by the silk I barely wondered how it'd gotten from my scissor blades into his hands. The silk was iridescent, nearly silver in the sunlight, and the thickest thread I'd ever seen.

He lit a match and set the spools on fire.

"Don't!" I cried.

Edan blocked me with his arm. "What makes their silk so special is that fire cannot consume it," he reminded me. "It can't be frozen, either, for that matter."

With a triumphant grin, he blew out the fire and held out

the spider silk to me. "Behold, Master Tailor, the first step to conquering your quest and taming the sun and moon."

Mesmerized by the glistening silken threads, and the possibility that my task wasn't so impossible after all, I hugged him without thinking. "Thank you!"

Edan quickly peeled my arms off. Pink tinged his cheeks, and he wore a frown.

"Sorry," I said, backing away.

"I'm not one of your brothers," he reminded me tersely, "and I'm not your friend." He sounded like he was trying to scold me but couldn't quite muster enough edge in his tone. "I'm here to make sure you don't get killed."

I swallowed. "It won't happen again."

We rode in silence for the rest of the day, but I didn't mind. In spite of the brutal sun, I was in good spirits. Finally, I could do something other than sketching while riding Milk—I could knit!

Eagerly, I took out a needle and cast on the first row of stitches. Knitting gloves was tricky, for if I wasn't careful, I'd end up with holes between the fingers. So I took my time, starting with a rib pattern for the cuffs, then crossing stitches at the finger splits to reduce holes. I was so absorbed in my work I didn't even notice the lone tree ahead until Edan's camel stopped in front of it.

Anywhere else, a tree might not have been so exciting, but in the middle of the Halakmarat, the sight of one was enough to make me fall off my camel.

The tree was gnarled and spiky, with empty branches that reached like claws into the vast, cloudless sky. Surrounding it were parched, sickly shrubs and rocks that bulged from the ground like bones of the earth.

To my endless disappointment, I found not a drop of water by its roots.

Edan tied our camels to the tree. "Set up your tent," he said, brushing his forehead. "Tomorrow will be a long day. We'll head east to the heart of the desert. That's where we'll capture the sun."

Obediently, I staked my walking stick into the ground and unfolded my tent over it. But when Edan wasn't looking, I stole a glance at him.

His cheeks were red, and sweat glistened on his brow. No, it couldn't be—he'd said he couldn't feel heat . . . unless it was extreme. He'd been fine this afternoon during the brunt of the day. Now the sun was setting, the air finally cooling down . . . yet he didn't look at all like his tireless self.

What was happening to Edan?

# CHAPTER TWENTY

A hawk's cry tore into my dreams. I bolted up, my head brushing the flap of my tent. It was difficult to hear any-thing over the howling of the wind, but then the hawk cried again. Louder. It didn't sound far.

"Edan!" I called, kicking off my blanket.

No answer.

I poked my head out of the tent. The moon shone bright against the black, starless sky. There was no sign of my travel-ing companion, but the hawk had plunged into one of Edan's saddlebags. Now it flew away with a bright red pouch in its beak.

I started chasing after it, but the camels caught my atten-tion. They pulled against their ropes, hooves kicking up sand. They were trying to flee, but from what?

I stilled. There was no sandstorm. And I didn't hear any horses. Horses were afraid of camels, not the other way around.

Bandits? No—

I squinted, picking out a pack of moving shadows in the distance. My chest tightened.

Wolves.

They were close. I'd mistaken their howls for the wind. De-mon's breath, no wonder the camels were jittery! I staggered back, their screams drowning the thump of my racing heart.

My hands trembled as I dug through Edan's trunks and satchel. Books, papers, pens, and more books. Amulets that were of no use to me. Did he not bring any weapons?

There! A dagger. I pulled it out but couldn't get it free of the sheath.

*No, no, no.*

Tried again. Still wouldn't budge.

Blood rushed to my ears. In desperation, I ran back into my tent and rummaged through my things. Silk, satin, linen. I couldn't throw my blanket over a pack of wolves, or toss needles at them.

Then I saw my scissors.

I bit my lip. Edan was sure to scold me later for losing our camels, but I wouldn't let them be eaten. I dashed out, snipped their reins, and slapped them on their rumps.

"Hut hut!" I cried. "Go!"

Our campfire was just embers now, so I couldn't light a torch to scare off the wolves. And there was nowhere to run. I'd have to stay and fight.

All I had was the scissors. They glowed, and for once, I was thankful. I set them against my tent's coarse muslin, and they snipped and cut, aiding me as I braided and knotted furiously, fashioning a sturdy rope. I tossed it over the tree and clambered up, each touch of the dry bark scraping my skin. The low growls behind me grew louder and louder.

And then the wolves were upon me. In the moonlight I saw their black fur and bloodshot eyes, hungry. There were five, no, six of them.

I swallowed a scream. *There's food in the tent,* I wanted to tell them. Part of me pitied their lean, scraggly figures. But then their eyes set on me. I was the prize.

The first wolf pounced. It caught my rope in its gleaming jaws and pulled. I let the rope go, wrapping my arms around a branch. The pack leapt at my dangling legs. I screamed, kicking and trying to haul myself higher.

Above me, the hawk returned, Edan's red pouch in its beak. Down it swooped to strike the biggest wolf.

The hawk retreated, only to dive again. This time it sliced the leader behind the ears with its talon, then thrust the red pouch into the beast's jaws. The wolf's fangs snapped shut on the hawk's wing, but it was I who let out a scream.

The wolf swung its head violently as the hawk batted its free wing to escape. I wanted to help, but the rest of the pack was still waiting for me at the bottom of the tree.

Then something strange happened. The leader snarled and turned on its pack, as if it were possessed. It let go of the hawk and lunged, tearing into one of its brothers instead. Soon I was forgotten as the wolves fought one another. The sight was gruesome, blood on fur on sand. I buried my face in my hands until the snarls became whimpers, then nothing.

My head was still buried in my hands when the hawk returned, perching on the branch above me. The tip of its wing brushed across my back, and I looked up. Its feathers were ink black, wings tipped milky white, and its eyes a bright, gleaming yellow—and curiously familiar.

Exhausted, I wrapped my arms around the tree, and I slept.

. . .

"Maia!"

The sound of my name jolted me awake. I squinted, seeing Edan's tall, lean shape below me. Milk's and Snowfoot's, too.

I fumbled down the tree. "Where were you? I almost died."

"I was retrieving the camels that you lost."

How could he be so calm? "Did you not hear me?" I shouted. "I nearly died." I pointed at our camels. "*They* nearly died. Where were you?"

Edan wouldn't answer, which only angered me more.

"How are you supposed to protect me if you're not even here?"

"You're still alive, aren't you?"

I gave him a scathing look, then dusted sand from my pants. Everything was so dry. My mouth, my tongue, my throat. If Edan could make a spring appear out of thin air, this would be the time. But I didn't want to hear another one of his lectures about conserving magic.

His lips were dry too. I noticed that he kept his right arm inside his cloak, and his left hand was bruised. Normally when he spoke, he gestured with his hands, so their stillness made me suspicious.

I poked his shoulder, and Edan let out a small cry. "What was that for?"

"You're injured," I confirmed.

Edan rolled his eyes. "I scraped myself."

"Let me take a look."

"No." He shrank back. "I'll heal myself."

I glowered at him. "I thought you said magic was scarce in the desert."

"It is. But I'll heal. Eventually."

"At least let me clean it."

He jerked his arm away. "We need to get going."

I stared again at his parched lips. "You should drink some water."

Edan's lip quirked upward. "Should I call you Mother now?"

I scowled at him and crossed my arms. "How far are we from the Temple of the Sun?"

"Not too far."

"How come I've never heard of it?"

"Few have. It was abandoned hundreds of years ago, and most of it is buried in sand. But you'll be able to catch a sliver of raw sunlight there." Edan struggled to unscrew his canteen. "With the help of the gloves."

Seeing him struggle with the canteen softened my anger. "You helped heal my hand. If magic is scarce here, then let me help you with your arm."

Edan shook his head.

"Your eyes are turning black." I'd thought that meant he was angry; maybe it was also a sign of pain.

A muscle in his jaw set; then he relented. "Make it quick." He rolled up his sleeve. "We need to be fifty miles east by sunset."

Edan had already tried patching up his arm. Gently, I unwrapped his bandages. The wound was deep, some of the flesh torn away. I noticed his nails were ringed in blood, and I thought of the hawk. It had dug into the wolves with its talons.

My pulse quickened, and I struggled to look calm. "Your stitches are crooked. I'm going to have to take them out and redo them. It'll hurt—do you have any rice wine?"

"Just do it," Edan said with a grunt. He clenched his fists, knuckles whitening as I carefully began to undo the threads.

"I used to patch up my brothers," I said conversationally, trying to keep his mind off the pain. "Finlei and Keton were the worst. They'd fight each other over the stupidest things. Then Sendo would try to stop the brawl and end up right in the middle of it."

"Is that why you're so good at stitching skin?"

"I practiced on my brothers, but my father taught me before that. When work was scarce, sometimes the doctor would call him to help—mostly out of charity. Often I would go in his place."

"I was once an apprentice like you," Edan said through clenched teeth. "Only, my teacher taught me how to open up a man's skull, how to dissect scorpions but leave them alive, how to tell the difference between hemlock and ivy." He coughed. "Useful skills for an overly curious young enchanter. But not very useful skills for looking after myself."

"I had no choice but to learn," I replied. "My mother died when I was only seven. I had to take care of three growing boys and my father." I pursed my lips, remembering the time when my family had been whole. It seemed so far away now, so deep in the past. "What about your parents?"

"I hardly remember," he said. "They died a long time ago."

"I'm sorry," I said softly.

"There's nothing to be sorry about." His voice was distant. "My mother passed when I was born, and my father—I wasn't close to him. Or to my brothers. I had brothers once, too."

He didn't say anything more. He looked lost, so unlike the self-assured enchanter I knew that I wondered if I'd caught a glimpse of the true Edan—the boy behind the magic and power.

"There." I wrapped the bandage over his arm and tied it with a knot. "Finished."

"Nice work." He rolled down his sleeves and regained his usual poise. "I wish I'd been there last night, but you defended yourself well."

"Are you *sure* you weren't there?"

Edan let out a dry laugh. "I would know, wouldn't I?"

I didn't laugh. "The wolves began fighting one another, as if they were bewitched. And there was a hawk—it went into your belongings."

"Oh? What did it take?"

"A red pouch from your saddlebag." I lingered to let my words sink in. "It seemed to know exactly where to find it."

"Hawks are intelligent creatures," Edan replied. "It must have been looking for food."

"Perhaps," I said, but I didn't believe him at all.

I was sure of it now.

The hawk was Edan.

# CHAPTER TWENTY-ONE

When at last we saw the Temple of the Sun, I feared it was a mirage. Framed by dark, charred-looking trees, it stood amid a sea of dunes, with a pool at the foot of its entrance that looked wide as a lake and long as a river.

I clambered toward the pool. My body ached for water, my throat was shriveled from the need of it. But as I knelt to receive its glorious waters, all I saw was my glassy reflection.

This was no pool at all! Only a mirror lying flat against the sand, awash with the gray-blue of the sky. I let out one quiet sob. I had no tears left.

The temple might have been ivory long ago, but like everything else in the desert, it had taken on the color of sand over time. My eyes burned when I tried to see the domed top, shimmering in the violent sunlight.

"You'll have to go in alone," Edan said, stopping at the mirror.

I blinked. "You're not coming?"

"I can't," he said. "Emperor Khanujin has forbidden it."

"What does that matter? He forbade you to come on this trip, and here you are."

His expression darkened. "That's not entirely true. I worded my request carefully. He forbade me to acquire Amana's children for you. He didn't specifically say that I couldn't come on the expedition." Edan folded his hands, looking apologetic. "I'm afraid you'll have to do the hard work your-self."

"And my father always said *I* was the obedient one." I sniffed. "Very well, I won't tell the emperor if you come into the temple with me."

Edan shook his head, strangely adamant. "You'll go alone. Don't worry—it's nowhere as dangerous as the next two tasks."

I didn't like the sound of that.

He handed me his canteen, only a quarter full. "The temple is a labyrinth. Always take the brighter turn, no matter how unbearable it feels. You'll find a round mirror in the center that directly reflects the sun. You'll have to get to the ledge just above the glass. Put on the gloves and reach out only with your hands." After a long second, he added, "Any unprotected part of your body will burn."

I gulped. "What do I do then?"

He unclenched his fist, revealing the last thing I'd expected to see.

"A walnut?"

"You didn't think you could trap sunlight and moonlight in a jar, did you?" Edan licked his lips to moisten them. "I take it you don't know the tale. After the god of thieves stole the sun and the moon, he stored their light—"

"In walnut shells," I said, remembering now. "Walnuts were his favorite food, and who would think to look in a nut?"

Edan nodded. "Coincidence or not, walnuts have unusual magical properties. Not only can they store magic, but they are capable of concealing it as well—from other enchanters, or the like."

"Your trunks are made of walnut wood," I observed. "As is the hilt of your dagger."

"Correct." He passed me the shell. "Crack it open when you are at the mirror and the sun is at its zenith. Do not look into the sun. Say it."

"I won't look into the sun."

"Good. I'll wait for you here."

One step into the temple, and the blazing heat already threatened to suffocate me. There was no roof to block the brutal rays, and I didn't dare touch the walls. I trod on, shedding my tunic and tying it around my waist. My skin simmered with sweat, the heat pricking my eyes.

The sun *was* a brutal god, I remembered from Sendo's tales. Brutal and merciless, he blinded those foolish enough to look at him. Was he watching me now, as I ventured into his labyrinth? Would he punish or help me on my quest to make his mother's dresses? More likely he'd do nothing at all. The gods rarely showed themselves.

Deeper into the temple, the paths narrowed and forked. As Edan had described, there was always one path in shade, the other in bright sunlight. No matter how I longed to shelter in the shadows, I always chose the brighter path. The labyrinth was a furnace, trapping all the heat of the desert. If this was the easiest of the three, I didn't want to know what the other two tasks involved.

Most paths were littered with broken bricks that slowed my progress, but the passages buried in sand were the worst, for I had to wade through slowly enough not to sink, yet fast enough that I didn't bake under the sun.

At last, I arrived in the heart of the labyrinth, where the sun's power nearly blinded me. I caught a glimpse of the courtyard with the round mirror before I had to shut my eyes for protection. The mirror resembled the pool outside the temple, its light magnified a thousandfold. I blinked, spying a wooden ladder propped against one of the courtyard walls. At the top was a ledge that extended out above the mirror.

Half blind, I moved to the ladder. The wood creaked under my feet, and I prayed that the dry beams wouldn't snap. The wind kept knocking me to my knees, and I dug my nails into the wood so I wouldn't blow off.

*Amana, have mercy,* I thought as I climbed, stealing glimpses of the ledge above. It jutted over the mirror like an outstretched hand, sand sifting through its fingers.

The sun bore down on that wretched mirror, so bright its reflection was a wall of white gold beaming back into the sky.

Each glimpse lit my eyes afire. They watered, the tears trickling down my cracked cheeks.

The ledge's surface chafed my palms and knees and burned my skin. I thought of Baba as I kept my head bent down and crawled. *You were always the strong one,* he'd told me on my last day at home. *Like your mother.* I couldn't fail him.

I dragged myself toward the edge—toward that waterfall of sunlight. The sun was reaching its zenith, and the heat made my hands swell until they could barely fit into the spider-silk gloves. I yanked them over my fingers, ignoring the pain.

I wasn't going to give up now. I wasn't going to die here.

I closed my eyes. *Gather the sunlight.*

My heart hammered and my stomach churned with fear, but I ventured one last inch forward.

I reached into my pocket for my walnut and dug my nails into the seam to crack it open, but the gloves blunted my grasp, so I had to use my teeth.

I held the walnut out carefully.

Sunlight stroked my fingers. The shell grew heavy, hot. It

trembled, shuddering as though the light within it were alive. Quickly, I shut the other half of the shell and shuffled backward. My foot wobbled off the ledge, and the sun hissed, greedily scalding my skin.

I screamed, but my throat was so dry that no sound came out. My eyes snapped open and a flash of white blinded me.

Little by little, I pulled myself up until I knelt on the ledge. Gasping. Panting.

All of me was blistered and raw. I just wanted to lie down—I had no energy for anything else.

*No! You can't give up now.*

Was that my voice or Edan's? I couldn't tell. But it was enough to give me the strength to crawl off the ledge. Shielding my eyes, I slipped the walnut into my pocket and took the first step down the ladder.

One step. Then another. And another.

Mercifully, the path out of the labyrinth was straight and wide. When I could finally see the sand outside, I started to run, so fast I nearly slid out of the temple gate. My whole body ached like fire, but I let out a strangled, dry laugh.

Edan pulled me up and thrust his canteen to my lips. "I see the Temple of the Sun has left you half baked. . . ." His voice faltered. Worry etched itself into his features. "You don't look well, Maia."

I drank greedily; then I got up slowly and dusted myself. "I'm fine. I did it." I held out my walnut to him, but instead of taking it, he caught me in his arms.

"So you did," he said, holding me upright with his good arm. "Well done." He touched my cheek with the back of his hand. "You're burning up."

It hurt when he touched me; my skin was scorched and I was almost delirious.

Blisters swelled on my eyelids, and I winced when he covered my eyes with his hand.

"Keep your eyes closed."

"I'm fine. It's just bright."

Without any warning, he picked me up, his chin touching my forehead, and carried me into the shade of the trees. The winds were strong, but he shielded me from the gusting sand.

I started to wrap my arms around him, but his eyes were yellow and bright like the sun . . . they frightened me. I struggled out of his hold and ran toward Milk before collapsing in the sand.

. . .

Edan was reading by the dim light of his lantern when I awoke. My movement startled Milk—and me. I was secured to the saddle, but now that I was awake and flailing, I lost my balance. She kneeled just before my legs tipped off her back onto the sand, and she blinked her large amber eyes at me. Then she licked my cheeks.

Edan made a tutting sound at Snowfoot and dismounted. "You're awake."

As he untied the ropes holding me to the saddle, I tried to stand. My body was stiff, the pain from the burns a dull throb. My face and arms were sticky, plastered with salve.

"You had heatstroke," said Edan. "Try not to wipe it off or your burns will fester and become infected."

Steadying me with his arm, he gave me a canteen. I took a

long, long drink, suddenly thankful he had been managing our supplies so carefully.

"How are you feeling now?"

"Fine," I replied tersely. "Hungry."

"No wonder. You were asleep for nearly two days."

"Two days!"

He passed me a bag. Inside were crackers and dried fruits and jerky. A feast.

Edan jumped onto his camel and picked up his book again. The shadows blooming under his eyes were darker than before, and his irises were paler than I'd ever seen them—almost gray. "Don't finish it all," he said, waving his book at me. "We still have four days until we reach Agoria."

Agoria, where the Mountains of the Moon awaited, and where Keton had fought the shansen's men during the Five Winters' War. Where Sendo had died.

"The shansen's men and the emperor's army came to a standstill in the Mountains of the Moon," Keton had told me when he returned home. "I was there. Arrows got me, and Sendo dragged me to safety. There were bodies everywhere, scattered over the mountain. By the end of the night, thousands were killed. Including Sendo."

I chewed and swallowed, suddenly losing my appetite. Tightening the drawstring on the bag, I turned away to gather myself. Edan was still reading on his camel.

"Where's the walnut?" I asked as I tapped Milk to kneel and mounted.

Edan replied, "I'll retain it for safekeeping, if you don't mind."

"Have any tailors sewn with sunlight before?"

"Not that I know of," said Edan, removing his hood. His

214

black curls glistened with sand. Sand, and *sweat*, I noticed with a frown.

"Sewing with magic is a rare gift," he said. "Rarer still in the hands of a talented tailor such as you. Between friends, I will admit Lady Sarnai has set you up for failure, but I have faith you can make the dresses. I'll help you any way I can."

I raised an eyebrow. "I thought you said we weren't friends."

"We weren't. But enchanters are fickle." He offered me a small grin. "I might have changed my mind."

I felt a rush of warmth. If not for Edan, I would not have known where to begin. Even though we bickered, he was the only friend I had out here. Maybe anywhere, to be honest.

"Your father was not able to wield the scissors, was he?" Edan asked.

"No. He said they were my grandmother's."

He leaned close, as if he were studying a fragile specimen. "Odd." He touched my chin. "Enchanters don't usually leave descendants."

I didn't know why the comment made me blush. Or why his touch, so quick and gentle it was practically nothing, sent a rush of tingles trilling over my skin. I pulled back, hoping my embarrassment didn't show. "I don't know much about my ancestors."

"Never mind that," Edan said, letting a comfortable distance settle between us again. "You have three tasks: to acquire the sun, the moon, and the stars for Amana's dresses. These tasks translate into three trials: one of the body, one of the mind, one of the soul. Sunlight was a trial of the body. How much suffering you could endure."

I stroked my cheeks, still sticky with salve, but my skin wasn't so raw anymore. "You're only telling me this now?"

"I didn't want you to be afraid." He inhaled. "The hardest will be the last."

"The blood of stars?" When he nodded, I pressed, "What can you tell me?"

"I don't know exactly what you'll have to face," he admitted. "What I do know is when. Once a year, the stars open up to the mortal world."

I knew the tale. "On the ninth day of the ninth month, the goddess of the moon is reunited with her husband, the god of the sun. Only for this one night each year can they be together. They walk toward each other on a starlit path, a bridge the god of thieves must hold up on his shoulders as punishment for once stealing the stars. When their time has passed, the bridge collapses and the stars, wrought with their pain from being apart, bleed into the night."

"Yes," Edan drawled. "Rather romantic, isn't it?"

I frowned. The ninth day of the ninth month. That was forty days away. And Lake Paduan was on the other side of the continent.

"I thought it was just a legend."

"All legends have a spark of truth. Sometimes more than a spark." Edan shielded his face from the sun. "You should start making the shoes. Having something to do will help you recover faster. Be sure to—"

"Make them watertight," I finished. After weeks of slowly burning to death, I couldn't even imagine needing to protect myself against water.

"You remember." Edan turned away and dabbed at his temples. "Good."

I finished my jerky and licked every crumb off my fingers. My pants were so loose they sagged from my hips. If I was hungry, Edan had to be hungrier. He always ate less than I did, saying, in his proud way, that enchanters didn't starve.

I wasn't sure I believed him anymore.

Edan whistled, maintaining a mask of cheerfulness as he led us toward mountains too far for me to see. I worried that even if he was in danger, he'd never tell me. He was arrogant like that. Too proud to admit any weakness.

Tonight, I resolved—tonight I would stay awake and find out what he was hiding from me.

# CHAPTER TWENTY-TWO

My head jerked up. Milk's reins were in my hands, and I was in the saddle again, my legs folded just in front of her hump. I didn't remember falling asleep.

Rubbing my eyes, I turned to Edan, then to the sky. It was just past dawn, and he was human.

I gritted my teeth. Edan had thwarted my plans somehow. There was no way I would have fallen asleep—not unless he'd . . .

I crossed my arms indignantly. "Did you enchant me?"

"Why, good morning to you, too."

"Did you enchant me into falling asleep?" I demanded again.

Edan raised a hand, motioning for me to be quiet. He pulled Snowfoot to a stop, and after a rebellious second I did the same with Milk. I shielded my eyes, wishing the wind would stop blasting my hair over my face.

Edan pointed ahead.

Beyond the haze of the desert, I thought I could make out the promise of trees. Trees, flowers, colors I hadn't seen in days. I looked down. The sand beneath Milk's hooves had become grittier, almost dirtlike. Around us, brown and yellow bushes rustled. We were close to the end of the desert.

But that wasn't what had caught Edan's attention. The smoke of a campfire. Horses. Camels. Men.

"Bandits?" I whispered.

Edan waited a beat before answering. "No."

Without another word, my companion dismounted his camel and waved at the group ahead.

The strangers had their weapons up in an instant and sprang toward us, but Edan took off his hood and made a courteous bow. "I'm Delann," he said. Once I'd caught up with him, he touched my shoulder. "This is my cousin, Keton."

The lie was so smooth I hardly flinched when he introduced me.

I bowed, my movements far stiffer than Edan's. Hurriedly I removed my hat to cover my chest. I'd stopped binding it weeks ago. "Hello."

"Orksan," replied the leader. His skin was bronze, and he wore his dark brown hair braided with beads red as wolfberries. A style popular among Balardans.

I smiled nervously, then bit my lower lip to stop. This was not the time to look like a dolt.

"What brings you two to the Halakmarat?" asked Orksan. He hadn't lowered his guard. His hand was on the hilt of a sword, and I wished Edan or I carried a weapon. Where was the dagger he'd brought? I didn't see it on his belt.

"We're leaving it, actually," Edan replied.

Orksan eyed our trunks, amplifying my apprehension. "Going into Niyan to trade?"

"Nothing left to trade," said Edan. "Once we leave the Halakmarat, we're traveling the Spice Road."

"What brings you onto the Road? You don't look like mercenaries. Or merchants."

"My cousin is a tailor," Edan said, rather proudly. "The best in the land."

Orksan cast me a cursory glance. He didn't look impressed.

My pants were torn, and my tunic's color had faded from a rich green to a dull olive. I shifted self-consciously.

"And yourself?" Orksan asked.

"My father was a merchant on the Road. Married my mother and had me." Edan faked a charming grin. "I'm no good with coin, I'm afraid, so I'm an explorer. We're traveling to find my cousin some dyes, then we'll go to A'landi to open him a shop."

Without warning, Edan reached for the satchel slung over my shoulder. Orksan and his men raised their weapons, but Edan's fingers were swift. He withdrew a sleeve I'd been working on for Lady Sarnai.

"See," he said, displaying the sleeve as if it were a prized jewel. "This is my cousin's work."

The sleeve was unfinished, but I'd embroidered gold flowers along the seams, and I'd sewn dozens of tiny pearls along the cuff. Anyone could see that the work was exquisite.

Orksan looked at me with new respect. "Can you mend?"

I opened my mouth, but Edan spoke over me: "In his sleep."

Orksan's distrust faded a notch. By now he must have observed that we were unarmed. "My wife is a remarkable cook, but she can't sew a stitch." He drew back his cloak, revealing tattered sleeves. "Perhaps your cousin can teach her a thing or two."

"He'd be happy to," Edan said, slapping me hard on the back. I stumbled forward and frowned at him, but his pleasant grin didn't waver.

"Then there's my three brothers and two brothers-in-law," Orksan went on, introducing the group. "We're headed northeast ourselves. Why don't you two join us for a few days? Celebrate the midsummer with us. We've plenty of wine to share, and Korin makes the heartiest stew you'll find on the Road!"

The thought of food and drink had already sent a pang to my belly, but my eyes widened with alarm. We couldn't join a group of Balardans!

"We'd be honored," Edan said, ignoring my distress.

"Good. These roads are treacherous. I'm surprised you two are traveling alone."

"Have you run into any bandits?" Edan asked casually. "Or soldiers?"

I twisted my face into a frown. Why was he asking about soldiers?

"None, thankfully," replied Orksan. "But we were detained in the Buuti Passage for a few weeks. The prince of the province wouldn't let us leave without papers. He said we were smuggling wine out of the country to sell to A'landans." Orksan snorted. "As if we'd want to sell his wine. It tastes like horse piss."

"Our journey takes us north," Edan said. "We're heading for the Mountains of the Moon."

"That's quite a way from here," Orksan said. "You'll be traveling off the Road."

"We're aware of that," said Edan, offering no further explanation.

Orksan didn't ask any more questions. "You can come with us into Agoria. But the boy'll have to do some mending." He looked at me, and I bobbed my head in assent.

"He's jittery as a cricket," Orksan said to Edan. "Is he mute?"

"He's recovering from desert fever. First time traveling so far from home."

Orksan's eyes deepened with understanding, and he motioned for us to follow him toward the campfire.

"Are you sure about this?" I whispered to Edan once Orksan was out of earshot.

"We need food and drink, and they're offering it. Why turn it down?"

"They're Balardans," I said, still clutching my hat over my chest.

"Balar is a vast country," Edan chided. "Not everyone is a barbarian. And not every Balardan fought in the Five Winters' War."

I frowned, staunch in my distrust. Until I saw Orksan's children.

Their clothes were tattered and frayed, flapping in the wind as they rushed up to greet us. A boy tugged at my pants, holding out a pile of ragged garments. "Will you fix this? Da says you can."

I knelt beside Orksan's two sons—they couldn't have been older than four or five—and took their clothes. "They'll be good as new," I said with a smile.

Orksan's wife, Korin, chuckled, then gently peeled her children off me. "Run along and play with the camels. Mama needs to work on sewing with our new friend."

"Is that yours?" Korin said, lifting the lid of one of my trunks, where the hem of Lady Sarnai's dress peeked out.

I jumped up. "Don't touch that!"

Hurt etched itself over Korin's face. She immediately dropped the lid. "I'm sorry."

I clamped my lips shut. Then I sighed. *Stop being rude, Maia. She isn't going to put a knife in your heart.* "No, I'm the one who should apologize. It's just . . . it's been a long journey."

I lifted the trunk lid and took out what I'd sewn so far of Lady Sarnai's dress. I hadn't yet used the sunlight I'd collected, but the shape of the gown was coming together, with its ruched bodice and one flowing sleeve. The trim sparkled with golden leaves and flowers.

Korin held her breath, marveling at my work. "Did you embroider this yourself?"

"Yes," I said firmly. The truth was, I'd used the scissors, but I was gradually coming around to the idea that their work was also mine. I saw now how they enhanced my natural abilities and let me experiment with designs I'd never dared before. I carefully folded the gown and began teaching Korin how to mend her family's garments.

While she practiced on Orksan's clothes, I lost count of how many pants I hemmed and sleeves I patched, but I was glad to have something to keep my hands busy. Though Korin seemed happy to have me around and tried to talk to me, I kept my guard up. I wasn't very clever at making small talk anyway.

"My first proper buttonhole," Korin said, wiping a bead of sweat from her forehead. We were under the shade of a tent, but it was still brutally hot.

I examined her work and offered a nod. "That looks good."

She let out a sigh of relief. "I don't know how you do it so quickly. Sewing's hard work."

"It's my trade. Orksan says you're a fine cook. I couldn't imagine having to feed all these men every day."

"Yes, it *is* easier with only two of you." She chuckled, and paused. "So, how long have you and Delann been married?"

My breath caught in my throat, and I yanked and broke the thread. *Married?*

I stared at my stitching and picked out the mistake I'd just made. I slipped the thread into my mouth to moisten it, then rethreaded my needle and began again. Korin waited expectantly for my reply.

"How could we be . . . married?" I said, faltering at the end. "We're cousins. Almost like brothers."

"You don't fool me," she said with a laugh. "Or Orksan. I knew you were a woman the moment I saw you. It's the reason Orksan didn't shoot at your companion out there."

"Oh—oh," I stuttered, looking down at my chest. We'd seen the caravan so suddenly I hadn't gotten a chance to bandage it before meeting Orksan.

Korin laughed at me. "It had nothing to do with that, my friend. I saw how protective Delann is of you. Yet he respects you. Took me years before I could convince Orksan to take *me* out with him on the Road. But now that the boys are older and the war's over . . . he is more amenable to the idea. He didn't make me dress as a man, though—but it's probably a good idea, since it's only the two of you traveling together."

I returned to my needlework. "Did Orksan and his brothers fight in the war?"

"Is that why you're so quiet around us?" Korin asked. "Because you think we fought with the shansen?"

I didn't say anything. I'd heard terrible stories about Balardan fighters pillaging towns, killing women and children.

"Nah," Korin said. "My husband's no soldier. His knife is for fur and meat. . . . The shansen hired mostly mercenaries—professional fighters."

I pursed my lips. "I hope I haven't offended you."

"It's understandable." Korin put a hand on her hip. "I'm from Balar myself, unlike Orksan. Born and raised on the Spice Road, my husband. He gets anxious when he's not on the move in a caravan or a ship."

"I've never sailed on a ship," I confessed, trying to open up a little. "Though I grew up in a port town."

"And Delann? He doesn't look like he's from A'landi. Where did you meet?"

Best to keep to the truth, given my clumsiness at lying. "In Niyan."

"He's a charming one, your husband. You're a lucky girl."

I knotted my thread, plucking the needle from the fabric. "He's not . . ." I closed my mouth. Maybe it was better to let her think I *was* Edan's wife. Fewer questions would be asked that way. "He's not . . . *always* charming," I said instead. "Sometimes he can be quite annoying."

"Ay, but you trust him," Korin said. "And your trust doesn't come easily."

I didn't know what to say, so I simply smiled at her. She was a stranger, and a Balardan at that, but I could be friendly. And after weeks traveling alone with Edan, it was nice to talk with another woman, *as* a woman.

For the rest of the afternoon, I showed Korin how to knot a net to protect herself from mosquito bites, to darn socks, and to properly patch a hole. She in turn taught me how to make a hearty stew out of as little as three ingredients. While we worked, she regaled me with tales about her children and Orksan's travels.

When dinner was nearly ready, I left Korin's tent. Edan was outside playing with the children, pulling coins out of their ears and making desert flowers appear from his sleeve.

"You're good with children," I remarked.

"You sound surprised," he teased. "I was a child once too, you know."

"Maybe a hundred years ago," I said dryly. My retort earned

me a quiet chuckle. I was learning that the less I asked about Edan's past, the more comfortable he felt telling me about it.

He didn't offer more, but he settled on the ground beside me. "There's going to be a flushed moon tonight," he said. "Will you watch it rise?"

"Will you be there?"

He nodded, but only after some hesitation. "Yes. At least until the light is gone."

This was the closest he'd come to acknowledging his disappearances at night.

I studied him, watching his pale blue irises flicker with hints of gold. Though I hadn't seen the black hawk since that night with the wolves, I felt certain it was Edan.

It was as if the sun and moon were helping him keep his secret. The past few days had grown so long that night lasted merely a few hours. And when night did fall, the moon hid behind the clouds, wrapping such a dark blanket over the landscape, it was impossible to stay awake. Soon, though, the days would grow shorter again.

"How did you make that coin disappear?" I asked.

"With the children?" Edan said. "Just a little trick I picked up during my travels, not real magic. I could show you if you like."

I realized I wouldn't learn his secret tonight, not while we made camp with Orksan's family. I stood. "Maybe when I've finished the dresses."

I left to sit alone on a rock near the camels. There, with my back to the sun, I worked on my embroidery. The light was gentle yet brilliant, casting upon the sand a red-orange glow. After my ordeal in the Temple of the Sun, I'd never expected to enjoy basking in its light again.

"Enough with the knitting," Orksan said, coming up behind me.

I pushed my needle into the edge of my embroidery so it wouldn't drop into the sand. "I'm not kn—"

"We've opened three casks to enjoy, and your husband is already partaking. Come join him."

So everyone *did* think Edan and I were married. My eyes widened. "I don't drink much. I really have to get back to work—"

"Woman, you have all your life to sew pretty things," Orksan said. "Enjoy yourself for a night. What, is the world going to end if you don't finish your needlework?"

*Yes,* I almost muttered.

But then I saw Edan. He was smiling, and he raised his hand to wave me over. How happy he looked here. Happier than I'd ever seen him in the palace.

"My wife loves good food," Edan said, wrapping his arm around me, "though the desert's offerings make it hard for her to make a decent meal."

I wasn't as mortified as I thought I would be when Edan called me his wife. And that was mortifying in itself!

"Will you stop blabbering so we can start eating?" I cried.

Everyone laughed at me, and I blushed. I hadn't meant to cry out like that. I'd gotten so used to being around only Edan that I'd forgotten to mind my manners.

No one seemed to be offended, though, and I got up to help Korin serve the men and children. The stew smelled delicious. It was a feast of spices, with chunks of cactus and juniper, though I didn't recognize the meat.

"What are we eating?" I asked Korin.

She glanced at me, as if I didn't want to know.

"You can tell me."

"There was a storm a few days ago, and the morning after, our camp was crawling with rats." I eyed the pot skeptically as she continued. "Never heard the men curse so much while hunting." Her shoulders shook with amusement. "I started drying some of them into jerky, but we're so close to getting out of the Halakmarat, Orksan wanted a nice stew."

"Oh . . . ," I said, spooning an extra-large serving for Edan. My hunger had subsided.

Korin smiled at me. "They're delicious, I promise. And there's some beans I've been saving. Since we're almost out of the desert and have new friends, what better time?"

We ate, laughing and getting to know each other until one of Orksan's brothers claimed the blanket next to me. He didn't smile as the others did. A string of coins interlaced with human teeth dangled around his neck, and a copper earring hung from his left lobe. He made me uncomfortable.

"You don't look A'landan," Orksan's brother said, eyeing Edan suspiciously. "Your trunk is full of books and amulets. Books in languages I've never seen."

"Vachir!" Orksan barked. "Did you go through his things?"

Edan waved him off, but I could tell his smile was forced. "It's fine."

Vachir's stare didn't leave Edan. "There's word Emperor Khanujin's enchanter is away. The shansen has offered a great deal of money for his capture."

Edan chuckled. "Do I look like an enchanter?"

"The enchanter is away on a quest," Vachir repeated. His icy stare moved to me. "With the imperial tailor. They were seen in the Samarand Passage."

My breathing became shallow.

Had Norbu seen Edan, too? He must have spread word we were traveling together, knowing it'd cause trouble for us.

Gritting my teeth, I summoned my courage. "The imperial tailor is a man!" I said in as shocked a tone as I could muster. "I couldn't sew for the emperor. It wouldn't be proper."

"Perhaps the girl is who she says," Vachir said gruffly, "but you—" He pointed his jug of ale at Edan. "You are not just an explorer."

"Vachir," Orksan cautioned. "It's rude to interrogate our guests."

With a growl, Vachir got up. He gave Edan a long, dark stare before he stalked off behind the horses.

"Don't mind him," Orksan apologized. "My wife doesn't like him either. Luckily, he comes and goes from our camp."

That did nothing to soothe my worries. Edan laughed with Orksan's men, trying to brush off the incident. But the muscles around his eyes were tight—he was worried.

"Drink!" Orksan's men said, passing around a wine gourd. "Drink!"

I lifted the gourd to my nose and sniffed. I made a face—the wine smelled sour.

"Women can drink too. No law against it."

"Just a sip," I said, taking a swig. I coughed. "It burns."

Edan took the gourd and patted my back. "Never had wine before?"

"Of course I have," I spluttered.

"Wine at the temple doesn't count," he teased.

He'd got me. I'd only ever drunk rice wine at the temple and had never had more than a sip. But once, my brothers had brewed ale out of barley, and it was awful. They drank it all in one night, and afterward their clothes reeked so badly I spent an entire day washing out the smell.

My eyes watered with memories of Finlei, Sendo, Keton, and me as children. I wondered how Baba was doing, whether he'd gotten the letters I'd sent from the Samarand Passage and the news that I was now the imperial tailor. I hoped he was proud of me, that he and Keton had spent the money I sent, and had enough to eat. Winter would come to Port Kamalan all too soon. I vowed to write them tonight.

"It wasn't something my father kept in the house," I said evasively, remembering the difficult months Baba had spent after Mama's death.

"But you had three brothers."

"Three *overprotective* brothers," I reminded him. "I still have one."

"I'd like to meet him someday," Edan said after finishing his stew. There was a dot of sauce on his cheek, and I fought the urge to wipe it off with my finger. "Do you think he'd approve of me . . . as your husband?" He winked, and I had to clench my fists to keep from punching him in the ribs.

"You haven't met the girl's family yet?" Orksan said.

"We're on our way to her home now," replied Edan smoothly.

As Edan launched into a ridiculous tale about how we'd met and gotten married, I wanted to cover my face with my hands. I'd run away from a terrible match with the local butcher, he told them, stowing away in his caravan, only for Edan himself to fall in love with me—I was so mortified I simply took another drink. And another. The more I drank, the less it burned my throat. The less I worried, too, about Lady Sarnai's dresses or Vachir or Keton and Baba at home without me.

230

"Easy there," Edan said, pushing the gourd from me.

"He doesn't want you to sleep *too* well," one of Orksan's men piped up.

The men chuckled, but Edan didn't. I dipped my head low, not knowing if the flush on my cheeks was from embarrassment or from the wine.

The men began exchanging stories, and when it was Edan's turn, he drew a little wooden flute from the folds of his cloak. He whistled often when we were traveling. But I'd never heard him play.

"I never can remember the words to songs or stories," he said with a laugh. "But I can remember the notes to a tune."

He pressed the flute to his lips. The sound was sweet, and there was an innocence about the melody, one that tugged at my heartstrings. Even the children were quiet as Edan played, the little boys tapping their feet to the rhythm.

Above us, the flushed moon rose. The sky was brilliant amber, streaked with honey and persimmon. The moon climbed steadily, a pink rose blooming amid soft flames.

I sat cross-legged on my blanket and gazed at Edan. Normally I wouldn't have stared at him so obviously, but the wine had washed away my caution. There was a tickle in my stomach as I listened to him. I didn't want this night to end.

Edan looked peaceful when he played, as if he were serenading the moon. His face was burnt and tanned, as mine must have been. The sky slowly darkened to mahogany.

Then the song was over. Everyone clapped, and Edan bowed his head. He looked tired, but there was a faint smile on his lips. "The wife and I should retire. It's getting late."

"It's not late," I protested. I lifted my head to the sky. "You just want to leave so you can fly away."

If I hadn't drunk so much, I would have caught Edan's flinch, but it was fleeting, and I barely noticed. He forced a laugh and patted my shoulder. "Up we go. The wife needs her rest."

"No good-night kiss?" Orksan teased.

Orksan's brothers chimed in. "Kiss her."

"You can't leave without a kiss."

That tickle in my stomach returned. My head weighed more than I remembered as I turned to face Edan. He was already looking at me, a strange, hesitant flickering in his eyes. Was he going to kiss me? Orksan and his brothers chanted in the background, and my heart quickened. Was he leaning forward?

I couldn't bear the suspense. So hastily I surprised even myself, I kissed Edan on the cheek. A quick peck, then I shot up so fast that Edan had to grab me by the waist so I wouldn't fall.

Edan wrapped my arm over his shoulder. I couldn't argue. My heart pounded, and blood rushed to my head when he pressed a gentle kiss on the side of my lips, just missing my mouth.

His lips were soft, despite the desert's unrelenting dryness. A shiver flew up and down my spine, even though his breath was warm, and his arm around me even warmer.

The world beneath me spun. I felt Edan's hands clasp under my knees, and the pressure of standing disappeared. He was carrying me! But I was too tired to care. He was strong, and he crouched low to enter a tent. I turned away from the light.

"Don't enchant me into falling asleep," I warned him drowsily.

"I don't think you need any help with that tonight."

I knew he was right, even as I defiantly tried to stifle a yawn. "I'm going to stay up. I'm going to watch you change into a hawk. Don't you dare touch me. I know you enchanted me last night."

Edan's hand hovered above my forehead, but he pulled it away and didn't touch me. "Sleep well, my Maia."

Curse him, I couldn't keep my eyes open. They closed, and my mind lingered on a forbidden thought before slipping into slumber.

*I wish Edan had kissed me.*

# CHAPTER TWENTY-THREE

$P$ain roared in my ears. My head throbbed so violently I
feared it would split in two. Standing up only made it
worse, and every step sent a pang to my skull.

Edan's grin didn't make things better. "Morning, *xitara*."

"Don't you have something to make the pain go away?" I
pleaded.

"I brought medicines for cuts, burns, and bruises," he replied with a laugh. "Not for the aftermath of drinking oneself
into a stupor."

Miserably, I glared at Edan. "You're the one who told me to
drink."

"I didn't know you'd finish the entire gourd!"

"I don't remember that." I clutched at my temples, groan-
ing. "My head feels like it's being attacked by demons."

"It's not as bad as that," Edan assured me. There were shadows under his eyes again, and I wondered how much sleep he
had gotten. "Trust me."

He passed me a canteen full of lemongrass tea Korin had
brewed. "Here, it'll help." As I drank, he looked at me ear-
nestly. "I shouldn't have goaded you into drinking, especially
so soon after a fever. I'm not used to taking care of another
person."

I softened in spite of myself. "Being an enchanter sounds

like a lonely job. Tailoring is too." I cleared my throat, feeling suddenly awkward.

Edan chuckled. "Come on. The others are getting ready to go."

We were out of the desert by midday the next day. I almost kissed the Road when I saw it. On this side of the continent, it was merely a narrow, pebble-strewn path, but I didn't care. Dirt, birds, even the buzzing gnats I had once despised so much—my eyes welled with tears of relief to see them all. And the river in the near distance—so much water!

Leaving the desert also meant parting with our new friends, including the two camels that Edan had agreed to trade for two of Orksan's horses.

Korin and I hugged each other. "Good luck with your dresses," she told me. "And thank you for your help. Write to me when you and Delann have settled into your new shop."

"I will," I said, pursing my lips. I wished we hadn't had to lie to her. "I hope our paths will cross again."

Edan and I waved goodbye as Orksan and his family left. Vachir wasn't among the group; I hadn't seen him since midsummer's night. That unsettled me, but there was nothing to be done.

"I think you'll like her more than Pumpkin," Edan said, handing me the reins of my new horse. "Balardan mares aren't as strong as A'landan ones, but they're fiercely loyal." He chuckled. "She's even got freckles like you."

I approached my new horse carefully. Pumpkin used to kick whenever I got too close. "Does she have a name?"

"In Balardan, but Orksan welcomed you to pick a new one. I'm naming mine Rook."

"I'll call her Opal."

Opal's freckles were like dots of honey, but the rest of her mane and coat were white as silk. She gave off a little neigh when I reached out to touch her cheek. I fell in love with her immediately.

"You like her more than me," Edan pouted.

"That's not hard to do." I petted her mane again; then I offered Edan a small smile. "But thank you."

He cleared his throat. "Have you finished the shoes?"

I huffed at the reminder. By my calculations, I was at least a week behind in my sewing. I took out my needle, certain I could finish embroidering one of Lady Sarnai's sleeves before we were off again. "No. My own are in good repair, and I need to work on the sun-woven dress."

"I suggest you readjust your priorities." He pointed to the Mountains of the Moon rising in the distance. While most of the mountains had gentle, sloping curves, one was so steep I almost mistook it for a pine tree. Even in the summer, it was capped with snow. "See that?"

"Rainmaker's Peak," I said, nodding. My hands worked while I glanced up. "It looks like a needle piercing the sky."

"You'll be climbing that."

"What?" I gasped. "It'd be suicide."

"Not with the proper shoes."

With a sigh, I put aside my work and riffled through my sketchbook for the design Edan had drawn. I reached for my scissors to start cutting the leather. It was becoming habit to use them now, and I appreciated the help. They instinctively knew the size of my foot, and within minutes I had a perfectly good sole to work off.

"How will you enchant them?" I asked, holding the sole up to my foot.

"With magic that'll get you to the peak. Alive."

"What about down?" I asked.

Edan mounted his horse, motioning for me to do the same. "We'll worry about that later."

Up ahead was the Dhoya Forest, but we followed the river until we absolutely had to leave it.

We stopped to rest at a small, bubbling spring. I washed some of my clothes and fought the urge to leap into the water for a bath. Not in front of Edan, anyway. Still, it was good to wash my face for the first time in weeks. My skin was still healing, but already the cooler, more humid weather was helping with the blisters and peeling.

Edan watched the sky, a grim expression darkening his face. "We can't take too long here."

I scrubbed at my palms. "Why not?"

"We're close to the mountains, but we need to cut farther north if we're going to reach Rainmaker's Peak. The next full moon is in four days. And night in the forest is dangerous."

I frowned. I hadn't seen him work his magic since we'd collected the silk thread from the desert. "Now that we're out of the desert, can't you use your magic to bring us through the forest safely?"

Edan pursed his lips. "That's not how it works."

"Then tell me."

"You should learn to use a dagger," he said, changing the subject. "There will be far more dangers here than in the Halakmarat."

"Why?" I wrung the bottom of my shirt dry. "Because you're planning to disappear again at night?" I didn't wait for him to come up with an excuse. "Where do you go, anyway?"

"I go to my tent, just like you," said Edan, wariness tightening his voice.

My fists curled at my sides. "Stop lying to me. I'm tired of it. You might think me a fool, but I've been around you long enough to know you're keeping something from me—"

"Maia," he said. "Calm yourself."

"I will not calm down!" I shouted. "I was attacked by wolves, and where were you? You came back with a gash on your arm and never explained how you got it. And every time I ask for an explanation, you—"

"I'll tell you," he interrupted. He held my hands, but I didn't remember him taking them. I tried to pull away, but he held on tightly. "I've been wanting to tell you."

I was still upset. "Then why didn't you?"

"I wanted to protect you," Edan said, letting go of my hands. "And myself. I didn't want you to see me for what I am."

All traces of his usual arrogance were gone. I crossed my arms, not wanting him to know that he'd mollified me so quickly.

"You're right," Edan continued. "You *should* know. It would be good to keep traveling at night, and you'll need to know the limits of my magic."

He removed his outer robe and pulled up his sleeve; then he pointed to the gold cuff on his wrist. The one I'd noticed before.

"This is a symbol of my oath," he said, holding out his arm. "My oath to serve the one who holds my sigil—the amulet you so perceptively noticed the emperor wearing."

Edan rolled down his sleeve. I swallowed. "So . . . you didn't choose to serve him?"

"Whoever owns the amulet is my master."

"Your master," I repeated. "Emperor Khanujin."

"He doesn't like it when I call him *master*," Edan said dryly. "But yes, that's what he is."

238

"But—why?" I whispered. I'd thought enchanters were like mercenaries, free to serve whoever could afford their exorbitant fees.

He shrugged. "It is the price we pay for our power. All enchanters must swear an oath—it prevents us from becoming too powerful, or greedy. Magic is . . . addictive, you see. And over time, it can corrupt."

I did see. I remembered how my scissors hummed to me, how *good* it felt to sew with them. They filled me with such irresistible power, my hands tingled and throbbed even after I used them.

"Can you be free?" I asked softly.

"That's a challenging question," Edan said. He lifted my chin and took my hand gently. "Khanujin's been good to me. It isn't as bad as it must sound."

I shivered from the intimacy of his touch. My heart—my rebellious heart—began to race. "And . . . what if you leave him?"

Edan let go of my chin. "Then I would be trapped in my spirit form forever."

His spirit form . . .

"A hawk," I breathed.

"Clever girl," he whispered, letting go of my hand.

"But you're only . . . only a hawk at night."

He nodded. "When I'm near my master, I can change at will. It's useful for spying on people—during the war it was especially helpful. But as I go farther away from him, my nights are stolen from me and I must spend them in my spirit form. My magic grows weaker the longer I am away from my master, until I can no longer transform back into a man."

A cold knot of fear twisted inside me. "How much time before . . ."

"Out here?" He kicked the dirt, then sat cross-legged on the ground. "Long enough for us to get back to the palace. Don't worry about me."

But I *did* worry about him. Now I understood the fatigue written on his brow, the hiding and evasive answers.

He brought his forehead to mine. "Cheer up," he said, his voice husky. "It isn't so bad being a hawk. I can travel more quickly than I do in my human form, and I don't need as much food."

An ache rose in my throat. "Your skin is getting burned." I'd noticed this days ago, but only now did I bring it up. "You said you didn't feel the heat or the cold."

"As I said, the farther I go and the longer I stay away from my master, the less attuned to magic I become."

"You said that magic was scarce in the desert."

"That is true. But being away from Khanujin is the real problem. My spirit form instinctively tries to fly back to him every night; narrowing the distance—even for a short while—helps. But we've been too far from the palace for quite some time."

I felt a surge of compassion for Edan, and I knelt beside him. "So your oath . . . it is for eternity?"

He shook his head. "All enchanters become free eventually. Once we have served a thousand years, our magic leaves us, and we live out the rest of our days as mortals."

Hope glimmered in me. "How many years have you served?"

"I'm a little more than halfway through my term."

"Oh." I swallowed painfully. Edan was over five hundred years old! I could hardly believe it. He didn't look older than twenty. "Can't you ask Emperor Khanujin to free you?"

Edan leaned forward, resting his elbows on his knees. "I used to think so," he said finally, "but not anymore. His father promised to free me after he unified A'landi. I waited years, but he was always afraid the shansen would rise against him. When at last he resolved to fulfill his promise, he died. And his fears about the shansen came to fruition."

"But the truce—"

"Tensions with the shansen are still high. The wedding may hold things together for a while, but Khanujin is worried the shansen will betray the truce."

"That would be dishonorable."

"Perhaps," Edan allowed, "but so long as he remains a threat, Khanujin will never free me. Especially since the shansen knows that Khanujin is weak without me."

"What do you mean?"

Edan's gaze was piercing. "Khanujin draws upon my magic to make himself stronger, more powerful . . . more charming. It's how he wins everyone over. Even you."

*Even me.* I flushed, but I couldn't deny it. The magnetism of being near Emperor Khanujin was hard to ignore. I pursed my lips. "But not Lady Sarnai."

"I don't know how she resists. She has no magical ability herself."

So many things made sense to me now. This was the secret Lady Sarnai had been trying to discover. A secret her own father, the shansen, had kept from her. It was all about Edan. "So that's why the emperor won't leave his rooms—because you're away from him. That's why he wouldn't let you go with me."

"I left his side because a wedding between Lady Sarnai and the emperor is the best option for peace, and I promised Khanujin's father I would do everything in my power to bring peace to A'landi."

"You helped Emperor Khanujin win the war."

"Yes," Edan admitted, "but at great cost to your people."

I plucked a handful of grass, then let the wind carry it from my hand. It was blasphemy to speak my thoughts aloud, but I couldn't help it. "Would you be free if he died?"

Edan turned to watch the horses. They were so happy, munching on a patch of grass. "No, the oath does not work that way. The amulet would return to the sands or the sea, and the first man to find it would become my new master."

"And during that time—"

"I'd spend it as a hawk," he said. "During my years between masters, I've seen much of the world this way." A faint grin. "So I'm not *really* as old as you think."

His attempt at humor was lost on me. My lip trembled. "What if I steal the amulet?"

"You'd become my master, yes, but also the target of every assassin in A'landi. Maia, it isn't that easy. Owning the amulet always makes my masters . . . change. I wouldn't want that to happen to you." He became wistful. "I used to be passionate about magic before my oath. I used to believe in the good of magic. In the good of people." The wind flattened his hair, emphasizing his boyishness as he turned his gaze at me. "You make me remember a part of myself I'd forgotten."

"Sounds like I'd have liked the old Edan more," I said quietly.

"Probably," he admitted. "He was less proud. More earnest, but also more reckless. More boy than man."

I gave him half a smile. "You're still a boy. No man would name his horse Valiant Grace."

Chuckling, he reached out to touch my cheek. "I wish we'd met in different circumstances, Maia." He pulled his hand back. "But I came with you to help you. Gods know you need it."

His closeness made my stomach flutter.

"Which reminds me," Edan said, as if reading my mind. "No more pretending to be a boy. If people are looking for the Lord Enchanter and the imperial tailor traveling together, it's better if you're a girl."

I brushed back a lock of hair, feeling it curl around my shoulder. It was long enough to braid now, but I missed the way it used to hang down my back.

"Besides," he added, "I like your hair long."

My stomach fluttered again, and a blush crept up my cheeks.

"You can pretend to be my cousin again."

*Not your wife?* I almost dared to ask. "That didn't work so well last time. Besides, how can we be family? We've been traveling together for weeks, and I don't even know where you're from!"

"I don't know much about you, either," he pointed out.

The realization took me aback. "You know more about me than I know about you! You spied on me while I was in the Summer Palace."

Edan's shoulders shook as he laughed. "Khanujin asked me to keep an eye on Lady Sarnai, who was in charge of the trial. I had no choice but to spy on you all."

"You spied on me the most," I said stubbornly.

"Only because you were a girl pretending to be a boy. It was interesting. The others were not so interesting. Or pretty."

I hid a smile. "So what did you learn about me?"

"You have a weakness for sweets," he said slowly, "and steamed buns, especially ones with coconut or lotus paste. You're a talented artist, though your choice of subject is questionable at times." I blushed, remembering my drawings of Emperor Khanujin. "And your favorite color is blue. Like the ocean."

*And your eyes,* I couldn't help thinking. They were sapphire now, almost, like the depths of the sea. I cleared my throat, certain I was red enough to pass for a tomato.

"But I don't know what makes you laugh and what makes you cry." Edan leaned forward, stopping before he drew too close. "Only that you miss your family and your home. Most girls your age are married. Maybe you have some boy in Port Kamalan pining after you."

Edan's light tone belied the intensity of his gaze.

I averted my eyes. "The baker's son asked me to marry him." I grimaced. "I wasn't interested."

"Well, I'm glad. He wouldn't have deserved you." He cleared his throat, a tinge of red creeping up his own neck. "I'd love to meet your father and your brother one day." His lips bent into a grin. "As your *husband,* it's scandalous that I haven't yet."

"I thought you were my cousin."

"You were right, that didn't go so well last time." His eyes twinkled. "Maybe we should keep pretending to be married."

"I didn't say we should be *married.*"

"And now you're annoyed with me," Edan observed. "You twist your lips whenever you're irritated. It happens often when you're with me."

I quickly untwisted my lips. "You enjoy teasing me, don't you?"

"Being near you is the only thing that makes *this* enjoyable for me."

*This.* Being away from the emperor. Spending each night as a hawk.

"Now that you're too far to fly back to him," I began, "where do you go once you change?"

Edan gave a dark smile. "Hunting."

To my credit, I didn't cringe. I swallowed hard. "Edan . . . I'm sorry."

"It isn't so bad," he said. That weary look passed over him again—exhausted, almost haunted. "Not yet. But it will get worse."

I waited for him to explain.

"The oath knows that I am straying. It will compel me to go back to my master, and punish me if I don't. There are other dangers as well—the emperor and I have many enemies. If they can't steal his amulet, they'll come for me. Especially if they know I am away from him."

Could Edan be killed? I shuddered, not sure I wanted to know the answer. "Will the shansen send his men after us?" I asked with trepidation.

"It's likely," said Edan in a tight voice. "Men first. Then perhaps others."

A chill swept over me. "Demons?"

"They would be a last resort. Demons are bound in a fashion similar to the way that enchanters are, but to a place—not a master. That makes them harder to control, and often they require a dear price for their services."

I thought of what Lady Sarnai had said about her father's dealings with demons, and Yindi's warnings. "Have you met one?"

"One of my teachers became a demon. Long ago." Edan saw my fear and said, "Don't worry yourself over this, or over the shansen. I chose to come with you, and I will stay with you."

"Except at night," I said quietly.

"Yes," he said. "When I am a hawk, you cannot depend on me to help you, but I will if I am able."

Thinking of Vachir and the other enemies we might

encounter on the rest of our journey, I said resolutely, "Show me how to use the dagger."

Edan had it on him. It was the one I'd seen in his room and in his trunk, with the silvery scabbard and thin red cord.

"The dagger's blade has a double edge because it is two weapons," he explained. "One side is best used against man. The other side is made of meteorite and is best used against . . . creatures I hope we won't encounter. To unsheathe it, you must grasp the hilt and say my name."

"Grasp the hilt and say *Edan*," I repeated. "That's simple enough."

He shook his head. "Enchanters have many names, sometimes thousands. Edan is only one of my names."

"Emperor Khanujin has a thousand names."

"He has titles. And a thousand is an exaggeration. It's more like fifty-two, and they're all variations on the same thing."

I crossed my arms, skeptical. "But you, almighty Lord Enchanter, you have a thousand names."

"Close to a thousand," he admitted.

"I'll believe it when I hear them."

"I wouldn't want you to hear *all* of them," he said, amused. "Some are quite insulting. And untrue."

"Oh?"

"Sorcerer Who Feasts on Eyes of Children—Enlai'naden. Hateful Master of the Wicked—Kylofeldal. It goes on and on."

"And the one that unlocks the dagger?"

He waited a beat before answering. "Jinn," he said. "One of my first names."

"Jinn," I repeated.

"Carry it with you always." He passed the dagger to me, still sheathed. "If someone attacks you, the quickest way is to slice his throat." Edan pointed at his own throat, drawing a line. "Aim the blade where the pulse beats, then cut across."

Finlei had tried teaching me to fight when we were children. *When will I ever need to fight someone?* I'd asked him then.

If only I'd known. I copied Edan's movement.

"Or you can stab his chest. Here." Edan wrapped his hand over mine so that we held the dagger together. He raised the blade to his chest, pulling me closer to him. "Aim between the ribs for the lungs, then thrust up for the heart."

Again I copied the movement, but Edan didn't let go of my hand. His heart beat against my palm as it landed on his chest. His pulse raced, almost as fast as mine.

Edan's other arm found my hip; then he leaned forward until he was so close I felt the warmth of his breath on my nose.

His breath touched my mouth, the softest brush of his lips over mine. I closed my eyes. I couldn't hear anything, not the symphony of the forest, not our horses snuffling impatiently behind us.

A beat. Two beats. My heart squeezed with anticipation.

Then . . . Edan let go of my hand.

My eyes flew open, and all the breath I'd been holding in was expelled from me in one quick burst. "What—"

"It's getting late," Edan said abruptly, lowering the dagger so that it no longer came between us. "That was a good start, but no more for today."

I closed my mouth, feeling cheated and dejected. I could have sworn he'd been about to kiss me. I could feel that he wanted to.

"I know you want to bathe. Come on, I'll find you a better place."

I followed mutely, kicking at a pile of dirt when he wasn't looking.

What a confusing, confusing man.

# CHAPTER TWENTY-FOUR

The Great Spice Road continued around the Mountains of the Moon, a narrow and winding path through the thick forests hemming in the range. A chill clung to the air as we traveled deeper into the woods, and when I looked up, I saw snow on some of the mountaintops.

I took out the shoes, humming to myself as Opal trotted toward the mountains, and I checked my work from the night before. Only after a while did I realize I was humming the little tune Edan often whistled.

Of course, his enchanter's ears had heard me. Chuckling, he brought his horse closer to mine so that we rode side by side. "It's a good song. Quite catchy, if I may say so."

I wasn't ready to talk to him. Ever since he'd almost kissed me, the air between us was heavy. Different.

I gave Opal a kick so she'd break from Rook's side and ride ahead.

"Don't ride in the sun," Edan called after me. "Your freckles are multiplying."

I glared at him, shouting, "You know exactly what a girl wants to hear!"

But I did guide Opal into the shade, cursing Edan under my breath—and my hammering heart. How his teasing got under my skin! How it made my heart pound and set my cheeks aflame. My brothers' jokes had never done that to me.

Edan caught up with me, looking more solemn than before. "Are you upset with me, Maia?" He managed a little grin. "I was joking about your freckles. I like them very much. Every one of them."

His eyes were too blue. I looked away from them and groped for the right words. "Why do you enjoy tormenting me?"

He paused for an agonizing second; then, curse him, he simply blinked, looking confused. "Tormenting?"

Demon's breath! How dense could he be?

A tight reel of words had been weighing on my tongue all day, and now I could not stop it from unspooling. "All this teasing, and pretending to care about me." My hands wheeled in wild circles, as if mimicking the way Edan's moved when he talked might help him understand. "And the other night when you tried to kiss me, I thought—I thought you might—"

I stopped, a hot burst of embarrassment flaring across my cheeks. Suddenly I wished the earth would open and swallow me up.

Gods, what had I just done? What had I just said?

I jumped off my horse, but Edan caught my arm before I could go. "You thought I might what?" he asked. All humor had fled his voice, and I couldn't bear the intensity of his gaze.

"Nothing," I mumbled.

"Maia—Maia. Look at me."

I couldn't. I wouldn't.

Edan wouldn't let me go. His voice turned soft. "You thought I might care for you?"

I pinched my eyes shut, mustered a scowl. "I said it was nothing."

"It wasn't to me," he said, still quiet. "I wasn't pretending. I do care."

Now I looked at him, half sure I'd find a grin on his lips and a mischievous twinkle in his eye, but there was none.

"I do care," he repeated. "But when you're an enchanter, there isn't much time for romancing. No girl has ever caused me to question this." His voice became even softer, if that was possible. "Then again, none of the girls were you."

My knees wobbled then, and my scowl fell out of place. "Me?"

"You're quite oblivious at times, my *xitara*."

"Stop teasing me," I said, my lower lip quivering. "It isn't funny."

Edan's broad shoulders tensed, but his eyes—his deep, sapphire eyes—were clear. "I tried to tell you, but I thought—" He inhaled. The Edan I knew was never at a loss for words.

"Thought what?"

He took a step closer to me. "I thought you found me disagreeable."

Another step. "I do," I said, my breath catching in my throat. Edan's gaze burned through me, and despite what I was saying, my body did not rebel against his coming closer. "Highly disagreeable. And impossible."

"And arrogant," Edan murmured. Our noses touched. "Let's not forget arrogant."

"How could I?" I said breathlessly.

He drew me close, practically lifting me off my feet, and kissed me.

His lips pressed against mine. Gently at first, then with increasing urgency as I started to respond with my own need.

His hand was tight on my waist, holding my wobbly knees

steady. His other hand slid up my back, finding the end of my braid and undoing it. Then his fingers raked through my hair, loosening it into waves off my shoulders.

He let me go then, as if he remembered I needed to breathe.

Edan took a step back. His jaw was tight, his shoulders squared.

"What's the matter?" I asked.

"No," he said, raising his hand to keep distance between us. He sucked in a breath. "This is wrong. It was a moment of weakness."

A twinge of hurt sharpened in my chest. "Oh, I see." My face was hot, and I turned away before my humiliation could become too much to bear.

"Wait, Maia." Edan reached for my arm. My sleeve slipped through his fingers. "Don't—"

"Don't what?" My voice came out wounded when I'd meant for it to sound harsh. "Make up your mind, enchanter."

"I told you the other day . . . that you . . . you make me wish things were different." Edan opened and closed his fists. He let out an uneven breath. "I don't want to give you false hope. And I don't wish to be selfish. You deserve someone who can be with you. That someone isn't me."

"Then you *are* being selfish," I said. "Don't kiss me, then tell me I should be with someone else. Don't—" *Don't make me fall in love with you.* My tongue stopped, unable to say it. "Just don't."

I ran for my horse, bounding onto the saddle and kicking her to a gallop. The rush of wind did little to help my heart stop pounding in my ears, but it was good to be alone. I needed to be alone.

My emotions were tangled, and I didn't know how to sort them. What did I feel about Edan? Did it even matter? He was a servant to his oath, unless Emperor Khanujin freed him.

He would spend a thousand years as a slave to magic—while I would sew a few dresses for the new empress, then be lost in the vast sea of time and history.

How was there any hope for us?

"Maia," he called. "Maia, please. Wait."

I wouldn't look at him.

Opal and I sped for the Mountains of the Moon. This time, Edan didn't try to catch up.

. . .

Opal reared back and snorted as soon as we entered Moonwatcher's Basin. A shower of haze and mist greeted us from the pass ahead, and I looked up at Rainmaker's Peak, so tall it pierced the clouds. A shiver came over me.

"Let's not go this way," Edan said. They were the first words he'd said to me all day.

My back was to him, and I sucked in my cheeks.

"Why not?" My voice came out thick with irritation, my tongue heavy from lack of use. "I studied the map. If we don't go this way, we lose two days. Time isn't on our side, as you often point out."

"I'd rather avoid danger than take a shortcut to save time," Edan replied.

I pressed my lips into a tight line. I wouldn't look at him.

I patted Opal firmly. "Come on, love. It's fine."

Obediently, she trotted forward. The land sloped downward like a shallow bowl. But my breath caught when I saw a sword staked in the ground. Beyond were arrows, many with crimson plumes, some erect and others slanted, as if a careless tailor had punctured the earth with his pins and needles.

Then Opal balked. She wouldn't go any farther, so I dismounted.

The scene before me turned my stomach. Broken drums, slashed war banners, mounds of bones—human bones. And bodies.

"Soldiers," I whispered with a shudder. I'd never seen a battlefield. Never even seen a dead person.

Over time, rain had washed the grass clean of blood, but the soldiers' uniforms were still stained. Some of the men had frozen to death. I could tell from their ashen faces, tightly drawn blue lips, and curved-in shoulders—the snow had buried them and preserved them until the thaw. Others weren't so lucky: vultures and other scavengers had long since eaten their flesh. Only a few still had their eyes—which stared ahead blankly as I approached.

"Maia!" Edan called from behind. "Maia, don't."

But I'd already crouched beside the nearest corpse. The smell made me want to retch, but I kept it in me. What was left of the boy's face was moist from recent rainfall. He'd been struck three times—arrows in his knee, his abdomen, his heart.

He couldn't have been older than Keton.

I hugged my arms to my chest, holding back a sob. Finlei and Sendo had died this way—alone, yet not alone. Hacked by a sword or impaled by an arrow. Sendo . . . *Sendo* had died in these very mountains. His body was somewhere among the thousands strewn around me, rotting under a coat of earth and snow. I wouldn't even recognize him if I saw him. Just thinking about it made me want to weep.

"Are you all right?" Edan said quietly when he caught up with me.

"Were you—" My voice choked. "Were you . . . here?"

"No."

Of course not. If Edan had been here, more of the emperor's soldiers might have survived. We'd heard of Khanujin's miraculous victories. I'd always thought they were because he was a fighter equal to none, like his father. But now I knew . . . it was Edan. Edan whose magic was worth a thousand soldiers. Edan who had enchanted the emperor into a ruler, a warrior, a man A'landi loved and esteemed.

It had always been Edan.

"But you were a part of the war," I said, clenching my fists. "How could you . . ."

Edan didn't reply. He simply wrapped his arms around me. I could feel his steady heartbeat, and it soothed me. It felt too soon when he let go.

I didn't venture deeper into the pass. Nor did I complain when Edan led me back the way we'd come.

We were almost to the horses when the wind began to bluster. Something was wrong—I could tell by the way Edan stiffened.

"Mercenaries," he said, pulling me behind a rock and pushing my head down.

My pulse spiked, and I peeked out.

Balardans. I recognized Orksan's brother among them. *Vachir.*

My muscles tensed, and I reached for the dagger. I counted at least a dozen, no, two dozen men. We wouldn't stand a chance against them.

Edan crept back to my side. He'd gone to the horses for a bow that I'd never seen before. It was almost as long as I was tall. "When I tell you to run," he said, "take Opal and make for Rainmaker's Peak."

"I'm not leaving here without you."

"I'm a decent marksman," he said sternly, "but you're not. Together, we're not going to cut down thirty men."

I swallowed. "I thought they wanted to capture you."

"That would be preferable," Edan said tightly. "But the shansen isn't a picky man. They'll settle for killing me if I prove too difficult."

As if Edan had summoned them from their hiding places, men rustled among the bushes on the hills. Arrows glinted in the sun. Archers.

My world began to reel, and all of me went numb. If we fled to the valley, the archers would kill us.

But if we stayed where we were, the foot soldiers would kill us.

I couldn't move. My feet had rooted themselves into the earth. All I could do was watch the men run toward us, shaking their weapons and shouting battle cries that were lost in the wind.

Vachir led them, the string of coins and teeth around his neck jumping as he ran. He wore the same faded tunic I'd seen at dinner with Orksan and Korin—the tunic whose frayed sleeves I had mended for him.

"Surrender!" he boomed, loud and deep. "Surrender now, enchanter."

Edan lifted his bow, pulling the string wide across his torso as he aimed. He fired three arrows in quick succession. Vachir eluded each shot, but the men behind him weren't as lucky. Two fell. Vachir let out a shout, and his mercenaries stopped running. They reached behind their backs for their bows to return Edan's favor.

Edan grabbed me by the wrist and pulled me behind a wide oak, pressing my back against its trunk. Arrows zoomed straight for us. Three, four, five arrows plunked into the oak's bark, grazing Edan's thigh and missing me by only a hair's-breadth.

"Go!" Edan barked, pointing at the mountains up ahead.

I didn't budge. "I'm not leaving you." I held Edan's dagger in my left hand, and with my right, I brandished my magic scissors.

"Happy as I am that you're using your scissors," he said dryly, "I'm not sure if this is the appropriate time to sew something."

I ignored him and began cutting at the bush in front of me. As the scissors snipped, all I could think of was something to shield us from the furious onslaught of arrows. A minute later, I had crafted a brambly, densely woven thicket around us.

A round of arrows arced into the air. "Get down," I cried.

Edan and I fell to our stomachs. "I must commend the creative use of your scissors," he said between breaths.

The arrows pierced my barrier with strident plunks, and I choked back a cry. The thicket was dense enough to trap the arrows within its branches, but it wouldn't hold for long. "Will you stop talking and get us out of here?"

Edan threw his cloak over me. His pupils dilated, his eyes yellowed. "Stay very still."

Birds exploded from the trees. Swallows, falcons, hawks—there had to be thousands of them, so many that their wings raised a powerful wind, blowing apart my wall. I covered my face with my hands as the birds flew over us toward our attackers. Wings beat, shrieks echoed, and talons glinted as the birds dove and clawed at the mercenaries. Vachir yelled at his men, who had stopped shooting at us and instead pointed their weapons at the sky. "Push forward! Fire at the enchanter! The enchanter!"

Few listened to him. Dead birds fell, thumping to the ground, and all around them men screamed, clawing at their faces to try to get the birds off. But it was as if Edan had instilled in them some wild, violent spirit. The creatures were mad and blood-thirsty. They moved like a turbulent black haze, following the men who tried to run away. I almost pitied them. Almost.

Edan's eyes blazed yellow now, and his face had gone very pale.

Then the clouds darkened. Rain pounded from the sky, and lightning struck the trees, making them topple down upon our attackers.

Beside me, Edan crouched, his arms folding over his legs as he began his transformation. Feathers sprouted over his skin and spine. A pair of wings erupted from his shoulders and fanned down across his arms. And with a flash, that familiar golden cuff anchored itself to his left talon.

*Go.*

He flapped his great black wings and soared up to join the birds, a shadowy fold against the dark sky.

I picked up Edan's bow and ran toward Opal and Rook. "Come on!" I shouted at them. I vaulted onto Opal, grabbing her by the mane. "To the peak!"

The horses didn't need a second warning. They galloped at full speed through the storm. I glanced over my shoulder once to see the birds descend again and again upon the men. Their screams grew distant, fading as I left them behind.

I didn't look back again.

# CHAPTER TWENTY-FIVE

Edan found me at the base of Rainmaker's Peak, sitting under a tree, sewing.

I jumped to my feet when I saw him. His cloak was torn, and there was a gash on his cheek. I gasped with relief. "You're alive!"

He flashed me a disarming grin. "I hope it hasn't been too boring without me."

"Where have you been?" I bit my tongue before I blurted that I'd tried searching for him, only the horses wouldn't take me back to the site of the battle, no matter how much I coaxed them—they'd been hell-bent on reaching the peak and staying there.

"Is that concern in your voice?" Edan teased.

"You've been gone a whole day," I said, more tartly. "I thought you'd died."

"That was inconsiderate of me," he allowed, "especially since I'm the one with the map to get us home. But I'm here now." He picked up the shoes I'd left by my campfire. "Ah, excellent. You've finished."

I threw him a sidewise glare. "All you can do is comment on my shoes? Did using all that magic addle your wits?"

He sat against the tree, his long legs stretched out. Rook trotted up to nuzzle his neck. "At least *someone* is glad to see me."

Edan looked thinner. His cheeks were more sunken, and that gash looked like a knife wound.

"I was so worried," I said, softening.

"I was sleeping," he confessed. "I didn't mean to worry you."

Tension gathered in my shoulders. "I thought you didn't have any magic left in you."

"I've stored a little," he said, plucking a leaf from above. He chewed, then spat it out. "Enough to enchant your shoes and get us to Lake Paduan. And some left over for emergencies. My body paid a price for it, though." He rubbed his back, then plucked and chewed another leaf. "Aches and pains everywhere. But some willow leaves will help. Good on you for building camp near this tree."

I hadn't even noticed the tree. "You could have been killed."

Edan *must* have been tired, because he didn't argue. That, or it was true. "What's done is done."

Sitting down beside him, I stabbed my needle into Lady Sarnai's golden skirt, vexed by his calm. He had saved us. Yet my fear had been so raw. It had punched me in the gut, leaving me with a sinking nausea I could still taste. Not because I needed his silly map or his magic, but because I needed *him*.

"The moon will be full tonight," Edan said, unaware of my thoughts. "If you leave soon, you can reach the peak before dusk. The days are shorter here in the mountains, so once night falls, I'll fly up to meet you on the peak. Will you put down that damned skirt!"

I carefully made another knot in the back of the skirt. Finally, I looked up.

"Put on the shoes," he said, clearly exasperated.

"If you can fly," I muttered, "I don't see why I have to climb this mountain. *You* could get the moonlight for me and we'd be two dresses down."

"You know I can't," Edan said gently.

I tried to calm myself. "What are you going to be doing all day?"

"I'll ride to the other side of the mountain and find a safe place to store your trunks." He winked. "Then I'll try to finish hemming that skirt for you. If you'll let me."

"Absolutely not!"

Edan laughed, and I glowered at him while I reached for the leather shoes and put them on. They were simple but sturdy and fit snugly over my feet. I'd waxed the outer leather to make it as watertight as possible, but the sun's heat hadn't been strong enough to properly set the wax, so I'd have to be careful not to get them too wet. At least I'd double-lined the insides—the weather in the mountains would be brisk. Already I felt the chill.

Edan took off his scarf and wrapped it around the one already on my neck. When I tried to protest, he said, "It'll get colder the higher you go." He tied it so it wouldn't fall off. "The full moon will rise over the mountains, illuminating a pool somewhere on the peak. When you find it, dive in and capture the light in a walnut. You can swim, yes?"

"Of course I can swim. Can you?"

There was a long pause.

"That sounds like a no."

"I grew up near a desert," said Edan defensively. "Never had time to learn." He puffed out his chest. "Besides, I can walk on water. And fly."

I rolled my eyes. "You should learn. What if you're flying over a lake one day and dawn comes? It isn't hard. You start by putting your face underwater and blowing bubbles . . . like this." I began to show him but stopped. What did I care if he couldn't swim? Edan was my guide, nothing more. And I was the one who'd be in the pool, not him.

Turning away from him, I pressed my palm against Rainmaker Peak's pale, coarse granite wall and took a hesitant first step up. As my shoe pressed against the mountain, I craned my neck and stared at what awaited me. A dangerously steep climb, with few fissures or crevices to latch on to, and a nose-shaped overhang at the top. One misstep, and I'd slide down to my death.

This was where Edan's enchantment came into play.

The shoes stuck to the rock, as if made of glue. On my belt, I had two sharp climbing picks—compliments of Edan's foresight and bartering skills—which I staked into the granite when necessary. Step by step, I hauled myself up the mountain, feeling like an ant crawling up the edge of a sword. My balance wobbled, for at first I did not trust the shoes to stay in place. But it got a little easier once I did. A little.

I swallowed and staked one of my picks higher into the wall. Repeat. One foot at a time. One foot at a time.

I wasn't far up before Edan shouted, "Remember not to get the shoes wet! There's snow when you get higher!"

"I know!" I yelled back. Then I continued my ascent. It wasn't long before Edan was too far below me for us to continue shouting at each other. That was when the loneliness set in, and the worry. Edan was weaker than he let on. I hated leaving him, especially so soon after I'd thought he'd died fighting Vachir's men.

But the window for collecting moonlight was narrow—I'd have to wait a month for another full moon. I had no choice but to go on.

Rain clouds drifted toward me, but they were still far away.

My concern was the snow. Patches of it coated the peak, and snowmelt dribbled down the rock. The thin rivulets sparkled in the sunlight, deceptively beautiful. But I knew better. Getting any part of my shoes wet would counteract their enchantment. My heart stopped every time I made the mistake of looking down, and I imagined stepping into the water, slipping, and falling to my death.

Fear of falling kept me attentive, even as I climbed for hours—almost all day. My palms became raw from clutching the picks, my nails blackened, and my back sore. But I was starting to see how this was the trial of the mind, not the body.

The higher I rose, the colder and icier it became. Choosing my route to the peak became a series of calculated gambles. Should I go around that glistening patch of ice, or did I dare step over it? Was that a shadow on the rock, or a stripe of snow? Grappling with the fear that every next step could be my last made my head spin and my breath come short.

*Stay calm,* I reminded myself as a blast of wind tore at me. *Stay tough.*

I trained my tailor's eyes on the mountain, focusing on the light and colors to avoid ice and snow.

*This isn't so different from sewing,* I said to myself. *Pretend you're a needle stitching up the mountain, trying to find the way to make a perfect seam. One wrong stitch, and the fabric of the mountain will be torn.*

*Sometimes finding the way is tricky, but you always do. As long as you don't give up.*

My courage swelling, I moved doggedly. One hold after another. While I searched for the next, I leaned against the rock, digging my picks as deep as I could. I'd been gripping them so tightly, their wooden ridges had imprinted themselves on my palms.

Eventually, the sun began to set. I left one pick jammed in a fissure and reached into my pocket for my tinderbox. Carefully, I lit the lantern hanging from my belt.

I was at the Rainmaker's overhang when I felt Edan's wings rippling behind me. A gust of wind followed, breezing through my hair and lifting my spirits.

I shouldn't have let him distract me. It was dark now, and in my hurry to reach the peak, I didn't watch where I was climbing. Just as I pulled one pick from the rock, my left shoe grazed a patch of ice. Panic shot through my nerves; my heart jumped madly in my chest. I tried desperately to regain my balance. But the shoe wouldn't hold anymore.

I screamed.

My lantern plummeted, leaving me in darkness. I held on to my right pick, left arm flailing as my shoe slipped uselessly against rock. As I dangled from the precipice, I could feel the muscles in my arm tearing, my grip on the pick slipping. The seconds collided into what felt like an eternity.

Wind roared in my ears. *I'm going to fall. I'm going to fail. No. Not here. Not now.*

I slammed my left pick into a crevice and slowly, trying to keep my fragile control, pulled myself up.

Only after I hauled myself onto the summit and rolled away from the edge of the precipice did I dare exhale, the vapor of my breath dispersing into the cold air. Then I lay on my back, panting, looking up at the moon, my arms throbbing like they were about to fall off. I'd never been this close to the sky—close enough to feel the power of its light humming in my bones.

Edan was perched on a rock, chirping and whistling as he did in his human form. I rose and lifted one tired arm, beckoning him to approach me.

His wings lifted, and he swooped onto my shoulder. To-gether, we walked, exploring the summit of Rainmaker's Peak. It was quiet here. Even the wind was gentler than it had been on the ascent. The moon was enormous. It hung in the night, a massive round lantern, its watery light so bright I almost reached out to touch it.

Edan flew off toward the shadow of the overhang. I fol-lowed him, mindful of my footing. Veins of ice snaked across the rocky summit, so brittle they crunched under my shoes. All was still but for the flap of Edan's wings—and the rattle of grit and tiny pebbles cascading down. My ears perked. Where was that sound coming from?

I broke from Edan and trailed the falling debris to the north side of the summit, watching the pebbles spill into a rocky opening just wider than my hips.

"I found a cave!" I shouted, beckoning Edan to me. I crouched to begin lowering myself. Its mouth was narrow, so I inched inside slowly. I had the unnerving feeling that I was entering some great beast's jaws. Toothlike stalactites pricked me, and dripping water kissed the top of my head.

Bats fluttered, their wings beating so powerfully I staggered forward.

Edan bit my hair and pulled back hard.

I froze. Let out a sharp breath. Moonlight filtering through the ceiling cracks revealed a silvery carpet of ice. One more step forward and I would have fallen through the ice into the pool beneath it.

I peered down. A city of crystal glimmered beneath the ice, illuminated by slivers of moonlight.

*You'll have to swim for the moonlight,* Edan had told me

when he handed me the second walnut. *And carry this with you,* he added, also giving me the walnut now filled with sunlight. Its shell glowed ever so slightly, a warm, bright bulb of light.

*Keep it near your heart,* Edan had said as I tucked the walnut into my tunic. *It'll give you warmth.*

I knelt by the pool, Edan the hawk on my shoulder.

"There?" I pointed to the center of the still water, where moonlight glistened brightest. "That's what I have to get, isn't it?"

The hawk's neck jerked. *Yes,* I assumed. It was impossible to tell how deep the pool was.

My body shook as I removed my cloak, pants, and shoes. I folded them into a neat stack on a rock. Then, as I'd done before with the sun, I put on my spider-silk gloves and grasped my scissors.

The cold numbed my fear. Sucking in the biggest breath I could hold, I jumped.

Nothing could have prepared me for the shock of the cold water. Without the walnut of sunlight spreading warmth through my blood, I would have frozen within seconds.

I dove down, away from the dim light of the surface. It was so quiet all I could hear was the sound of my pulse slowing.

The pool was bottomless. The air stored in my lungs grew thin. Pinching, pinching. Tight.

*Go back!* My mind screamed at me. *Go back now!*

But I kicked on. After nearly dying on the climb, I couldn't give up now. I tried to think of Baba and Keton, that I couldn't fail them. But this trial wasn't about my heart.

*Stop kicking, stop swimming. Relax.*

I let go. Released everything. My body began to float back toward the surface, and my throat burned, nearly out of air. *No . . .* Had I made a terrible mistake?

Then a strong current caught me, pulling me down so fast and deep into the pool that my stomach surged into my throat. There below, a soft, silvery light penetrated the water, illuminating the city of stone and crystal surrounding me. At first, the light was gauzy, thin and faint. But as I was carried deeper, it separated into thick, bright beams that blinked like eyes—tears of the moon! Around me they shimmered, long whorls of melting silver. All I needed to do was catch one.

The moonlight was slippery. Even with my spider-silk gloves, it curled and twisted out of my grasp. The next beam I caught, I quickly tied into a bow, as if it were not light but a ribbon. The beam flickered and glowed, becoming so bright I had to look away. I cut the end, clamping my scissors over the light before it could flee.

I coiled the ribbon of light over the blades and forced it into Edan's walnut. Underwater, the task was harder than with the sunlight. My breath leaked out of me, the bubbles gurgling to the surface.

*No one can rescue you, Maia.*

Above, I saw Edan's hawk form fluttering over the water.

At last, I sealed the nut and swam up. As I broke the surface, my lungs exploded with a gasp. Each breath was like inhaling ice. If I didn't get out, I would be dead.

I kicked the water. It felt thick, and every kick wearied me, the ice lacing into my bloodstream. I stretched out my arms, reaching for something to hold. A rock, an icicle—anything.

Frost bloomed over my lashes, forcing my eyes shut. I was

so cold I couldn't see and I couldn't feel. But at last something blocked my way. The edge of the pool, surrounded by rocks. I gripped one as tightly as I could, dragging my legs up onto the stony bank.

I had never been so cold. My skin was blue-gray, the moisture in the corners of my eyes hard as ice.

Edan wrapped his wings around my chest, which helped, but it wasn't enough to thaw the cold in me. With trembling fingers, I reached into my tunic for the sunlight, and I clutched it to my heart.

· · ·

I didn't know how long I languished on the cave floor. When my eyes fluttered open again, it was snowing outside. My body was cocooned in warmth, hot tea steaming by my side.

And Edan was human.

He lay beside me, his arms bare and wrapped tightly around me, his powerful shoulders casting shadows behind him. Both our cloaks were draped over me, and I was wearing his tunic—a realization that made me draw in a sharp breath, even though I was too cold to care.

He let go of me quickly, but I wished he hadn't. The warmth of his touch washed away and I shivered uncontrollably.

"You fell asleep," he said, sounding stern yet worried.

I sat up, poking my hands out of the coverings to reach for the tea. "Y-you m-m-make it—it sound . . . like a—a c-c-crime."

A fire burned, my clothes and enchanted shoes drying next to the flames. Edan's magic tablecloth was out, a small square anchored by a steaming pot of stew. The aroma of garlic, star anise, and mutton sharpened my hunger.

Edan was already scooping some into a bowl for me. "Has anyone ever told you that you talk in your sleep?" he said. "It's adorable."

My cheeks warmed, and I peeled off his cloak. "What did I say?"

"Mostly you babbled nonsense, but there were a couple of outbursts of 'Edan, Edan, Edan.'" He passed me the bowl and grinned. "I take it you were dreaming about me."

"Y-y-you wish," I retorted between bites. "I didn't dream about anything."

He clutched his heart. "Oh, well, that's devastating to hear."

I rolled my eyes, but I was used to his teasing by now. "Ar-ar-aren't you c-c-cold?"

"Not while I'm near you." When I blushed, Edan drew back, as if remembering my earlier outburst. He kept a small distance between us and cocked his head at the modest fire he'd made. "The fire helps. And I can bear it easier than you. I *am* an enchanter, after all."

Still, there were goose bumps on his bare arms, the dark hairs standing on end. I scuttled closer to him and wrapped his cloak over his shoulder. Our arms touched, and he didn't move away. "I—I think I like you better when y-y-you're a bird," I joked. I inhaled, taking in his scent. "Your enchanter form is obnoxious."

"Don't get too used to it," Edan returned, but I heard the anxiety in his voice. "I look forward to my full powers returning once we're back."

We sat in comfortable silence, me sipping my tea, Edan observing the snowfall outside. "We'll have to wait out the snow before we descend the peak," he said. "Some rest will be good for you."

"I'm not tired," I lied in protest. The air stung my throat even before the words formed. My teeth chattered once more, and I folded my body inward and scooted closer to the flames. I tried again: "I j-just slept. I'm n-not t-t-tired."

Edan took my cold hands. He rubbed them, transferring back some of that heat I'd already begun to miss. Then he breathed into my palms. It felt nice, the warmth of his lips on my skin.

"Liar," he whispered. "Of course you're tired. You were swimming in a freezing pool. Your body's in shock."

He drew me to him, enveloping me with his warmth. I wanted to push him away, but my body drank in his heat, my arm instinctively hooking under his. When I noticed what I'd done, I tried to pull back. But he tilted my chin and kissed me. Heat flooded me from my lips to my toes, and my heart hammered, its beat rushing and skipping to my head.

I opened my mouth, only for Edan to stifle my words by kissing me again. I didn't stop him, but I tried to get a word in. "I told you I'm not—"

"Shhh," he said, brushing my lips with his. "Sleep."

I leaned into him, resting my head against his chest. His pulse skipped, a sound that sent a shock wave of thrills jolting through me. He wrapped a warm arm over my waist and pulled me closer.

He fell asleep first. I listened to him breathing, in and out, in and out. A rhythm I matched even without knowing it.

A strange, wonderful contentment filled me.

Edan had been right—this journey *had* changed me irrevocably.

And for the first time, I stopped counting the days until it was over. Now I didn't want it to end.

# CHAPTER TWENTY-SIX

When I woke and saw that the world outside the cave was white, my first thought was that the clouds had fallen, so soft and satiny was the snow.

I began my descent. The climb down Rainmaker's Peak was easier than the ascent. My enchanted shoes had dried, and with Edan's help on the summit, I used a rope to rappel down the other side. But still it took me the better part of the day. At nightfall, Edan joined me in his hawk form. He made a glorious sight, his night-black feathers and milky-white wings gliding down. He landed neatly on my shoulder, his talons curving gently against my collarbone. I smiled at him. "Show-off."

In his beak was a knot of wildflowers, which he dropped onto my lap.

"For me?" I asked.

Edan the hawk merely blinked. With a laugh, I put the flowers in my hair and kissed his beak. Then I readied our mounts, me riding Opal with Edan perched on my shoulder, and Rook pacing behind.

Moonlight lit our path through the mountains, so we had no difficulty traveling by night. Sometimes Edan disappeared for an hour or two. He was a predatory bird, after all, so I didn't wonder about him. He always found his way back to me, sometimes with a spider or a snake trapped in his beak.

I touched his throat, rubbing it with my finger. "Wonder if that'll give you indigestion tomorrow, Edan."

It was so easy talking to his bird form that I found myself telling him about my brothers, about Finlei wanting to explore the world, and Sendo writing poems about the sea. About Baba and Keton, and my dream to become the best tailor in A'landi.

It made the time fly, and it helped me stay awake. When sunrise came, Edan flew off my shoulder and onto Rook's back. And as the first rays of sun shone upon us, I was no longer traveling with a bird.

"Tired?" was Edan's first word to me.

I shook my head.

He smiled, seeing the flowers tucked behind my ear; then he cleared his throat. "You accepted them."

"Was I not supposed to?"

"A man who wishes to court a woman brings her flowers."

I blushed. "You were a hawk. Besides, there's no such tradition in A'landi."

"I'm not from A'landi," he reminded me. He cleared his throat again. "But I once served in a land where it was customary to make one's intentions known to the object of one's affections. I like the idea very much. And," he said, leaning closer, "if a woman accepts a man's flowers, it means she's willing to be courted by him."

A rush of warmth heated my face. "But . . . how could you court me?" I blurted, wanting to take the words back as soon as they came out of my mouth. "What about your oath?"

Edan looked vulnerable for once. "You told me to make up my mind, so I have," he said softly. "It is an illusion to assume we choose whom we love. I cannot change how I feel about you. I would move the sun and the moon if it meant being with you. As for my oath . . . I cannot promise to break it, but I would do every-thing in my power to make you happy, Maia. That I *can* promise."

His words stirred a want inside me. I longed to kiss him and tell him all that I felt, but I bit my tongue.

He reached for my hand. "Do you not want me to court you? Simply say the word and I'll stop."

I *wanted* him to, more than anything. Yet something held me back. I withdrew my hand and made a show of picking a snarl out of Opal's mane so I didn't have to look at Edan. "Where do we go now?"

Edan's hands fell to his side. "South. To Lake Paduan."

"That's where we'll find the blood of stars?"

"Indeed," he said quietly. "It will be the hardest of the three to acquire."

I ignored the swirls of dread curdling in my stomach. "I take it that's a hint to start on the carpet."

I had two bundles of yarn that Edan had bought in the Sa-marand Passage. The colors were poorly dyed—a washed-out blue and a dull coppery red. I began knotting the base for a rug to the dimensions Edan specified. The rest, I'd leave to my scissors.

"Why didn't we stay on Rainmaker's Peak?" I asked as we rode through a flat stretch of forest. "Surely the top of a moun-tain is the closest we'll come to the stars."

"You haven't studied the Book of Songs, have you?" chided Edan gently. "In one of the odes, the Great Eulogy to Li'nan, it's written that 'the stars are brightest in the dark, and the dark is in the forgotten.' We must go to the Forgotten Isles of Lapzur in Lake Paduan. The Ghost Fingers."

"Where the god of thieves shot the stars to make them bleed," I said. "I know the myth."

"The myth doesn't tell you everything."

"And *you* know everything?"

"No." He spread his palms. "But I've had many more years to study and learn than you. A knowledge of A'landi's classical poetry would enrich your craft, Maia. And I think you'd appreciate its beauty, even better than I." He tilted his head, lost in thought. "I'll pass you my books once we reach the Autumn Palace. I only hope the servants brought them all."

The Autumn Palace. It felt so far from here, both in distance and time. The red sun was less than a month away now, and I still had much work to do on Lady Sarnai's three dresses. What reception could we look forward to when we returned?

I was the imperial tailor, he the Lord Enchanter. Edan would be busy advising the emperor . . . and I'd be pretending to be a boy again. Even if we didn't have his oath to worry about, how could we be together?

Edan didn't say anything further, which made me nervous. The silence between us was charged, like waiting for lightning to strike. Every extra beat grew heavier, so that being near him was like brushing against fire. It was only so long before I couldn't take it anymore.

"Sendo used to scare me with stories about the Ghost Fingers," I said with a shudder. I hadn't believed in ghosts when I was a child, but the last few months had changed much. "He said that Lake Paduan was once home to a great civilization, an ancient city of treasure beyond our imagination. Legends of it spread, and men grew greedy. But they could never cross the water—storms and dangerous conditions would force their boats to turn around.

"Then one day, a ship made the crossing. It was the first to trespass on the islands for hundreds of years, so the city welcomed the men as a sign from the gods. They posed as traders, but they were really barbarians who had used magic to reach the city. At night they killed everyone. The residents became ghosts; the lake rose, flooding the city until only what we know as the Forgotten Isles remained, and the barbarians were cursed to be demons, rich with treasure but never able to leave."

"A high price to pay for their greed," Edan commented. "The people of the city didn't deserve what happened to them. You know the story well."

"I didn't know it was real."

"Your brother got part of it right."

"Which part?"

"The part about the ghosts," said Edan. "If you see one, be wary. If you touch one, you will die and become a ghost yourself."

The warning brought goose bumps to my skin. "What about a demon?"

"If you see a demon," Edan said darkly, "my advice would be to run."

"Will we encounter any there?"

He paused. "We must prepare for that possibility."

I swallowed. I'd learned by now that Edan was always prepared, but the gravity of his tone meant that what lay ahead was going to be very dangerous indeed.

"And how are we going to cross the lake?" I asked.

"We're going to fly." Edan pointed at the carpet I was weaving. "On that."

I was incredulous. "You mean we could have been flying this whole time? You could have told me that before I climbed that mountain!"

Edan shook his head. "Magic must be conserved. And Lake

Paduan is full of—surprises." A cloud passed over his face. "I've been there. It is a place not easily forgotten."

"Why were you there?"

"An enchanter's training is shrouded in secrecy," he said, "but we are tested much as you are—trials of the body, mind, and soul."

"And one of them was on the Forgotten Isles?"

"The last one." Edan hesitated. "We had to drink the blood of the stars. It is the final test every enchanter must take."

*The blood of the stars!* "What happens when you drink it?"

"Your powers increase a hundredfold, and you are gifted with a thousand years of life," replied Edan softly. "It is the aspiration of every young enchanter. We are so foolish in our youth. So eager to believe we can change the world. And I was younger than most when it was my turn." He paused. "More reckless, too. Most who take of the stars do not survive. I was lucky . . . or unlucky, depending on how you look at it."

I pursed my lips. Immortality and power, in exchange for being a slave. Of course, they probably didn't call it slavery in the oath. How strange Edan's youth must have been.

"Why would you *want* to become an enchanter?" I asked.

"We don't think of being bound to the oath as a sacrifice, but as an honor. It is an honor to use our powers to better this world."

"But you might have a terrible master."

"That is the balance of fate. We are not invincible, and our numbers dwindle as new eras dawn and people forget about magic. When you have served as long as I have, it is impossible not to grow disillusioned with the oath." His voice fell soft. "It becomes impossible *not* to wonder if you might be happier without magic."

His gaze bored into me, deep and penetrating. Melting my resistance.

"I know one thing, Maia Tamarin—being with you makes me happier than I have ever been."

I couldn't fight my heart any longer. "I'm glad you became an enchanter," I said fiercely. "I know you've suffered, far more than you let on. But if you hadn't, I wouldn't have met you."

I picked the flowers from my hair and buried my face in them, inhaling their scent. *Somehow,* I swore to myself, *somehow I will find a way to set Edan free.* Then, so softly that I almost didn't hear myself, I whispered, "You may court me."

Slowly, Edan traced a finger over my lips and kissed me, then moved on to kiss every freckle on my nose and cheeks until I was intoxicated by the sweetness of his breath.

"But only if you tell me your names," I said, surfacing for air. "One for each day."

He groaned. "I'm going to have to court you for a thousand days?"

"Is that too long?"

"I was hoping for a hundred at most."

"And?" I held my breath. I didn't know what courtship had been like in Edan's home country, but he'd been in A'landi long enough to know that a man didn't court a woman without serious intentions.

"It would be no fun for me if I told you all my plans for us."

"Edan!"

He smiled mysteriously. I had no idea what he was thinking, but the happiness on his face was contagious. I smiled too, warmed.

"It would be easier if you didn't have to pretend to be a

boy," Edan admitted, "and if I weren't under oath to serve the emperor. But we'll figure it out, day by day. I promise."

"I already know four of your names," I whispered, placing my hand over his. "And Edan. So it'd be nine hundred and ninety-five days. Tell me your first name."

"My first name was Gen," he said. "It's the most ordinary of names; it means *boy*."

"Boy!" I exclaimed. "That's hardly a name at all."

"It isn't," he agreed. "My father had seven sons, and by the time I was born, he had run out of names. So that was what he called me. I had no other name until I was much older."

I opened his hand and traced the lines of his palm. They were long and smooth, seemingly without end. "And what does Edan mean?"

He smiled, his lips parting slightly before they covered mine. "It means *hawk*."

# CHAPTER TWENTY-SEVEN

Autumn was coming. The summer heat mellowed, and I could feel a chill in the wind; it made the hairs on the back of my neck tingle and my fingers dance past each stitch a beat slower and stiffer than I was used to. In the forest the edges of the leaves were gilded amber, and the verdant landscape bloomed with reds, oranges, and even purples.

We left the Dhoya Forest behind us and made our way back to the Great Spice Road. On the way to Lake Paduan, we passed through a town or two, where I posted letters to Baba and Keton, but we never stopped for long, and always made camp some miles out. Now that we knew the shansen was searching for Edan, we needed to be careful.

Every day I woke at dawn to rekindle the campfire and greet my enchanter when he returned to me, hungry for my touch. Our mornings and days were dedicated to kissing—whether on foot or on horseback. It had to be an enchantment that our horses knew where to go, for Edan and I paid little attention unless they veered off the Road.

The nights grew longer and darker the closer we drew to Lake Paduan, and my sleep grew deeper. One morning I arose late and was just stirring the fire when I spied Edan's hawk form gliding down toward me.

He landed behind the flaming hearth, transforming into a man. An intense, now-familiar heat rippled through me.

Edan's eyes were still yellow, and sweat beaded on his temples. He looked tired.

I knelt beside him as he sat against a poplar tree by the campfire. His shirt was misbuttoned, and I fought the urge to fix it for him. "How can we lift your curse?"

"It isn't a curse; it's an oath."

"An oath you can't break. What's the difference?"

"There's no easy answer," he said grimly. "Khanujin isn't going to free me unless he is compelled to."

"Not even after the wedding, when there's finally peace?"

"I wouldn't depend on that."

I lay on the ground next to him, taking in the grove of poplars around us, most of the trees so tall they obstructed my view of the sunrise. I didn't mind. There was something beautiful about these woods, and I was content simply watching the trees sway, like feathers ruffled by the wind.

"I think about Lady Sarnai sometimes," I murmured. "Her heart is with Lord Xina. Do you think she'll ever love Emperor Khanujin?"

Edan softened. "It doesn't matter. They're to be married for the peace of A'landi."

"That's sad."

"It's the way of kings and queens," he said distantly. "Doesn't matter where you are. It's all the same."

I wondered then how many kings he had served. Whether his boyish grin and lanky figure were part of another enchantment . . . were part of his oath.

"And what about you?" I asked, feeling bold. "Will *you* ever marry?"

A rare blush colored Edan's neck. "I hope to."

"You hope?" I teased. "You're courting me—you can't renege now!"

"Marriage isn't advised while bound to the oath," he replied slowly. "You would age while I stayed young."

"I don't care about that."

"You say that now, but your opinion might change." A note of urgency strained Edan's voice. "And if my amulet were ever lost, I'd become a hawk again. It wouldn't be fair to you."

"Let *me* decide what's fair and what isn't."

He turned and held my hands, rubbing the calluses along my fingers. "It's just . . . I don't want you to have regrets, Maia. You're young, with dreams and a family to care for. And now that you're the imperial tailor—I don't want you to throw it all away on a foolish boy like me."

"I wouldn't stop sewing for you, Edan," I said lightly. "I'd open a shop in the capital—one by the ocean, preferably. I'd draw by the water and sew all day." I wiggled into the hollow of his shoulder and rested my head there. "And you're not foolish—not for chasing magic. I can see in your eyes how much you love it. Enough to pay such a terrible price." I paused to chew on my lower lip. "Would you lose it, if you were freed?"

"Enchanters are born with magic," he answered, "but yes, I would lose my sensitivity to it, and my ability to channel its power. Something I would welcome if it meant being with you."

I swallowed, feeling an ache rise in my chest—but one that wasn't entirely unpleasant. "What would you be, if you were free?"

The deepness in his voice faded, and he sounded like the boy he was. "If I were free? Perhaps I'd be a musician and play my flute, or work with horses in a rich man's stable."

"You do love your horses."

He winked at me. "Or I'd be an old, fat sage with a long beard. Would you still love me then?"

"I can't imagine you with a beard," I said, touching his smooth chin. My fingers slid down to his neck, stopping just before his heart. A throb in my chest again. "But yes. Always."

"Good." He grinned, the dimple on the left corner of his mouth making an appearance. "I'll be in charge of tutoring the children. I hope you know I expect many. At least eight."

I slapped his shoulder playfully. "Eight!"

"I had six brothers, after all. I'm used to a big family." He sat up to kiss me, and despite the tiredness on his face, his eyes shone with a contentment I'd never seen before.

"We couldn't afford eight children in the capital."

"Then I'll grow a money tree when we're back in the palace."

I couldn't tell if he was joking. "A money tree?"

"How else do you think freed enchanters become wealthy?" Edan snorted. "I have the seeds tucked away in a secret hatch in my room. We can use it to buy a nice mansion for us and your father and brother, with a hundred servants." He looked worried. "Do you think your baba will like me?"

"My baba cares nothing about wealth," I said, laughing. Happiness bubbled in me as I thought of Edan trying to impress Baba and befriend Keton. "He'll only want you to be good to me."

"I will be," Edan promised. "Better than good." He reached into his pocket and took out a small leather book with a blue cover and a thin golden cord and tassel for tying it together. Its edges were slightly bent from having been in his pocket. "For you."

"A new sketchbook?"

"I picked it up in Samaran," he said sheepishly. "You looked like you were almost done with yours."

"You *are* observant." I brought the sketchbook to my nose, inhaling the scent of fresh paper. I reached for Edan's cheek and traced his hairline to his jaw. A brief shiver tingled down my spine. "I wonder who should be my next subject."

Edan made a face. "Enchanters don't often sit for portraits. We're too restless. However, I will be in need of a new cloak soon." He gestured at his fraying one. "In case you wish to thank me, Master Tailor."

"A sketchbook for a cloak? Hardly seems like a fair trade."

"It's a *magic* sketchbook," Edan said, reaching for it.

I rolled my eyes. "Really."

"See, when you turn it upside down, sand falls out." Edan smiled widely as he caught the desert's golden grains in his palm. "Sand, sand, and more sand."

"Oh, you!"

He laughed. "So, Master Tamarin, can I count on you making me the best-dressed enchanter in all the Seven Lands?"

I turned out his collar, straightening it. I clicked my tongue. "You can hardly be the best-dressed enchanter in *any* land if you can't even button your shirt properly."

"Ah." Edan looked down at his shirt helplessly. Laughing, I reached out to fix it. But the laughter on my lips faded as he drew me close.

My whole body trembled, but my fingers most of all

as they undid his buttons one by one, and try as I might, I couldn't steady them. As my hands traveled down his chest, my heart hammered, betraying a need I didn't know lurked inside me.

He locked his hands around my waist and kissed me again, more tenderly than ever before. "Thank you, Master Tailor," he murmured. He started to rebutton his shirt, but I placed my palm on his bare chest.

Surprise flickered in his eyes; I felt a spike in his heartbeat, and that pleased me. I liked seeing him like this. Vulnerable, and tender. More boy than enchanter.

Before I lost my nerve, I slowly slid his shirt off his shoulders. Edan went very still, almost rigid. There was a tingle ripening in my core that wouldn't quiet. A hunger I'd been suppressing for days, maybe weeks. The hairs on his chest bristled as I ran my fingers down him, and I placed the softest of kisses on his throat.

Edan's breathing quickened. "Maia," he whispered, almost a gasp. A question hovered on his lips, but I placed my finger over them before he could ask. I unfastened his belt, then moved for the one holding my robes together, unthreading my arms from my clothes until they tumbled behind me.

The wind swept across my bare back, and I shivered, feeling suddenly shy. Edan pressed a warm hand on my spine and drew me against him. He kissed me, exploring my mouth with his tongue, then tantalizing my ears and my neck until I was dizzy and feverish. Finally, when my knees weakened and I couldn't bear to stand any longer, Edan eased me onto his cloak against the soft, damp earth.

Our legs entwined; then we became flesh upon flesh. All of

me burned, my blood singing wildly in my ears, my senses soaring. Above, the stars faded behind the misty sky, and the sun fanned its light upon us. We melted into each other until the dawn slid into dusk, and the sun paled into the moon, and the stars, once lost, became found again.

# CHAPTER TWENTY-EIGHT

We arrived at Lake Paduan three days later than scheduled, but they were three days I wouldn't have traded for all the magic in the world. Admitting my love for Edan was like succumbing to a beautiful, rapturous dream and wanting never to wake. If not for Edan's oath and my promise to the emperor, we might have forgotten ourselves completely and stayed forever by that poplar tree under the sun.

The morning we were to make our journey across the lake, I unrolled the carpet over the dry yellow grass. I heard Edan rustle behind me. Every time I saw him, my heart became fuller, yet heavier. A faint golden crown still rimmed his pupils; he'd just finished his night as a hawk.

"Good morning," Edan greeted me, kissing my cheek. The fatigue weighed on him more heavily with each passing day. Sometimes, in the early morning when he slept, he would cry out from a nightmare; when he woke, his eyes would be almost entirely white.

He didn't seem to remember. I knew it would only hurt him if I asked about it.

I unrolled the carpet at my feet. "Is this good enough?"

Edan surveyed my work. "It will do nicely."

"Thank you." I flexed my hands. I hadn't realized how sore my fingers were from constantly knitting, knotting, and sewing. The magic scissors helped, of course, but only to a point.

Edan rolled up his sleeves, and the cuff on his wrist glowed slightly, the way my scissors did when they knew I was about to use them.

He knelt and touched the carpet, tracing its border with his fingertips.

Nothing happened. I could tell Edan was getting agitated, though he tried not to show it. His shoulders tensed, his brow creased, and he wouldn't look at me.

Finally the carpet began to tremble, so subtly I thought I'd imagined it. Its fibers stretched, wiggling and vibrating until they hummed a low, deep song. I hoped I'd woven it strong enough to weather Edan's enchantment.

Then, miracle of miracles—it floated. A mere inch above the grass at first, then higher and higher until it was level with my hips. My head grew dizzy from the impossibility of it. Familiar as I'd become with Edan's magic, I'd never seen anything like this.

"After you," Edan said, gesturing with a note of triumph in his voice.

Once we'd both settled on the carpet, it swerved up into the air, soaring until it scraped the clouds. I clung to the edge, staring at the hundreds of tiny islands dotting Lake Paduan below, lit up like stars in the misty sunlight.

"It's so beautiful," I breathed.

"Don't let its beauty mesmerize you," Edan warned. "This land is full of dark magic."

It was hard to imagine that. The islands appeared lush with vibrant green trees and golden beaches. But I'd come to trust Edan's warnings since our brutal days in the Halakmarat; I still

286

had nightmares about baking in the sun and finding my canteen full of sand.

I followed his gaze to a group of islands covered in mist. I could barely see them, for the sky there was dark and the water murky. We dipped down, and I grabbed a tassel, glad I had taken the time to add them to the carpet. My excitement quickly turned to fear as the wind picked up strength.

"I made this too thin, didn't I?" I cried. "We're losing control!"

"It'll pass—just hold on!" Edan shouted back, but something in the carpet ripped.

I let out a shriek as we plunged through low-hanging clouds.

"I've got you!" Edan yelled, hooking his arm around me. Reaching for a corner of the carpet, he twisted it as the wind hurled us across the sky and steered us toward a dark pocket of land. The mist was so thick there I could hardly see.

Violent gusts of wind tore at us until I couldn't tell if we were flying up or down. Then the carpet lurched, and we plummeted. My gut was sinking and being crushed all at the same time. Cloth whipped behind me—Edan's cloak or mine, I couldn't tell. I could see the water beneath us, its hungry, bottomless depths roaring toward us, drowning out my screams.

I grabbed Edan's hand. He started shouting, the same words over and over until his voice was hoarse. The carpet careened toward a shadowy stretch of land, but the wind thwarted it. Whether we crashed on land or on the sea made no difference. The speed at which we were falling guaranteed death either way.

Edan flung his arms up, and the carpet folded around us, tight as a cocoon, surging for the island. Once we were over land, the carpet hung back, fighting the wind. We hovered in midair, barely long enough for me to catch my breath.

Then we fell again, this time into a crooked tree whose branches pierced the fog. Down the trunk we slid, the coarse bark shredding the edges of the carpet.

We hit the ground with a thump, and fireflies fled into the misty fog above us.

After a long pause, Edan stirred. "Maia?" he whispered, rolling to his side to face me. "Are you hurt?"

"I don't think so." My neck tingled, but I could move my head and my limbs. "Are you?"

"Nothing's broken."

I peeled myself off the moist, cold ground. The carpet lay at my feet, beaten and battered, its yarn half unraveled. I wove my arm through Edan's and pulled him up. Using magic had drained him, and he was breathing hard. "Are you sure you're all right?"

"No more close encounters with death, please," he joked feebly. "I don't have it in me to save you anymore."

"Save *me*?" I retorted. "Vachir's arrows would have made a pincushion out of you if not for me and my scissors. And don't forget you were on that carpet too."

"True, true." He chuckled. "Save *us*, then."

I hid a smile and shook the dirt from my sleeves. "Is this the right place?"

He looked around, his sharp eyes discerning things that lay beyond my field of vision. "It is."

Through mist and shadow, the island revealed itself. A graveyard of dead trees, their arms gnarled and crooked, raked across the sky. Aside from fireflies, the only signs of life were vultures, ravens, and crows. How odd that their shrieks comforted me in this eerie silence.

Even the water, which had slapped against the shores from

which we departed, had become oddly still. Only if I listened closely could I hear the waves whispering restlessly from afar.

A lone gust of wind hissed, rippling through my sleeves and bristling against the back of my neck. The fog was thick, but the stars above shone so brightly their light cut through. They seemed so close, hanging in the sky even though dawn had broken just a short while ago. It disoriented me, how dark it already was on the island.

In the distance, I could see the shadows of a city's ruins. I started toward it, but Edan pulled me back. "Don't venture off," he said. "Not here."

Edan shed his cloak, but I kept mine. Goose bumps crawled over my skin, my fingers stiffened, and the cold air seeped into my bones.

The isle was larger than it had looked from above. It became even quieter the deeper inland we ventured, until not even the birds breathed.

"Was it this quiet the last time you were here?" I asked.

"Yes." He pointed to a tower off in the distance. "They say that the god of thieves leapt from the top of that tower to steal the stars. Of course, back then, they were much closer."

"Did you go inside?"

Edan nodded. "It was the last rite before I took my oath. When enchanters are deemed ready, we journey to the Thief's Tower. On the night the blood of stars falls from the sky, we drink from the well there." He cupped his hands to show me. "If we survive, the blood stains our hands and binds the oath." He held up the wrist with his cuff. "And we must serve the ages with magic . . . for better or for worse."

"How many don't survive?" I wondered aloud.

"The blood of stars is not meant to be drunk," Edan said,

by way of a reply. "And this isle is full of surprises." His tone darkened. "You're going to hear things . . . maybe even see things that are . . . are not of this world."

I swallowed. "I understand."

"Don't listen to anyone but yourself no matter what you hear," Edan said quietly. "They're ghosts. They will call to you, say things that no one else could know to lure you close. Do not touch them."

I nodded. He had already warned me. "What about demons?"

Edan clenched his jaw. "No two demons are the same—but demons have magic, whereas ghosts do not."

"But there might not be any demons here, right?"

"I pray not." He hesitated. "I told you I had a teacher who became a demon. He was bound to these isles." Edan reached for my hand. "If he is still here, he would be more interested in me than you."

"That doesn't make me feel better."

"I'm not trying to make you feel better," Edan reminded me. "I'm trying to keep you alive."

Hand in hand, we passed through the gate into the city. Crumbled buildings lined what must have once been a street. Broken signs in a language I couldn't read hung from shattered windows. Everywhere, I saw smashed glass and fallen bricks, even cups and kettles outside what must have been a teahouse. There were no bones, no traces of life. All was still.

Then I began to hear the whispers.

*YOU! Enchanter . . . You shouldn't be here. Turn back. Now. NOW.*

"Edan," I said, gripping his hand sharply, "did you hear that?"

Edan's body was taut as a bowstring. "Just walk on," he said. "Ignore whatever you hear. They feed on fear."

I walked faster.

*Turn back, enchanter. Turn back now or stay forever.*

*Perhaps the girl will stay with us. She'd like it here. More than you did.*

My heart beat faster. Edan squeezed my hand, and it helped. I gathered in a deep breath and concentrated on the tower ahead of us.

Against the darkening sky, the Thief's Tower resembled a beacon, except there was no light, no hope at the top. Its stones were even and straight, like kernels on a withered cob of corn, untouched by the destruction around us.

One step after another, we walked steadily forward—until I could make out the statues crouched by its door. Statues of the god of thieves, I surmised. Sunlight piercing the mist touched his eyes, making them glow as if from within.

*Maia. Maia, you're here.*

I froze. I would recognize that voice anywhere.

*Maia, breakfast is ready. Won't you come join us? Have a taste.*

Against my will, I sniffed. The fragrant aroma of chicken porridge, with fried dough, wafted invisibly through the air. That smell was so taunting . . . so real.

I couldn't move. My legs were leaden.

"What's wrong?" Edan shook my hand, pulling me forward. "Don't stop walking."

I stumbled after him. "That was my mother's voice."

"It wasn't. Remember what I told you."

"It sounded so much like her."

Edan shook me again. "It wasn't her." His voice was stern.

*Maia! You've found us.*

I felt the blood drain from my face. "Finlei," I whispered.

I started to turn, but Edan grabbed my shoulders. "Don't look back. Promise me, Maia. You need to ignore them."

I stared at him blankly. "Do you hear them?" I whispered.

Edan caught my hand. "Maia," he said harshly, urgently, "they're not the ghosts of your family. They're trying to trick you. Be strong."

I pursed my lips. My palm was sweaty against his, and I tried to pull my hand away but Edan wouldn't let go. *I am strong*, I thought. *I've always been strong.*

*Maia, Maia, my girl*, my mother's voice rang out. *Don't listen to him. He's lying.*

*Maia.* Sendo spoke now. *Come to us.*

Over and over, they called out to me. Mama and Finlei and Sendo. *Why are you ignoring us, Maia? Dear sister. Speak to us. Come to us.*

How I yearned to run to them! But Edan wouldn't let go of my hand, and I remembered his warnings about ghosts.

"Don't let go," I whispered to him, "not until you have to."

Edan nodded. He looked so tired, so withered. What was eating away at him here? What hadn't he told me?

We walked on, climbing over fallen debris. Salt was strong in the air, salt and dust and little else. Gone was that smell of Mama's chicken porridge.

Edan shook my arm. "Maia," he pressed, "tell me about your brothers."

He was trying to distract me from the ghosts. I swallowed, picturing my brothers. My real brothers. It hurt so much to think of them. "Finlei . . . Finlei was the leader. The brave one." My voice shook. "Sendo was the dreamer." Edan squeezed my hand, encouraging me to go on. "Keton was the trickster, the funny one . . . but not so much after he got back from the war."

"And you?"

"The obedient one."

"No," Edan said. "You're the strong one."

The strong one. The one who held the seams of my family together.

I inhaled, hoping that would be enough.

All too soon, we arrived at the gate of the Thief's Tower. The air was hollow, deathly still.

"I'll wait for you here," Edan said, lighting a candle and passing it to me. The flame flickered, even though there was no wind.

"What do I do?"

"It's the ninth day of the ninth month," Edan said. "The sun sits high in the sky, waiting for the moon to rise. Once a year, the two are reunited for a precious moment, linked by a bridge of starlight." He opened his palm, revealing the third walnut. "When the bridge collapses, the stars will bleed dust from the sky, and some will fall into the well at the top of the tower. Collect what you can."

Edan caught my sleeve just as I started through the gate. A wild look haunted his eyes, and his skin was so ashen I worried he might collapse.

"Only seek the blood of stars," he rasped. "Do not be tempted by anything else."

"Edan." My eyes widened with concern. "Are you all right?"

"I will be," he whispered. "Once you come back to me." He pressed a gentle kiss on my cheek. "You are strong." He managed a smile, but it was merely a turning up of his lips. "Go. Find the stars."

I climbed the stairs to the base of the tower. My steps echoed into the night, the loneliest sound I had ever heard. There was no door, so I simply walked inside, into a round, empty room, open to the sky. I felt like I was inside a spool of thread; there were no windows, and the walls around me had no edges or corners.

Where were the stairs up to the top? The room seemed to stretch the deeper I went inside. Its stillness reminded me of a temple, but there were no deities to worship. No incense, no offerings to the gods. And I no longer felt alone.

No, I heard voices. Voices humming . . . from within the walls.

My blood turned to ice. I recognized Sendo's voice. He was singing. *There once was a girl in blue. Her hair blacker than the night.*

"Sendo," I whispered. I strode quickly now, almost running. *She fell in love with the ocean, this girl in blue.*

I stopped. Turned.

There, atop a stairway, stood my brother.

"No," I whispered. "You're not real."

*Remember how we sat on the pier, Maia? And I told you stories about fairies and ghosts?*

"I remember."

*I miss those times.* Sendo began to fade up the stairs, his voice sounding faraway. *Will you come with me? Don't leave me, Maia. It's so lonely here.*

While I began to climb up, the stars shot forth, and the moon emerged from the fog. It was a faint but luminous orb, a gleaming white marble slowly rising to meet the waiting sun.

As I went higher and higher, a wondrous, horrible thing

happened. The chamber shifted. Gone were the gray, unpolished stones, the dank smell, the dust from the debris outside.

I was home.

I smelled it first. Baba's incense: cloves, star anise, sandalwood—and cinnamon. Baba's incense was always heavy on cinnamon. I inhaled, letting the scent enfold me until I was awash in it.

I whirled around. No, this wasn't our shop in Port Kamalan. It was too large, too crowded. This was Gangsun—now I saw Baba was in the front, talking to customers, and Finlei was in the back, arguing with our supplier over a sheath of turquoise brocade that apparently had the wrong flowers embroidered on it.

There was my embroidery frame in the corner—ah, I was almost done making a purse for Lady Tainak. She'd wanted it embroidered with a scene of the Three Great Beauties. I still had to finish the Beauty who was playing the lute. Her face was difficult to sew—I'd never been good at embroidering noses.

But where were Keton and Sendo?

I stepped into Baba's shop, and my fingers brushed over our inventory of silks, satins, and brocades.

Sendo must be hiding somewhere, his nose in a pattern book. An adventure story tucked into its pages, of course.

"Maia!" I heard someone shout. The voice was deep and familiar, but distant.

I glanced out the shopwindow and saw a hawk. His yellow eyes shone, bright as two fervent flames. He let out a small cry, but it dwindled into oblivion as the wind carried him away.

# CHAPTER TWENTY-NINE

All my fear dissolved, forgotten, as I walked deeper into Baba's shop. I moved slowly, taking everything in—the wooden counters freshly wiped clean, the tapered cut of Baba's trousers, the blue porcelain vases full of fresh orchids and lilies, the satin jackets that hung on the southwest wall.

And the dresses! At least a dozen beautiful gowns, ready for their owners to collect. They were so fine. The skirts flared like lanterns, the sleeves light and wispy, trimmed with embroidered silk.

Had I helped make any of them? I couldn't remember.

I picked up my pace. I needed to find Sendo. Where was he?

The aroma of Mama's porridge was back. It wafted across the shop, sending pangs of hunger to my stomach. I followed the smell toward the weaving room, but Finlei waved me away from the looms.

"Maia," he called. "Let's go to the marketplace."

I whirled to face my oldest brother. "Now?"

"Of course now. Seize the wind, Maia! There's a new shipment of wool from Samaran that's supposed to be softer than a camel's foot. If we go early, we can buy some before our competitors beat us to it." His jaw squared into a protective brotherly look. "And you can point out that ruffian who Keton says always bothers you by the temple."

I chuckled. "I can take care of myself, Finlei." Tempted as I was to go with him, I drew back. "You're just eager to leave the shop. Go ahead, I'll join you after I greet everyone."

I pushed past a rosewood screen, past a room of workers at their spinning wheels, into the kitchen. Keton was there, his hair longer than I remembered. Then again, why would he have cut it? He'd never gone to war. He was washing dishes—no doubt it was a punishment for something he'd done this morning—and a stalk of sugarcane stuck out of his back pocket. I was tempted to tell him to put it away before Mama saw—she didn't like it when he indulged his sweet tooth. But he didn't turn around to greet me, so I left him alone.

And continued deeper into the kitchen.

"Mama," I breathed.

"Lunch will be ready soon," she said, wiping her hands on her apron. Behind her, a large pot boiled. I inhaled, savoring the smells of chicken with cabbage and salted fish.

"Do you need help?" I asked.

"No, no," Mama replied, pouring rice wine into the pot and covering it. "I've the maids. They're outside with the oven now, baking coconut buns and taro puffs. Your favorite." She started frying pork with cabbage and cracked a salted egg into the pan. Oil splattered, and the fumes wafted to my nose. I inhaled greedily.

"Are you hungry?"

My stomach rumbled. "Famished."

"Good," Mama said over the crackling meat. "Make sure Baba eats. He's been working so hard he forgets his meals." She chuckled; then she turned.

Why did it feel like it'd been years since I'd last seen her face? I almost didn't recognize her—the soft freckles on her nose and cheeks, the gentle curl of her black hair, her round, smiling eyes. She took a step toward me, her arms open for an embrace.

I wanted to hug her more than anything, yet for some reason I held back. "Do you know where Sendo is?"

"He's upstairs," Mama said.

Was there a staircase in Baba's shop? "Upstairs?"

Mama pretended not to hear me. She dipped a ladle into the pot, stirred, and offered me a taste. "Come, Maia. Try this."

"Later, Mama." I shook my head, still puzzling over this mysterious staircase. But as I left the kitchen, there it was. The stairs were steep and uneven, and I clutched the rail as I ascended. There were many more steps than there ought to have been. They wound up and out of the shop, so high I could no longer smell Mama's cooking.

My legs grew heavy, and my breath grew short. But the sound of someone singing and the soft strumming of a lute lured me to the top, promising that my search wouldn't be in vain.

*"East of the sun, the sapphire seas gleam. Dance with me, sing with me. . . ."*

I hummed along. I knew the melody, but I always forgot the words.

Like Edan. I shook my head. *Who in the Nine Heavens is Edan?*

The song grew louder as I finally reached the top of the stairs. There a narrow hallway awaited me. This was familiar, yes. My parents' bedroom was to the right. Which meant Sendo's was—

I turned left, and my hand pressed against the door to slide it open.

The singing stopped; my heart gave a lurch.

There was Sendo. Alive. Breathing. Whole.

Relief bloomed in me. Then the relief grew into wonder, so that whatever string tethered me to the earth snapped and I floated up and up with joy.

Of course he was alive. Why would I think he wasn't? His warm brown eyes blinked at me, as real as the dirt we used to play in by our shophouse, and so were his freckles and the jagged scar on his left thumb from cutting himself with scissors. This was my Sendo.

I wanted to touch him—to stick out my fingers and rub the soft stubble on his chin. I wanted to sit at his feet and listen to his tales of the sailors and merchants who'd come by Baba's shop since I'd been gone. I wanted everything to be the way it used to be . . . but something held me back. Maybe it was the fear that if I got too close, he would disappear. For the life of me, I could not remember why I had this fear.

"Shouldn't you be working on that scarf for Lord Belang?" Sendo teased.

His voice startled me. I tried to crush the emotions roiling in me, but my voice cracked slightly when I spoke. "The one . . . the one with all the tassels?" My fingers twitched, remembering something about tassels. *A carpet.* I shrugged away the memory. "I hate knotting. I can do it after lunch."

Sendo held a round-bellied lute—I hadn't realized he knew how to play. A sailor's hat slanted on his head, like a soupspoon about to slide off the uneven slope of his black hair. Seeing it, I felt something in me melt.

"Since when do you play the lute?"

"Don't you remember?" he said. "You bought it for me for my birthday. I've been practicing every day ever since."

Oh, I did remember now. Baba had let me take on my first

customer, and allowed me to keep the money I earned from the order. It'd been enough to buy presents for everyone. My parents and my brothers. I hadn't bought anything for myself.

I sat on his bed, stretching out my legs and crossing my ankles. A breeze tickled my bare arms from the open window.

"Someone needs to provide entertainment on a ship," Sendo said, strumming again. "Why not me? I can write poetry *and* sing. And I can tie knots better than anyone in Gangsun."

"Sewing knots are very different from sailing knots," I rebuked him gently. "Besides, Baba will never let you become a sailor."

"He doesn't need me in the shop," Sendo persisted. "Business is doing so well. We have twelve hired hands now." He stilled the lute strings with his fingers. "Will you talk to him about it?"

I softened. Seeing him had brought an ache to my heart, as if we'd been separated for a long time. "Anything for you."

"Thank you," Sendo said.

I made a motion to stand, but Sendo tilted his head. His thick brows knitted.

"What's the matter?" I asked him.

"Come closer."

Again, I hesitated. What was holding me back?

Sendo dropped his lute on the bed. "Why are you carrying a dagger, Maia?"

I looked down. I was wearing my usual navy dress, with a sash for my needles and scissors. But Sendo was right—a dagger hung at my side.

There was something familiar about it, but the memory teetered at the edge of my thoughts . . . ready to slide off and never be recalled again.

I bit my lip. "I don't know."

"Give it here," Sendo said.

Obediently, I handed it to him. My brother stood and walked to the window. I followed, basking in the warm sunlight. The day outside was perfect. I could see the merchants' carriages parked along the road, and children playing with dragon kites.

Sendo twirled the dagger's silken cord. "It looks valuable. The hilt's walnut, and the scabbard is laced with a silver stone of some sort. Meteorite, I'd say."

"Meteorite?" I repeated. "Like from the stars?"

My stomach flipped, again with that pang of having forgotten something. Sendo tried, but he couldn't unsheathe the dagger.

"Here," I said. "Let me try."

The dagger was light in my hands, and the cord was dirty with sand. Strange, I didn't remember dropping it. Then again, I didn't remember much of anything about the dagger.

"Jinn," I uttered, and the scabbard released. The blade, half iron and half meteorite, flashed, catching the sun and nearly blinding me.

I shielded my eyes, and Sendo took the dagger from me.

"What was that?" he said, looking impressed. "You said something."

I shrugged. "Some nonsense word. I guess it unlocks the scabbard."

Sendo admired the blade by the candlelight, studying its two different sides. The metal side gleamed, while the stone edge glowed, so brightly the glare made my brother shield his eyes. "I've never seen a double-edged blade like this. Did someone give this to you?"

The question took me aback. "I . . . I don't know."

"Don't let Keton see it," he said, sheathing the dagger and putting it on the table beside him. "He won't give it back."

Suddenly, the sky darkened. Only minutes ago, the sun had bathed Baba's shop, but now night fell upon us. Thick clouds drifted above, obscuring the moon, but I could see it was full and bright, as if it held a net of stars and they were about to explode into the sky.

"You aren't going to leave us, are you?" Sendo said.

"Leave?" I repeated. "Where am I going?"

"Your memory is terrible today, Maia. The emperor invited you to become his tailor. You're supposed to decide tonight. That's why Mama is cooking for you. She doesn't want you to go. Neither do I."

"The emperor?" I repeated, blinking. "And the stars . . ."

What was I forgetting?

"Maia?" Sendo's lips twisted into a scowl I'd never seen him wear before. His voice grew thick, slightly impatient. "Maia, are you listening to me?"

Sendo was never impatient. "What's wrong?"

"You need to decide. Are you staying or are you going?"

"I don't want to leave the family—"

"Then don't," Sendo said sharply. "Stay here."

I stared at the ground, then lifted my head. Someone had told me to get rid of that bad habit. Who was it—Keton? Why would Keton say that to me? He never talked to me unless it was for a prank. But I remembered his voice. He'd sounded so sad . . . so grown-up.

"You look unhappy," Sendo said, opening his arms to me. "Come here, sister."

I started to reach out. "Wait." I frowned. "I'm not supposed to touch you."

Sendo laughed. It wasn't his usual, carefree laugh. I heard an edge of irritation in it. "What?"

I tried hard to remember. *I think there's something I'm supposed to—*

A gust of wind stroked my hair. I looked outside and saw a black bird with white-tipped wings. A hawk.

Something sharp stirred in me. "Edan."

"What did you say?"

"Edan," I whispered again. What did that mean? Why couldn't I remember?

Sendo took slow steps toward me. He'd taken the dagger and pointed it at me. "Little sister, you're acting strangely."

Shadows danced along the walls. The sun had disappeared, but now so had the moon and the stars.

"Sendo . . . ," I said. "It's dark." My voice sounded small. "I'm going now."

My brother moved to block the door. "You're not going anywhere."

His lute vanished, along with the window and the bed and the little bamboo stool by his dresser. As if they'd never been there.

Then his eyes sank into his skull, flaring red. In the dark, they glowed like rubies. Red as blood.

I held back a scream. "You're not Sendo!"

"No," he rasped. My brother's skin withered before me, and his hair grew long and wild. Gray fur coated his skin, and his eyelids folded back, pupils constricting into tiny beads, like a wolf's. His robe became white as bone, and a black amulet—with a crack in the middle—hung from his neck.

Around me, the walls of the bedroom flickered out of focus, then vanished, nothing more than hallucinations. I was outside, on the ramparts of the Thief's Tower. I'd been outside the entire time.

"You're a ghost," I whispered. Grief welled up in me. Grief for my family, for Sendo, for the dream of everyone being happy together ripped suddenly away.

The shock scorched my insides, but my breath was cold.

"Those other creatures were ghosts," said Sendo, dropping Edan's dagger. He didn't need it, not with his claws. They were curved, with razor-sharp tips that could flay my skin to ribbons. "I am something else entirely."

# CHAPTER THIRTY

I reeled away from the demon who'd taken Sendo's form, staggering back until I hit the parapet. The stone grated against my elbows, and I looked down. Below was Lake Paduan, its waters thrashing violently. A terrible fall, but I might survive it if I didn't hit the rocks.

The demon laughed. "Little Maia, lost and alone. Did you think your family was all together again?" He sneered. "Foolish girl. You fell for it so easily. The others usually fight harder."

I bit my lip, choking back a sob. I'd wanted so badly for my family to be whole, and he'd used that against me. "How do you know so much about me?"

"I know everything, Maia," rasped the demon. "You want to be the best tailor in the land. You want to be loved by your enchanter. You want to save what's left of your family—to see your father happy, and your brother walk again." His red eyes glittered at me. "Well, you can't have it all. But you know that already, don't you? You learned that when your oldest brothers died. All those nights wishing and praying you'd see them again." He raised a claw. "Allow me to grant that wish."

I dove just before he lunged, barely making it out of harm's way.

Blood rushed to my head. Edan's dagger glinted behind me, not far from the stone stairway leading to the top of the tower.

I sprinted for it and, unsheathing it, dashed up the steps as fast as my feet would take me. I didn't know what the demon was, but I'd learned from scaling Rainmaker's Peak not to let fear overcome me. If I did, I'd be lost. Up and up I went.

The top of the tower was empty, save for a stone well in the center. Above me, the sun and moon were side by side. The bridge connecting them arced across the sky, a vein of shimmering silver. Once it collapsed, the blood of stars would trickle down into the well.

Still panting, I bent over the well. Inside was an endless black abyss, as deep as the tower was tall. I prayed the blood of stars would fall soon.

My ears perked at the sound of scraping, knives against stone.

The demon had followed me. His claws grated against the side of the tower, red eyes glowing as he leapt up, landing on the other side of the well.

He laughed at my raised dagger. "You barely know how to use it."

*One side is best used against man,* Edan had said. *The other side is made of meteorite and is best used against creatures I hope we won't encounter.*

I held the weapon close. The edge made of meteorite began to glow, and the demon's stare turned vicious. He sprang for me and I darted away with a scream. I didn't know how to attack him. He was thin as air at times, solid as iron at others. He crouched atop the well, leaping at me and blocking my way whenever I tried to get past. Laughing. Playing with me.

It was a game I couldn't win. He was too fast. Just trying to avoid his razor claws left me gasping with terror. I would have to attack soon, before I became too tired.

I stopped running and faced the demon, swinging the blade with all my strength. This surprised him, but only for a second. He twisted away, and I missed, but the meteorite burned through the chain of his amulet. I grabbed it and wrenched it from his neck.

The demon retreated. His eyes still glowed with rage, but he made no move to attack.

"Give it back," he demanded. His claws retracted, and his voice became sweet again. Honeyed, almost, like my mother's. "Give it back, Maia."

I backed up until I was against the well. Above me, the glittering bridge between the sun and the moon collapsed in one great flash of light, and a white veil swept over the night, smearing light across the sky. It didn't last long. Darkness returned, and the blood of stars began to fall, a firework of silver dust that trickled down like raindrops. The stones in the well hummed and trembled, the dim light shining from its depths growing brighter and brighter.

"There is nowhere for you to go," the demon growled. "Return it and I won't kill you."

I brandished the meteorite blade with one hand and held the amulet over the well with the other. "One step closer and I throw it in."

The demon assumed Sendo's voice again, knowing it would torment me. "The ghosts will see you dead before they allow you to leave with the blood of stars. Return the amulet to me, and I will give you safe passage off this island."

"Safe passage?" I snapped. "You tried to kill me."

"Give me my amulet, and I will let you go." A deliberate pause. "Or I can give you something your heart yearns for."

I was breathing hard. "What do you know of my heart?"

"Edan," the demon whispered. "You love him, and yet he pledged an oath that cannot be broken. Hand over the amulet, and I will break the oath."

I hesitated. "How?"

"Let me show you," he hissed, inching closer with the lethal grace of a wolf. "Just give the amulet back."

I was torn. *Are you crazy, Maia? You can't trust a demon.*

But what if he was telling the truth? What if he *could* free Edan? We could be together.

*Listen to yourself!* the logical part of my brain screamed at me. *The demon is manipulating you. If you don't take the blood of stars now, then there will be no hope of peace for A'landi. Thousands more will die. Their blood will be on your hands.*

*But Edan . . .*

*We'll find another way.*

"I don't bargain with demons," I said shakily.

"That's too bad," the demon said. "I was looking forward to freeing Edan. Death would be a gift for him, after serving so many hundreds of years."

A chill rippled down my neck. The demon would have killed Edan. He had tried to trick me *again*!

Hatred thickened my blood. *No more of this.* Heart racing and fingers fumbling, I cracked open my walnut and leaned over the well, reaching deep for the shimmering silver liquid within. Just an inch more!

The demon's shadow loomed over me. I jumped, feeling his icy-cold breath on my neck, and the walnut slipped out of my hand into the well.

"No!" I shouted.

My gut twisted with despair, and the demon cackled. "Such a useless girl," he murmured, shaking his head.

A small vial materialized in his palm. He held it out, sharp nails glittering. "Give me back the amulet, and you may have it."

I tightened my grip on his amulet, studying its rough black surface. Its round face was scratched and dented, likely hundreds of years old. Maybe more. It resembled the one Emperor Khanujin wore, only with a wolf in place of a hawk.

I glared at him. I desperately needed the vial. "Fine."

With all my strength, I hurled the amulet at him. His claws rose to catch it, and in a moment of madness, I lunged forward and slammed my dagger into his shoulder. He cried out, an anguished scream that made my blood curdle.

I swooped for the vial before it shattered on the ground. The well was nearly full now. As quickly as I could, I filled the vial. I should have run immediately, but the glass shone with an intensity that transfixed me.

The blood of stars.

I held it close, staring into its sparkling depths. It would be easy to stare at it forever, mesmerized by its ever-changing colors. How many men had died trying to obtain this priceless substance, I couldn't begin to guess. But I hadn't escaped yet, so I capped the vial and whirled around to run—

Straight into the arms of the demon.

He was back. Black, velvety blood seeped out of the wound in his shoulder, but it was already healing in a whirl of smoke and shadow. I tried to flee, but he blocked me and wrapped his claws around my neck. The shock of his touch was like lightning. It tore through me, boiling inside my veins, silencing my thoughts, my nerves. My dagger clattered, the clang of its double-edged blade against the stone floor sounding a thousand miles away.

My blood thickened. I could see nothing. Not the brilliant star-flooded sky or the horrible red eyes of the demon before me.

He laughed in my ear and brought me close to him. "You aren't going anywhere," he whispered. "My ghosts are hungry. Don't you hear them wailing?"

I heard the howling, but I'd thought it was the wind. I shut my eyes, wishing I could shut my ears, too. I writhed and kicked at the air, tearing at the demon's face to free myself. But he was too strong.

"It's been so long since they've had a visitor," he continued. "And one with such sweet, sweet memories. Wouldn't you like to stay with them, Maia? My ghosts. You could all be one happy family again." He squeezed my neck, right where my pulse beat. I gasped. My heart stopped. Started. Beat. "Ghosts devour memories, did Edan tell you that? One touch, and they take away your past. You forget everything and become one of them." He squeezed me tighter. I wheezed. No more breath. "Or should I keep you for myself? Demons devour you slowly, piece by piece, memory by memory. Until you are nothing."

I was too weak to fight the demon anymore. My hands fell to my sides, limp and useless. But my scissors throbbed at my hip, and with one last spurt of strength I unhooked them and stabbed their blades into the demon's heart.

He let out a gruesome howl. This time I didn't linger. As soon as the demon dropped me, his terrible form peeling into smoke and his bones charring into ash, I was already on my way.

I picked up my dagger and careened down the tower, my feet moving faster than my breath. Ghosts began to rise, screeching whispers and taunts. The sounds chased me, so close that my ears rang.

310

The meteorite half of my blade glowed, and I kept it raised. Its magic was the best defense I had.

A ghostly horde waited for me below—all white hair and wet red eyes bulging out of their sockets. Their screams stabbed into my skin, resonating in my bones until I thought I might shatter.

I wouldn't give in. I wouldn't touch them.

I burst out of the tower, hurrying down the stone steps into the abandoned city. But there was no way off the island. There was nowhere to run. Then—

Edan. His great wings beat against the wind. Somehow, he'd managed to carry our carpet in his beak. Its weight hindered him, and he flapped hard to stay aloft. When he got close enough, he dropped it before me and squawked.

The carpet's edges were frayed, and the rest was tattered and torn. I kicked it, hoping to awaken it. No good.

My fingers trembled as I took out my scissors and got to work, mending holes and tears to breathe new life into the carpet. *Please fly, please fly.*

Edan circled me, waiting with me. *Oh gods, there is no way out of here.* I could see the ghosts swarming toward me now.

Threads looped and knotted under my scissors. I cut and cut, as fast as my fingers could move. Behind me, the night had become quiet once more.

My fingers burned as I frantically knotted the tassels with the scissors' magic. Finally, the carpet jerked to life. I bolted onto it. "Fly!" I shouted at it. "Fly!"

It started to rise, but the ghosts were upon me. With a chorus of whispers and shrieks, they swooped forward, their long, skeletal arms outstretched. They were so close I could see the hollowness in their eyes. Their mouths hung open, tongues thin and long as a snake's.

*STAY, Maia. Don't you want to be with your family, for-ever? STAY WITH US.*

I swung my dagger in every direction, and for a while, it worked to keep the ghosts at bay.

But there were too many of them. I couldn't hold them *all* off.

Desperately, I dug through my pockets, searching for any-thing that might help. Pins pricked me, but I kept searching. My cloak pocket, my tunic. I was about to give up when my fingers brushed over a walnut—the one storing sunshine.

Hope sprang, then courage.

I ripped a piece of my sleeve off and hurriedly tied it over my eyes. Then I squeezed them shut and pinched the shell open. The briefest second had to be enough.

Sunlight exploded over the tower, and the ghosts screamed.

The carpet rose. I grabbed on to its threadbare fibers and hung my chin over the edge, watching as the Forgotten Isles disappeared one by one, like candles snuffed by the mist, until finally Lake Paduan was gone from sight.

# CHAPTER THIRTY-ONE

We flew until the next dawn, then landed in a clearing near the horses. The sky was a tumultuous gray, thick and pregnant with rain. But the young sun threaded through cracks in the clouds, and I basked in its watery light.

I had no idea where we were going, but I didn't care. As long as I was away from that wretched island, I was content. Not even the sun, whose rim grew darker and redder by the hour, worried me. I would far rather face Emperor Khanujin's wrath than the creatures of Lapzur.

Edan shifted into his human form, sprawled on the ground. His eyes fluttered open, and he bolted upright. "Are you—"

"I'm fine," I lied quickly.

I wasn't fine. What I had seen on that island still wrenched at my heart—Mama and Finlei and Sendo alive . . . I hated the demon for twisting my precious memories of them, and for re-opening a wound I had struggled so hard to close.

A little voice inside urged me to tell Edan about my encounter with the demon: I could still feel his claws on my neck. Yes, he had touched me. But nothing had happened. I'd defeated him—his terrible howl still rang in my ears, the sight of his charred bones burned into my memory.

"I'm fine," I repeated. I looked up at Edan and nestled my head in its special nook on his shoulder. I had so many questions for him, but the words wouldn't come out. Instead I said, "You were right. It was the hardest of the three."

"It's different for everyone," he said slowly. "What did you see?"

I rubbed my temple, my fingertips buzzing with heat and my body tingling. Edan would be overly dramatic about it if I told him, so I didn't. No doubt it was from exhaustion.

"Finlei and Sendo. And my mother. They were still alive, and we were all so happy. Baba was happy too, and he was still sewing. And Keton . . . he'd never fought in the war." My voice was choked with emotion, my throat raw and tight. "I didn't want to leave. I almost forgot . . . everything."

Edan wound a stray piece of my hair around his finger and tucked it behind my ear. "Even me?" he asked softly, but with a hint of mischief.

"Even you."

He touched his forehead to mine. "Then I'll have to insinuate myself into your life more deeply, Maia Tamarin."

That made me smile. "I suppose so."

Edan lifted his head and traced my smile. "There, my fierce tailor is back."

"No more *xitara*?"

"I thought you didn't like it."

"It grew on me," I admitted.

Edan's mouth set into a line; he was about to make a confession. "I didn't mean it as *little lamb*, you know. You were always too strong and brave for that."

"But—"

"In Old A'landan, it *does* mean *little lamb*. But in Narat, what I grew up speaking, it means . . . *brightest one*."

314

"Brightest one," I whispered. The words sang in my heart. "You called me that, even when we'd just met?"

"I meant it for your tailoring skills then," Edan teased. "And now for what you are to me." The playfulness on his face faded. "The whole time on Lapzur, I was afraid I'd never have a chance to tell you. I was afraid I'd lose you."

I wanted to hug Edan close and tell him he'd never lose me. But a sudden hollowness overcame me as I remembered the demon's touch.

Unaware, Edan placed a warm hand on my shoulder. "The magic of those islands is strong, but you did well. It was brilliant, using the sunlight to ward off the ghosts. If not for you, we might both still be there." He stroked my cheek. "And now you have the blood of stars."

To my relief, Edan didn't ask to see it. He simply kissed me on the nose, then left to tend the horses. When he wasn't looking, I took the demon's vial from my pocket. Its iridescent contents sparkled in my hand, the colors so rich and infinite it was as if I held a handful of diamonds under a rainbow. But when I held the vial by its stopper and did not touch the glass, everything dulled, becoming dark as slate. It could easily be mistaken for a bottle of ink, not a precious liquid capable of granting immense power. Not the blood of stars.

I closed my fist over the vial, the intensity of its light making my fingers glow.

The hardest part was over. Once we got to the Autumn Palace, I'd have to sew Amana's children into three dresses: a challenge that had once agonized me, but not anymore. Now I couldn't wait to thread the magic of the sun and moon and stars through my fingers, to sew it into three magnificent gowns worthy of the gods, and finally be done with this quest.

Edan returned with Opal and Rook, and Opal cantered toward me. I ran to hug my horse. She nuzzled me back, but she was more focused on the wildflowers brushing against my calves. As she bent her head to graze, I stroked her neck fondly. How good it felt to be back among the living.

I reached for my canteen and took a long sip. "It's very warm here."

"No, it's not," Edan said, frowning.

I exhaled sharply. The tingling in my body hadn't stopped. Now it rose, creeping up to my neck. How my skin burned there, so hot it hurt just to breathe. Dread curdled in my stomach. "I don't feel so well. I feel . . . feverish."

He touched my forehead and took my hands. My knuckles were pale, almost white. "Maia, look at me," he demanded. "What happened to you on the isle? Did you . . ."

"Not the ghosts." I wavered. "But the demon . . . touched me . . . just before I stabbed him."

Edan pushed aside my hair. Whatever he saw on my neck made his jaw tighten. "Damn it! We need to get you as far from the islands as possible." He pushed me toward the horses and lifted me onto Rook's saddle before I could protest.

Dazedly, I leaned forward. "I thought we were out of danger."

"Not far enough." He leapt behind me onto Rook. "It'll be best if we stay off the Great Spice Road. I know a shortcut to the Autumn Palace." He pressed two fingers to my pulse. "If you start to lose feeling in your limbs, tell me at once."

I gulped. "All right."

Thunder boomed above us, and a storm spilled from the sky

in a relentless shower. Edan tucked my head under his chin, but rain still streamed down my cheeks. I pressed my ear against his chest, listening to his heart beat steadily against the counterpoint of Rook's hooves.

We rode in the rain for hours. The horses galloped at a valiant pace, over hills and valleys, until we finally reached a canyon where the Leyang River curved through the walls like a ribbon. We had to stop for the horses to rest. Edan reined them into a shallow cavity in the rock, barely big enough to fit all of us. By the middle of the afternoon, the rain finally weakened, but I still heard it dribble down the cliffs.

"A-are my dresses in the trunks?" I asked, my lips moving even though I couldn't feel them. I shivered. "They c-c-can't g-get wet."

"They'll be all right." Edan cupped my chin, sweeping rain from the side of my nose with his thumb. His own face was slick with rain, but he didn't bother wiping the water from his eyes. "*You* will too. Just rest."

"I can't sleep," I said. "My body feels stiff. Hurts to move." My teeth chattered uncontrollably. "T-tell m-me what's h-h-happening to me."

Edan threw his cloak over me and I waited for him to explain. He seemed reluctant to.

"He has marked you," he said. "It means he has a piece of your soul . . . and until he chooses to devour it, he can follow you."

Even in my state, I knew that was very, very bad. "F-follow m-me where?"

"Anywhere," Edan said woodenly.

The tingling reached my lips. "I thought . . . I thought I'd killed him."

"Demons are difficult to kill." Edan wouldn't look at me.

"I blame myself. I thought I would be enough to distract Bandur. . . ." His voice trailed off, and he turned to me. "No harm will come to you. I swear it."

The horses neighed, and Edan straightened, his body tense and alert.

I didn't hear anything, other than that the rain had stopped. "What is it?"

A beat. Then Edan replied gravely, "We're not alone."

"B-b-bandits?"

Edan put a finger to his lips. "The shansen's men. They must have been tracking us."

"What do we do?"

Edan was already taking out his bow. "*You* do nothing. They're not after you." He threw a blanket over our trunks. "Go east. Get out of the forest as fast as you can. If anyone follows you, don't hesitate to use the dagger as I taught you."

I tried to protest, but Edan's mind was made up. He lifted me onto Opal. "Hiyah!" he shouted, slapping her back.

Opal burst into a gallop, and I clung to her neck, my pulse racing unsteadily. I was so weak I couldn't turn back to see Edan vanish into the canyon; simply holding on to my horse was a struggle enough.

I might never see him again, I realized. If he died, I wouldn't know for days, maybe more. He'd be alone, like my brothers.

Whatever sense I had left begged me to keep going—what use was I to Edan like this? I'd only get in his way. But my heart overruled my jumbled thoughts, and I pulled back on the reins. Opal reared, her forelegs pawing the air.

With a cry, I fell off her back onto the slick road. I sprang to my feet, my knees barely holding me up. My vision was blurred, my body sweating from the fever. Where the demon had touched my neck, it burned hotter than before, but I endured the pain. I had to, if I was going to help Edan.

"Shhh," I said, holding Opal's cheek. "Stay here. You'll be s-safe."

I didn't see anything, only an empty expanse of craggy, red-veined canyon. No soldiers. No mercenaries. No Edan.

My heart hammered as I reached for my dagger, then into my satchel for my scissors—just in case—stashing them in my boot. Edan had shown me how to slice a man's throat, how to stab a man in the back—I tried to recall the lessons, fervently hoping I wouldn't need them.

Armed, I rushed to catch up with Edan. The rain had stopped, but the ground was wet as I ran along the Leyang River.

I heard the soldiers before I saw them around a bend. Their horses snorted and neighed from across the river, and the soldiers' armor clattered. They marched in a line that curved along the canyon floor, their iron shields and swords a stark contrast to the lush greenery. I gritted my teeth when I picked out Vachir among the men, riding a white stallion.

Crouching behind a tree, I scanned the area for Edan. He wasn't far, and he was on my side of the river, directly facing them. I ran toward him.

"There's quite a heavy price on your head, Lord Enchanter!" Vachir yelled. "You, sir, are going to the shansen. We'll take the trunks, and the girl."

That last part made Edan's eyes darken with anger. No sane man would dare threaten an enchanter, but the shansen's men were recklessly confident.

Did they know that Edan's magic was weakened?

I joined Edan by the river. He took one step to the side, shielding me. But he kept his eyes trained across the river, on our enemies. He raised his bow.

"I thought enchanters didn't need weapons," one of the soldiers sneered.

"You do not want to fight against me," Edan said. "I suggest you be on your way."

Vachir waved his sword, and his men began to ford the river.

A few of them turned their attention to me, shouting lewd words and making kissing sounds. Edan's eyes blackened into cinder. He stiffened and raised his bow and fired three rapid shots. The men fell into the river, never to rise again.

Already the soldiers were on our side, rounding on Edan. Edan grabbed my wrist and pushed me away from the river. "Go!" he shouted.

I ran, but two soldiers sprang on me from behind the trees. My dagger was out, but the men surrounded me, laughing.

"Where you going, girl?"

I slashed at the one who'd spoken, but I missed his throat and scored his cheek instead. I made a long, jagged gash—one that wouldn't be pretty once it healed. The man growled. As he moved to strike me, I raised my dagger again. But the second soldier came from the side, caught my arm, and twisted it until I dropped my weapon.

His teeth were yellow and crooked, and his breath smelled of spoiled meat. Before I could scream, his cold, sweaty hand covered my lips. I saw the dirt and blood in his nails, and my knees buckled. He laughed in my face as he held his knife over my throat.

"Stop fooling around and just kill her," his friend spat, wiping his bleeding face on his sleeve. "She's not the one with a price on her head. The enchanter is."

"Do you know how long it's been since I've felt a woman?" My captor yanked my hair back, forcing my neck to crane upward. "Not so feisty now, are you?"

I began to feel afraid. Two men, both larger and stronger than me. No dagger. No Edan. The world swayed.

*No,* I snapped at myself. *You've come too far to give up now. Have to fight.*

Using both my hands, I grabbed the arm holding the knife at my throat and pulled it away from my neck. I twisted out of my attacker's grip, jabbing my elbow into his side and quickly grabbing the hilt of his knife, kneeing him in the groin until he let go.

His friend lunged after me, but I swung the knife at his face, scoring yet another cut. As he howled in pain, I dropped the knife, picked up my dagger, and made my escape.

The two men chased me, their footsteps thudding, growing dangerously closer. I ignored their shouts, didn't look back. Then an arrow zinged past me, followed by a scream from one of the soldiers on my trail.

When I looked up, there Edan was, storming toward me with his bow raised. The soldier I'd cut tried to turn back and run away, but he was the next to fall. His body slumped into the dirt.

I couldn't have been more than twenty paces from Edan when someone grabbed me from behind. His grip was strong enough to bruise my ribs, and he pressed his sword against my throat. "Put down your weapon, enchanter. You're outnumbered."

I recognized the voice. Vachir.

"Let her go," Edan said, lifting his bow.

Vachir spat at Edan's feet. "Make me. If you had any powers, you would have used them already."

Edan gritted his teeth. It was true—he had almost no magic left. There was no way for us to escape.

I clawed my nails into Vachir's arm, smashed my heel into his foot, but his skin was tough as leather and he only held me tighter.

"Let her go," Edan repeated. "This is my last warning."

The other soldiers arrived. Too many to fight. They circled us until we were completely surrounded, and they laughed, their bows and swords raised at Edan's head.

Edan still wouldn't lower his weapon.

Vachir's blade pressed deeper into my skin, and I squeezed my eyes shut. *This is not how I die—my throat slit by a Balardan!*

My fingers slid slowly toward my sash, clasping my scissors.

Behind me, Vachir's body tensed. He craned his neck to look at the sky.

A tide of clouds had appeared from nowhere, casting a great shadow upon us. Lightning crackled, and thunder broke. The ground trembled, and several of the soldiers fell to their knees. I raised my scissors and blindly stabbed Vachir in the thigh.

As he hollered in pain, I twisted out of his arms.

A pile of dead soldiers surrounded Edan, but he was running out of arrows. Vachir and his remaining men charged for us. Then the earth bucked beneath us, and the river began to rise.

"Are you doing that?" I shouted, picking up my dagger.

"No." Edan pulled my hand, urging me to climb the rocks ahead. "They're coming."

"Who?" My voice trembled.

Instead of answering, Edan said, "Get to higher ground."

I followed him, scrambling up the steep slope away from the

river. The world spun, and with each step my head felt lighter and lighter, while my skin burned hotter. But I kept my eyes open and glanced below us. I soon wished I hadn't looked.

Ghosts. I'd thought they were confined to Lake Paduan, but I was wrong.

A sharp shiver raced up my spine. I tugged on Edan's sleeve, unable to speak.

He pulled me forward. "Don't look. Keep going."

I couldn't tear my gaze away from the ghosts. I counted dozens, maybe a hundred. Most took the shape of animals—bears, foxes, and wolves, all with red eyes. But here they did not screech or even whisper; they sailed across the land with eerie silence, so that only the soldiers' screams could be heard. The men slashed at the beasts with their swords and then shouted when there was no blood. "Magic!" they cried. "Ghosts!" These words were the last they uttered before the ghosts bared their teeth and encircled the men, folding over them—until there were no more cries.

One creature stood out from the rest. He was distressingly familiar, and more powerful than all the ghosts combined.

*Bandur.* The demon who had taken Sendo's form in the Thief's Tower. The one who had nearly killed me. He was horrible to look at in the light of the sun. All smoke and shadow, his eyes dark as dead blood. He wore armor today, and his amulet hung on his neck.

Bandur caught me staring, and with a smile, he vanished from the battle. Knowing I'd made a mistake, I hurried after Edan. Too late. I screamed when Bandur materialized, breaking Edan and me apart.

"You!" I cried. "I . . . I killed you!"

"Didn't you listen to your Lord Enchanter?" Bandur

mocked. "You can't kill one who's already dead, girl. Though I applaud you for trying. I do enjoy a good chase, and it has been too long since I've been able to leave that accursed island. Unfortunately, it will cost you."

The dagger at my side trembled. Edan was calling it to him. It flew to his hand, then shuddered and shook—as if confused.

"Silence!" Bandur shouted. His mouth formed a cruel smile as Edan's weapon clattered to the ground. "Your power is weak, Edan. You shouldn't be so far from your master."

Edan picked up his dagger. "You cannot have her."

The demon's terrible red eyes turned to consider me. In the wicked gleam of his pupils, I saw a reflection of the claw marks on my neck. "She is marked. You are a fool to open your heart while under your oath. She will not be free of me unless I will it."

"Then tell me what you want. I shall pay it."

"No!" I shouted. "Edan!"

The demon raised a hand to silence me. A low groan escaped my mouth, but my tongue no longer moved—I was frozen in place.

"Do not fancy that you have something I want, Edan," continued Bandur. "You knew the price you would pay when you drank the blood of stars. You gave your freedom, and it will not be yours again—not in the girl's lifetime. There is nothing you can give me while you are under oath. Unless . . ." Bandur retracted his claws. "I doubt you would sacrifice so much for a mere girl."

"She is not a mere girl," Edan spat. "I love her."

"But she is free, and you are under oath."

Edan blocked me with raised arms. "I am of more value to you, even under oath."

324

"Are you, now, Edan?" Bandur taunted. His hollow eyes bored into me. "I can sense magic in her. It is still weak, but as you said earlier, she is no *mere* girl."

"Tell me what you want in exchange for releasing her, and I will do it—oath or not."

"You know what I want, enchanter," Bandur said harshly. "I grow tired of being a guardian. You will take my place."

*No!* I wanted to shout.

But Edan nodded. Slowly. "Give me a year," he said, "to return Maia safely to the palace and see that peace is established under Emperor Khanujin—"

"You have until the red sun, Edan," Bandur interrupted. "Take the girl home, then return to the Isles of Lapzur before sunset. If you run from this debt, the consequences will be great. I will come for her and tear her apart, scattering her remains across Lake Paduan so she lives the rest of eternity broken. She will never leave the island."

"I understand," Edan said unflinchingly. "The red sun, then. Upon my honor and sigil as a lord enchanter, you have my word."

"Fine," Bandur rasped. If a demon could be giddy, he was so. His claws pierced the tree behind me. It withered, the bark graying and the leaves wilting brown into dust. "You have accepted. We are done."

"We are done," Edan echoed.

Bandur grasped his amulet and, along with his army of ghosts, vanished. The forest rustled again with life, and but for Vachir's fallen men, it was as if Bandur's shadow had never touched it.

My fever was gone, but I was shaking, rocking back and forth, hugging my arms to my chest.

"What did you do?" I whispered.

"Nothing I wasn't prepared to," he said. "Let's go."

I grabbed his sleeve. "Edan, you're hurt," I said, pointing at his wounds.

"Let's deal with it later. I want to get out of this damned place first."

Mutely, I nodded. We collected the horses and the trunks and set off for the Autumn Palace. My heart was heavy, and it only grew heavier as we rode, for Edan didn't speak to me. Rain pattered down, slicking back his black hair. His eyes were normal now—blue as the sea. But he held his reins so tightly his knuckles were white.

"Bandur . . . was your teacher, wasn't he?" I asked finally. "The one who became a demon."

At first I thought he hadn't heard me, he was so slow to reply. "Yes."

I leaned over to touch Edan's arm. My throat grew thick with emotion, and I swallowed. "How did he—"

"There are many types of demons, Maia. Some are born, or cursed. Not all begin as men or enchanters or even as animals. But guardians such as Bandur are among the strongest of demons and are always enchanters who have broken their oaths. Bandur killed the man he was sworn to serve—the man who owned his amulet. As punishment, he was forced to become the guardian of the Forgotten Isles for all eternity. Or until another took his place."

"And now you will become the next guardian of the islands," I whispered.

Edan gave a sad laugh at my horror. "Don't worry yourself over it, *xitara*." He kissed my cheek so softly I almost didn't feel it. "I would far rather endure this fate than allow Bandur to possess your soul."

A part of me shattered. My gut twisted and churned, and I couldn't hold in my emotions. I reined in Opal and threw my arms around Edan's neck. "You stupid man!" I cried. I held his cheeks and drew him close so our foreheads touched. "Promise me now we'll find some way to fight this. Promise me you aren't going to turn into a demon . . . like Bandur."

Edan pushed me away gently. "I love you, Maia. My life has been long, so let me do something good for you. You will become the greatest tailor in A'landi, and you will find some lucky boy to marry—"

"I won't."

"Be sensible," he said, squeezing my hands. "I cannot give you a future. You will forget me. I can make that happen."

I jerked my hands away from him, stung. "Don't you dare!" A sob wracked me, and my chest throbbed. Edan drew me to him and held me tight, kissing my cheek, then my neck.

"Don't touch me," I said, twisting out of his arms. I needed air. I needed to be away from Edan. "What about all your promises?" I couldn't bring myself to speak—of the shop we'd open together by the ocean, of waking every morning to the sound of Edan's laugh, of sewing to the song of his flute, of the towers of books strewn beside my looms and frames as I grew old with him. My mouth went dry, the loss of a dream I'd finally dared to hope for swelling in my throat.

I was hurt and angry—at myself and Edan and Lady Sarnai and Emperor Khanujin. I wanted to reach into my trunk and rip Lady Sarnai's dresses to shreds. They were the cause of everything—if I hadn't gone on this journey to make them, none of this would have happened.

Now Edan was condemned to be a demon.

All because of me.

Dusk fell, and Edan the hawk tried to perch on my shoulder a few times, but I waved him away until he disappeared. I didn't look back to wonder where he was.

I held in another sob. My body ached, and my eyes were raw from weeping. I was so tired. From the raid, from Bandur, from being so close to the stars.

From knowing that I was about to lose the boy I loved.

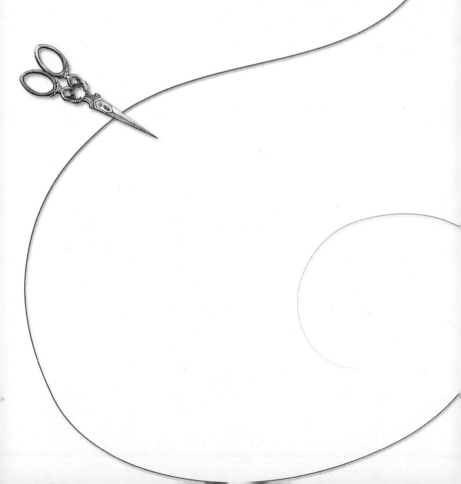

PART THREE

# THE OATH

# CHAPTER THIRTY-TWO

Once we were out of the canyon, Edan and I traveled for days without seeing any signs of civilization, until we finally came upon a monastery. Wedged between two great willow trees, it had a roof whose edges curled out like wings and a bronze bell that rang from a pillared courtyard by the entrance.

I didn't know whether to be hopeful for a warm meal and bed that night or anxious that we would have to deal with company. Edan and I had been riding in silence, him behind me, keeping a careful distance. Every time I stole a glimpse at him, his arms were folded over his lap, hands only moving to push his dark, unruly curls out of his eyes. I wished he would at least whistle or hum, but he didn't dare. Even his shadow didn't touch mine.

"You should get a good night's rest," he said, his voice crackly from disuse. "The monks will take you in."

I inhaled. The air was crisp, fragrant with pine and dew, and the shadows drifted west as the world slowly tilted toward night. "What about you?"

"Magic and religion have been at odds for centuries. I doubt a monastery would welcome me with open arms."

"I'm not going in if you aren't."

Edan overlooked my petulance. "Does that mean you want me to go in with you?"

I wouldn't answer, and he reined Rook toward the monastery.

We left the horses outside. There was a modest stables next to the grounds, well supplied with hay and water for Opal and Rook. Edan hid our weapons under a bush nearby.

I saw the monks before we reached the gates, outside sweeping the monastery's wide stone steps. Their heads were shaved, and they wore plain muslin cloaks over their robes. They greeted us with polite bows, but Edan was right—the senior monk eyed him suspiciously. Still, he did not turn us away.

We left our shoes outside, and one of the younger monks brought us water to wash our feet. A thread of saffron floated in the wooden bowl, scenting the air. I dipped my toes, shivering as the cool water washed over my skin.

Edan tried reaching for my hand, but I shoved his away. I saw his jaw stiffen, his mouth drawing in a tight, cautious line, and the twinge in my heart sharpened. I was hurting him, but I couldn't help it. Deep down, I yearned to have his arms around me, to have his warm breath touch my hair and his heart beat against mine. But every time Edan's promise to Bandur bubbled up in my memory, a flare of anger burned deep in me.

Going with Bandur had been *my* choice to make, not Edan's. *Mine.*

I pursed my lips tight, refusing to look at him. Instead, I stared at the sun. I couldn't look for much longer than a blink, but still I saw the ever-widening red tinge in its crown. Two weeks left of making Lady Sarnai's damned dresses. They were the reason everything had gone wrong.

The senior monk, whom I'd heard the others call Ci'an, approached. He was very old, his frame thin and shrunken, but his eyes were sharp. "We welcome guests to the monastery as long as they make themselves useful during their stay. Can you cook?"

"I can," I admitted. "But I am better with the needle."

This pleased the old monk. Unlike the others, he wore a faded burgundy sash, which was frayed at the ends. "Then you'll help with mending." He cautiously addressed Edan. "And you?"

"I can help with the horses," Edan said curtly.

The old monk grunted, then motioned for us to follow him into the monastery and to our rooms. The chambers we passed were sparsely furnished, save for several altars and a smattering of statues, mostly of Amana and Nandun, the beggar god who gave away his wealth to the poor.

"We are an enclave of men here," Ci'an said, addressing Edan. "Should you wish to bathe, you are welcome to. However, we ask that your wife wait until nightfall."

I stiffened. Of course I'd known Edan and I would have to pose as husband and wife to stay here, but hearing it pained me—because now I knew it would never be true.

"I understand," said Edan.

Edan was wise enough to retreat to the stables and give me time alone. Another monk delivered a change of robes, and my clothes were taken to be washed.

I tucked my scissors into my sash and started on the mending I'd promised to do. There were holes to patch and sleeves to shorten, but sewing had always been as easy as breathing for me. I finished so quickly that when I returned the clothes, the monk in charge balked, hardly able to believe it.

Wasting no time, I dipped into my trunk for the moonlight dress and sat cross-legged on my cot to sew. Of the three dresses, this one had the most layers: a jacket, a bodice, a belted skirt, and a shawl. It was also the most faithful to A'landan fashion, though I'd taken liberties with the cut. I worked on the jacket now, assembling its pieces and sewing the sleeves into place.

The looming deadline took my mind off Edan and Bandur's curse. A distraction I sorely needed. Little by little, I let my work fill my heart, let myself revel in the moonlight dress as it came together. I let myself remember how much I loved my craft, and how much pride I took in it.

When daylight was fading, someone knocked on my door. Edan.

He closed the door behind him. "Monasteries haven't changed much in a few hundred years. All the monks still do is hum and pray. The smells have gotten better, though." He tried to smile. "I am grateful to whichever god insists that everyone bathes twice a day and sweeps the halls at dawn and dusk."

He was trying to amuse me, but it felt like we were strangers again.

"They've been very kind," I said stiffly.

"To you. And for that I am grateful."

"Have you always disliked monks so?"

He shrugged.

I turned away and started embroidering gold on the hem of Lady Sarnai's dress.

Edan knew I was ignoring him. He let me, for a while. Then he spoke. "I was raised in a monastery," he said at last. "The gods worshipped there were different, but being here . . . still brings back memories."

How little I knew about Edan's past! Even though I wanted to ignore him, I was still curious. "Where?"

"Nelronat," he said. "It was a city thousands of miles from

here. It doesn't exist anymore. Barbarians destroyed it centuries ago."

I was quiet. I'd never heard of Nelronat.

"After my mother died in childbirth," Edan continued, "my father was left to raise seven sons alone. He hated me. Blamed me for my mother's death, and it didn't help that I was a scrawny boy who preferred to read rather than herd the cattle."

The sadness in his voice made my insides melt, but I wouldn't look up. I focused on knotting a stitch into place so I could change to a new color of thread.

"My father took me on a trip one day. He said he was going to put me in school, since I was so inclined toward reading. It wasn't a lie . . . not really. I was so happy."

"He left you," I said, looking up now.

"At a monastery a four days' journey from our farm. I tried many times, but I could never find my way home. The monks I grew up with were different from the ones here. Not generous and kind. And the gods we worshipped were harsh and unforgiving.

"I stayed with them for years, until soldiers overran the temple and I was deemed old enough to fight for their cause. I was barely eleven." He chuckled, though the laugh was dry of humor. "Six months into soldiering, my talent for magic was discovered. That led to me serving in more wars, but more as a weapon than a boy . . . until my first teacher found me." He stopped, as if he heard something in the distance. "You should go down. Dinner is ready."

I set down my needle. "What about you? You're going to change."

"Just tell the monks I wanted to rest," he said solemnly.

"Should I bring you dinner?"

He managed a grin. "I'll be out hunting. But I would be grateful if you left a window open for me."

"Will you be able to find your way back?"

His grin widened, and I realized I'd shown him a sign that I still cared. "To you, always."

His words made my heart unsteady, and I stiffened, then nodded and left.

Dinner consisted of boiled lettuce and carrots harvested from the garden, with a bowl of rice with sesame seeds. No one ate with me—the monks ate only in the morning, it appeared. But a few of the younger ones sat with me and sipped soy milk from wooden bowls.

When dinner was finished, I washed and dried my dish; then I sought out Ci'an. "You said I could take a bath once the sun had set."

"There's a spring past the washhouse you may use," he told me. "Walk with me. I'll take you there." As I followed him out of the monastery, he said, "Your husband did not wish to partake of dinner?"

"He wanted to . . . to rest," I said, staring at my hands. The guilt of lying to a monk made me unable to look him in the eye.

"I see," Ci'an said. The elderly monk walked slowly, for it was dark and there were many steps in the garden.

"Monks are taught to seek peace," Ci'an said, breaking the silence, "but even my brothers bicker with one another from time to time. Yet no matter how great their discord, they come to remember that harmony among them is greater."

I swallowed. Ci'an must have sensed that Edan and I had quarreled.

"You care much for your husband," he went on. "That is easy for anyone to see. But he cares for you more."

I frowned. "That isn't—"

"True love is selfless," the old man interrupted. "And I can see you are very young."

I kept quiet and watched my step. We had passed the wash-house, and the stone path we'd been following had disappeared.

"Your husband carries a heavy burden. I can see it in his eyes. He is not the first of his kind to pass through these walls."

I inhaled sharply. "Sir?"

"This monastery is a thousand years old," Ci'an said. "Many enchanters have come for the solitude and peace it offers, particularly before taking their oath. Your companion is the first I've met . . . the first to come here *after* taking his oath."

"I thought monasteries did not welcome enchanters."

The monk chuckled. "The rift between religion and magic *has* grown. But I was not always a monk, and I have seen many things the younger ones have not. Many things they will never see.

"In my time, we called the enchanters gatekeepers, because they guarded magic from the rest of us. It is a heavy responsibility. Respected even by men of religion. To this day, I still hold that respect."

Ci'an took my arm to lead me. "One thing I have never seen is an enchanter in love. They aren't supposed to love, you know. In some ways, they are taught to be like monks—compassionate and selfless. Only they love no one, and we love all. Your enchanter is different."

A lump hardened in my throat. "He's served a long time," I said, staring at the ground.

"So he has," Ci'an said. "Many wish for such power for themselves, but I do not envy his path. The toll is heavy."

I said nothing. I didn't want to talk about Edan. It hurt too much to think about his promise to Bandur, knowing there was nothing I could do about it.

Finally, we arrived at the spring. The young moon illuminated a clear pool before me, as well as three statues of Amana standing on the banks. Her eyes were closed in all, her hands clasped together and lifted toward the sky.

"Long ago, these waters were sacred to the priestesses of the mother goddess," Ci'an explained. "Some still come once a year, on the ninth day of the ninth month, to see the stars form a bridge between the sun and moon. You've only just missed it."

"I'm aware of that," I whispered, staring at the statues. The two wearing the sun and moon glittered under the silver moonlight, but shadows eclipsed the statue wearing the blood of stars.

"As a seamstress, Amana's dresses must fascinate you," Ci'an said.

"I always thought they were a myth," I replied, "as far from us as the gods were. But that was before I believed in magic. Now that I've seen what it can do, I'm no longer sure that the boundary between Heaven and earth is as solid as I believed." I thought of Bandur and the ghosts. "What if there are no gods? What if there is only magic, only enchanters and demons and ghosts?"

"You must keep your faith," said Ci'an. "The gods watch over us, but unlike the spirits of this realm, they do not interfere in our lives. Not unless we anger them greatly, or impress them."

"Yes," I murmured. "When Amana forgave the god of thieves, she returned light to the world, but only for half the day. She gave us night."

"She was still angry with him," Ci'an said. "Deservedly so. But you forget the tailor who actually made the dresses for the god of thieves. What few know is that Amana rewarded him with a gift."

"What gift is that?"

"It's said that she gave him a pair of scissors," Ci'an replied. "Enchanted to imbue their owner with a piece of her power."

I went very still.

"No one's ever seen them, but I imagine they must still exist, passed from generation to generation."

I held in a deep breath and reached into my sash, where my enchanted scissors rested. My fingers traced the design engraved on the shanks—of the sun and moon. These had to be the scissors Amana had given the tailor.

Did that mean the tailor's family was my own? Did that explain why magic flowed in me? It had to. And why only I could use the scissors.

Why Bandur had said I was more special than I looked.

"What if someone succeeded in making Amana's dresses?" I said in a rush. "Would the mother goddess interfere?"

"Many have tried to make them, lured by the legend that Amana would grant a wish to any who succeeded."

"Is it true?"

"I'd imagine that if someone *did* succeed in making Amana's dresses . . . such a feat might incur her wrath more than her blessing." Seeing my stricken expression, Ci'an smiled. "Then again, I would also wager that tale was made up by priests of Amana's children to keep their temples prosperous and well visited."

"I see," I said quietly.

"Speak to her here," Ci'an said, gesturing at the spring. "Amana is always listening, but perhaps here, among her children, she will listen more carefully." He patted my shoulder before leaving. "Make peace with your enchanter. He loves you very much."

Alone, I stood at the edge of the pool a long time, listening to the trees and the wind. I understood now why so many revered Amana's dresses, why some called them her greatest legacy. Because of them, she gave us the world as we knew it. Day after day and night after night, she spun the dawn and unraveled the dusk.

And somehow, I was closer to that legacy than I had ever dared dream.

Slowly, I slipped off my robes and stepped into the spring. The water was mild, and fish tickled my feet. Then I held my breath and sank down until I was fully submerged, coming up for air only at the last moment with a quiet gasp.

The crescent moon shone above me, a broken pearl in the black sea of night.

I reached into the pile of my robes and took out my scissors, holding them in my hands as if in offering. "Amana," I whispered, "Amana, I thank you for this gift you have bestowed upon my family. And I pray for your forgiveness. If you do not wish me to make the dresses, I will stop. But please, please do not punish Edan for my foolishness. Please let there be a way to free him from Bandur."

I waited a long time. But, as I feared, Amana did not answer.

. . .

Dawn arrived, with no sign of Edan. I kept expecting to see his shadow glide across the walls, the last caress of night on his wings as he soared through the window.

I'd never worried about Edan as a hawk before. But now I

couldn't stop—what if he was flying over a lake when dawn broke? He couldn't swim. He would drown!

Or what if a hunter had shot him? Or one of the shansen's men, perhaps—did they know what Edan became at night?

I sat on my bed, untangling knots in my hair with my fingers. It had grown long during my journey. I'd have to cut it soon, before we returned to the Autumn Palace. Then again, before the war, it had been tradition for men to wear their hair long.

I touched the ends of my hair. Would the emperor let me remain as the imperial tailor after I finished the three dresses . . . and after Edan left me?

These questions were painful, sharpening the loneliness already aching inside me. Getting up, I moved to the small table in my room and started a letter to Baba and Keton. *My journey is nearly over,* I wrote. *I'll soon be in the Autumn Palace.*

My words felt stiff and distant, yet no matter how I tried, I couldn't muster a lighthearted tone. My own heart was too heavy.

*And Maia—ninety-five steps,* I finished. *I hope I'll be home to walk with you soon.*

I set down my brush to dry and covered the inkpot. As I folded my letter, the air shifted.

"Morning," Edan's voice greeted me from the door.

I hadn't heard him come in. "Where were you?"

His hair was wet, and his monk's robes flowed loosely on his thin form. He raked a hand through his hair, slicking it back. The effect made him look impossibly young. "I promised to help with the horses. So I did."

I wanted to tell him what I'd learned about my scissors. But seeing how awkward he was there, by the door, I bit my lip. "Are you tired? You usually sleep as soon as you turn back."

"I'm fine."

The ensuing silence between us was heavy. Edan stayed at the door, and he gestured at the dress I was working on. It lay on the other side of my bed.

"It's beautiful," he said. "Lady Sarnai would be a fool not to appreciate it."

I could hear the monks chanting. I didn't understand the words, but they were rhythmic and steady, blurring together into a deep hypnotic drone.

"Did you have to chant every day?" I murmured. "When you lived in a monastery?"

"Yes," Edan said. His voice lifted with cautious hope. "Every day."

"I could get used to a monk's life," I said. "It's not so different from a tailor's. Sewing all day, chanting all day—I used to count my stitches out loud when I was a girl."

"You'd hate it." Edan leaned against the frame of the door. "You don't belong here, chained to a monastery. You should see the world."

My breath caught in my throat. I walked to him. "Edan . . ."

"I know you're angry at me," he said. "And you have a right to be. But I love you, Maia."

I swallowed. How unfair it was, that our time together was so short. That soon I would never see him again.

"I love you, too," I whispered, touching his cheek. It hurt to speak any more loudly—my voice was hoarse with emotion. "And I'll have you. The sun and moon only see each other one day out of the entire year. Even if it's an hour or a day—I'd rather be with you for that time than not at all."

A light brightened Edan's face. He didn't smile, yet somehow he looked happier than in all the months I'd known him. "May I kiss you?" he whispered.

"You may."

He touched my chin, tilting it up, but I was already on my toes. My mouth drifted forward, my eyes half closed.

Edan laughed softly. "Eager, aren't we? Then you shouldn't have denied me so long."

Slowly, he traced his fingers down my neck to my collarbone. His touch made me shiver, and my skin tingled as he traced back up my neck and around my lips. Then, when I was about to protest that he was tormenting me, he lifted me up.

I crushed my mouth against his, wrapping my arms around his neck and my legs around his hips. His kisses moved to my cheeks, my neck, my breasts, back to my lips. Passionate, then tender. Then passionate again, as if we couldn't make up our minds. As if we knew our lips would be bruised tomorrow, but we would laugh about it.

It was so easy to forget—and I felt myself slipping into the illusion that everything was fine.

I pushed his hair out of his eyes and cupped his chin. "Let me come to Lake Paduan with you."

Edan was still catching his breath.

"There has to be a way to defeat Bandur," I said slowly. "That amulet he wears—I took it from him when I was on the Thief's Tower, and that seemed to weaken him. Maybe if we can destroy it, you'll be free of him."

"A demon's amulet is already broken," Edan said. He pressed my back against the wall. "Destroying it won't kill Bandur, nor will it weaken him."

"But I saw—"

Edan put two fingers to my lips. "Bandur is cunning," he said. "He wanted to trick you into thinking he had a weakness so you would let down your guard—then he could mark you."

I fell silent, knowing that he was right. "I'm still coming with you. My mind is made up."

Edan sighed. "Maia, you know the isles abound with ghosts and demons. Even if you were safe from them, I won't be the same."

"Do you think I care?"

"You should," he said darkly. "I'll be a demon."

"Then I'll become one too. A ghost, demon—whatever the isles want of me. You don't have to be alone."

"That is the most foolish thing I've ever heard in my life," said Edan sharply. "And I beg you never to repeat it."

My shoulders started to slump, but I straightened. "My scissors are from Amana," I said fiercely. "They're from the legend of the god of thieves. Did you know that?"

"I suspected—"

"That means I'm part legend myself," I said over him. "Maybe even part enchanter. There is magic in me, so let me help you."

Edan pressed his lips tightly together. "There's no arguing with you, is there?"

"I'm the brightest one, remember? You said so yourself."

He laughed and kissed me again, ever so tenderly. Then he held me—as he had when we lived under the invisible morning stars—until the day washed into night.

I knew then that we were like two pieces of cloth, sewn together for life. Our stitches couldn't be undone.

I wouldn't let them.

# CHAPTER THIRTY-THREE

We arrived within sight of the Autumn Palace five days before the red sun. I didn't want to count the days until Edan surrendered himself to Bandur, but I couldn't help it. Too frequently I glanced up at the sky, watching the red slowly bleeding into the sun's crown. Only at night, when darkness swallowed the sun, could I put it out of my mind.

I could feel the magic rippling in the fibers of my dresses—more and more now, as they approached completion. Maybe I imagined it, but sometimes when the walnuts carrying the light of the moon and sun were nearby, the dresses sang to me. It was a soft, quiet song—like the hum of a peaceful brook. Edan couldn't hear it, but the song beckoned to me, as if imploring me to finish my task.

I craned my neck to study the Autumn Palace. It sat atop a hill, surrounded by trees that were sleeved with red, gold, and orange leaves. From where I stood, it looked alight with fire.

"You don't seem eager to go back," Edan half teased. "I'm sure Ammi will have plenty of cookies and cakes waiting for you in the kitchen. That's something to look forward to."

I said nothing, only sighed and began twisting my hair onto the crown of my head.

Edan drew closer. "Don't forget this," he said, passing me a pebble to put in my shoe. I'd left Keton's cane in the Summer Palace.

It had been so long since I had to pretend to be a boy, I wasn't sure I could do it again.

I nodded silently, but my face must have shown my anxiety, for Edan held my cheek in his hand. "Everything will be fine."

"Will it?" A hard lump rose in my throat, making it painful to speak.

Edan kissed me, so long and deep that even after he let go, my lips burned.

"It will," he whispered. "I'll make it so."

I knew he was trying to make me feel better. But nothing could erase the pain of his departure.

Numbly, I said, "When will you leave for Lapzur?"

"The morning of the red sun. I won't go until you finish the dresses. Not until I see that you are safe."

His words did nothing to comfort me. I wiped the corner of my eye with my knuckle. "I told you I'm coming with you. . . . I won't have you go alone." I swallowed the lump in my throat.

He held me and thumbed off the tears falling down my cheeks. "Do you recall when I healed your hand?" he said quietly. "You said you wanted to repay me."

It felt so long ago. I lifted myself from his arms. "Yes."

"I want you to do something for me."

I didn't like the tentativeness in his voice. "I'm listening."

"When I leave for Lapzur," Edan said slowly, "I want you to go home to your family and give them this." He opened his palm, revealing a fourth walnut no different from the ones I had used to trap sunlight and moonlight.

"A gift for your father and your brother," he said. "It has

a drop of Niwa spider blood, among other things—it'll bring some happiness back to your family."

My breath grew ragged. "Edan—"

"Put it in their tea," he interrupted. "And yours. It'll make you sleep. And when you wake, you'll be happy too."

I frowned, unable to read his dark, impenetrable eyes. "No magic tea is going to make me happy, Edan. Not without you."

"Please." He touched my lips. "Trust me."

I tucked my head under his chin and inhaled. But I made no promise.

• • •

It was nearly dusk when we reached the Autumn Palace. The moonrise cast a glow on the red and orange leaves, and I couldn't help but feel we were like moths inside a lantern. Trapped.

I had wondered if we would arrive before Edan changed. I could tell he was about to—the yellow in his eyes grew brighter as the moon overthrew the sun. But as soon as we reached the palace gates, the glow in his eyes dimmed.

"Tell His Majesty that his Lord Enchanter and imperial tailor have returned," Edan commanded the guard.

The great red gates before us creaked open, and we dismounted. Edan took a deep breath. Suddenly he looked fuller, taller.

He opened his palm, and there was a blue wildflower for me, like the ones he'd given me in the Mountains of the Moon. "This one won't wither."

I wouldn't take it. "I like the old ones," I replied. I'd pressed them in my sketchbook.

Edan nodded mutely, and the flower disappeared. The gates were open wide enough now for me to see the gardens inside. Shadows flickered. The last few moments Edan and I were free.

"I'll try to see you whenever I can," he said. "I can't promise it'll be often. Khanujin won't be pleased that I've been gone so long. He'll keep me by his side."

Before I could reply, Minister Lorsa arrived to escort us into the Autumn Palace. From his expression of surprise, I knew he'd expected me to fail.

I wished I had.

Lorsa folded his arms, his bright blue sleeves billowing behind him as he set off at a brisk pace. It was like that first day I'd arrived at the Summer Palace. Lorsa's clothes were the same, and the same jade pendant and giant red tassel swung from his sash. Only this time, I didn't try to keep up with him. This time, I hobbled and took my time, considering it a small victory whenever Lorsa stopped to wait for me.

I immediately hated the Autumn Palace. I missed the gold roofs and vermillion columns of the Summer Palace, the brilliant gardens and the smell of jasmine and plum blossoms. Yes, the trees here burned a lurid riot of colors even in lantern light, and the stone floors were awash with golden leaves, freshly fallen—but the air smelled stale, like damp ink. There were no dragonflies or butterflies, no larks or swallows. Only a thin mist that cloaked the earth, as if readying it for a deep, long sleep.

To my surprise, we saw Lady Sarnai in one of the gardens. She betrayed no reaction when she noticed us, but she rose, her skirts blooming as she stood, and stared at something far off in the corner—as if she, too, would rather be anywhere but here.

Minister Lorsa ushered us into the emperor's private chambers. The doors were painted with red-eyed lions that made me shudder and think of Bandur. Inside, Emperor Khanujin awaited us, a deep blue veil obscuring his face. Once Lorsa had left, he lifted it.

Edan had told me that the emperor relied on his magic to enhance his appearance, but still it shocked me how different he looked now. The real emperor was unimposing, shorter and less muscular than I remembered, with a weak mouth and small, merciless black eyes.

Trying not to stare at him, I fell to my knees as Edan bowed at my side.

"I should have you hanged, Lord Enchanter," Emperor Khanujin said through his teeth. "You left without my permission."

"I accept the consequences of my actions, Your Majesty," said Edan. "I thought it necessary to aid the imperial tailor, to ensure your marriage and peace for A'landi."

"You thought leaving me would be wise?" The emperor threw his teacup to the ground. It shattered at Edan's feet. "Wise for the shansen to know you were away? To give him the opportunity to hunt you?"

"If he did so, he failed."

Emperor Khanujin sniffed, slightly mollified. He drummed his fingers on the arm of his wooden chair, hardly a throne. His nails were long and uncut; they made a clacking sound that set me on edge. "Was your journey successful?"

"It was, Your Majesty."

"Then at least your absence wasn't for naught. I wonder, how should I punish you, Lord Enchanter? After all, there is nothing you fear, to my knowledge. And I cannot have you executed for your disobedience, since I need you at my side."

Edan was silent.

Emperor Khanujin touched the amulet pinned to his robe.

"I suppose your very existence is punishment enough. You, a vessel of such power at my command."

Edan didn't flinch, but I did. My fists curled at my sides, and I had to bite my cheek to keep from lashing out at the emperor.

"Master Tamarin, you have work to do. Leave us."

I glanced at Edan, who gave an almost imperceptible lift of his chin. A sign to obey.

The emperor knew my leg wasn't truly lame, but I made a show of struggling to get up from my knees anyway. I bowed to him. "May you live ten thousand years, Your Majesty," I said, the familiar words now foreign on my tongue.

Then I left, to return to the life I'd once dreamed of living. What I wouldn't have given for it to have stayed a dream.

• • •

My satchel and trunk were already in my new quarters. I opened my trunk to air out my dresses. Seeing them comforted me. I might be back in the palace, but I wouldn't forget my adventures outside. Wouldn't forget the battles Edan and I had fought, the magic I'd seen.

These dresses would always remind me.

A plate of almond cookies sat on my cutting table. No note accompanied the treat, but I knew it was from Ammi. *Welcome back!* I could hear her exclaiming.

Remembering my one friend in the palace cheered me, and I gobbled the cookies quickly, filling my empty stomach. Just after I set down the plate and started to unfold my dresses, the door to my chambers swung open.

"Her Highness, Lady Sarnai, honors you with her presence!" a voice shouted from outside.

Lady Sarnai entered. Her furrowed brow and pursed lips made it clear she wasn't pleased I had returned alive, but the shansen's daughter no longer frightened me. I grabbed my cane and bowed.

"The red sun draws near," she said in lieu of a greeting. The reminder pained me, though she couldn't know why.

"I'm nearly finished, Your Highness."

"So you found them?" she said hollowly. "Amana's children?"

"Yes, Your Highness."

Lady Sarnai held a fan, as always, but she twisted it in her hands, so hard I thought it must break. When she spoke next, her voice was tight. "Show me what you've done."

I knelt by my trunk, glad I had taken the time to clean it of sand and dirt. One by one I carefully took out my three dresses.

Lady Sarnai snatched the first one from me, lifting it by the sleeves to view.

"That is to be the gown of the moon," I said. "I haven't sewn in the moonlight yet."

Even without its magical element in place, the dress was breathtaking. I could tell from Lady Sarnai's silence that I had created something otherworldly.

The sleeves were long and wide and, when held up, curved like the elegant base of a lute. White-gold floss sparkled from the cuffs and the cross-collar, which I'd painstakingly embroidered with tiny flowers and clouds, and the skirt was silver, layered with five sheets of the thinnest silk to create the illusion of pale, shimmering light.

It moved her, how beautiful the dress was. I could see tears misting in her eyes, even though she blinked and struggled to hold them back.

Lady Sarnai dropped the gown to the floor. The color had drained from her face, and her eyes flooded with a mixture of wonder and horror. "It was supposed to be . . . impossible."

"It wasn't easy," I said tiredly. I couldn't gloat—the dresses had come at a great cost. "We faced many obstacles, magical and not. Some of your father's men pursued us."

Lady Sarnai's face darkened at the news. I thought she would lash out at me for insinuating that she'd sent Edan with me so her father could capture him, but she said nothing. Still, she wasn't surprised. I wondered if she was torn between her duty to the shansen and her hatred for him—for forcing her into marriage with Emperor Khanujin.

Lady Sarnai lifted her chin, reconstructing her careful mask of stone, but it was not quite as convincing as it had been before. "Very good, Master Tamarin." She kept her gaze high to avoid looking at the dress, as if the very sight of it wounded her. "I'm sure Emperor Khanujin will be pleased that you have delivered his wedding gift. But don't fool yourself into thinking this is your first of many great feats for him. The Son of Heaven's promises are as empty as the clouds that bore him. You should never have come back."

Her fan snapped in her hands, and she dropped the broken pieces on my dress. Without so much as a glance at the other two I'd made for her, she stormed out.

# CHAPTER THIRTY-FOUR

I survived the next few days by immersing myself in my work. I was so engrossed in finishing Lady Sarnai's dresses that I barely heard the bells ringing every morning and night, or the rain battering my roof during the storms that pounded the Autumn Palace. I scarcely even paid attention when Ammi chattered away about the emperor's miraculous recovery from his illness, though I perked up once—when she complained the Lord Enchanter wasn't eating much at dinner. Whatever magic I was working into the dresses muffled all the noise outside, making my deadline for Lady Sarnai feel far, far away.

After nearly three months on the road, I'd forgotten how exhilarating it was to lose myself to my craft. Not long ago, it had been my heart's desire to become the greatest tailor in A'landi. Life had been so different then—before I came to the palace, before I wielded my magic scissors, before I met Edan.

He hadn't come to visit me. It stung, but I couldn't blame him. Emperor Khanujin must have forbidden it, though sometimes from my window I felt sure a hawk watched me work late into the night. Deep down, when I pushed aside my anger for the emperor, I told myself it was better this way—for both of us. It would hurt less when we had to part.

And so, with the help of my magic scissors and spider-silk gloves, I spent the days spinning sunlight into golden thread so delicate it wouldn't blind or burn. Sunlight wasn't something I could spill onto my cutting table and measure with a stick. So I worked straight from the walnut, sifting rays of light onto my gloves and cutting with my scissors as thin a beam as I dared. Then I curled it over the blades and spun it into thread so fine it glided through the eye of my needle. With the moonlight, I did the same, only I braided the silvery beams, teasing them into slender, shining cords.

The night before the red sun, I wove sunlight into the first dress. The laughter of the sun did little to lighten my heart, but as its rays bounced off my scissors, I wanted to laugh—not with joy, but with wonder and relief. For when it was complete, the dress of the sun was so radiant my eyes watered from its brightness; even when I looked away, coronets of light stung my vision.

I blinked, flexing my fingers. The vial of the blood of stars sat warm on my lap, and my scissors hummed as I went next to embroider tears of the moon into Lady Sarnai's second dress. As I worked, I remembered my trial up Rainmaker's Peak, and my dive into the icy pool. A tear rolled down my cheek—not one of sadness, but of the bittersweet knowledge that the Maia finishing these dresses wasn't the same as the girl who'd started them three months ago. They were my journey, and soon I'd have to let them go.

I made the final stitch on the dress of moonlight. Only one dress left—the blood of stars.

My fingers trembled, and I wiped my eyes with the back of my hand. I hadn't slept in days; my exhaustion caught up with me now, making my mind wander, my determination waver.

My needle hovered over the last dress. What would happen to me after I finished?

The emperor knew I was a woman. Once these dresses were done, would he truly keep me in the palace? That was all my old naïve self had ever wanted, to win His Majesty's favor and be the imperial tailor. But now I knew better.

If he did allow me to stay, it would be as a reminder of his power over me. And a reminder of what I'd lost.

Tomorrow, Edan would return to Lapzur. He'd become a demon like Bandur.

All because of me.

Only my work kept me from losing hope. And now, that was to be taken from me. My dresses were all but done, and in the morning, Lady Sarnai would claim them.

I expelled a long, ragged breath and threw myself onto my bed. So many months of being strong. Strong for my family, strong for myself, then strong for Edan.

Finally, I let go. Everything I'd worked so hard to keep inside, all the hurt and grief I'd buried, I poured out of my heart and sobbed.

Why couldn't I just be Maia, the obedient daughter? The girl who loved to sew, and who only wanted to spend the rest of her days with her three brothers and her father?

But Finlei was gone. So was Sendo. And Keton—his spirit was but a phantom of his former self.

Edan had filled the void left by my brothers. He'd brought out the adventurer, the dreamer, and the rebel in me. But now I was about to lose him, too.

I couldn't lose Edan.

I wouldn't.

I slowed my thoughts, putting the pieces together. If Edan were free of his oath to Emperor Khanujin . . . then he would no longer be an enchanter. He couldn't become a demon. He couldn't take Bandur's place as guardian of Lapzur.

I rolled off my bed and picked up my scissors. Using my teeth, I popped off the cork holding the blood of stars in the vial, and I carefully poured its precious contents over the scissor blades. Then I touched them to the smooth white silk of my final dress.

Slowly, gradually, the blood of stars spread, paint rippling across an empty canvas.

The night was dark and starless, but inside my little room, I'd spun a world of light.

My dresses shone so brightly their power seeped through my closed doors and windows. Seeing all three dresses at once should have blinded me—but I was their maker, and that protected me from their intensity.

I stepped back, exhaling a long breath as I looked at my creations. "One woven with the laughter of the sun," I whispered. "Another embroidered with the tears of the moon, and lastly, one painted with the blood of the stars."

I searched for something to fix, a loose thread or button, but the scissors and I had made no mistakes. The dresses were perfect. Worthy of any empress. Worthy of a goddess.

With a sigh, I brushed my hand over the last dress. The paint had dried unnaturally quickly, and as my fingers lingered over its fine silk, I knew it was the most beautiful of the three, my masterpiece. The dress of the sun was wide and full, a glorious, incandescent gold with rounded flaps at the hem that flared like the sun's rays, and the dress of the moon was sleek and silvery, with flowing off-the-shoulder sleeves and a slim-fitting skirt that rippled down to a train. But the dress of the stars—it was black as night, yet when I touched it, a spectrum unfurled, shimmering with gold and silver and purple and a thousand other colors I could not name. I held the bodice to my chest, imagining myself in it.

*Why not, Maia? You've spent your whole life sewing for others, dreaming up dresses that you've never dared to try on.*

Before I could change my mind, I undid the hundred buttons I'd painstakingly sewn onto the star-painted dress, stepped into the skirt, and pulled up the bodice, threading my arms into the sleeves. Whatever power Amana's dresses held, I was going to find out. Tonight.

By magic, the skirt bloomed, the buttons knotted together one by one, and the sash tied over my waist. I touched my hands to my heart, trying to rein in my excitement. The dress fit perfectly. It hugged me neatly at the hips, the soft silk flowing outward like the petals of a rose. The fabric itself was warm, in a way that made me feel it was somehow alive.

I let my hair down and hid my face with a thin veil made of leftover silk.

Then I ventured outside. The palace was dark; the lanterns illuminating the garden paths flickered, their candles growing scarce of wax. But I needed no lantern or torch to see my way. My dress sparkled and lit my path.

The guards who saw me stared, their jaws agape. A few fell to their knees, touching their foreheads to the ground as if I were a goddess. No one asked who I was or where I was going.

I reached the Great Temple. My shoulders tensed, but I pushed past its wooden doors and made my way to the shrine.

An altar to Amana awaited me, lit by candles and incense so that the statues glowed, though the temple was unattended.

Gently, I took a bundle of incense, parted my skirt so I could kneel. "Amana, bless me and forgive me. For I have made the three dresses of legend, of your children: the sun, the moon, and the stars."

I staked the incense in its pot, bowed, and stood to leave. Then the wind began to hum. No, not the wind. The sound reminded me of my scissors—a quiet song that resonated with my very being, as if only I could hear it.

I turned around. Amana's statues glowed brighter.

*So you have found my children,* a woman's voice said. It was low and powerful, yet kind. *And you have made my dresses.*

I fell to my knees again. "Mother Goddess, I have."

*They hold great power, power too great to remain in your world.*

I bowed my head at the admonishment. "I see that now, Mother Goddess." My voice trembled as I spoke. "I will serve whatever penance you wish."

Amana considered me. *No punishment is necessary. You have suffered much, and the power of the dresses may cost you more yet.* She paused. *I shall take mercy on you and lift one of your burdens. Ask me your heart's greatest desire, Maia. And I shall grant it.*

My heart flooded. I didn't need to think twice. "Please, Amana. Release Edan from his oath to Emperor Khanujin, so that he may be free."

The incense grew strong, as did the eyes of Amana. *Your wish will have great consequences, Maia. Edan will not be able to fulfill his promise to the demon Bandur. You will have to pay the price for his broken oath.*

"I do not care," I said fiercely. "I love Edan."

A pause. I held my breath, waiting.

*Is your wish truly out of love alone? There is anger in you, child. Anger, and great sadness. Is there nothing you would want for yourself?*

At her words, my shoulders fell. One could not lie to the mother goddess. "For many years I've wished that my family could be together once more," I admitted quietly. "But that is a loss I know even you, Mother Goddess, cannot undo. Whereas Edan . . . there is still hope for him."

*Then it shall be done,* Amana said at last. *Upon the light of the blood of stars from whence he was bound, your love shall be free.*

"Thank you," I whispered. "Thank you, Mother Goddess."

I bowed three times, pressing my forehead to the cool wooden planks of the temple floor. Then I ran down the steps, my heart heavy with Amana's blessing and my arms spread wide with hope—that tomorrow would spin a new dawn.

# CHAPTER THIRTY-FIVE

I slept past the gongs of breaking dawn, even past the toll of the regular morning bells. When Ammi burst through my door, she found me asleep atop the blankets, both feet hanging off my bed.

She shook me, hard. "Everyone's waiting for you!" she cried, her braids whipping in agitation. "You were due at Lady Sarnai's apartments twenty minutes ago."

I jolted up. The first thing I saw was the red sun. It glared at me from the door Ammi had left open, casting a crimson glaze over my room, even over the breakfast tray Ammi had set on the floor hours earlier. Some soup had spilled onto the lacquered tray, and in the light it looked almost like blood.

My eyes wandered over to the dresses. The sunlight and moonlight gowns were folded into a neat stack, both ready to present to Emperor Khanujin and Lady Sarnai. But the last dress . . . it hung over my chair, skirts sweeping the floor.

It *had* to have been a dream.

"Get up. Get up." Ammi pulled me by the arm, struggling to lift me from my bed. "At least you slept in your clothes."

So I had. Strange, I didn't remember putting them back on the previous night. There was a mirror on my left, long and rectangular and framed with a rosewood lattice. I saw myself in the glass, my sunken eyes tired from worry and lack of sleep, wisps of black hair over my face and the rest tangled at the ends. Nothing out of the ordinary.

I tidied my hair, straightened my pants. "I'm awake."

Ammi took a step back and crossed her arms. "No time for breakfast." She knelt to wipe the spilled soup off the tray. "I'll leave this here for you to eat later."

I nodded, clasping my tailor's belt. My scissors hung at my side, their weight familiar.

She dusted my hat and passed it to me. "Your hair's gotten long."

I hesitated, wishing that Edan's spell over the palace hadn't affected Ammi, too. It would have been nice for another girl to know my secret.

"I know," I replied, taking the hat. "Thank you."

I gathered the gowns into a basket and hurried to Lady Sarnai's apartments, almost forgetting to hobble and use my cane. Like at the Summer Palace, the Orchid Pavilion was on the other side of the grounds, and as I passed through the open corridors and courtyards, I avoided looking at the sky. I could tell from the corners of my vision that the clouds were inflamed, that even my shadow had a tinge of red. But I wouldn't look up, wouldn't view the flaming red sun.

I hurried up the steps and fell to my knees after the guards let me in, bowing. "Your Imperial Majesty. My deepest, deepest apologies for—"

The sight of Emperor Khanujin made me forget my words.

Gone was the short, weak ruler I had encountered only five days ago. Thanks to Edan's magic, Emperor Khanujin was again the regal king beloved and feared by all. His hair was black as ebony, tucked under a headpiece made entirely of gold, and his eyes were bright, if not kind. The façade was so stunning I forgot what his real self looked like.

I pulled my eyes away from him, refusing to let magic toy with my perceptions and feelings. At his side was Edan. I pursed my lips. It'd been days since we'd been together. Edan's hair was shorter, his curls tamed behind his head, and he was dressed in the black robes he always wore when he was near his master.

He stood tall. Stiff, almost. *Bound*. That golden cuff still shackled his wrist, and the emperor's aura radiated as violently as ever. I must have imagined my meeting with Amana the previous night. Seeing Edan this way, I felt as if my heart wanted to burst.

I turned my head slightly, taking in Lady Sarnai's chambers. They seemed smaller than her rooms in the Summer Palace, perhaps because there were so many gathered here: Minister Lorsa and three other eunuchs, a line of courtiers, several of Lady Sarnai's maids—and Lord Xina. All here to see if I'd succeeded in making Amana's dresses.

"You're late," said Emperor Khanujin as the doors shut. He wasn't looking at me, and it took me a while to realize someone else had arrived after me.

Behind me, Lady Sarnai approached. Her bow was slung over her shoulder, as if she'd only just returned from hunting. In her hand was an arrow, as sharp as the animosity in her eyes. I wondered if she was considering shooting *me*. She certainly didn't look pleased to see me here.

She gave her weapon to one of the emperor's eunuchs and dropped the arrow in her hand, as well as her quiver, on the floor. If she was surprised to see Lord Xina here, she concealed it well as she bowed to the emperor.

"Rise," he said, taking a seat on one of the two scarlet lacquered chairs set out for him and Lady Sarnai in the center of the room, incense burning beside them. I noticed Edan's amulet on his sash. It looked the same as always—old and dull, with that carving of a hawk.

"The red sun has arrived," Emperor Khanujin declared. "Master Tailor, we have long awaited your completion of Amana's dresses. Present them to Lady Sarnai so she may attire herself in one to honor the shansen's arrival at our celebration banquet tonight."

I swallowed, keeping my head low and my hand on the head of my cane as I rose. "Your Highness," I said, addressing Lady Sarnai, "I have completed your dresses and present them to you in anticipation of your marriage to Emperor Khanujin."

As I lifted the dresses and unfolded them, I marveled that not a wrinkle marred their fabric. I heard Lady Sarnai's maids gasp as I held up each dress, one after another. The skirts puffed like clouds, shimmering and sparkling with such intensity, they looked like they were made of beams of sunlight and moonlight, of gold and diamonds and other precious jewels.

"One dress woven with the laughter of the sun," I narrated as the maid took the dresses from me to present to Lady Sarnai. "And one embroidered with the tears of the moon."

Lady Sarnai barely looked at them. It was difficult to do so. The dresses were blinding up close, but my eyes were used to their light.

"Lastly," I said, "a dress painted with the blood of the stars."

"Wait." Lord Xina stepped forward to inspect the dress. His large hands hovered over the fabric, which strangely did not glitter or sparkle. Even in my hazy memory, I could have sworn it had come alive last night when I had worn it. As if I carried the light of the stars.

But no, the dress remained black. Black as coal, as ink—as death.

"An inauspicious color for a wedding, isn't it?" said Lord Xina, slinging the words at the emperor. "You insult the shansen."

A corner of Lady Sarnai's lips twisted upward. "Even if the color did not repulse me, it is exceedingly plain, Master Tamarin. Hardly a dress evocative of our great goddess."

I drew closer to the maid holding the dress and tried to get her to step into the light. But the light was crimson and did nothing to bring out the colors of the stars.

"It catches the light, Your Highness," I said, trying to hide how mystified I was by the lackluster dress. "Perhaps because today is the red sun, the light is different."

Emperor Khanujin folded his arms across his chest, his long silken sleeves draping over the ground. "Don't look so sullen, Lady Sarnai. I think the color will suit you quite well."

"I won't wear it," she said. "Lord Xina is right. It would be inauspicious."

"Perhaps Your Highness should try on one of the other dresses," Edan prompted. "The dress of the sun."

Lady Sarnai's eyes narrowed at him. "What difference does a different dress make, if this one fails to dazzle? I asked for the three dresses of the goddess Amana, not imitations."

"They are not imitations," said Edan sharply.

"Indeed not," Emperor Khanujin said. He rested his hands on his knees, looking strangely calm. "Last night, my guards swore they saw the goddess Amana at the Great Temple wearing a dress made of the stars."

Several of the eunuchs murmured to one another that they, too, had heard this tale.

Lord Xina turned to Edan, his face taut with anger. "Did you think to fool us with your magic? To make us believe the goddess Amana would actually walk the earth in this . . . this vile gown?"

"Put on the dress," Emperor Khanujin commanded me.

Mine was not the only head that snapped to face the emperor. "Sire?"

"Master Tamarin, demonstrate its power, as I believe you did last night."

"I don't see how that would be appropriate," interjected Lord Xina. "Master Tamarin is a man. He couldn't possibly—"

"That is where you are wrong, Lord Xina." A smile smeared the emperor's lips. "Master Tamarin is Kalsang Tamarin's youngest child. His daughter, Maia."

A gasp escaped my lips, and shock rippled across the room from face to face. Why was he doing this?

"An impostor!" I heard people murmur. Minister Lorsa's hand jumped to his mouth, and the eunuch beside him began scribbling into his records fiercely. Lady Sarnai's smirk washed away into bewilderment, but I was too busy watching Edan to savor it. His face remained quiet and brooding, though he lifted an eyebrow at me, a sign that he had no idea what the emperor was thinking. Nervously, I twisted my fingers.

"Maia Tamarin, put on the dress."

Edan moved to assist me, but the emperor raised a hand, stopping him.

Aware that everyone watched me, I retrieved the star-painted dress and went behind the changing screen. I could feel Lady Sarnai's eyes burning through the screen, waiting for my dress to fail to bring Amana's magic to life.

A chord of fear twanged in my gut that she might be right. None of the maids moved to help me, and the buttons didn't fasten themselves this morning. I reached for my scissors, and that was all it took for the magic to return. The buttons knit together, closing me into the dress.

Without any hesitation, I lifted my hat; my hair tumbled down just past my shoulders. Then I stepped out from behind the screen.

My dress threw off dazzling bursts of light, intense enough to wash over the entire chamber. Overwhelmed, Emperor Khanujin raised his hands to shield his eyes. Lady Sarnai and Lord Xina did the same.

But Edan did not look away. A silent breath escaped his lips. Marvel sparked in his eyes, awakening him, and for a moment *my* Edan had returned, not the Edan who was Emperor Khanujin's servant. Yet it wasn't the dress he was looking at; it was me.

"You're glowing," he whispered, so softly only I could hear.

I looked down, confused. My dress had come to life, as it had last night. It was a different color today, more purple than black—richer even than the dyes only kings and queens could afford. The fabric rippled and shone, radiating every color imaginable across the ceiling and walls. Then I saw my reflection in the mirror. I *was* glowing—my skin, my hair, my hands, my entire body radiated a soft, silver light that grew more brilliant as I became aware of it. Edan reached for my scissors. I'd been gripping them so hard the bows had made indents in my fingers.

The dress grew brighter as his hand brushed against mine, but then he stepped back, and Emperor Khanujin took his place.

Wonder filled the emperor's face. His sneer slid from his

lips, and he touched my chin, raising it to him as he had in the prison cell.

"What a glorious transformation," he said, studying me from every angle. "Now I see why they mistook you for Amana herself. Walk for me."

My legs were heavy, but I obeyed, taking one small step at a time, circling before the emperor so that all could observe me. Their eyes followed my every movement, drinking in the dress's radiance.

Although I knew how Emperor Khanujin's power worked, its strength was hard to resist. What I'd once mistaken for charisma was force—it poured out of him, strongest when he was near Edan. I steeled myself against it, and my mind was able to resist, but my body couldn't. The emperor told me to twirl in my dress, and I did so. He told me to take his arm, and I did so. He touched my face, and I let him.

Edan watched, his hands twisted behind his back. His jaw was tight; I knew he was furious with the emperor for using his powers to manipulate me. And furious at himself for not being able to stop it.

"Do you still doubt that these are the dresses of Amana?" Emperor Khanujin asked. "Only such magic could transform a simple girl like Maia Tamarin—into a goddess."

Lord Xina and Lady Sarnai said nothing. The light from my dress danced about their eyes, but it did not fill them with wonder. Only torment.

"Show us Amana's power, Maia." The emperor's voice rang with authority, yet the sound of it made my body tense.

"Your Majesty," interrupted Edan. "The dresses are not meant for this world."

"Quiet," rasped Emperor Khanujin. Edan's amulet

swung from his robe, but now it glimmered among his other pendants, particularly as the light from my dress brushed against it.

*Upon the light of the blood of stars from whence he was bound,* Amana had said, *your love shall be free.*

Edan had told me once that he became an enchanter by drinking the blood of stars. That the cuff on his wrist had appeared once he took his oath on Lapzur.

My gaze wandered from the amulet on the emperor's sash to the cuff on Edan's wrist. Could it be that simple?

"Maia Tamarin," said Emperor Khanujin again, "show us Amana's power."

A light sang within me. I would unleash the dress's magic for Edan, not for the emperor. As my determination grew, the fabric burned brighter and brighter than ever before, with a dazzling silver light that eclipsed whatever it touched. My mind reeled, spinning with so much power that I didn't feel Edan grab me by the shoulders, didn't hear Emperor Khanujin laugh or Lady Sarnai scream.

I spun to face Edan, intertwining my fingers with his. A whirlwind of blue and purple light encircled us, a tempest of radiance. "What are you doing?" he shouted.

Instead of replying, I squeezed his hand and placed it over my heart. The light grew so bright no one could see us, not in the eye of its storm. I stood on my toes and kissed him, thinking of *all* my heart's greatest desires: for Keton to walk again, for Baba to be happy. For Edan to be free. One by one, I'd make those happen, no matter the cost to me.

*Be free, Edan. Be free.* I parted my lips and touched my forehead to his, seeing astonishment sweep over his eyes. His hand jerked against my chest as the gold cuff began to smoke and hiss and gold dust trickled to the ground like nothing more than sand. The wind whisked it away before the light of my dress faded and the palace's wooden walls surrounded us again.

It was over. As calmly as I could, I stepped away from Edan. Everyone else in the room had collapsed. Vases and chairs were overturned, teacups shattered, and linens scattered over the floor. The emperor recovered first. I saw Lord Xina help Lady Sarnai stand, then settle into a respectable distance from her. His large jaw was clenched, his mouth a tight, unhappy line. How familiar that look was to me! I'd often seen it on Edan.

"Behold the splendor and power of Amana," said the emperor, folding his arms to shake the sleeves of dust. "My congratulations, Master Tamarin. None can deny that you have satisfied Lady Sarnai's wishes and earned your position in my court."

I sank to the ground, bowing. The amulet in his sash was dull, with a thin crack in the center splitting the hawk. But the emperor hadn't noticed. I had a feeling he wouldn't, not until he saw his own glory fade in the mirror.

"You are relieved of your duties for the remainder of the day."

I barely heard the rest of the emperor's words as he dismissed me and everyone else in the Orchid Pavilion. All I could do was simmer under the heat of Edan's stare. His face had gone ashen, his eyes stricken and confused, his movements heavy. He tried to catch my gaze, but I didn't dare look up at him, not when he returned my scissors to me, or when his cloak brushed my shoulder as he followed the emperor out.

The guards threw the doors open, letting in a cool blast of air. As the room emptied, Lady Sarnai's maids hurried to clean up the mess. No one was brave enough to help me out of the dress, so I did it myself, and left it wilted against the emperor's red lacquered chair.

Lady Sarnai watched me, but her glare lacked its usual menace; this one looked forced, resigned. Turning her back on me, she glided to a corner and sat beside her embroidery frame, as far as possible from the dress I'd left on the emperor's chair. Her fists did not unclench, not even when I turned to leave her apartments.

I did not put on my hat; I held it at my side while I walked back to my quarters. The guards straightened when they saw me. "Master Tamarin," they murmured, bending their heads with respect. Minister Lorsa was nearby, and he bent his head as well before quickly turning away.

I should have felt triumphant. After all, I, a simple seamstress from Port Kamalan, had made the legendary dresses of Amana. I had become the imperial tailor of A'landi, the first woman ever to do so. And I had freed Edan, a Lord Enchanter, from his thousand-year oath.

Yet there was a hollowness in my gut. The moment I'd freed Edan, an intense cold had rushed over me.

*He's free,* I reminded myself as I collapsed onto my bed. *That's all that matters.*

And with that, I fell asleep with the saddest of smiles on my lips.

# CHAPTER THIRTY-SIX

Edan was not smiling when he woke me. His arms were crossed over his chest, and he sat on the edge of my bed. The change in him was subtle, but I noticed it right away.

His shoulders looked lighter, as if a terrible weight had been lifted. His hair was lighter, too, closer to the black of poppy seeds than the black of night, the bridge of his nose slightly more crooked, and for the first time, I noticed small imperfections on his face—a thin scar above his eye that hadn't been there before, a small mole on his cheek. My heart swelled to see them.

He spoke, sounding strained. "You summoned Amana."

It wasn't a question, but I nodded. I sat up. "Last night. When I put on the dress, I went to the Great Temple, and she came to me. She granted me a wish."

He cursed. "Maia, of all the impulsive, foolish—"

"What else would I wish for?" I said softly. "I love you."

Sunlight touched Edan's face, casting upon him a ruby glow as his anger dissipated. The sorrow in his eyes spoke a thousand words. "I should have made you drink."

"Drink?"

"That potion for your father and brother—there is enough in it for you, too. You would have forgotten me. You would have been happy."

Now I remembered what he meant. My answer hadn't changed. "How could I ever be happy without you?" The words choked me, and I realized how true they were. I'd been happy for a fleeting moment this morning, when I'd freed Edan from his oath. But I couldn't be happy forever. Though I'd refused to acknowledge the truth, deep down I'd known that, in setting him free, I'd ensured that Edan and I would never be together.

"Don't you realize what you've done?" he said. "Bandur will come for *you* now."

"It would have devastated me if you became like . . . like him."

Edan shook me by the shoulders. "It will devastate *me* if Bandur takes you. Do you not care about that?"

My heart wrenched. I'd never seen Edan look so vulnerable, so sad. I wanted to be with him. My soul burst with it.

*You will have to pay the price for his broken oath,* Amana had said. But Bandur had not come for me. Not yet, anyway.

"Bandur won't take me." My voice shook. "He can't."

"I don't understand, Maia." Edan's eyes, so clear and blue I no longer remembered them being any other color, wavered. "What do you mean?"

"You said these dresses are not of this world," I replied, slowly formulating my lie. "They freed me as well."

Edan's gaze was piercing. He didn't believe me.

"Look," I said, pushing aside my hair to show him my neck. "There is no mark."

"There hasn't been a mark since Bandur transferred his curse to me."

"And now that curse is broken," I said. "You're free—of your oath and of Bandur." My tongue grew heavy; it pained me to lie to him, yet it was easier than it should have been. A strange, cold feeling washed over me. "We both are."

A muscle in Edan's jaw ticked as he searched my eyes. I numbed my emotions, startled by how easy it was to feel nothing—to make Edan find nothing. He had no more magic, no more spells to detect my lie. "You swear it?"

The seams holding me together threatened to burst. I clung to the coldness; I needed it to help me protect Edan. "I do," I said calmly.

His features softened then. He believed me. "If you and I are truly free, then why do I feel as if we still cannot be together? That the little shophouse by the ocean you dream of is still so far away?"

Drums began to pound, taking away my chance to answer.

"The shansen will arrive soon," I said. "You need to go. It won't be long before Emperor Khanujin realizes you are no longer bound to him. He'll . . . he'll change."

Edan didn't budge. "Come with me."

Oh, how I wanted to. But even if I hadn't been lying about Bandur, I couldn't. I couldn't risk what would happen to my family if Emperor Khanujin found out *I'd* broken Edan's oath.

I shook my head sadly. "Go. The longer you stay, the more danger you are in." I could tell that wasn't enough to convince him, so I added, "And me."

Edan opened his mouth to argue, but I cut him off.

"I'll be safe here. The court is abuzz with the news that I'm a woman—that I made Amana's dresses. It will intrigue the shansen and the emperor long enough for you to disappear."

"When did you become so brave, my *xitara*?" He took my hand and looked down at it. "Your hand is cold, Maia."

"It's . . . it's from wearing the dress," I said, pulling away. A hard lump rose in my throat, and I swallowed painfully. More lies. "Please. You must leave."

He held on to my hand, tightly. Urgency tore away his grief and anger at what I had done; he knew I was right—there was no time. "Guard the dresses. They have great power, and they speak to you. The emperor will be weak without me. I cannot protect A'landi any longer. But perhaps you can."

"Where will you go?"

"To find a source of magic that exists beyond the oath."

"Is that . . . possible?"

"Enchanters are born with magic. Even when our oath is broken, some of it remains in us, only we cannot rekindle it. But my teachers told me of a freed enchanter in Agoria who could still wield some magic. If he is still alive, perhaps he can help me."

"Edan, I made my wish for you to be free, not to—"

"This is how I choose to be free," he interrupted gently. "Until I know you are safe from Bandur—and Khanujin—I must find a way to protect you. And when I do, I will come back and take you with me. You are my oath now, Maia Tamarin. And you'll never be free of me."

I took his hand and pressed it against my cheek. His warmth spread across my face, melting away the cold. "I know."

He touched my forehead, his fingers caressing my skin. "May Amana watch over you until I find you again."

I mustered a weak laugh. "I thought you didn't believe in the gods."

"I'm beginning to," he said in earnest. "Just as I'm beginning to believe you are A'landi's best hope." He reached to the floor and passed me our carpet. "Take this. If you are ever in danger, use it to flee. Use it to find me."

"You should keep it."

"It can't hear me any longer." Sadness seeped into Edan's voice, despite his effort to hide it.

He pulled me close and kissed me. Roughly, then deeply, as if the intensity of his love would change my mind and make me go with him. It left me breathless. I clung to his neck, listening to the steady pounding of his heart.

He stroked my hair; then he took my cheeks between his hands and lifted my head so our eyes were level. "Thank you, Maia, for freeing me."

"Be safe," I whispered. "Remember, you're mortal now. Don't do anything foolish, and don't take too long coming back to me."

A faint smile touched his lips. "I won't."

He unthreaded his fingers from mine; then, with one last kiss, he turned and was gone.

I wanted to cry, but the tears wouldn't come. Cold gripped my heart, twisting it tighter and tighter as if preparing it to break. Numbly, I closed my curtains, letting shadows fall over my room.

Drums pounded from the temple, a sign the emperor had arrived for his noon prayers to celebrate the red sun. The sound made the water in my washbowl quiver.

I dipped my fingers in the water and splashed my face.

"You freed your enchanter," murmured a dark, rippling voice. "A mistake, Maia Tamarin. A grave mistake. I warned you that if Edan broke his oath, I would return for you."

I froze. I couldn't pick out where the sound was coming from. It seemed to resonate from the walls.

"Look again," the voice whispered.

I swallowed, then moved into my workroom. The loom

was empty, as were the chairs and table. I went back into my bedroom—there was Bandur, in the mirror.

"Did you know," he said, "they used to play drums to scare off demons?"

I pulled back my shoulders and straightened. "If you've come for me, I'm not afraid."

"Your trembling voice gives you away, Maia Tamarin," Bandur purred. "I only wish to have a word with you." The demon took on Sendo's visage, and my brother smiled at me in the mirror. "Perhaps this will help."

"Leave my brother out of this," I spat.

Bandur laughed, and his features rearranged themselves into his usual form. "You surprised me, Maia Tamarin. Edan's soul was a great prize, but you, the tailor who summoned Amana to life—you might be more valuable yet."

"If you've come to take me to Lapzur, then do it." I clenched my fists so tightly that my nails bit into my palms. "Or have you not the strength to cross this far from your realm?"

Bandur floated in the glass, his flat, obsidian eyes that bled ash and death gazing at me. "I don't need to take you to Lapzur." His hand pierced the mirror, and I staggered back. "You will come of your own volition."

"I'll never go back to that treacherous place," I snapped. "Never."

"We shall see," Bandur said with a laugh. "Now that your beloved enchanter is free, he cannot protect you from me. In due time, you'll beg to take my place as guardian of Lapzur."

His certainty prickled my stomach with dread. "You're delusional, demon."

"Am I?" he rasped. "If you had been a mere girl, your fate would have been easier. I would have spread your bones across the earth so your soul would wander restless. But no, Edan was right. You are no mere girl. So now, the price you pay must be higher. Amana warned you of this."

My knees should have shaken, and my stomach should have clenched, but I felt nothing. I looked at him defiantly. "I'm not afraid."

"Then it has already begun," said Bandur. "Demons do not feel fear."

The cold surging in my chest rioted, and I let out a suffocated gasp. "No. *No.*"

"Yes, with every second, you become more like me. Soon the drums will only remind you of the heart you once had. Every beat you miss, every chill that touches you is a sign of the darkness folding over you. One day, it will take you away from all that you know and cherish: your memories, your face, your name. Not even your enchanter will love you when you wake as a demon."

"No!" I shouted, pounding my fist against the mirror. "What you say isn't true."

Bandur caught my wrist, his black nails scraping against my skin. "Be happy, Maia. It will not last."

Then he was gone.

Slowly, I crumpled to the ground. Bandur had to be lying. It wasn't true. It couldn't be true.

I wanted to weep, but no tears would fall. And no matter how I tried to summon fear, I could not. Deep down I knew Bandur was right. There was a crack in my soul, a new hollow where shadows seeped in and folded over my heart. Soon it would shatter me, and I'd become like him. A demon.

"I am Maia Tamarin," I told the mirror. "Daughter of Kalsang and Liling Tamarin, sister of Finlei and Sendo and

Keton." I swallowed. "Lover of Edan." I said this over and over, remembering the faces of my parents and brothers and Edan, remembering my childhood by the ocean and my love for silk and colors and light. I remembered what I had lost, and what I had gained, and the pain of Edan's leaving without knowing I'd deceived him. Finally, the tears came, choking me with emotion as I rocked myself back and forth.

I missed Baba and Keton so much. So, so much.

*Be happy,* Bandur had taunted me. *It will not last.*

How could I be happy without my family? I'd thought coming to the palace would save Baba and his shop, but I'd been so wrong. And now, without Edan—

Suddenly I remembered Edan's gift and his words: *It'll bring some happiness back to your family.*

I rubbed my eyes and dug furiously in my trunk for the last walnut Edan had given me. When I found it, I clenched it in my fist, clinging to its warmth.

I would not let Bandur take my soul. Not without a fight.

I needed to see light in Baba's eyes again, to see Keton walk again. I needed to remember what it was like to be happy. If only for one last time.

Reaching for my scissors, I attacked the remains of our enchanted carpet until it quivered with life.

Home. I was going home.

# CHAPTER THIRTY-SEVEN

It was a few hours before sunset when I arrived in Port Kamalan. The roads were empty; everyone was at home to celebrate the red sun, and not even the street peddlers were out selling their wares. I spied Calu's father in his bakery, stirring flour, oil, sugar, and water as he did every afternoon, preparing the dough for tomorrow morning's buns, but he didn't see me. No one did.

Our shop was closed, but I knew Baba was absentminded and would have forgotten to lock the door. With my carpet rolled under my arm, I quietly pushed my way inside.

Nothing had changed—piles of linen shirts sat folded on the counter, cobwebs were slung across the corners, and Baba's pan with charcoal rested against a low stool.

"Who's there?" a voice rasped from far behind the counter—if I were to guess, from our little altar beside the kitchen. Baba shuffled slowly into the storefront.

Seeing my father made me choke with emotion. "Baba!"

He recognized my voice before my silhouette; then his eyes widened.

"Heavens, Maia!" His breath hitched. "You should have written that you were coming."

"I can't stay long," I said, trying to remain in the shadows.

My eyes were bloodshot from crying, and I didn't want Baba to see.

Baba ushered me inside. "Did the emperor give you a holiday?"

"Yes."

"I didn't think he would, now that you're the imperial tailor." Baba held my shoulders. "*My daughter*, the emperor's tailor. It's been difficult keeping your secret, especially when I'm so proud of you."

"You don't need to anymore. The emperor has told everyone that I am a woman."

"Truly?" Baba stood taller. "Then, praise Amana, he is as magnificent as they say."

I pursed my lips instead of responding. The red sun hung lower in the sky, but its light poured in from the kitchen window, and I shielded my eyes from the glare. "Where is Keton?"

"Home in time for dinner?" came a voice behind me. "Thank the gods. Baba put me in charge of the cooking. But now that you're back . . ."

"Keton," I said softly. My hand slipped into my pocket with the walnut Edan had given me, and I held it as I watched Keton struggle forward, dragging himself along the wall. I rushed to help him, dipping under his shoulder and wrapping my arm around his waist so he could lean on me.

"Careful, Maia," he scolded me, half teasing. "These bones are still healing. You'll crush them with that grip of yours."

The corners of my vision glistened, and my throat swelled. I let him go. "You can walk?"

"Hardly," Keton replied, wearily leaning against the wall.

"You said you'd take a step for every day I was gone."

"Maia," said Baba sharply.

At my side, Keton hung his head. "I tried. I really tried, Maia."

My heart sank, but I smiled so Keton couldn't see the sadness in my eyes.

I rested my carpet against the wall and looked about the shop. It was neater than before, but only barely. I saw my letters strewn over the cutting table, their edges worn, and I briefly wondered if the sand caught between their folds had made it to Port Kamalan. I couldn't bring myself to check.

On the kitchen table was a line of half-burnt candles and a pile of half-sewn silk. I stroked the silk; it was satiny and lustrous, the kind you could only buy from merchants on the Road.

"You've been sewing again," I marveled, hearing Baba's box of pins rattling in his pocket as he followed me. "Was the money I sent enough?"

"You sent us *too* much money," Baba scolded me. "I had to give half of it away so our neighbors would stop asking where it came from and where you'd gone. They're shrewd ones, those fishermen's wives, but they're no snitches . . . at least not after a hundred jens."

"I was worried you wouldn't have enough food," I said, relieved.

"Be more worried about Keton's sewing skills."

"I'm getting better," my brother protested.

"Yes, he can finally sew buttons now."

Keton made a face. "What about you, Maia?" he said, studying me. "You look . . . different."

I was wearing his old clothes—the ones I'd taken the night

I'd decided to leave home. Yet I knew what he meant. I *was* different.

I'd battled ghosts and touched the stars. I'd climbed a mountain to the moon and conquered the fury of the sun. How could I be the same girl who used to sit in the corner mending rips and practicing embroidery all day?

But I said none of this as I helped Keton to his chair and spread a blanket over his legs. Drums thundered in the near distance. The sound startled me, and I jumped. "What's that?"

"They're from the temple," Keton said, frowning at my unease. "Maia, are you all right?"

"Just tired," I said quickly. "I've had a long journey."

It was the first lie I'd ever told my brother. I wasn't fine, and when I glanced at Baba, I could tell he knew it. I clutched Edan's walnut in my hand. Somehow, it gave me strength to know that if this was the last time I'd see my family, I'd do some good for them.

"So," Keton said. "Tell me everything."

I sat on the stool beside his chair, still unsettled by the drums. Their pounding was a steady counterpoint to my unsteady heart. "What is there to tell?"

"Come on, Maia. You've been gone for months. You're the imperial tailor. You've met the emperor and the shansen's daughter. You must have a story to tell."

I touched his knees and looked back at Baba's pile of clothes to be mended. It would be so easy to stay here with them, to take care of the shop and forget everything that had happened. If only I could. "I don't even know where to begin."

"Start at the beginning," Baba said. "Make it a tale, like the ones Sendo used to tell you. Then the story will come to you."

Yes, Sendo used to tell me fairy tales. How he'd love mine

if he were still alive: the tale of a girl who'd sewn the sun, the moon, and the stars into three dresses, the tale of a girl whom a demon had vowed to possess.

It was the tale of a boy, too. A boy who could fly but not swim. A boy with the powers of the gods but the shackles of a slave. A boy who loved me.

It was a tale still being written.

I took a deep breath, then told them about the trial, the master tailors I had met and competed against, and Lady Sarnai's request for the three dresses of the sun and the moon and the stars. I recounted my journey with Edan across A'landi and the Halakmarat Desert and Agoria, even to the Forgotten Isles of Lapzur, and what enchantment surrounded Emperor Khanujin whenever Edan was near. But as I approached the end of my story, Baba's brow creased. No matter how I tried to hide what I was feeling, he could always read me. He could tell I was leaving something out, and he was right.

Shadows fell over me as the day aged, and I sank into them to hide from the scrutiny of Baba's gaze. I couldn't tell him I'd fallen in love with the emperor's enchanter, or that the power of Amana's dresses had set him free—or that I'd been cursed by a demon.

"That's quite the tale, Maia," said Baba when I finished. "So it is thanks to you that the emperor and Lady Sarnai will wed."

"Tell me more about the ghosts and the demons," urged Keton. "And this enchanter."

"Later, Keton." Baba looked at me and frowned. "Maia, you don't look well."

"I'm just tired." I managed a smile, but my fists were clenched. A chill seeped in from one of the windows. "Keton, you're shivering. Let me get you some tea."

"I'm not shivering," my brother protested, but I was already up.

Reaching into my pocket, I retrieved the walnut. Deftly, I cracked it open like an egg. A golden liquid, thick as honey, glistened before me, and the scent of ginger wafted into the air. I started to empty its contents into the teapot, but at the last moment, I wavered. I'd witnessed enough of Edan's enchantment to have faith in it, and yet . . . magic had never been what made Baba call me the strong one. It had changed me, but it had never made me stronger—or happier. How could it, for Baba and Keton?

They were waiting for me, so I shoved the walnut behind one of our potted plants. I scooped up the nearest cup and filled it. The weight of the tea pressed the cup against my palm, and the heat settled in a second later. My skin tingled from the warmth, and I handed the cup to Keton, then poured a cup for Baba. Then a cup for me.

"Let us celebrate my appointment as imperial tailor," I said, hoping my voice didn't come out strangled. "Let us toast Emperor Khanujin's wedding to the shansen's daughter. And pray its success will allow me to come home more."

"To peace," Baba toasted. He drained his cup, and Keton too drank the tea in one gulp and wiped his mouth with the back of his hand.

I watched them both, hoping with all my heart I had made the right choice.

"You're staring at me, Maia," said Keton teasingly. "Do I have tea leaves up my nose?"

I crouched beside him, taking his hands in mine, and smiled. "No, I'm just happy to see you. And Baba. And to be home again."

He drew me close. "Remember our last morning in Gangsun?" he asked quietly. "I refused to leave, and I climbed a tree to hide so no one would find me."

I remembered. "You fell and broke your arm."

"It hurt so much I was afraid I'd never be able to use it again, but I was more afraid of Finlei." Keton let out a soft laugh. "He scolded me until my ears rang. But afterward, he splinted my arm and, once it healed, he helped me exercise it to make it strong again."

Keton's hands steadied, his breath evening. "I'd forgotten that morning for so many years, and yet, after you left, I thought about it every day." Finally he confessed, "I think I was afraid of you, too. Not that you'd scold me. But that I would let you down."

I was glad he was holding my hands, for my balance wobbled as I rocked back with surprise. "Keton . . ."

"I did try," he said, silencing and steadying me both at once. "Every morning, every night. Some days were better than others, but every time, I fell. I didn't want to fall when you came back."

Before Baba or I could say anything, he peeled off the blanket. His knees trembled, and he reached out to keep them still.

"You've been away a long time, sister," he said, "and I promised a step for each day. But I didn't promise that they'd all be at once." He inhaled, and pulled himself to the edge of his chair, planting his feet firmly on the ground. He struggled to stand without help from the walls or from Baba, but he wouldn't take my arm when I held it out to him.

Folding his fingers tightly over his cane, he stabbed it a cautious distance ahead, dragged his foot forward, and closed the gap with a step. Then another. And another, until I heard Baba gasp as Keton staggered toward him.

Three steps, and my brother collapsed against the chair beside Baba. I wrapped my arms around him.

"Three for now," said my brother, smiling as he ruffled my hair. "Will you count that, Maia?"

"I would rather count your smiles than your steps, dear brother," I said. "What means most to me is being here, home with you and Baba."

Baba came to us, and we embraced him. It'd been so long since we were together like this, I never wanted to let go.

As I knelt beside my brother, Baba told stories about us as children, how Keton used to put worms in my hair and how Baba worried I'd never be recognized as a tailor in my own right. And he laughed. I heard my father *laugh* for the first time in years.

Dusk bloomed too soon. Baba began to light the candles, but his eyelids drooped, heavy with tiredness. I ushered him to his room to get some rest. Then gently, I helped Keton to his bed.

I found the walnut where I'd left it, its contents still warm and glistening. Still there for me to drink. For me to be happy, as Edan had told me. But it was too late for me. To see my father laugh and my brother walk, and to see Edan become free . . . that was all the happiness I needed. I'd cling to it, as long as I could—until Bandur took my soul, piece by piece.

The drums thundered, still distant, but quicker. My heart lurched. Maybe if I stayed here, Bandur's prophecy wouldn't come true. Maybe if I didn't go back, I could salvage who I was.

No. Amana had warned me of the price I'd pay to save Edan. And even in a thousand lifetimes, I would not have made a different choice.

I poured the walnut into a potted bamboo shoot on the windowsill. The plant grew greener as it absorbed Edan's magic. A sight that both stung my heart and made it swell.

I sat beside Keton on his cot. His eyes were already half closed, and a smile touched his lips. I kissed his forehead, and I pressed his cheek to mine. "Sleep, dear brother."

"Is this real?" he murmured, clasping my hand. "Are you really here? Did Baba really laugh?"

"Yes, yes," I said. "I'm here. And Baba did laugh. He will, again and again until we never forget the sound—because we're together. And we will be again, soon. Now sleep."

I listened as his breathing slowed. In and out it wove, in and out—that steady rhythm meant he was fast asleep. I wrapped a blanket over Baba's shoulders and pulled up Keton's so it covered his chest. Then, careful not to make a sound, I left our shop.

The last vestiges of the red sun painted the horizon in crimson. I shielded my eyes from its light and sat on my carpet. In the glass window of Baba's shop, a shadow flickered in my reflection's eyes—making them sparkle blood-red.

A shiver coursed down my spine. *Just a trick of the light,* I told myself. *From the red sun.*

I watched the sky until the last strains of daylight faded, washed over by the black of night. Yet as I soared over Port Kamalan's glittering waters back to the palace, that shiver settled in me. I knew I had ended my tale to Baba and Keton on a wondrous note. I had been afraid to tell them the truth, that my homecoming was not the end of my story.

But a new and terrible beginning.

# ACKNOWLEDGMENTS

My book would not be in your hands without Gina Maccoby, my stalwart agent. Thank you, Gina, for seeing something special in my writing and giving me a chance, for helping me hone my writing to be the best it can be, and for believing in me through the ups and downs of my path to publication. You are the mentor I always dreamed of having.

To Katherine Harrison, editor extraordinaire. I knew from the beginning that Maia had found her home with you, and I'm thankful that fate landed my book in your hands. Thank you for making her story even stronger with your keen edits, and for championing *Spin the Dawn* in ways I didn't even know were possible.

A hearty thank-you to the Knopf BFYR team: Alex Hess, Alison Impey, Julia Maguire, Mary McCue, Jaclyn Whalen, Alison Kolani, Tracy Heydweiller, Jake Eldred, Artie Bennett, Janet Renard, Amy Schroeder, and Barbara Perris for the incredible enthusiasm, time, and effort you put behind making this book not just a reality, but also a work of art to read, hold, and cherish.

Thank you, Tran Nguyen, for a tremendous cover that breathed life into Maia Tamarin. I've lost count of how many indulgent hours I've spent staring at it. I couldn't have imagined a more fitting cover, and I love it so much. To Virginia Allyn, for your breathtaking map; my heart still flutters every time I notice a new detail on it.

To Doug Tyskiewicz and Leslie Zampetti, my critique partners: I'm convinced one of the hardest things about writing is finding a steady critique group with fellow authors whose work and company you enjoy. I am so lucky to have found you two and even luckier to call you both my friends.

To Patti Lee Gauch, for her life-changing advice on voice (don't flinch!), and for inspiring me to light the spark in my writing. To Gregory Maguire and Patricia McMahon, for reminding me to unravel the threads of my favorite fairy tales and keep Maia tough. And I'd be remiss not to include Nancy Sondel and the wonderful teens and adults at the Pacific Coast Children's Writers Workshop, who gave me valuable feedback on *Spin the Dawn* during its early days.

To my fellow writers Liz Braswell, Kat Cho, Bess Cozby, Suzi Guina, Joanna Ruth Meyer, Lauren Spieller, June Tan, and Swati Teerdhala, for their friendship and advice, and for squealing with me over bookish updates and agonizing together over drafting and revisions. I've learned so much from you all. Thank you also to Roselle Lim, for her insight into Chinese embroidery schools and for her sewing expertise; Sarah Neilson, for her thoughtful feedback, so much of which has strengthened *Spin the Dawn*'s story; Heidi Heilig, for being such an encouraging force for aspiring writers; and Jen Gaska at *Pop! Goes the Reader*, for graciously hosting *Spin the Dawn*'s cover reveal.

A big shout-out to the Electric 18s, for being the most amazing debut group a girl could ask for. You have all made me feel like part of one big, happy family. I also want to take a moment to thank the teachers and professors I had the privilege of studying with during my journey to become an author: thank you for encouraging me to take risks and be creative.

And, of course, thank you to all the fellow writers, readers, booksellers, Goodreads librarians, and bloggers I've met in the past two years—virtually or in real life—who've done so much to make me feel welcome in the kidlit community. Thanks to you, the future of books and storytelling—*our* future—is brighter than ever.

My heartfelt thanks (along with big hugs) to Diana Link, Joyce Lin, Eva Liu, Evelyn Lu, and Amaris White—a few of my dearest and oldest friends—for reading my earlier novels, cheering me on throughout the years, and keeping me sane over countless IMs and phone calls while I sought to become a published author, as well as lending your critical eyes and ears (not least, for telling me what it's really like to ride a camel and climb a mountain with ice picks).

This book would never have happened without the support of my family. Thank you to my po po, for sitting me with her at the sewing machine when I was little as she worked, and telling me all her stories. You are one of the strongest women I know.

To my parents, for teaching me the value of persistence from a young age. To Dad, for sparking in me a love for fairy tales, for being proud of me no matter what I chose to pursue—but wisely advising me to work hard and be the best I could be in those pursuits. Everything I have done is thanks to your wisdom. Mom, whose talent for arts and crafts never ceases to amaze me: thank you for emboldening me to be creative. I wouldn't be the musician or writer I am today without you.

To my sister, Victoria, for pushing me to make the book more romantic (always, ha-ha!), for being a sounding board whenever I needed an honest opinion, and for giving me design and fashion advice. My life would be far lonelier (and less entertaining) without you.

Most of all, thank you to my husband, love, and best friend, Adrian. Thank you for nourishing me with countless breakfasts and dinners and for reminding me to eat lunch when I was so immersed in editing that I forgot to, for spending hours reading my drafts and giving me the brutal edits (and no-less-valuable encouragement) I needed, for hugging me during the lows and laughing with me during the highs, and for buying me a more comfortable desk chair. You are my inspiration and my joy.

Thank you to our baby, Charlotte, whose infectious smiles and giggles make me anxious to wake up every morning to spend time with you. Already I can't wait to read and sing and dance—and write with you.

And lastly, thank *you*, dear reader. For picking up this book and giving it a chance, for following me through the wilds of my imagination, and for (hopefully) making it all the way to the end. Until next time!

READ ON FOR AN EXCERPT FROM
THE BLOOD OF STARS, BOOK II

# UNRAVEL
## THE
# DUSK

I had a mother once.

She taught me to spin the finest yarn and thread, made from silkworms raised in our court of mulberry trees. Patiently, she would soak thousands of cocoons, and together we wound the gossamer threads onto wooden spools. When she saw how nimbly my little fingers worked the wheel, spinning silk like strands of moonlight, she urged my father to take me on as his seamstress.

"Learn well from Baba," she told me when he agreed. "He is the best tailor in Gangsun, and if you study hard, one day you will be, too."

"Yes, Mama," I'd said obediently.

Perhaps if she'd told me then that girls couldn't become tailors, my story would have turned out differently. But alas.

While Mama raised my brothers—brave Finlei, thoughtful Sendo, and wild Keton—Baba taught me to cut and stitch and embroider. He trained my eyes to see beyond simple lines and shapes, to manipulate shadows and balance beauty with structure. He made me handle every kind of cloth, from coarse cottons to fine silks, to gain mastery over fabrics and feel how they draped over the skin. He made me redo all my stitches if I skipped one, and from my mistakes I learned how a single seam could be the difference between a garment that fit and one that did not. How a careless rip could be mended but not undone.

Without Baba's training, I could never have become the emperor's tailor. But it was Mama's faith in me that gave me the heart to even try.

In the evenings, after our shop closed, she'd rub balm onto my sore fingers. "Baba's working you hard," she would say.

"I don't mind, Mama. I like sewing."

She lifted my chin so our eyes were level. Whatever she saw made her sigh. "You really are your father's daughter. All right, but remember: tailoring is a craft, but it's also an art. Sit by the window, feel the light, and watch the clouds and the birds." She paused, looking over my shoulder at the patterns I'd been cutting all day. "And don't forget to have fun, Maia. You should make something for yourself, too."

"But I don't want anything."

Mama tilted her head at me thoughtfully. As she changed the burnt-out joss sticks by our family altar, she picked up one of the three statues of Amana lining the shrine. They were plainly carved, faces and dresses washed out by the sun. "Why don't you make three dresses for our mother goddess?"

My eyes widened. "Mama, I couldn't. They're—"

"—the most beautiful dresses in the world," she finished for me. She tousled my hair and kissed my forehead. "I'll help you. We'll dream them together."

I hugged Mama, burying my face in her chest and holding her so tight a laugh tinkled out of her throat, like soft strokes of a dulcimer.

What I would give to hear that laugh again. To see Mama one more time—to touch her face and comb my fingers through her thick braid of black hair as it loosened into waves rippling against her back. I remember no matter how I tried, I could never weave silk as soft as her hair. I remember I used to think the freckles on her cheeks and arms were stars. Keton and I would sit on her lap, me trying to count them, Keton trying to sweep them off.

The stories she'd tell us! It was Mama who dreamed of leaving Gangsun and living by the sea. She recounted to us the tales she'd grown up with—of fearless sailors, water dragons, and golden fish that granted wishes—tales Sendo drank with his soul.

She believed in fairies and ghosts, in demons and gods. She taught me to sew amulets for passing travelers, to cut paper clothes to burn for our ancestors, to write charms to ward off evil spirits. Most of all, she believed in fate.

"Keton says it isn't my fate to become a tailor like Baba," I sobbed to her one afternoon, weeping from the sting of my brother's words. "He says girls can only become seamstresses, and if I work too hard, I won't have any friends and no boy will ever want me—"

"Don't listen to your brother," Mama said. "He doesn't understand what a gift you have, Maia. Not yet." She dried my tears with the edge of her sleeve. "What matters is, do *you* want to be a tailor?"

"Yes," I said in a small voice. "More than anything. But I don't want to be alone."

"You won't be," she promised. "It isn't in your fate. Tailors are closer to fate than most. Do you know why?"

I thought hard. "Baba says the threads he stitches into his work give it life."

"It's more than that," replied Mama. "Tailoring is a craft that even the gods respect. There's something magical about it. Even the simplest thread has great power."

"Power?"

"Have I told you about the thread of fate?"

I shook my head.

"Everyone has a thread tied to someone—a person who's meant to be by your side and make you happy. Mine is tied to Baba's."

I glanced at my wrists and ankles. "I don't see anything."

"You can't *see* it." Mama chuckled gently. "Only the gods can. The thread may be long, stretching over mountains and rivers, and it may be years before you find its end. But you'll know when you meet the right one."

"What if someone cuts it?" I worried.

"Nothing can break it, for destiny is the strongest promise. You'll be bound to each other no matter what happens."

"The way I'm bound to you and Baba, and Finlei. And Sendo?" I was mad at Keton, so I didn't care if my youngest brother and I were tied together.

"It's similar, but different." Mama touched my nose and rubbed it affectionately. "One day you'll see."

That night, I took a spool of red thread and cut a string to tie around my ankle. I didn't want my brothers to see and make fun of me, so I tucked the loose end under the cuff of my pant leg. But as I walked with my secret tickling my ankle, I wondered if I'd feel something when I met the person I was fated to be with. Would the string give a little tug? Would it stretch and bind to its other half?

I wore that string around my ankle for months. Little by little, it frayed, but my faith in fate did not.

Until fate took Mama from me.

It came for her slowly, over many months, like the cypress tree outside our shophouse. Every day, leaves trickled from its spindly arms, only a few at first, but more and more as autumn loomed. Then, one day, I woke up to find all the branches were bare. And our cypress tree was no more, at least until spring.

Mama had no spring.

Her autumn began with a stray cough here and there, always covered up with a smile. She forgot to add cabbage to the pork dumplings Finlei loved so much, and forgot the names of the heroes in the stories she'd tell Sendo and me before we went to sleep. She even let Keton win at cards and gave him too much money to spend on his errands in the marketplace.

I hadn't thought too much of these slips. Mama would have said if she weren't feeling well.

Then one winter morning, just as I'd finished adorning our statues of Amana with our three dresses of the sun, the moon, and the stars, Mama fainted in the kitchen.

I shook her. I was still small, and even her head was heavy for me to lift and rest on my lap.

"Baba!" I screamed. "Baba! She won't wake up."

That morning, everything changed. Instead of praying to my ancestors to wish them well in their afterlife, I prayed that they spare Mama. I prayed to Amana, to the three statues I'd painted and clothed, to let her live. To let her see my brothers and me grow up, and not to leave Baba, who loved her so much, alone.

Every time I closed my eyes and pictured the future, I saw my family whole. I saw Mama next to Baba, laughing, and teasing us all with the fragrant smells of her cooking. I saw my brothers surrounding me—Finlei reminding me to sit straight,

Sendo slipping me an extra tangerine, and Keton pulling on my braids.

How wrong I was.

Mama died a week before my eighth birthday. I spent my birthday sewing white mourning clothes for my father and my brothers, which we wore for the next one hundred days. That year, the winter felt especially cold.

I cut the red thread off my ankle. Seeing how broken Baba was without Mama, I didn't want to be tied to anyone and suffer the same pain.

As the years passed, my faith in the gods faded, and I stopped believing in magic. I shuttered my dreams and poured myself into keeping our family together, into being strong for Baba, for my brothers, for myself.

Every time a little happiness seeped into the cracks of my heart and dared make it full again, fate intervened to remind me I couldn't escape it. Fate took my heart and smashed it piece by piece: when Finlei died, then Sendo, and Keton returned with broken legs and ghosts in his eyes.

The Maia of yesterday picked up those pieces and painstakingly sewed them back together. But I was no longer that Maia.

Beginning today, things would be different. Beginning today, when fate caught me, I'd meet it head-on and make it my own.

Beginning today, I would have no heart.